Throstleford

SUSAN EVANS McCLOUD

DESERET
BOOK

Salt Lake City

This book is for
my Sister in flesh and spirit
DIANNE ELIZA EVANS

Library of Congress Cataloging-in-Publication Data

McCloud, Susan Evans.
    Throstleford / Susan Evans McCloud.
        p.   cm.
    ISBN 978-1-59038-942-3 (paperbound)
    1. Clergy—Fiction.   2. Mormons—Fiction.   3. Church
membership—Fiction.   4. Great Britain—History—19th century—Fiction.
I. Title.
    PS3563.A26176T48 2008
    813'.54—dc22   2008013528

Printed in the United States of America
Publishers Printing, Salt Lake City, UT

10   9   8   7   6   5   4   3   2   1

The throstle bides in the hedgerow,
And waits his time to sing:
Old are his ways, and old his songs
And the memories they bring.

The robin calls in the morning,
The cuckoo cries to the moon,
The raven circles the wild trees round,
And the lark rises all too soon.

But the throstle hugs to the homeland,
To the field and the mead and the moor,
The throstle sings in the hedgerows
His heart's song, o'er and o'er.

—Traditional

"Calls from all quarters to come and preach were constantly sounding in our ears, and we labored night and day to satisfy the people, who manifested such a desire for the truth as I never saw before."

—*Life of Heber C. Kimball*

Throstleford Village
Major Characters

⟨≈≈⊃⊃⊃⊃≈≈⟩

Christian Grey	minister, Church of England
Esther	daughter
Mary	wife (died eight years ago)
Pearl	housekeeper
Nicholas Shepperd	minister, Methodist
Rhoda	wife
Andrew	son
Jonathan Feather	squire
Sophia MacGregor	wife
Jonathan	son, "young squire"
Tempest, James, Nathan	sons
Sarah, Diana	daughters
"Betts"	servant in squire's hall
Archibald Sterne	doctor
Janet	wife
Paul Pritchard	miller
Paisley	wife
Daniel	son (crippled from fall)
Obey	daughter
Zacharias Kilburn	blacksmith
Louisa	wife
Matthew	son
Laura	daughter

Samuel Weatherall	grocer/farmer
Margaret "Meg"	wife (herbalist)
Michael Bingham	stone mason
Hannah	wife
Edwin Sowerby	tailor
Evaline Madora	wife
Adam Dubberly	farm laborer
Rose	wife
Sallie Brigman	beekeeper
Dorothea Whitley	spinster
Lucius Bideford	bachelor farmer
Peter Goodall	retired farmer
Martha & Mary	granddaughters
Wilford Johns	constable
Hilda	wife
Oliver Morris	shepherd
Roger Coleman	stableboy
Harvey Heaton	innkeeper, Stragglers' Inn
Spencer, Alan, David, Ben	sons
Marjorie Pool	maid, Stragglers' Inn
Jem Irons	ruffian mate of Heaton's
Monkman Smedley	ruffian mate of Heaton's
Elder George Hascall	Mormon missionary
Elder Levi Walker	Mormon missionary

Chapter One

⁓⟡⟡⟡⁓

Esther was the first to see the strangers wend with weary walk into Throstleford. They came by the narrow back road that crossed through the mill meadows close to the pond. It was a raw day in March, raw and windy. She pushed a tendril of hair back from her face, where the wind wanted to plaster it, and stood uneasily outside Sallie Brigman's cottage to watch them walk on, and up the path to the doctor's doorstep. A shudder passed through her frame. She was to remember that shudder, with all else about these first moments, for the rest of her life. And yet, she had no premonition of ill or of trouble. Rather, in a singular way, a sense of quickening anticipation seized her, which she could not explain.

She entered Sallie's house and remarked casually on the fact that two strangers had just come into the village.

"Stopped at the doctor's, did they?" Sallie raised herself from her sick bed on one elbow and squinted up at her young visitor. "He's got a brother in London, you know, missy, and who can guess what other connections. They could be anybody, come to see him about who knows what matters, highfalutin and consequential. Did you bring the lovage for my rheumatic?"

Esther nodded. This was a clear dismissal of the subject, and she would not allow her curiosity to press her further. Sallie was old enough to be her grandmother, and crotchety as a wet hen left out in the rain. She possessed the warmest of hearts, thank goodness, but her manners could be off-putting, to say the least.

"That and some of Pearl's hot biscuits," Esther smiled. "Would you like me to put the kettle on and brew the lovage for you and a bit of mint for myself?"

"That would be cozy, m'dear."

Esther moved easily about the tiny kitchen, for she knew where every crock and plate had its place, and she hummed under her breath as she worked.

"You be just like my bees," Sallie crooned. "Always have been, since you were a littl'un, hummin' and singing that way."

Esther smiled. Sallie had been a part of her life since she could remember; but then, it was the same with most of the villagers, who thought of themselves as separate and distinctly individual—yet very loyal—members of one family. Esther was nine when her mother died, and every heart quickened to the sorrow of the quiet, wide-eyed child, who had her mother's mild disposition and tender ways. And they kept their eye on the kindly young vicar who seemed to go gray and haunted at the terrible loss of his wife. Only Esther had power to reach him, to draw him out of himself, and that power grew as she emerged into a young woman, with many of the canny ways and perceptions of her sex.

"I found a bit of lace the other day in my sewing box," Sallie mumbled, sucking the hot tea up through her teeth. "Here, I set it out to give ye."

"You mustn't!" Esther protested. She picked it up and ran her fingertips along the finely-stitched designs. "It's far too precious for giving."

"Made it when I was a slip of a girl," Sallie continued, ignoring her. "I remember doing up half a dozen like pieces, I fancied the pattern so well." Esther moved to replace it on the low table. "'Twere meant for you, Esther. I ask you, who else would I give it to? You'll take care of it, see, and use it with love."

"Yes, I shall do that," Esther promised, bending to kiss the soft wrinkled cheek of the woman beside her.

"I know what you're thinking," Sallie blurted. "And I agree that 'tis a pity I have no fine girls of my own." They both sighed, picturing the three small graves in the churchyard, unaware of the wistful sound their breaths made in the quiet room. "But I've yourself to take care of me, Esther, and that means the world."

Esther reached for the hand that lay on the counterpane, so slender, yet so capable, so cunning. "I know, I know." She sighed, and rose reluctantly.

"Ye must away, then?"

"Father does not like his supper to be late, as you remember." She moved to the door. She felt happy inside; she felt like smiling. *Was it only the gift of the lace?* "I'll bring you some celery seed from Meg first thing in the morning, along with a cup of new milk, I hope."

Sallie nodded. "Wrap your shawl against the wind, dear, and give my respects to your father." She smiled, and for a moment her lined face lit with a remnant of the woman's beauty that once had been hers.

Esther leaned into the press of cold air that greeted her and kept her head down, though her eyes sought the doctor's closed door and closed, silent windows, lit by the last of the sunset so that the small panes seemed to tremble and throb with a shimmer of gold. *I wish I had a fair excuse for knocking on that door,* she thought. The curiosity was stirring inside her again. But her hands were empty, as was the basket she carried, save for the circle of fine lacework she had tucked inside.

So she walked on to the vicarage, which was set deep in the wedge of the churchyard, where old trees and old stones leaned against each other and where, beneath an arch of weeping birch, a gentle mourning dove sat watching her. He uttered his plaintive coo, tender with longing, and Esther stood still to watch him, until he lifted his feathers and glided away. She knew that longing; she had known it all her life. Perhaps she had even been born with it. She cupped her heart around the sound and entered the dim, lonely house.

Esther found a place for the lace doily on the table beside her bed.

It set off the picture of her mother, the candlestick, and a small stack of books she kept there. She was pleased with the effect and smiled to herself as she hurried down to supper.

"Has Father come in yet?" she asked Pearl, who was bustling about the steamy kitchen, looking a bit ruffled.

"That he has not. I've not seen hide nor hair of him."

"Well, that is strange; neither have I."

Pearl fairly bristled. "Some busybody, choked with care for himself, has kept him since tea is my guess," she fussed. Esther frowned slightly. It *was* a bit unusual for her punctual father not to be home in good time for his hot evening meal. She reached for her shawl, draping it over her head and shoulders as she called, "I'll step out and take a quick look 'round for him, Pearl."

But her father was not on the path, nor could she spy him in the shadows that were beginning to loom from the dim light that gathered into darker pockets beside hedge, stone, and tree. She came inside slowly, wondering what could be keeping him, sensing from long experience that it must be something of import. But what in the world could that be?

At length the two women set out the food, and just as the steaming chicken was lifted from the oven, Christian Grey walked through the door. He lifted his eyes and smiled thinly at his daughter, barely moving his mouth. "So sorry to worry you both," he apologized, "but it could not be helped."

He pulled out her chair and sat Esther at the table before seating himself. He was preoccupied still; it was easy to see that, and Esther hesitated. Should she tell him her news? He might not even take note of it, or he might wonder, when he heard, what import it might possibly hold. How could she explain how she felt? That little lift at her heart when she saw the two strangers, that grew into a warmth as she had watched them—the whole thing made no sense.

Thus they ate in silence, her father quickly and methodically, his mind elsewhere. After a very little time he laid by his napkin and scraped back his chair. "I'll be in my study," he announced. Then, as a bit of an afterthought, "That was an excellent meal, as always, Pearl."

How proper he is, Esther thought. *But how kindly. No matter what his own concerns may be, never neglecting consideration of others.* She took up a plate of scraps to feed the cats who, hearing her come out on the porch, scampered up and made a pool of moving fur around her legs as she bent down to them. The large ginger male was her favorite. He possessed a certain dignity that the others lacked. She scratched the soft spot behind his ear and drew her hand through his fur. The wind had settled into an uneasy slumber, and the tree branches were still. Esther had none of that stillness within her, only this restlessness which was new to her, and which she could not explain.

Back indoors, she lit the lamp in the sitting room and settled down with a book. This was one of her favorite pursuits, but tonight she could not turn her mind to the words on the page. There seemed, unaccountably, to be something in the air, almost an *expectation* that destroyed her ability to concentrate, so that she found her thoughts wandering and her hands fidgeting in her lap. She discarded the book and took up her knitting from the basket beside her chair. Now her fingers could fly of their own accord, and her thoughts might also fly where they would.

She jumped, startled at the sound of her father's voice calling her name. At once she rose and went to him, pushing open the door to his study with a trembling hand.

"Come in, come in, Esther, and draw the door shut behind you. There's a good girl." The preoccupation was still in his tone of voice, and in an uneasy tightening along the muscles of his face.

"What is it, Father? May I be of assistance to you?"

"I think, perhaps, Esther, you can." He ran his fingers through his hair, an anxious gesture, and the ruffling of his pale, wheat-colored locks made him look younger and suddenly vulnerable. Esther drew her chair a bit closer to his desk. "What is it, Father?" she asked again.

"I have been with Doctor Sterne," he began, "and he has introduced me to two strangers—gentlemen—who are, in fact, staying with

Archibald and Janet for"—he coughed into his hand—"for I know not how long."

Esther's heart gave a jump, ever so slight a sensation, but she placed her hand on the front of her dress as if to quiet the stir. "These men are clerical men, ministers of a new religion." He paused. Drawing the words out was not easy for him. "An *American* religion, Esther. And apparently Archibald's brother, in London, has become involved with them, and the good doctor himself is interested—most interested—" The nervous hand through his hair again. "And the long and short of it is that he has asked me if they might preach on the Sabbath *in my church.*" He stressed the words ever so slightly, but Esther already knew how confused and affronted her father felt. "My good friend, Esther. One of my *dearest* friends." He paused, gazing at her, gazing through her, gazing inside his own self.

"Did you meet these men?" Esther scarcely breathed the words.

"As a matter of fact, Esther, I did."

"At the doctor's? What were they like, Father?" She could not help pressing him.

"Good men, it appears. Reasonable, well spoken. Clear eyes, honest eyes—you know that is one of the first things I look for, Esther—" She nodded. "Eyes reveal so much that we can in other ways conceal or disguise."

"You were favorably impressed with them?"

"I was." He may as well have said, "*I fear I was,*" for she knew him so well, and could read that thought in his mind.

She drew in her breath, gathering courage. "I saw these men myself, Father, on my way to Sallie's house."

Her father lifted an eyebrow. "You saw them?"

"Well, not to speak to; only from a distance, really."

"But? There is more to the matter?"

"Only *within myself,* Father."

"Yes—" He leaned unconsciously toward her, where she sat demurely, her hands folded in her lap and her face a bit pale.

Esther had always been honest with him, entirely open and honest with her thoughts and her feelings since she was a child. It seemed the most natural and right thing for her to share everything with him, everything that impressed or frightened or delighted or amazed her. "As soon as I saw them my heart gave a leap, truly, Father, as silly as that may sound. And I felt—oh, I don't know, not exactly happy, but *expectant*, as though, as though—" She let her voice trail away, then added, "It was nothing greater than that."

Her father nodded, and a slight frown creased into lines between his eyes, giving him a quizzical aspect. "I see." He was thoughtful; Esther could almost see him thinking, *This is most singular, Esther.* He might have said the words; it was a phrase he was fond of and often used. But this evening he refrained. Looking up, he attempted a smile. "Thank you, daughter, thank you for coming to me."

"When must you make your decision? Must you tell the doctor soon?"

"Today is Wednesday. By tomorrow or the day after at the latest, I should think."

Esther nodded, and rose slowly. "Will you be all right, Father?"

At her words his smile broadened. "Indeed, I shall. Be on your way now; I've kept you long enough troubling yourself over my concerns."

He made a sweeping movement with his hands, but she planted a kiss on his forehead before turning and leaving him, quickly and quietly. *How I love him,* she thought, as she stood in the hall and leaned against the cool wood of the closed door. *He is lonely without Mother, though he tries to hide it. But the loneliness is always there. Something he lives with, but I do not think he is entirely reconciled to.*

Within the study Christian Grey rose from his chair and went to the window, pushing it open to let in the night air. *I need something to clear my head,* he thought. But it was really his feelings that were troubling him. What disturbed him about these men? It was a common enough request, really, that his good friend had made. Why did he hesitate? Why did he feel that there was something portentous in the decision he was to make? For good or ill, what he decided would somehow make a *differ-ence*; of that he felt sure. But, beyond this he could see nothing, discern nothing. All was silence and shadow, both without and within. He stood for a long while leaning on the sill, gazing up at the trees, watching them reach in the night wind, long-armed and eager, toward the stars: cold inimitable stars, realms of light and splendor set in the canopy of heaven that stretched above this small earth and beyond, always beyond. He sighed. *Men,* he mused, *understand so little.* And perhaps that was how it should be, how God intended it. *Faith—was faith meant to be all?* He wished he knew. He wished—with another sigh he drew in the window and tightened the latch. Then he moved to his desk and reached for his Bible, the volume he had known and trusted since boyhood, its leather covering frayed and thin because it had come so much under the touch of his hand. He thumbed through the pages, selected a favorite part, and settled down in his chair to read.

Chapter Two

Throstleford was as common a village as any. By Friday morning every person in the vicinity knew of the presence of the strangers, and what their purpose there was. Most knew, as well, that the kindly minister of the Church of England had generously granted them the privilege to preach in his church. Many thought this a goodly, magnanimous gesture; others railed against it as being weak and foolish and likely to bring forth no good.

"We've two churches as it is, one more than we stand in need of," grumbled some.

"They'll come and go," reasoned others. "American upstarts looking to make hay in the old country that bred 'em. We want none of their ways."

Whatever the opinion, it was thought pleasant to have something new to discuss. And that was the way of it as Friday made way for Saturday and the Sabbath approached.

For Esther there was that same strange expectancy. Indeed, there had been a heavy, soaking rain all the night before, and the air, cleansed and sweetened, seemed to bring spring on its breath and all sorts of promises unnamed.

She had not yet met the strangers herself. They had left the village on Friday to preach at a nearby town, and were not expected back until the very late hours of Saturday night.

"What possesses them?" her father grumbled, returning from the doctor's, where they had made arrangements for the service. "I asked Archibald that question and he said, 'They want all England to hear their message; they want the whole world to hear.' Said it with a smile, that boyish smile of his." He shook his head. It was seldom her father either complained or criticized; thus Esther knew how uneasy he was. "That's Americans for you—always in a hurry, always sure of themselves." Yet when Nicholas Sheppard, parson of the Methodist congregation, pounded on their door late Saturday evening and was admitted to her father's study, Esther could tell by the soothing sound of her father's voice that he was defending his friend the doctor and the strangers as well.

She did not need to listen at the latch to guess what Mr. Sheppard would be saying. He was a big, blowy sort to begin with, and 'twas an uneasy peace he held with her father, for in a village this small two churches were bound to come to loggerheads now and again. If her father had not been of such a temperate and tranquil nature, abhorring conflict and avoiding emotional encounters as he would the plague, why things may have been considerably worse.

"You'll make a laughing stock of both of us, at the least," Parson Sheppard blustered. "My own flock scurrying over to see what all the excitement is about! Really, Christian!"

Esther heard that much when she knocked and brought in a tray with tea and the last of Pearl's scones. The parson barely nodded to her, but her father inclined his head and thanked her graciously.

She meant to wait up, but her eyelids grew so heavy with sleepiness that she found herself stumbling through her scripture reading and prayers, unable to pay proper attention. So she just lay her head on the bed, meaning to rest atop the coverlet for a few moments, and fell at once into sleep. When she awoke the sun was struggling its way out of the heavy cloud cover and morning was here, and she not even out of her day dress! What would Pearl say if she was found out? So the Sabbath had come, and she scarce prepared for it! There was no time at all for her to draw her father away for a moment; he would be at the church hours before she was ready. And, if she *were* given the opportunity, it would be futile, for what might she say to him, either by way of question or of encouragement?

Esther could not help being expectant herself. After washing and dressing with more than the usual care, she walked her own short distance that separated the vicarage from the church, between a row of dripping plane trees. As she walked, she noted many new faces among the stream of regular parishioners. She was intrigued to see more than a few from the Methodist congregation; how vexed Nicholas Sheppard would be.

It had amused her ever since she was a child that the two "men of the cloth" in their village, ministers of the gospel, so to speak, should bear such singularly appropriate names—not merely one of them, but both. Her father was Christian, and she thought the name fitted him, for indeed he was a Christian in all he did; while the head of the United Methodists was truly a "shepherd" to his flock, driving and rounding them here and there as he best saw fit. She and Andrew Sheppard, his son, used to giggle about the oddity of it when they were children. She wondered where Andrew was now; right now, at this moment. Would he come to listen to the strangers preach—would he dare?

Esther caught sight of Janet Sterne, the doctor's wife, talking to another woman near the entrance, and her attention was instantly piqued by the hat Janet wore. It had a shorter brim than was customary, and curled close to the head, setting off Janet's blue eyes and high cheekbones.

Perhaps Doctor Sterne's brother sent it from London, Esther mused. *Or even the strangers may have brought it.* Then she felt instantly sorry for her worldly and frivolous thoughts. She entered among the rest and worked her way up to the far left of the pulpit, to the small half bench which, even when her mother was alive, had been their family pew.

"You and I do not require much space," her mother used to explain.

"And up here we are out of the way, and yet close to your father. I like that, for I can see the expression in his eyes, my dear, and now and again he is able to send a special little smile our way." Esther settled in, looking neither right nor left, trying to listen to the music of the organ that filled the old sanctuary with melody. She closed her eyes, for with her eyes shut, all the real and true things filtered through, like light through the tall stained-glass windows high in the nave. The music, like the light, was an essential part of the memories: her mother was with her once more; she could almost feel the light touch of that cool hand resting over her own. She was young and the world held nothing but beauty: no fear, no ugliness, no sorrow or pain. Only here, and in the narrow space beside her mother's grave, could she recapture some of that feeling and find some remnants of peace.

The prayers were over. Her father was speaking. Esther bent forward to listen, feeling the breath suspended within her, as though she was a child again.

After they were presented, both of the strangers rose and spoke in turn, and very differently from anything Esther had experienced before. George Hascall was English, a convert to the new religion. The other, whose name was Levi Walker, came from the United States, a place called Nauvoo, on the great Mississippi River, and the romance of the names added an extra attraction for Esther. He called himself a *Latter-day Saint*, but the word *Mormon* had already been introduced, and when it was first spoken there was a bit of a stir in the congregation. Esther had heard nothing, either good or evil, about these people; she wondered if her father knew more.

Mr. Hascall called his companion "Brother Walker," with obvious respect and deference, though Walker was younger than Hascall by perhaps a good dozen years. Yet from the moment this Brother Walker began to speak to the people in earnest, Esther felt herself drawn to him, struggling to follow what he was saying, to understand.

He spoke of Christ's true church being restored to the earth through revelation, assuring them that revelation, along with the power and authority to act in the name of God, were essential to true knowledge and to the salvation of souls. He drew pictures with his words so that Esther could see what he called "the Sacred Grove" where the young boy, Joseph Smith, knelt in prayer on a mild spring morning and was answered with a vision of the Father and the Son.

The words were startling; they struck like small pebbles against Esther's senses. Could such an experience be true? Or did those termed religious fanatics only dream or contrive such remarkable things? Joseph Smith had read a verse in James with which she was familiar: "If any of you lack wisdom, let him ask of God, that giveth to all men liberally, and upbraideth not; and it shall be given him." With the confidence of a young and pure spirit, he retired to pray, to ask God which of all the churches he ought to join, for they were all contending one with another, and his mind was confused.

What astonishment to have this heavenly personage answer him with the admonition that he must join none of them, that they were all wrong, that "they draw near to me with their lips, but their hearts are far from me, they teach for doctrines the commandments of men, having a form of godliness, but they deny the power thereof."

For a moment Esther's heart stopped as she heard that terrible condemnation, spoken with such quiet and dignified conviction. Her eyes sought her father's face, but his head was bowed. *Surely not!* A fiery indignation leapt within her, a desire to protect more than defend. *Her father!*

But then a voice within her head said: *Your father is a good and true man. It is not he who stands under condemnation, but the system he serves.* She glanced around her; the impression was as strong as if a voice had spoken. She clasped her hands until the knuckles went white. The American speaker was talking of the Book of Mormon, this new scripture shown to Joseph Smith by an angel, then translated by means of an ancient interpreter. *A second witness for Christ,* the man called it. *A record of God's dealings with his children upon the American continent, containing precious truths translated by the power and authority of God, not contaminated by the precepts of man.*

He went on, but it was difficult for Esther to listen. Her mind was all in a whirl. She was overwhelmed—she wanted to be angry and offended at the condemnation of all she had known since she was an infant! But something within her would not. And she felt the struggle like a terrible tug-of-war, tearing her thoughts and feelings apart.

After the sermons had ended, both men bore witness, bore testimony, of the truth of the things they had said. *Truth restored. Truth restored.* The words rang with a sweet sense of assurance. *Why in the world were they doing this? What could all of it mean?* When her father stood at the high pulpit in his long robes of office, he looked as dignified as an angel, but there were tears in his eyes. Esther felt herself reach for her mother. Then her hand clenched against the hard wood of the bench. There was no one sitting beside her, no soft fingers pressed over her child's hand, no eyes smiling into her own.

Suddenly she felt terribly alone.

It was over. Many people gathered round the strangers, with her father and the doctor making introductions and congenial comments to smooth things along. *My dear father,* Esther thought. *My dear father.* Most people appeared pleased rather than offended, and that surprised Esther. She could see questions in their eyes as they pushed past her, but also something else she could not quite grasp. A listening attitude, a sort of illumination.

She wished she could recall all the strangers had said to them; perhaps part of her had not really wanted to listen *or* remember. Yet their words seemed to move through her mind like a stream of sparkling water, sun-streaked and clear. She stopped in her tracks. *Why am I thinking this? Why am I feeling such things?*

She suddenly felt awkward at the idea of meeting with or talking to other people. How would she respond when they asked what she thought of this new doctrine—when they sought to know what her reactions had been?

She could reach home by going the back way down the half-hidden walk that led to the side door of the parsonage. Grateful for the shelter of the cluster of young hawthorns that half-screened her from view, she scurried the short distance, pulled the heavy door open, and slipped gratefully inside.

Janet Sterne, who had been keeping an eye out for Esther, saw the girl dart down the narrow path and disappear as she neared the house. Janet's brow, high and fine, knit into a dozen tiny lines of concern. She had been afraid this would happen. "We shall be imposing on your friendship with Pastor Grey," Janet had warned her husband, "by asking the use of his church, *and* his congregation, when it comes down to that."

"I hope not," Archibald had replied. "I do not wish to cause him any inconvenience, Janet, much less discomfort. But this is what is being done across the length and breadth of the country, dear. There is nothing unusual in it."

Yes, but there is something unusual in these Mormons. Janet had only thought the words, not spoken them. But that had been the feeling within her concerning these men from the start. Now, she knew of a certain. Now a spirit of truth had swept through her, like a cleansing, illuminating flame. Now she stood convinced of things she had before scarce had the hope to give credence to.

She watched the faces of her friends and neighbors, not covertly, but openly. For the strangers' sermons had created an openness, had seemed to turn on a light that caused people who were usually solemn, even taciturn, to smile upon one another, to grasp hands with a depth of feeling they seldom showed.

"There'll be another meeting Tuesday evening," Paul Pritchard grinned. "An' I'll be there with me questions, for I picked up one o' these books." He held up the Book of Mormon, waving it in an emphatic gesture for all to see.

"And I as well," muttered Peter Goodall, "I as well."

Adam and Rose Dubberly walked forth with their arms linked and their faces aglow. They were a happy pair, he a simple farm laborer, and they had just lately wed, so that all the hopes and dreams they cherished were still fresh in their eyes. What they heard in the church house had stirred them; they had looked questions and then wonder back and forth at one another. He whispered into her ear as they trudged up the still-muddy slope above Windy Strath; he whispered what he had felt. She lifted her wet eyes to his and nodded. It was passing wondrous, indeed. Truth come down from the heavens, and forth from the earth. God speaking to man just as He had in the ancient days. A Heavenly Father who loved and guided His children in such a way!

So they were marveling, but Zachie Kilburn, the blacksmith, was chewing on sterner fare. Revelation, restoration, *authority* to act in God's name. Oh, but the Church of England would smart at that, to be sure! What bold creatures for certain these Mormons were! Yet, it all made sense to him, the way that foreign preacher man had explained it; it all made sense. And, what's more, it made something happen within him. Something sure and warm, like the glow of the forge on cold mornings; something sure and steady that would not let him alone. He was glad there had been enough of the Mormon books for him to take one. He had to get to the bottom of this matter, that much he knew. He had to do it—he was *eager* to do it. Walking alone, striding ahead of Louisa and the children, he could admit this, albeit with wonder, in his own mind.

Sallie Brigman hugged her arms to her body as she shuffled along. She had scarce felt well enough to leave her bed, but she had wanted to be here. And now she felt all warm inside, almost a sense of well-being which seldom came to her now that she had grown old. *Something was in the wind;* even her bees had sensed it when she spoke with them in the early morning, amid the shafts of sunlight which fair blinded her gaze, streaking like thin, sharp swords through the tangled black branches of the old oak in her yard.

"No leaves yet, my pets," she had murmured to the humming bees. "Too early for leaves and blossoms. Wait yet awhile." But the stir that had greeted her was one she well remembered from when she was a child: the bees awakening early—too early? No, for their ancient knowledge was etched deep within them; something so still and so sure that it could not be denied. They knew when the spring would break forth. They *knew* what men, in their mortal ignorance, could seldom surmise. And Sallie minded the last occasion, long years ago, that this had happened to her. It had been as a portent to the sweetest and happiest time of her life. Her babe, whom the doctors had warned would be born witless because of the high fever Sallie had suffered while she carried her, was born beautiful, strong-limbed, and sound. Her husband, slipping while hewing logs in the squire's woods, suffered only a shallow slash along his leg—losing neither limb nor foot as those watching had been sure that he would. Half a dozen things happened fair for Sallie that year; oh yes, she could not help but remember it well.

"What now?" she asked the restive bees. "What is in the offing for old Sallie? Or is it for others of us in Throstleford, sleepy Throstleford, that good news is biding?"

She wished she knew. She hoped whatever it was, it would embrace that young Esther, sweet and comely girl that she was. She needed something to happen to set life aglow for her. The lass lived too much in the past, her own and her father's; too much of them both lay buried in the one quiet grave.

So Sallie mused as she walked to her cottage, nodding here and there to her neighbors as they passed.

It was early, too early to tell yet, but Parson Grey, standing calm and dignified, friendly, but not forthcoming, was watching, too. His quiet eyes were as keen as a hawk's, but his usually quiet soul was in a turmoil that his mind seemed unable to still. He had not anticipated this, despite the disquietude he had felt. He was simply being polite, gracious and gentlemanly, as a good pastor should. A passing courtesy, then the strangers would leave and life would go on as it had.

This sudden shock had knocked everything within him awry. He sensed the extent of the impact on himself and his congregation, and wished heartily that he might look ahead. *Would that he might! Would that he might prepare and protect himself!* Protect was the word that stood out, that throbbed in his head like an unseemly taunt as he walked to the house, wondering suddenly where Esther had disappeared to, and what she had thought. Wanting very much to learn his daughter's response and opinions, yet knowing, at the same time, that he would not ask. Knowing that he had not the courage for that.

Chapter Three

The awkward silence of the long afternoon and evening alone with Esther, which the vicar had feared, did not come to pass. To his astonishment he received a veritable stream of visitors, neighbors drumming up the weakest of excuses to call at the vicarage, either to air their views or to ask hearty, sometimes glowing questions of the small, patient man.

Some, artless in their enthusiasm, praised the new preachers, expressing hope that they be invited again. Others, less than subtle, probed the minister for *his* opinion of what had gone on in his church. Christian Grey treated each with the same solemn courtesy, and they went away knowing little more than when they had come but feeling vaguely happier with themselves, nonetheless. Esther observed, but kept more silent than was her usual wont, though curiosity was churning her insides painfully. They ate their evening meal in courteous, but rather dull, comradeship, Esther taking her lead from her father because she knew that she must. When he excused himself and went to his study, Esther paced the floor in frustration. It was the Sabbath; there was little she could turn her thoughts or her restless hands to.

She had often been told that her mother was a woman of great patience, like the patience of the stream making a path down the rugged, rock-strewn hillside—that was the way old Sallie always described it. Esther wished she could remember with more than a child's fair impressions what her mother was like. She had just reached the age of nine when her mother died, so she had memories in plenty of picking berries in the spring, of tending her mother's gardens in the summer, of churning milk and helping with bread and pie baking; all the common pursuits of a woman's life. She even remembered her mother washing the fine linens and laces. She remembered, too, reading stories aloud by the fire, and her mother singing her to sleep as she lay in her bed, with a voice high and thin, almost like a child's simple voice. The voice had never been raised to her in anger, that much she knew. But, oh, the laughter of it, childlike as well, bubbling from some hidden source of her mother's being where, surely, true joy must have dwelt.

With a sigh Esther took up the supper leavings to take out to the cats. Her mother's old ginger tom stood back to let the kittens hungrily devour, perhaps knowing that Esther would have kept back some tidbit for him. He had been a kitten himself when her mother died, and had now reached the venerable age of ten years. "You learned her patience, did you?" she addressed the sleek animal, whose large amber eyes blinked back at her. "I do wish, goodly sir, that a little more of it would have rubbed off on me."

She did not expect to see her father again for the rest of the night. She took up a candle and went to her own room. She could find solace in reading; there was always that, if nothing else. She found her place in the book and drew her chair up close to the window, an old blanket wrapped round her knees against the rising night cold. She wanted to see the last of the light over the grove of aspen that fronted the squire's old house, half concealing it, so that the untrained eye would see nothing but dark trees against a dark sky, and off to the south the rounded head of Raven's Knoll, glowing still where the sun had lit it and left the throbbing of her flame that took a long, gentle time to go out.

Esther awoke earlier than usual and found herself hurrying to wash and dress, tying her hair in a simple knot at the back of her head. But when she entered the kitchen her father's seat was empty, though the table was laid and hot porridge bubbled in the pot.

"Master hasn't come down yet," Pearl answered her unspoken inquiry. "Haven't heard a sound from his room." Nothing more needed to be said, for both women knew how unusual this was. Esther set off in search of him but, after knocking tentatively and then pushing the door, she found his chamber empty and his bed untouched. He must have fallen asleep over his books in the study; he was sometimes known to do that. She entered that inviolable chamber cautiously to find her father with his head pillowed on his outstretched arms, sleeping still despite her disturbance. As she drew closer, thinking to wake him, she noticed the book that lay open beside his hand. The Book of Mormon. She paused to stare at it. What strange things did this volume contain? What mysteries, what knowledge so intriguing as to hold her father in fascinated attention, even against his will?

She touched a page tentatively, then pressed her father's shoulder with the tips of her fingers, but he did not stir. Best to leave him. Who knew how long he had been reading. She tiptoed out of the room and set out reluctantly on her morning errands, her terrible curiosity not yet satisfied.

She carried a basket on her arm, filled with varied wares, and thought it best to first take the eggs to Dorothea Whitely and old Peter Goodall, then she would not need to exercise caution against jostling or breaking them during the rest of her walk.

Dorothea lived alone. She was a handsome woman who had reached life's midyears much like a ship that had sailed an ocean where no squalls and no tempests rose, only calm waters and sunny skies. She had inherited her father's house and a modest annuity to live on, augmented by her admirable skill with needle and thread. She was mild of nature and opinion, sailing neither to port side nor aft, but charting a safe middle course, asking favors of no man, but giving to all with a natural, disinterested ease and sincerity. She was out in her yard, raking up the twigs and debris of the last spring storms, and smiled her broad, easy smile when she saw Esther approach.

"Ah, you remembered! Eggs with my bacon tomorrow, then." She took the snowy cloth wherein the white eggs nestled and turned toward the house. "I've got that sleeve mended and ready for you in return, Esther. I'll just hurry inside and fetch it." Esther followed at a leisurely pace, enjoying the sensation of sun on her bare head, lifting her face to the weak warmth of it, wondering if spring would come on steadily now, or if winter would snarl at them once or twice more before loosing his hold.

Dorothea returned quickly and, as she handed over the wrapped parcel, spoke markedly, her eyes fixed on Esther's face. "What did you think then of the Mormon sermon? Did it strike any chords in your heart?"

The question startled Esther, though she was used to Dorothea's outrightness. "Did it with you?" she parried.

"Yes, yes, it did. Much to my surprise, I might add." She was smiling again, though still watching. "The idea of a prophet for our time, of revelation—well, it feels right to me."

Esther nodded. What could she answer and remain truthful? She dared not assent; not now, not in the face of her father's silence. "I must be on my way." She patted her fat basket as if to indicate all the stops that yet lay ahead of her and Dorothea nodded in response, seeming to understand.

"Good morning to you, then."

"Good morning, Dorothea."

Esther passed through the gate and down the road all the way to the end, to the small, sagging cottage that old Peter Goodall had kept from time out of mind, and which was now snug and filled with the acquisition of his two granddaughters who had come to look after him.

"Come to eat me out o' house and home, they two," he complained mildly, whenever anyone would grant him an ear. But there was little truth to his mutterings, for Martha kept his house swept as clean as a pin, and Mary ran errands for him, to save his old bones, as he said. He was really very fond of the girls, but had been accustomed to solitude for so many years that at times their bustle and chatter told on his nerves.

Martha, a paragon of energy, also took in laundry and, convincing her grandfather of the efficacy of milk cows, made and sold to her neighbors the sweetest, smoothest butter the village had ever known. They were pleased to get the eggs in return for a slab of cool butter. Martha was too busy to leave her labors, but Mary came out to chat with her visitor for a moment.

She stood leaning against the fence, altogether unbothered by the morning stresses, as Martha was. Her features were pale and indeterminate, and her eyes more gray than blue, while Martha's beauty was of a more forthright, overpowering nature: she was larger of frame, darker of color, more sharp and cunning of eye.

"Wondrous meeting, that," Mary began, seemingly unaware of any discomfort Esther may be experiencing. "Made me feel all strange-like inside, if you know what I mean. Grandfather says this is what he's been praying for his whole life, though I'm not certain just what he means."

Esther nodded, with a bit of a lump in her throat. "Yes, well, we were given much food for thought."

"Exactly! Well put!" Mary smiled and placed her hand lightly over Esther's where it rested on the edge of the gate. "Always a pleasure to see you, Esther, if but for a few moments. Will we see you tomorrow night then?"

"Tomorrow night?" Esther felt her face go hot as she suddenly remembered. "Well, yes, I suppose that you might."

She turned somewhat suddenly and headed back up the road, waving her hand to the girl, beginning to truly dread the remaining calls she had yet to make. *I should have known,* she fumed to herself. *So little happens in Throstleford from day to day that, of course, these strangers would take precedence over all other matters of interest or gossip.* She sighed. What harm was there in it, anyway? Why did she feel she had something to protect, something to defend?

Rolled tight like a ball of yarn round her fears and frustrations, Esther bumped right into Evaline Sowerby at the door of Sam Weatherall's shop. Evaline had just stepped outside and was preoccupied herself with the parcels she was balancing. Both women laughed as they looked up and recognized one another.

"Are you going inside?" Evaline asked, stepping back a bit.

"No, I'm off to the doctor's," Esther admitted, "with a book from my father."

Evaline's fair brow knit in perplexity. "Strange this, isn't it, Esther? These two young preachers, I mean. I suppose your father isn't entirely pleased." She paused and pushed back a strand of hair from her face; dark blonde, Esther would call it, a warm color and as fine as spun silk.

Esther liked Evaline Sowerby and so, with a sigh of acquiescence, replied, "Yes, I shan't pretend to you that it is not disturbing."

"They said some mighty powerful things though, didn't they?"

"Yes," Esther agreed. "Yes, they did."

"I liked what they said. It made something good and warm rise up within me." Evaline looked at Esther closely, her brown eyes open and guileless. "They answered—well, questions I have had, really, since I was a little girl."

Esther nodded. "Yes."

Evaline sensed that she had best press no farther. But she added one more thought, placing her fingers lightly against Esther's arm. "My Edwin didn't see it the way I did. He has no interest at all."

"I'm sorry," Esther said before she could stop herself.

Evaline looked down at the tips of her boots. "Well, Edwin is himself. He has always been sure of his own ways, his own opinions . . ."

Her voice trailed off as she lifted her hand and Esther began to move in her own direction. "Have a good day, my dear. Perhaps I will see you on Tuesday."

Why did everyone say that? Esther wondered. Could they not recognize the awkward position in which she was placed? And now there was nothing for it, she *must* stop by the doctor's before going home. Yet, despite her reluctance, she realized, with the honesty of her nature, that she felt an intense curiosity to set eyes on the strangers again.

As soon as she knocked on the door it opened, and Janet herself stood there to greet her—with warm enthusiasm, though it seemed to

Esther her face turned a bit white. Such a lovely face. Esther had always envied, just a little, her young neighbor's beauty: she had the light brown hair the Scottish poet, Burns, praised in his verse, thick and warm, like coils of resting sunlight wound on top of her head. Her skin was like honey, with a light sprinkling of freckles across her nose, giving her not the common impish look but a distinct air of mystery. She was all woman, but there was something girlish in every aspect of her being: her looks, her voice, even her bright, lithesome movements and step.

"I brought the book the doctor requested from my father." Esther held it out, feeling a cold wave of awkwardness that distressed her, for she and Janet had always moved easily and confidently in and out of each other's hearts.

"I was hoping you might. I have something for you to take back, dear." She started off toward the kitchen, and Esther followed, catching the promising waft of flaky crust and warm fruit as they drew closer. "You've been baking pies," she cried out. Janet Sterne was known for her pies in all the villages nearby.

"I had to do something to occupy my hands and keep my thoughts from tormenting me," Janet confessed, her voice dropped to a low, confidential tone.

"Are your visitors—difficult?" Esther asked, her voice almost a whisper.

"Heavens, no. They are gentlemen to be sure," Janet responded. "It is what they bring in their wake—it is *everything else*, Esther, that weighs on my heart."

Esther felt relief well inside her, and she let out her breath with a long sigh. "I understand," she said simply. "Whatever happens, wherever this leads, I know—Father knows—"

Janet lifted a pale, tormented face. "Does he, Esther? Has your father said anything about—"

"Nothing. He fell asleep last night over his books, and I have not exchanged one word with him since."

Janet nodded, placing the warm pie into Esther's basket and covering it with a bright cloth. "We must wait then. We must all be patient—" She spoke the words almost to herself. Esther couldn't help smiling. "That's what I have been telling myself," she confessed. "But you know what a sparing acquaintance I have with patience!"

They laughed together, and the laughter cleared off the last bit of awkwardness, so that it was with a sense of ease and reassurance that Esther walked to the door, no longer concerned over the strangers, only wanting to hasten home to her father, to see what awaited her there.

Thus it took her a moment to realize what was happening when a man loomed out of the front hall right before her and extended his hand.

"I am Elder Walker," he said in his unfamiliar accent, "and you are the parson's daughter, though I do not know your name."

"Esther Grey, sir." Esther took the outstretched hand cautiously and felt her fingers encircled by a grip that was at once firm and gentle, as was the expression in the face that smiled down at her: firmness and gentleness; qualities she had always attributed to her father. She blinked back at the kindly gaze, feeling a bit dazed and uncertain.

"We appreciate your father's great kindness to us," the man was saying, "in allowing us the freedom of his pulpit."

Esther inclined her head at a gracious angle, not knowing what else to do, but being unable, as she regarded the stranger, to ignore the goodness that emanated from him. *You can many times discern goodness in a man*, her father had often told her, *because the inward man is stronger than the outer; the integrity of the soul overwhelms the lesser effects of the natural man.*

"We have come to do him good." Mr. Walker was continuing, watching her closely. "It is my hope that, in time, he will come to realize that."

Esther removed the hand he still held, murmuring something she did not remember as she fled from the house. *What an unusual thing to say to me*, she thought, her pulse pounding. *And what does he mean by it? What "good" can he do to my father, which would not jeopardize or destroy all that he is, all that he ever has been?* This she sensed, along with many other things, vague and uncertain, that disturbed her peace as she walked the pleasant way home. She *felt* change approaching, as one feels a storm before one sees the mass of dark rain clouds gathering, as one feels the miraculous renewal of spring in the first sun-warm breezes that brush the earth so lightly with their heavenly breath.

She was disturbed, but not distressed; perhaps the day was too lovely for that. Perhaps—but her thoughts took her nowhere. Nothing but the same vague sensations assailed her and with these, for the moment, she must reconcile herself.

What will my father say to me? she wondered. *What will he ask?* She felt certain he would ask something of her, she knew him so well. She walked resolutely, but with no hurry, into the parsonage, depositing her basket and its fragrant contents in the kitchen before going in search of her father, knowing, somehow, that she would find him waiting for her.

Chapter Four

꧁ ∞∞∞ ꧂

I should like you to read this, Esther, if you would." Christian handed the book to his daughter. Esther felt her fingers shake as she took it.

"No word now, not until you've read it," he answered the look in her eyes. "Yes, my dear, I know you are burning with curiosity, but 'twould be a waste of your time and mine until you have *read what I have read.*" He spoke the last words as though they were outlined in flame. Esther looked into his face. "What of Tuesday, Father? Are you still allowing the strangers to preach again?"

"I gave my word to them, did I not?"

Esther nodded. "I shall begin this afternoon, Father."

"Good, give it as much attention as you can."

She nodded again, wondering at the strange feelings that assailed her, aware that her entire life had been fraught with new feelings, both uncomfortable and intriguing, since the strangers arrived.

She completed what chores she absolutely had to, made excuses to Pearl, and fled to the little bower in the heart of the churchyard, whose closely grown curve of yew and hawthorn, interspersed with a dense tangle of old rose bushes, encircled her mother's grave. Tucked into the shade and quiet of the spot was an old wooden bench, stripped of varnish and faded, and lost to the memory of most who walked here. Esther had fiercely claimed it shortly after her mother died and had held on ever since. So many hours, fair and stormy, she had passed here! So many tears shed, so many hopes sighed into the rich, listening air.

She sat now, with her feet tucked beneath her and a pillow at her back, and opened the book, which held the lingering fragrance of her father's touch. *"The Book of Mormon, an account written by THE HAND of MORMON upon plates taken from the Plates of Nephi. . . . Translated by Joseph Smith, Jun. . . ."*

Esther read the words slowly. *Scripture. New scripture.* From a man who claimed to be a prophet, in a land she had scarcely given a thought to in the whole of her life. *An American prophet, an American volume, like the Holy Bible, claiming to have been written under the inspiration of God.*

She turned to the first page of the first book of Nephi and began.

> *I, Nephi, having been born of goodly parents, therefore I was taught somewhat in all the learning of my father; and having seen many afflictions in the course of my days, nevertheless, having been highly favored of the Lord in all my days; yea, having had a great knowledge of the goodness and the mysteries of God, therefore I make a record of my proceedings in my days.*

A feeling welled up in her that she could not identify, except for its rightness. *"Having been born of goodly parents . . ."* the words read like scripture. But they carried a note of intimacy, as well, so that straight from the beginning this Nephi seemed a true, living man, whose words reached out to her with a sense of reality from thousands of years' distance of time and place.

❦

Christian Grey knew whence his daughter had retired. The house had grown still. Esther was out there reading, digesting, thinking. Would she come up with the same conclusions as he had? And, if she did, what then? *What then? What to be done now?* He paced the floor, back and forth, trying to concentrate on something other than this huge barrier of light that had come into his life with the threatening power to stop him cold, to alter and even abolish the things he held dear, the things he was wont to cling to and call uniquely his own. Esther's response would be telling. Esther's pronouncement would have a vital effect on his own.

❧

Paul Pritchard closed the mill early, leaving his assistant, Coleman Dunn, to tidy up. He told his wife, Paisley, to leave his meal sitting in the kitchen until he came back for it, didn't matter if it got stone cold. He had things to do that had to come first. She understood; she had been watching him these past days, and she gave him no fuss.

"I've no mind for anything but this," he muttered as he walked the bumpity, uneven field that lay behind his mill and his house. There was a spot beneath the big cool spread of the old chestnut where he could rest and seclude himself, and dig into this book with a vengeance. Why did it burn a hole in his pocket, as it were? Why did it call to him like this?

He scratched at the stubble of beard on his chin, then dug the book out of his pocket with hands still powdered with the fragrance of wheat dust. He put one big thumb on the first page and started to read.

❧

Old Peter Goodall thought the sun would never set, the chickens never take to their roosts, or his two noisy granddaughters take to their beds. He fussed and fumed like an old lady, itching to get back to his reading, which had gone by bits and snatches since the Sabbath afternoon. Tomorrow night was the meeting. He wanted to know something more about what he was hearing; he wanted to get deeper into that Mormon book.

He had experienced dreams since he was a young man, recurring dreams that he had never told another soul. He might have told Lizzie;

indeed, he might, if she had not died so of a sudden after the birth of their second child. One dream in particular came more often after that. And it came mostly on the darkest nights when he had been missing her, when he had humbled himself in the awful stillness to pray to God. As the dream began he was always standing alone at the edge of a deep meadow shrouded in darkness, which appeared as vast as the entire world stretching out before him. He felt lonely and afraid, until he saw a light begin far off in the distance, a light that slowly enlarged and drew near. As it came closer its brightness increased and the brightness brought warmth with it, until all fear and loneliness disappeared, and the warmth invaded his being with an incomparable sensation of joy.

Sometimes he stood alone, bathed by the joy, until the dream faded or he awoke. But lately, the past few years, other filmy, uncertain figures had come to inhabit his dream landscape, some of them wearing an air of familiarity, but none of them tangible or clear enough to recognize. Once or twice he thought it was Lizzie, herself, who approached him, and then his sweet joy was such that it made his whole body go weak. At these times, it appeared she carried something clutched in her hands—it appeared that she carried *a book*.

Was he naught but a silly old man to connect his dreams with this new and sudden reality? He did not think so. For the feeling that had come over him when he heard the Mormon preachers in Pastor Grey's church was exactly the feeling that overcame him so richly with joy when the light approached in his dreams.

Thus he sat late, with one sputtering candle, when the girls were abed. He bent his head over the pages until the words blurred and he nodded, despite himself. Tonight was the last of it before the next preaching, and he had to get as far as he could. At length he rose stiffly, walked to the door, and opened it a wedge to let in the chilling night air. Then he poured himself a cup of cold tea and bent over the book again, his senses cleared and drawn by the words on the page that were a kind of wonder to him.

A soft mist of a rain at last drove Esther inside. She had come in briefly two hours before to eat supper with her father. Now the light was fading, save for the lurid throb and glow of the slight storm over the hills, painting the bleached, waning sky deep shades of faded heather and dull pewter. She glanced reluctantly at the graceful curve of stone that marked her mother's resting place and, with one of her long sighs, rose. "I must go in now," she said aloud, talking to her mother as she always did on such visits. "I must go in to *him*. And what I have to tell him will not be easy for either of us."

She dug her toe into the soft, moist earth at the base of the old hawthorn that had sheltered her. *What would you have done, Mother? What would you have felt about all of this? More than ever, I wish you were here with us now.*

As she entered the house the warmth of the inviting rooms made her skin shiver. Pearl was nowhere around, so she went straight up to her father's study and knocked on the door.

"Is that you, dear?" he called out.

She pushed the door open and slid inside like a shadow, smelling of rain and the clean wetness of leaves.

"I have read much," she began, "too much really to take in at one sitting." She paused, drawing her breath.

"But you have reached a 'verdict'?" There was a forced lightness in his voice.

"Yes. Yes—this book astounds me, Father. It is rich and alive; it is truly as one speaking from the dust, from the grave." She looked up and realized that his keen eyes were upon her, and that he probably had guessed what she was going to say. Yet, he would require it of her to speak the words and state her profession out loud.

"It has touched my heart with a conviction of truth—I know no other way to say it, Father."

He was silent for a moment; indeed, the silence of the room seemed as heavy as a weight upon them. At last he nodded his head, but paused again before saying, quite softly, "Yes, I very much thought that was what you would say—what you would feel."

Silence once more. Esther shuffled her feet and shifted her weight. She could hear the clock ticking on the mantel. She could hear the liquid call of the little screech owl from his perch in the yews. She knew her father was not yet prepared to return favor for favor; she knew it was impossible for him to share any of his own feelings with her. Indeed, the awful weight of those feelings was part of the heaviness about them. "I am in the middle of King Benjamin's sermon," she began, struggling to make her voice sound natural. "Do you mind if I take the book with me and—and finish?"

"No—by all means—I mean, yes, take the book along with you, my dear."

His endearment released her. She moved quickly to his side, leaned her head for a moment against his shoulder and planted a kiss on his cheek. She wanted to tell him somehow how much she loved him, tell him what tenderness she felt inside for him, but the awkward words stuck in her throat; she feared they would sound stilted and unnatural, and she could not bear risking that.

"Good night, dear Father," she murmured instead. "Do not stay up too late."

"And the same to you, little one." He pushed a lock of hair back from her cheek with his fingertips, and the brief touch brought tears to her eyes.

Alone in her room she performed her toilette for the evening and climbed into bed, her pillows propped comfortably behind her. She would read for an hour, perhaps—but certainly no longer than two.

The night seemed to hang suspended outside her window and she realized no time at all. When she nodded to sleep, the volume open in her hands still, the candle guttering into dimness beside her, she could not have told what time it was. But a light from her father's window glowed as a thin, yellow silhouette that cut a brave path in the darkness long after Esther was safely sleeping and unaware.

∞

Despite the few unsettled hours he had rested, Christian Grey arose early, for he knew his visitor would appear at his doorstep as precipitately as he decently could. Even then he was scarcely prepared for the vigorous pounding that made the old manse windows rattle and sent the house cats scurrying.

"That will be Mr. Sheppard," he called out to Pearl. "Would you please see him into the parlor?" Pearl did so with the special reticence she reserved for the Methodist minister. She could not bide his rude manners and his effrontery in being high-handed with her master, and had no idea of how to hide her aversion, nor the least conception that it might be more proper and more seemly in her if she did.

"Is the proposed meeting still on?" Nicholas Sheppard demanded, rising as his host entered the room, but not bothering to take the hand held out to him.

"What do you mean, Nicholas? You've come all this way to ask such a foolish question?" The vicar's voice was soft and noncombative; one would have to know him well to catch the thread of steel that stiffened the silken fiber of it. Sheppard bristled at the implied criticism in the discreet, direct reply.

"You know I am a man of my word," Vicar Grey continued.

"Man of your word—sounds good, Christian," his visitor growled. "But it's nonsense, and you know it. You've backed yourself into a corner this time with your everlasting complacence!"

"I thought you might look at it that way."

"Don't be foolish, man. There is no other way to look at it, not for the likes of the two of us!"

Christian nodded agreeably and waited for his friend to continue.

"My people are more open-minded than yours. This thing has got them buzzing, Christian!"

"This thing?"

"These Mormons. This Mormonite Bible—"

"If we have our people, we have them. If we don't, we'd better know soon than late," Christian soothed. "There is still freedom of religion in England, my friend."

"Homilies, platitudes!" Nicholas glowered from beneath his thick, shaggy brows, eyes like coals that could burn into the hearts of his parishioners but touched Christian Grey not at all. "There is *no reason* for this kind of upset!" he cried. "How can I be naught but aggrieved with you, man?"

Christian moved until he stood close to his friend and placed his hand firmly on his shoulder. "This is good for us, Nicholas. I am convinced of that." As his companion began to sputter in protest, he continued firmly, his hand still resting with resolution on that thick, muscled arm. "If these men are two-bit charlatans, what lasting harm can they do?"

"And if they are not?"

"Ah, that *is* the question—" Christian left his words hanging uncomfortably in the air between them. But his colleague, after spitting it out, shrank from the directness of the query as well as all it implied.

"You snatch my parishioners from me, you bite into my living, you bite into my respect amongst the people."

"I don't think so," Christian replied with his maddening calmness. And just then, to the secret relief of both men, Esther entered the room.

"Good morning, Mr. Sheppard," she smiled. "Andrew is here to fetch you for—"

"Fetch me!" he bellowed.

"Some need at the house, he said," Esther answered meekly.

"Tell him to wait for me outside."

Esther did as bidden, happy to escape the tension that snapped between the two men, but more than that, happy to spend a few moments in Andrew's company. They sat down on the porch together. "We'll have a bit of time before your father comes out," she guessed.

"We'll have the better part of an hour," he laughed, "if I know my father."

Esther shook her head at him. Then, unable to help herself, she asked, "Are you coming to the meeting tonight?"

"Why should I risk the wrath of my father?" Andrew answered, his expression mildly astonished.

"Why should you not?" Esther countered. "Have you no interest at all?"

"Curiosity, I'll admit. But not enough to risk a tongue-lashing and a week out of favor with him, not when he's as fierce as this has made him."

"Curiosity," Esther mused. "It goes no further with you than that?"

"And why should it, Esther? Are you trying to tell me it goes further with you?"

She ignored him for the moment. They had been friends since she was a toddler and he was in short pants, as long as they both could remember. "Come walk with me," she invited him, rising. "It's lovely out under the trees."

Should she tell him that she had been reading the Book of Mormon? Should she share with him any of the thoughts or questions it had engendered in her?

As she mulled over the possibilities, Andrew made her decision for her.

"Religion. Why do people get so het up about it, anyway, Esther?"

"Strange thing for a minister's son to be saying," she countered.

"Not at all. I've had it up to my neck. I just want to get on with my life—" He glanced at her face and instantly modified his words and his tone. "I wish to be a good person, of course. You know I do, Esther. I want to live with honor—and with a good sight more kindness than my father ever has shown."

"But the depths of religion—the depths of the spirit"—Esther merely breathed the words, almost hoping that he did not hear them—"they do not draw you, they do not speak to the very core of your being?"

He did *not* catch the words, only the gist of her meaning, because he knew her so well. "I forget," he said, a little more gently. "I forget what such things mean to you."

"Yes, Andrew." Esther found she could not say more, so she turned her footsteps back toward the parsonage, and the space between them became as silent as the cool mossy grounds through which they walked, along a path that diminished as it wound its way between the flat slabs of raised rock and the taller tombstones that marked the vicar's domain.

"Esther," he attempted. "Have I made you angry? That was not my intent."

She shook her head and gave him a weak smile. *Why am I feeling so strange, so different within myself?* she wondered without wanting to face any possible answers. *Why does not Andrew understand—even a little—even for my sake?* She did not like being out of humor or out of harmony with him. He had remained in many ways her best friend, ever since they were children. Friendship—and always a little more—a tenderness which her own heart embraced and encouraged, despite her knowledge that her father held very different hopes: that the childish love would wear itself out and that, as a mature woman, she would look somewhere else for a mate.

She sighed. Andrew took her hand and squeezed it. "I shall try to be at the meeting for your sake," he whispered, "truly I shall."

Their fathers were waiting for them, Nicholas Sheppard striding toward them stiff-jointed with his eyebrows beetling into a scowl, her father standing a little stoop-shouldered and appearing weary. She went to his side and waved only a halfhearted good-bye to her friend. She found that her thoughts were elsewhere right now. And she was glad to enter the sanctuary of her home and see to her father's needs.

Chapter Five

Meg pinned the brooch her mother had passed down to her just beneath her collar with a sense of satisfaction. She had convinced Samuel to close the store a bit early. "No one will be coming for meat for the larder or fodder for their beasts at this hour," she cajoled him. "Most folk are preparing an early supper, would be my guess, and getting ready to go to this meeting the doctor has gotten up."

She had been gratified when he had so quickly agreed. She could not say what it was about the religion she had heard the strangers preach that drew her, nor why she felt this sense of anticipation as she secured the precious brooch in place and arranged her best hat over hair she had washed and braided that morning—entirely out of the ordinary habit and scheme of her days!

Something in the way of things, something good, she thought. *I can feel it. A renewing, reviving sort of thing, same as my herbs act, natural because they have both the sun and the earth in them: sweet flag for the stomach and the eyes, shepherd's purse for childbirth, chamomile for nausea and insomnia, mayweed for children's colds, yellow foxglove for the heart, angelica for sore throats—the list could go on and on. Something sound. Something the good Lord provided.*

She drew on her wedding band, then set about looking for her best gloves. Samuel had agreed to bring their three oldest children along: Tom, who was as goodly and hard-working a son as any woman could hope for, and Molly and Lucy. Her daughters were already serious about their prayers and their readings in the scriptures, in the way of women, whose nature cares more deeply for the things of the Spirit than does the more down-to-earth, pragmatic makeup of men. She found her gloves. "Good," she said out loud. "I'd like to be there early in order to get a close seat, and to see which of my neighbors come to this meeting, too."

Paul Pritchard had read the Book of Mormon from cover to cover, and he knew that his wife, Paisley, was a good halfway through. The words of Moroni were running round and round inside his head, and he felt that he must understand them and do something about them, some-how. He would like to bring his son, Daniel, to meeting with him, but the boy's leg was swollen and hurting, too sore for him to walk even the short distance into town. And it would not do to see him carried down the street by his father.

"Take the wagon," his wife suggested, but he had to remind her that they had loaned both wagon and horses to Constable Johns, whose best horse had just gone lame. Nothing to do for it. "There'll be another time," he told both of them. But, nevertheless, his heart constricted within him when he saw the boy's eyes.

Zachie Kilburn left his blacksmith's forge to the care of his only apprentice and donned his Sunday clothes, a mite unwillingly, since he did not want to be seen making a big to-do out of this. But Louisa had a bee in her bonnet, that was for sure, and was herding her five children in front of her like a ruffled hen with her unruly brood, he among them.

"What's gotten into you, woman?" he growled.

"Can't rightly say," Louisa admitted cheerily. "Husband, I can't rightly say."

They walked into the lane, which already held a file of people all heading toward the church.

Pastor Grey, from the high, mullioned window of his study, was watching the people, too. *This is a modest church,* he thought. *We are not much more than a village here, after all. Yet this building has stood since the year 1540; indeed, the old chancel arch goes back three hundred years before that. What has it seen through the long, slow centuries?* More than he could comprehend, he knew. He, too, had read the Book of Mormon all the way through to the end. He knew the peaceful old place of worship had never seen anything like this in its life. He knew, but he did not understand. And he could not see into the future, not even one day.

Michael Bingham pinned a few wild violets on his wife's bodice. "Found them in the woods," he told her. His eyes were shining as he brushed a kiss on her cheek.

Hannah smiled back. She thought him the handsomest man in the village and the kindest, as well. He worked with his hands, but it was his heart that drove them, so that the fine things he fashioned from wood took on the glow of his spirit; she was convinced of that. She loved him very much. They had been married four years—four years flowing swiftly and sweetly. And, although she wanted children, she was glad to have had him to herself for this while.

Children will come, she often told herself. *They're bound to. It would be impossible for a love such as ours not to bear fruit.*

They were among the stragglers, for their modest cottage stood at the very back of the village. And, besides, Hannah had to admit, they were both woefully tardy in their habits. She touched the delicate violets with her fingertips. She could smell their fragrance very faintly if she closed her eyes, placed her hand on her husband's arm, and let him guide her along. It was thus she walked the last few yards to the chapel, not noticing anyone or anything about her at all.

A prophet of God in a grove of trees in a place called Palmyra; only a boy who was chosen of heaven, who proved himself true. "Through Joseph the Prophet God restored His authority here on the earth, a new dispensation, the last dispensation of time in which all things shall be gathered, all things restored and revealed." Those were the words the speaker now used, and the words burned into Esther's soul. She ought to reject them; they ought to feel strange and unpalatable to her. Any exultation in her soul at the hearing of truth was mingled with a terrible sadness, and she found she dared not look up at her father's face. *What is he thinking now? What is he feeling? What can all this mean to him?* She was not free to choose for herself, and every word that fell upon her heart she must judge in respect to the effect it would have on the life and well-being of her father.

"The gospel of the Son of God that has been revealed is a system of laws and ordinances which, if obeyed, will assure that we may return again into the presence of our Father and of our Lord, Jesus Christ—"

The speaker's voice was unraised, but it rang with the harmonies of deep conviction. Adam Dubberly leaned forward in his seat, his elbows on his knees, the muscles of his face taut in an effort to comprehend what was said. He was nothing but a common laborer; he neither thought much nor expected much of himself. But *this.* He lifted his eyes, concentrating all his powers.

"The Lord did not create this world at random. The earth was created for certain purposes, one of these being its final redemption and the establishment of His government and kingdom upon it in the latter days. And this that a people may be prepared to meet Jesus Christ when He comes here to reign. If we are obedient to the principles of godliness we can become like Him, we can feel our spirits progressing, we can come to love all men, we can live in the peace of the Savior's love and the power of His Atonement in our day-to-day lives. What great promises He holds forth for the faithful!"

This could be understood, this could be understood by the heart as well as the mind. Adam had never heard doctrine so powerful and so pure. He reached for Rose's hand; it was small in his own. But he could feel the warmth of life pulsing in the slender fingers and it seemed, of a sudden, a miracle to his senses: the precious wonder of the life of the spirit put into the flesh, which these men, with their clear eyes and countenances, could explain in a way he had never encountered before.

Archibald Sterne had already heard these doctrines: at his brother's house on the outskirts of London, and at the conferences held in Preston. With each hearing they were becoming more familiar, as though they had somehow belonged to him all his life.

He opened his Book of Mormon and followed along in the fourth chapter of Mosiah:

> And they had viewed themselves in their own carnal state, even less than the dust of the earth. And they all cried aloud with one voice, saying: O have mercy, and apply the atoning blood of Christ that we may receive forgiveness of our sins, and our hearts may be purified; for we believe in Jesus Christ, the Son of God, who created heaven and earth, and all things; who shall come down among the children of men.

He glanced around him to see the effect of these words on the others who heard them. He seemed to see hope in their eyes and the same light that kindled in his.

> And now, as ye are desirous to come into the fold of God, and to be called his people, and are willing to bear one another's burdens, that they may be light; yea, and are willing to mourn with those that mourn; yea, and comfort those that stand in need of comfort, and to stand as witnesses of God at all times and in all things, and in all places that ye may be in . . . now I say unto you, if this be the desire of your hearts, what have you against being baptized in the name of the Lord, as a witness before him that ye have entered into a covenant with him, that ye will serve him and keep his commandments, that he may pour out his Spirit more abundantly upon you?

Covenant people of the Lord . . . that, according to your own desires, He may pour out His Spirit upon you. . . . There was still much Archibald felt he did not understand. He knew only that God had witnessed to his soul the truth of these words. He knew that he desired to enter into covenants with God through the priesthood authority that these men held. The meeting would come to an end soon, and they would announce that there was to be a baptism on the following day. He knew only that he desired to be among the first to present themselves for that ordinance— for baptism by immersion, then for the laying on of hands by one holding authority to administer to him, Archibald Sterne, the priceless and powerful gift of the Holy Ghost.

∞

The rain started early the next day, as if to taunt or at least sorely try the believers. There would be no baptisms at the side of the river while the thunder and lightning and fierce wind prevailed. It did more to appease those smug or disturbed souls who feared and resented this religious intrusion than it did to discourage the converts or dissuade the convictions newly born in their hearts.

Christian Grey knew this, and he winced inwardly when he opened the door to Pastor Sheppard's earnest knock.

"I'm not staying to plague you for your blindness and your sins, Christian," he announced, standing dripping and strangely triumphant under the small sheltered porch. "Though I might ask you if you feel the fool you've been made," he snapped. When he received no answer he shook the rain from his hat. "Well, we've our own means. We've waited too long for you, vicar, to take matters in hand."

He was turning down the wet, puddled walkway as he flung out the last words, but Christian stemmed the impulse to call after him. He didn't really want to know what the minister's foolish words meant, or what he might have in his mind. He shut the door on the storm without, wishing ardently that he could shut out in the same way the storm within.

∞

Doctor Sterne was not surprised when he opened the door and found the constable, looking stiff and uncomfortable, his hat in his hands and his eyes downcast.

"Might I have a few words, doctor?"

"Is there anything the matter?"

"Just some concerns," the man hedged. "Concerns—brought to my attention, is what you might say."

The doctor stood back. "Do come in out of the rain, friend," he said gently. He had half-expected as much. And, strangely, he found that he had no uncertainties and no fears in his mind.

The rain wore itself to a miserable dripping in time for the sun to make a tardy show and sweep away the dullness of the storm with a subtle gold that glowed through the tree branches and over the house-tops with the intensity of a beacon light. They could go now; the baptisms could go forward before nightfall. But the time had already been changed until the following morning, just after sunrise. Better then. A new day, the river calmed and waiting, perhaps the banks less muddy as well. Many preparations were made behind the curtains of a dozen silent houses. And in the doctor's study the yellow lamp burned late, past the still midnight hour, and on.

The vicar was generally an early riser, but he had debated whether to lie late abed this day and leave well enough alone.

A knock, then hurried steps along the corridor and up the stairs, startled him into wakefulness, and gave him just time to wrap his morning robe round him and run a comb through his hair.

"The doctor is downstairs asking for you," Pearl hissed through the keyhole.

"Tell him I shall be with him directly," the vicar replied.

One more ordeal. Something within him grew weary at the mere thought of it. Even his feet seemed heavy as he made his way down the stairs.

"Thank you for receiving me," the doctor began as soon as he entered the parlor.

Christian nodded. "What is so essential at this time in the morning, Archibald, and on such a day?" he asked gently. "Or is there trouble brewing?"

"I dearly hope not," his young friend breathed. "I simply—well, before things begin, before I take this step, I wanted to speak with you, friend to friend."

"You owe me nothing," Christian said, then he bit his tongue on the unwelcome words that had somehow slipped through.

"It is not a matter of that. It is a matter of our two hearts which have before moved in a rare friendship and harmony, and now perhaps hazard estrangement."

"Broken music," the vicar mused.

"It would grieve me very much. It grieves me enough to take this step away from you, as it is."

"Indeed." Christian did not wish to look into the eyes, so earnest and guileless, that were seeking—*what* from him? "Men of integrity follow the reasoning of their own minds and the prompting of their own hearts, my good friend," he attempted. "I hold nothing against you—none of what you choose to view as disruption or disrespect on your own part."

"Yes. Of course, you would understand." The words were spoken as a tribute, with a sense of respect and affection impossible for the vicar to miss.

"Enough, then." Christian coughed against the dryness in his throat, reluctant to clothe with words this thing he wanted to say. "The *details* of this matter, if you but think about it, Archibald, bring me pain, if anything does—for then I must think about, examine, and deal with what is happening more closely than I am yet willing to do."

The younger man nodded. His eyes, which were still seeking his friend's eyes, were tender, yet there was nothing apologetic about his manner. He possessed a singular kind of confidence, born of the Spirit; the vicar recognized that.

"God go with you," the churchman said, holding out his hand. The doctor clasped it firmly, gripping it tightly for a long moment before letting go.

❧

Peasant Lane ran behind the village and parallel with Ash Water, the narrow river that took its name from the ash grove that bordered the old squire's house. The squire lived to the east of Throstleford, but the ancient lane wound west with Windy Strath. The strath, dotted with a few farm cottages, stretched on the other side of the river before the farther-reaching woods and high moors. Only a few dozen yards out from the village the river widened, and an old stone bridge spanned the expanse like a dark humped rock, a bridge that had served the villagers from before their grandfathers' time. Here the strangers had come to perform their baptisms. The people were gathering, and Constable Johns stood atop Blind Man's Knoll to keep watch. The knoll was little more than a slight rising of ground, but it afforded an excellent view.

He walked back and forth, rubbing his hands together, for he could not seem to hold still. "Awkward business, this," he muttered under his breath. He knew who all the troublemakers in the village were, he knew the rough element not only by name but sometimes by the way they walked, by the sound of their voices in the distance. He knew the lot of them would be here this day. *And why?* He had no answer for that age-old question. For himself, he wished the Mormonites well. He could not see what threat or danger it would be to anyone if some of the good folk in this village were baptized by the Mormons this day. *Leave religion alone, and it will leave you alone.* That's what he had always held to. Belief was a thing of the heart, a thing of the conscience that generally made men better, not worse, unless they took to harassing one another in the name of that conscience and believing themselves justified. This other, which was gathering like the dark swells of storm clouds, came from fear and the powerful impulse to dictate to others, something else he did not understand.

He stopped and squinted his eyes to pick out faces among the people gathering near the water. *Good people all,* he pronounced to himself. He wondered how many had come to actually be dunked in that cold stream, and how many merely to stare. He wondered—ah, well! Wondering was of precious little value, and he was not paid to wonder, he was paid to keep watch. He began his pacing again, back and forth, back and forth, not aware that he had begun whistling an old tune under his breath. The candidates for baptism gathered in a loose halfcircle, while the two Mormon elders stood at the head. Doctor Sterne and his wife, Janet, were conspicuous, standing just to the right of the strangers. His face was composed, but his eyes were alive with a warm light, and he was holding her hand.

Dorothea Whitely stood as tranquil and sure as an angel, with Peter Goodall, stretching his old stiff body as straight as he could make it, there by her side. His granddaughters hung back in an unusually docile attitude, but Louisa Kilburn, with her noisy brood, pressed forward, Zachie right behind her, his wide mouth smiling so broadly that everyone who happened to look at him felt their own faces relax and lift into answering smiles.

But the miller and his wife stood with their heads half-bowed, and there were tears in Paul's eyes.

The Mormon elders and Doctor Sterne were there, but their good pastor was nowhere in sight. Perhaps there were not a few who sighed with relief, for they could go forward more happily into the waters of baptism and commitment to this new religion without his kindly, non-judgmental eyes upon them.

Levi Walker, from Nauvoo, Illinois, where the Prophet of God resided, spoke to the assembled people, encouraging and blessing them, then a hymn was selected and sung.

"Rejoice, the Lord is King!" Charles Wesley's words rang out. "Your Lord and King adore! Mortals, give thanks and sing and triumph evermore . . ."

Constable Johns was not watching the singers. He had his eye on the shadows of men slinking up on the assemblage like so many wolves, their backs hunched, their brows furrowed into dark lines of anger. He recognized every one, from Jem Irons, the teamster's son, to the Heaton boys. And the Heaton boys were the ringleaders, as they most usually were. "His kingdom cannot fail; He rules o'er earth and heav'n . . ." The singers were largely unaware of the danger that was approaching them. Constable Johns could see that some of the boys carried bulky sacks, probably filled with rank and rotting vegetables, which they intended to dump into the water, or over the heads of those being baptized. *"Lift up your heart! Lift up your voice! Rejoice, again I say, rejoice!"* Wilford Johns rubbed the rough stubble at his chin. Then he drew his stick from the bushes and headed toward the boys.

At the water's edge Archibald Sterne, dressed in white trousers and shirt, was wading into the water beside Levi Walker, who reached across and placed his hand on his shoulder. Each took his place before the elder's arm was raised to the square and the ordinance spoken that would make the doctor a member of the new Church of Jesus Christ: "Having been commissioned of Jesus Christ . . . in the name of the Father and the Son and the Holy Ghost. . . ."

The men came up out of the water slowly, and it seemed all the others assembled were holding their breaths. No one spoke. The doctor's gaze sought his wife's face and his eyes spoke of a joy that he had not words to express. He moved onto the land, dripping water, and someone placed a blanket around his shoulders. There were murmured words of kindness here and there that the doctor's ears could not catch.

Janet would be the next, but before she could enter the river a loud splash was heard, like a mighty slap on the water, accompanied by half a dozen piercing whoops of triumph and almost fiendish delight.

The converts turned their widened gaze up the stream to see a chaos of debris floating toward them: rotten vegetables mixed with kitchen parings, dirty rags, and pieces of broken boards, warped and rough, claimed the expanse of the water and quickly approached the clear pool where the group stood and helplessly watched. Constable Johns had his big hands on the scruff of two of the offenders, his booted foot holding another one down. They protested loudly, believing that the officer, as their fathers had told them, would be on their side. But they had already done their mischief, so their voices were still sharp with belligerence. The constable was calling to the blacksmith and a couple of the other large men. He had it in his mind to coerce the ruffians to undo their own pleasure and clear the stream by their own hands so that the proceedings might yet go on.

As he was wondering just how he was to effect such a triumph, a keen, high whistle was heard, long and sustained, and a black streak shot down from the low hills followed by the shape of a man whose movements were deliberate but unhurried. By the time he reached the riverbank, the border collie danced at his side, panting and grinning, his ears cocked and ready for his master's command.

"Be ye in need of a little assistance?" the shepherd asked the constable.

Their eyes met, and Mr. Johns nodded. "Indeed, your arrival is timely, my friend."

The young men knew, too, that their efforts had been defeated, and it was with a surly air and not a few muttered threats and curses, that they brushed themselves off and waded into the river, the two men with clubs watching, the collie nipping at their heels every time they stepped out of line.

The congregation sat in the shade to wait. The five strong young men cleared the river in no time, and the constable marched them off toward town. He knew he would have the dickens to pay when he faced their fathers, but he was not concerned about that. He knew what he had felt when that stranger from America raised his hand above the doctor's head. He may as well have been struck by lightning, the sensation had been so real.

Oliver Morris, the shepherd, retreated up the hill and watched from a safe place as the quiet baptisms proceeded. His dog lay still at his side. The grace of the scene affected him. The faces he watched were faces familiar to him. He felt their joy as much as he saw it. It disturbed him that this should be so. He watched through the last young person—for the very little children had not entered the water—and he watched the damp, happy people amble back to the town. Their voices, singing snatches of old hymns, seemed to wander back and remain with him as he made his way along the undefined trails to where his flock waited and where he would again be alone.

Chapter Six

*E*sther stood at her window and watched the merry group coming back through the meadows, happy as May Day revelers. They were heading en masse for the Pritchard's mill, where they would celebrate with roasted chicken and early greens, with Sallie's honey spread over fresh bread, and with Janet's warm pies.

She wanted to be with them. The parsonage felt like a tomb to her, echoing in a suddenly meaningless silence. She was young and the day was fair, and she wished to be with her friends.

She drew the curtains and turned from the window. *Are they my friends? They have all done something big and something solemn that has drawn them away from me.*

She did not know what she thought of it all; she did not truly know what she wanted. How distasteful it was, like a dizzying sensation, to be discontent and confused! It spoiled everything for her, even reading, which was generally her solace.

Where is my father? she thought. *What will he do without these people who have been so long a part of his life? It is as though a dozen, two dozen people were suddenly wiped out by a plague, as though they all died at once.* She shuddered. It did not seem just that these friends could so thoughtlessly turn from him, only because—only because . . . *I know why, I know why they have turned from him—because I have felt it, too!* She dare not think of her father, not at the present. Her own inability to help him was like a wound, like a sharp pain that played over her senses and rendered her weak.

∽

The festivities broke up early, for there were solemn feelings in the hearts of most, and much conversation concerning the experience they had passed through. At length women took tired children home to their own firesides, while several of the men repaired with the visitors to Doctor Sterne's house. There, in the front parlor, clean and quiet, with the rich golden rays of the late afternoon sunlight filtering through, hands were laid on their heads and the priesthood of God, by those holding authority, was conferred.

A quiet gladness sent tears to the men's eyes as they clasped hands and gazed at each other with wonder. Doctor Sterne was set apart as presiding elder and instructed to hold meetings often so the new Saints could pray together, read from the holy scriptures, and testify to each other in faith. The visiting elders would return in a fortnight to check on this new flock, see what their needs might be, and perform baptism for any who wished it.

Zachie Kilburn walked to his house in a quiet mood, studying in his mind all that had happened. He felt he could see in a new way, though dim and not fully formed yet, what it meant for him to be head of a household, head of a family. *An eternal entity,* Elder Hascall had called it. *The only divine institution that will go on through the eternities.* He gazed about him, the wonder within him coloring all that he saw, making precious what had before been commonplace. He felt his feelings expand, and the strongest that he took with him as he entered his warm lighted house was the feeling of gratitude—gratitude for wonders and blessings which he had accepted but could not yet understand.

∽

Paul Pritchard retraced his steps to the mill, and he felt that his heart was singing, like the whirr of Paisley's spinning wheel of an evening. He felt poetic; that is how his wife would describe it if she could see into his heart. He had special reasons for wanting the power of heaven to help him; had he joined this church simply for that? *Nah-nah,* he chided himself. He knew what he had learned, and he knew what that knowledge had already done for him. All his past life he had looked upon religion as a matter for the preachers and parsons, something they thought about and worked at and then presented, in appropriate bits and snatches, to the men and women who came and sat in their pews. Comfort was supposed to be there, and understanding, but Paul had felt little of that. When his son fell out of a tree at five years old and shattered his upper leg and hip bones, even the gentle Reverend Grey had little comfort to give him.

"We cannot understand the ways of the Lord. We must accept and trust him. You can pray for your son, commit him to God, and seek for the courage to go on with your life."

For all his goodness, Paul felt that was what Christian Grey had been doing, or trying to do, ever since his young wife died. The Book of Mormon and the words of the Prophet Joseph Smith that he had read gave Paul *reasons* as well as hope. They gave him *a road to walk on,* that's how he looked at it; assurance through the priesthood that his obedience would bring him close to heaven in a way he had never envisioned before.

"I am God's son. Very literally." He spoke the words out loud, under his breath, to the quiet night wind that wove itself comfortably, like a cloak, round his shoulders, seeming to ward off the growing chill. He felt changed and blessed—*changed and blessed*—the words were like a cadence to which he fit the rhythm of his steps as he walked home.

⟫

Paisley sat alone, waiting. Some of the other ladies had helped her to clear up before they left. Now even the children were calmed and in their beds, and only stillness surrounded her: the stillness of home. She knew this man, whom she had loved since the first time she laid eyes on him, was a good man. She had watched through the years how he dealt with his neighbors: always a full measure; always an *extra* measure if a family was pinched and in need of it; always a kind word and a helping hand. It ought to be about time. She listened for the fall of his footstep, and heard the night wind blowing from off the far moors, scattering its way through the town, then gathering sweetness again as it left the village streets behind and found its way to the mill. Always clean smells and clean sounds at the old mill; Paisley liked that. She liked making her home here. She liked the man who gave that home a texture and purpose it would not possess otherwise.

What will this mean to Paul? To the both of us? she wondered. *We have set our feet on a path we did not know existed a week ago. Where will it take us?* She knew the ending of all paths was hidden from view. She had taken a strange path when she left her home in Scotland to follow this man. She had never regretted it; she had only grown more and more contented and sure. But this new way—what twists and curves, what rough, stony stretches did it harbor? What long distances leading to something she could not yet envision—she shook her head. *Long roads . . . long thoughts . . .* She'd best set the big lamp in the window well so that Paul could find his way more easily and know she was waiting for him.

Janet was the last in the house to go to bed. She had tidied and fussed about longer than she needed to. She could not get her thoughts to lie still; they lumbered, like great shadowy dogs, round and round the tracks of her tired mind.

It had been a good day: her own baptism, and the way she felt when she came up out of the water, as though she were light as a feather—her body washed with water, but her *self*, her spirit, washed all over with light. Then the company of all these good people who had always been their friends, but were now something more, sharing a thing they were all willing to change their lives for—work for, *sacrifice* for, if necessary. Why did that word come to her mind?

I am more timid than people think. I must not be, she chided herself. *Now is the time to be brave.* But she had seen the expression on the face of one of the Heaton boys when he tossed an armful of wood, all shards and splinters, into the quiet stream. There had been *hatred* in his eyes; blind, stupid hatred, and the look had made her whole body go numb and cold. *Why? Why do people hate when there is no reason? What does the religion we choose to follow have to do with them?* She hugged her arms and rubbed her cold shoulders, because she could feel herself trembling through her thin nightgown.

Best go to bed. Best think about all this tomorrow. Or not at all. Archibald would be ashamed of her—no, not ashamed of her, not with his gentle spirit. But disappointed, surely disappointed, and she could not bear that.

She did not wish to wake him, so she dropped to her knees in the dark, chilly parlor. She would pray here; here where the Spirit, such a short time ago, had manifested itself through—*what did they call it?* the laying on of hands. She had felt it; she had no doubt of its validity. She closed her eyes. She would wait until this Holy Ghost came to her, until she felt its influence fill her and calm her. It would come, she knew it; and then things would be all right.

Evaline Sowerby attended the baptism, but had not dared to do more. Scurrying home on her own, she had watched the merrymakers, glowing with a happiness her heart longed for, make their way to the mill. Edwin was sewing when she arrived, sitting on a tall stool in his little shop at the back of the house, stitching patiently on a job of work needed up at the manor. Evaline began at once to cut the vegetables she would be cooking for supper. She had started her bread early, before leaving for the bridge pond, and it was rising nicely by now. She began humming; she often hummed under her breath while she worked, without really knowing she did. This time it was the tune of one of the hymns they had sung, one that the man from Nauvoo in America had brought with him. It had stayed fresh in her memory, speaking to something within her, awakening longings . . .

> *The Spirit of God like a fire is burning! The latter-day*
> *glory begins to come forth; The visions and blessings of old are*
> *returning, and angels are coming to visit the earth . . .*

She repeated the phrases over and over again in her mind. Edwin came into the kitchen. "Need to stretch my legs a mite," he said, reaching for the jar of buttermilk and taking a long swig. "Hope you've got all this religious nonsense out of your head now, Evie."

Evaline did not look up. She had not dared to ask her husband if she, along with the others, could be baptized. But she had to be brave now, at least brave enough to speak her mind to him. She had to begin somewhere. "I am interested more than before," she ventured. "I should like to—"

"I told you, I want no more of it." Edwin's voice had a bite to it that sent chills down her spine. He had never struck her before; he had seldom been really unkind to her. But this—this had awakened some hardness in him that lay like a stone on her heart.

"I am a good wife. I do all you ask of me, and more," she retorted. Edwin's glum silence she knew was assent. "Doctor Sterne and some of the best people of the town have joined with the Mormons—and, what's more"—she hurried to add—"they know of my desire to be among them—"

He understood what she was hinting at. "Let's leave it then, shall we? Let's leave it for a spell, Evaline."

She was partially satisfied; she felt she had made more headway than she had dared hope for when first they had started to talk. *Patience. Patience.* She spoke the word slowly inside her head and drew a deep breath.

Stubborn woman, Edwin thought. *I'll not risk the straight-on approach again. There are more ways than one to skin a cat, and I happen to know of another that ought to work for my purpose just fine.*

There was an unspoken sense of anti-climax following the baptism, as though, somehow, the village had been let down. Many had expected fireworks that morning by the river and went away not only disappointed but with all the energy of their emotions still pent-up. Others would have bet on a hell and damnation reviling by one or more of their ministers, especially Nicholas Sheppard, who guarded his flock like an old jealous sheep dog, shaggy head lowered and ready for the least bit of trouble he might smell out or spot. They were disappointed, and some took to murmuring over their teacups of an afternoon that Reverend Grey was too kind and too mild by half, and this all was *his* fault, was it not? Why, if he had refused the strangers when they came begging their favors of him, they'd have had to seek elsewhere for a pot to stir trouble in.

In truth, too many neighbors had been enticed from the fold: good neighbors, good folk, well respected and well thought of. What did it mean? What further changes would this change bring? It was morning. Early enough that the throstles still sang in the hedges and the larks in the sky. High thin clouds boding nothing but a fair day thinned as Edwin watched them, threading his way through the village streets toward Ravensquill Manor, his pack on his back.

He had done fine work; he always did fine work. No one cut cloth with as much skill as he, nor took stitches as fine. But what he was delivering today would please Madam and her tetchy daughters enough to purchase him a few moments in the midst of their pleasure to worm in a question or two. He had every intention of imparting information as well. *Stir things up a mite,* he thought with a sort of grim satisfaction. It had been all too easy for those strangers to waltz in here and turn their world upside down! What a to-do might break over their heads if the squire's wife deemed it—and Edwin hoped that she did. He whistled as he crossed the fields by the footpath and entered the protected silence of the squire's grounds. He walked back to the tradesmen's entrance and knocked on the door.

"Madam is home and anticipating your arrival," old Betts said with a kindly smile. He had been servant in this house for a long time. He knew its comings and goings; he knew its ways. He gave no sign of what he, personally, might think of the visitor, but moved aside to let him come in.

Just what I had hoped! Edwin inclined his head respectfully. "She'll not be disappointed," he asserted as he passed through the door.

There were regular and proper times for the squire to visit the pastor. Pearl, seeing his carriage outside the window, knew that this was not one. She called for Mr. Grey, at the same time thrusting her broom into the cupboard and straightening the cap on her hair. *What can this mean?* she muttered as she scurried through the passageway, but she thought she could guess. She cursed the good doctor for his highfalutin ideas, she cursed the strangers, and she cursed the stupidity of her neighbors, all in one breath.

When she opened the door it was to smile at the intruder, the great man who alone had no need to announce or make excuse for himself. She led him into the parlor where the pastor was waiting, then with an itchy reluctance closed the door on the two of them and went her own way.

Christian Grey also guessed what had brought the squire thither, and steeled himself for the encounter.

"What's this unpleasantness I've been hearing about?" Squire Feather began bluntly.

"Unpleasantness?"

"Don't bandy words with me, Grey. It's the matter of these strangers from America thrusting themselves upon our community—calling themselves Christians—having the audacity to *preach* to our people things they've never thought of before!"

The squire's huffiness was causing his already ruddy face to blush deeper, and Christian hoped that his own calm demeanor would give him the edge.

"Doctor Sterne invited them here; they are friends of his brother's in London."

"Don't care whose friends they are! You let them speak in your chapel, Grey—"

"That is a customary courtesy, sir."

"Don't care if it is customary. You ought to have looked into the matter more closely—now look at the mess we're all in!"

"I see no mess, no conflict; nothing that I am aware of—"

"God and highlanders, you don't, my man," Jonathan Feather thundered. "They've stolen your flock, as I hear it, right from under your nose."

"There was a baptism, yes. They have made a few converts." Christian could feel discomfort, like a fever, spreading through his system, and sitting like a weight on his forehead.

"Can't have that, can't have that!" His antagonist spoke stoutly, sure of himself and his stand with all the surety of four hundred years of ownership and rank to uphold him.

"People have their own will and agency, sir. This is the 1830s— England is a free country."

The squire glowered from beneath his black brow and hunkered his broad shoulders in displeasure.

"Sincere religion blesses and strengthens the lives it touches. Our community will not be hurt by the Mormons coming in here." Christian leaned forward in his seat and forced himself to meet the smoldering eyes across from his. "If you will allow me, sir, the only rancor and trouble comes from"—he paused—"the lower elements, the habitual troublemakers which every village suffers."

"Don't know that, don't know that of a certain, my good man. Religion stirs up strife in a family as well as a nation; you know that, Grey, as well as I do."

Christian began to wonder just who it was that had gotten hold of the squire. Not Harvey Heaton from the Stragglers' Inn, or any of his compatriots; clearly someone more respected, who would have a natural reason for intercourse with the big house. The squire rose heavily. He was a large man, just touching on stout, but tall enough to conceal his increasing bulk and to maintain the added air of authority his size afforded him. His black hair was thinning on the pate of his head, but he combed the long strands back to conceal it. His eyes were as black as his hair; raven-dark. All the Feathers, men and women, were the same—all but one.

"Can't have it, can't have it!" he repeated. "You're a Church of England man! I don't want to see these people making free in yon sanctuary again, Grey."

Christian nodded; curtly, he knew, but he could not trust his voice.

"See that you take care, my man—nip this thing in the bud, will you? Send the scoundrels well on their way."

Christian thought, with a wry regret, of how seldom the squire and his family ventured into *yon sanctuary*. If he had been in attendance these two weeks past, he would have known of events for himself.

The squire turned and began to take great strides toward the door. He had completed what he had come for; there were to be no banal pleasantries today, then, to soften the contours of their meeting. His heavy boots made loud scuffing noises along Pearl's scrubbed floor. So be it. If Christian had given thought to it, he would have expected no more.

I shall see you at Sabbath meeting, sir, I trust. Christian *nearly* said the words, but he could not quite get them out. *I am a coward,* he thought as he watched the coach draw away. *Mild-tempered, gentle-mannered, they call me. But it is a coward I am. My people know it. I know it.*

He walked back into the house and through to his study, very firmly shutting the door behind him. All about him looked threadworn and shabby, tainted with an air of disappointment, stained with the bitter dregs of his own pale inadequacies.

If Mary had lived, if she were still with him, things would have been different—*he* would have been different. He knew this for a fact; 'twas not a lame excuse he made to justify his weaknesses and failings. Sometimes, after all these years, it was difficult just to go on. He had Esther; he thanked heaven that Esther was a part of his life. She wove colors and melodies into the fabric of his being that enlivened the drab stuff with vigor and beauty that seemed constantly changing, shifting, renewing itself. He was fortunate; he should not need to remind himself of that fact.

But was she, his daughter, so blessed by his presence in her life? This question was new to him, and he was reticent to entertain it, even in the very depths of his thought.

He went to the window. There were still hours of daylight remaining, there was still work to do. There was his friend, Archibald Sterne. He must face him and disappoint him.

He clasped his hands behind his back and began to pace the small room. He struggled against an inclination very similar to the squire's: curse the Mormons for ever coming. His own religion, he knew, had much of sternness within it; a stern God who made demands and who punished; a far-off God who gave few explanations, whose nature was jealous and, at times, unforgiving and harsh. These Mormons—just what were they attempting to do? They were taking his placid and pleasant existence and stirring it ever so roughly and clumsily, with no apparent regard for the distress they generated—nor for the pain, old and deep, which their well-meant efforts inadvertently brought forth.

Chapter Seven

⟨───◈───⟩

Archibald Sterne anticipated him, and Christian Grey became all the more convinced of his own reticent nature because of the relief he felt when he opened his door to the doctor.

Archibald took over and did what Christian was loathe to do. "I am here to relieve your mind, Christian," he began. "You have done more than enough in harboring and encouraging those who, by their very nature, must become your antagonists. We are a small enough group to be able to hold our meetings at my home, or at the mill from now on."

Christian opened his mouth to respond, but the doctor held up his hand and continued. "These who were baptized, who have joined with us, are your people, your friends. Surely you know that I have a painful realization of that."

Christian nodded. This was difficult for both of them. He let the doctor go on.

"If it were not for the *truth*, for the depth of my own convictions, I would never sow discord and sorrow for you, my friend."

Christian nodded again, realizing that he did not trust himself now to speak. Something in the gaze of the man beside him caught at his heart and sent strange sensations through him. Besides, Archibald's desire was transparent: he wanted the pastor, his friend of many years' standing, to see as he saw, to feel as he felt—*to be converted, as well.* He knew that Christian had taken a copy of the Book of Mormon, and that he had read in it, and that he was a man of intelligence and integrity.

"I appreciate all you feel and all you are trying to do," Christian found himself saying. "But I am a minister of the gospel, dully ordained, trusted by those who have placed me here. You hope, you believe—"

"Yes, yes," Archibald hastened. "I hope much, and I am too hasty; that is my nature, I fear." He took a step forward and held out his hand. "We part friends still?"

"We *part* not at all." But as Christian said the words, he knew the truth was not in them. Religion had more power than anything else to divide men asunder, to divide *families.*

They shook hands and smiled, but the sadness behind their expressions tugged at Christian's heart. And Archibald, walking back to his own house, cursed himself for a fool. *Wait on the Lord,* he muttered to himself. *Wait and pray, show a good example, and give everything time. Be grateful for what the Lord has already given you.* And even there, in broad daylight, with his eyes open, he felt a prayer of love and gratitude stir in his heart.

The days passed. When Sunday came the Saints held a quiet, unobtrusive gathering in the doctor's parlor. But the sight of so many people traipsing up to his door, and the sound through the open windows of their voices raised in singing, could not be disguised nor ignored.

All the worse were the empty pews in the old church, upon which the vicar gazed down with his customary quiet patience and grace.

Esther's heart went out to her father. He had seemed to withdraw into himself ever since the morning of the Mormon baptisms. And the Book of Mormon had mysteriously disappeared from its place among the books on his shelves. She dared not speak to him concerning the matter, much less ask the questions that burned in her mind. She could only guess at the struggles he was undergoing, and she fought against a prickling sense of anger at Doctor Sterne and all the others who had let their minister down. She knew it wasn't as simple as that; she realized there was no "malice aforethought," but nevertheless, things had become sadly awkward and unpleasant ever since those two men came to town. It seemed many of those who were her dearest friends in the village were among the deserters, and she missed the strength of their spirits firmly situated there in the congregation, like actual sources of warmth and light who for years had cheered the aloneness of her young life. *What now? Would there forever be this barrier of sympathy and understanding that had seemed to spring up between them?* Esther could not bear the thought of such a possibility.

She slipped down to kneel as her father began the confession:

> Almighty and most merciful Father, We have erred and strayed from thy ways like lost sheep. We have fol-lowed too much the devices and desires of our own hearts. We have offended against thy holy laws, We have left undone those things which we ought to have done, And we have done those things which we ought not to have done, And there is no health in us . . .

The words, familiar since her childhood, Esther could say nearly by heart. But suddenly they jolted her senses, for she heard them in a new light: *We have erred and strayed from thy ways . . .*

No, surely not! Not as the Mormons believed it, that revelation had ceased with the corruption of the early church, and both revelation and authority direct from the Savior needed to again be restored.

Like the mild, naturally sweet taste of honey in her mouth were the words of the Mormon teachings to Esther's questioning mind. *Yet, how dare she embrace them, how dare she?* She trembled as she rose and settled back into her seat. From the corner of her eye she caught an unfamiliar figure sitting alone near the back. She turned around quietly to gain a better view of him, startled to realize that her first impressions were true: Oliver the shepherd sat straight-backed, with his shepherd's crook to one side of him and his dog sitting, statue-like, at the other. He appeared slender and stately, despite the common coarseness of his clothing and the unkempt length of his hair. His large hands, spare of flesh and finely-molded, lay still in his lap.

To Esther he appeared immutable, ageless. She knew he had known her mother, but he had been only a lad then and she a young wife. If her father was now fifty, her mother would have been only forty-six if she had lived. So the shepherd was younger than that, though his years sat on him with a certain weight, as though the wisdom of the quiet hills and skies, of the trees, of the animals he lived with was a burden nature compelled him to bear.

Oliver comes regular as the seasons, Esther thought. *Epiphany in the spring, Trinity Sunday, Harvest Home in the autumn, and Christmas Day. Why has he stepped outside his accustomed pattern?*

She noticed that other heads were turning, as hers had, to glance at the man. He was the only one of all the community and the area surrounding it who was allowed to bring a creature inside the church. No one begrudged him, for it seemed that the dog and the man were as part of each other: keen minds trained to perceive and judge together, eyes to see clearly, close or far, bodies to move in rhythm as one.

Esther sighed. *What are you doing here, Oliver?* She wished she could walk back and ask him directly. Perhaps when the service was out.

The prospect gave her no peace, and as soon as was decent after the last prayers had ended, she slipped out the side door and just caught him heading in long strides away from her. She called out to him in a low voice and he reluctantly paused.

"Wherefore did you come on this Sabbath, of all Sabbaths?" she asked outright.

He shaded his eyes with a hand that was mostly bone and knuckle. "You ought to know the answer to that."

"Was it for my father's sake?" She spoke the words scarcely above a whisper.

"What else could it be?" he replied.

All Esther's fears and uncertainties seemed to press against her lips as she gazed at him, and if she had not exerted an effort they would have tumbled right out. But his eyes, dark and recessed in the tanned creases of his long face, were clouded with a far-away expression that forestalled her.

He touched his cap to her and the corners of his mouth twitched into a kindly expression before he turned and walked on. Esther watched after him, beset by a longing that had risen within her like a sudden squall on the land: a terrible longing for something she could put no name to, and a sadness that brought tears to her eyes.

"There's to be another dunking in the river. I heard the doctor's wife speak of it last week when I went into town. They're whittlin' away at us, bit by bit, and that be the truth of it." Harvey Heaton spoke in a growl: the growl of authority which he had exercised as keeper of the inn these past twenty years, and as father of a half dozen scruffy, unruly sons. He had a meanness that made everyone who knew him give him a wide berth and never attempt to cross him. He could *put on* a pleasing manner when required and deceive the passing guest. But no one who knew him trusted him, nor received kind treatment from him for more than a scattering of hours at a time.

"Here be my plan," he continued, gazing round the tight-lipped group whose faces were all hollows and shadows in the uncertain light of the cellar room where they were meeting. "We carry off some mischief, dead of night, see, and lay it at the door of the Mormons."

Jem Irons scratched at his forehead. "What sort of mischief had you in mind?"

"This or that." Heaton ran his eye from face to face, and its coldness was like the heat of a live coal upon each brow. "For starters, we'll smash up some of those new jars and urns that the potter threw last week."

"Charlie Bates, you mean?" Monk Smedley's voice, coming out of his fat, overblown cheeks, sounded as if it were muffled with a mouthful of porridge. "He's countin' on them for his livelihood come winter."

Harvey Heaton made an impatient sound. "The doctor will have to stand good for them; we won't really hurt Charlie none. I chose him for a reason. He's been heard talkin' against those Mormons left and right through the village. And you know Charlie don't mince his words."

The half-moon of men nodded assent. Harvey knew what he was about; Harvey always had both the first and the last word in things. "Lean in close," he told them now, "and I'll give you the details and what I want you to do." He paused, and there was not a stirring or sound from the shadows. "*Each one of you.* So you'd best listen carefully and get it right the first time. And there'd better be no missteps or excuses about it." He grinned into the gloom and let out his breath with the sharpness of a razor. "But then, you lads know that."

The assent was unanimous. The details were hammered out, the assignments made. It was a given that no one ever spoke a word of what they were about to do—or what they had done—once they walked out of that low, dank room. The risks were too great for any man in his right mind to even give it a thought.

They stamped noisily up the narrow sag of stairs with their heavy boots and each went his way. Ben was the youngest of Harvey Heaton's sons, the furthest from being a man. Indeed, he had been considered a Mama's boy until he reached the considerable age of nine and his mother died. Since then he had been left largely to raise himself, willy-nilly, in the shadow of his older brothers, bossed and bullied not only by them but by the various chambermaids and barmaids that made their way through his father's establishment. Every now and again one came along who took pity on him and, with her instincts aroused, mothered the poor boy a bit.

Marjorie Poole was of this ilk. She had befriended Ben since she first came to work for his father, when she was a girl of fourteen, tall, well filled out and looking older than her meager years. Marjorie was eighteen now and Ben was fifteen, and they were still friends. Without daring to breathe the thought to any living person, he considered Marjie the best friend he had. He had gotten into the habit of telling her what went on with him and, from time to time, even coming to ask her advice.

He sought her out now. She had finished scrubbing the long tables and sweeping the floor in the public rooms and was settled in a favorite corner stitching on one of the garments from the endless pile of mending nearly overflowing the basket that stood at her side.

She spoke before she even looked up at him. "You been with your father and the others?" she asked. He nodded and sat on the floor beside her, his legs crossed beneath him.

"Rough business," she said. The words were a statement. She knew the boy's reluctance to be involved in what she called "thy father's black deeds." She did not commiserate; she merely listened to him with a calm, reasoned air that drew him out of the blackness better than too much tenderness would.

"In for another adventure. P'raps you ought not to tell me about it, Benjamin."

Ben ignored her hint of warning. She was the only person who called him by his full name, and it tended to give him a different sense of himself. He returned her smile and handed her one of the apples he had brought up from the cellar. He thought her slender fingers, as white as the breasts of pigeons, were lovely. She had grown into her size and moved with the easy grace of long legs and a supple body. She was attractive in Ben's eyes; she was easily the most lovely thing in the place.

He leaned close. He could smell the gentle scent of herbs, clean and faint, on her skin. Outside the triangle of light where they huddled, the empty room was a cavern of darkness that closed them off, to Ben's mind, like the tangled thickness of a dark wood that would let no danger in. He began to speak, outlining step by step what his father and his father's men were going to do.

Adam Dubberly awoke early, but he lay in bed with his eyes closed and listened to the birds from the hedgerow and the green summer branches greet the morning with song. He could pick out the gentle wren, the saucy robin, the exuberant, almost nervous, glee of the chickadee, and the melodious warbling of the throstles without any effort at all. A dozen others poured into his ears, nearly overwhelming his senses. He stretched his legs, pushed the covers back, and got out of bed. Rose

was still sleeping. She appeared years younger when she was asleep, like
the child he used to know, used to watch and wonder at, when they
played on the hills and the heath. He had always pictured the time when
they could be together, but the reality of her presence in his life was better than he could have imagined it. The companionship of her spirit was
a song as sweet as the birds sang. He pulled on his shirt and trousers and
unlatched the front door.

His cottage stood just off a narrow lane, really no more than an
uneven track that stretched through the squire's farmlands. His father
had been factor to Squire Feather before he died—unseasonably, at the
young age of forty, and another man had taken his place. Adam was in
the process of proving himself. "I must needs outgrow my raw youth,"
he had often explained to Rose. "Squire has his eye on me; that much I
know. He'll not slight me, in deference to the fine work my father did; if
for no other reason than that."

It was a good life, though modest and simple; he and Rose wanted
no more. They were content to trust what the maturing years might bring
to them. First of all, they wanted children, though so far that blessing
had not come to them.

"We need be in no hurry," Adam would soothe when Rose, from
time to time, drooped much like the flushed petals of a thirsty and sun-
needy rose. "The Giver of all things has His own times and seasons. He is
mindful of us; that is all we need to know."

Now, this new faith which they had embraced seemed like sun and
sweet rain on the petals of their lives; they could feel themselves blos-
soming; they could see nothing but beauty in each other and in all the
world round.

As soon as Adam opened the door he knew something was different;
he could sense that things were not right. He tightened his braces and
pushed his feet into his boots that stood on the door stoop, preparing
to have a look round.

He never got that far. From around the side of his cottage he saw the
constable coming toward him, with two other men beside, one of them the
old squire's factor, one Charlie Bates, the potter. Adam blinked his eyes.

"Is something the matter?" Adam's heart beat in his throat so that his voice came out all wobbly and weak. "Tipped off we were, Adam, or you might 'ave gotten away with it." Constable Johns's tone was not unkind. He was known for a fair man. Adam continued to stare and blink at him. *He's got no idea what I'm talking about; I can see it*, the constable thought.

"Seems somebody broke into Charlie's place last night and stirred up a regular wasp's nest, busting and smashing. Not many of his new pots and pitchers be left."

The constable caught the younger man's gaze and held it. "You wouldn't know anything about it, my lad?"

Adam swallowed, his throat suddenly dry and constricted. He knew his misery must show in his eyes and his face. "We'll wake Rose." He spoke the words without thinking and took a few steps away from the front of the house.

"You were seen near the premises, shortly after midnight." The factor, too, spoke in a kind voice, though he wore a scowl on his face.

Adam let his glance touch each in turn. "I in the town past midnight—I destroying another man's handiwork—his living—"

"You were seen," the constable repeated, somewhat reluctantly. "There are those who will identify and accuse you. Besides—" He kicked with the toe of his boot at a spot of upturned soil. Adam's eyes went to the spot. "Look what we have here."

A perfectly formed bowl had been unearthed, and a small pitcher beside it. The dull thought came to Adam, *Rose would love that little yellow pitcher to pour out her morning milk.* Then he swallowed against the sickness that was spreading throughout him. "They were planted, surely you know they were planted here—surely you know someone has—"

He was not allowed to go further. Charlie Bates had moved up close beside him and was waving his fist in his face. "You're a liar, Dubberly! It's the influence of those Mormons, I swear it! You've heard me speak hard against them; you know how I feel."

"So I did—this?"

"You did it in spite. You did it to show me!"

Adam was pale. He could feel a trembling pass through him that made him go dizzy and weak. "Have you ever known me to behave in such a manner—I ask each of you, all of you!"

"You'll have to come with me. We'll have to straighten this out."

What was the constable saying?

"Come along, lad." The factor put a hand on his arm.

Adam began to move woodenly, feeling that his feet would stumble at each step he made.

"I'll send one of the womenfolk back to explain things to Rosie," the constable said into his ear.

Adam nodded miserably. He watched the sun pierce through the branches and light up the trees that bordered the fields, tumbling across the green leaves and making them dance and shine like pieces of gold. He realized suddenly, with a dull sense of foreboding, that there was nothing but a heavy silence surrounding them: the birds were no longer singing; the morning was no longer new.

The constable had awakened Archibald, who had been out half the night on a late call. Once he had stumbled from bed he still had difficulty understanding what the good man was saying. When at last it sunk in it went deep, deep enough for his senses to tell him: *This is only the beginning. This is only the first time. There will be another and another. They have figured out how to get at us, how to drive us—to do God knows what.*

He passed his hand over his eyes that seemed blurred a bit, and thanked the constable. By the time the constable returned, with a stunned Adam in tow, the doctor was dressed and waiting at the village hall, pacing and praying, pacing and praying until he saw them approach.

It hurt him to see the look of betrayal and hurt in young Dubberly's eyes. *They would pick on the least of us, the least in station*, the doctor thought. *No one would have dared to lay this at my door.* "Who are the witnesses who claim to have seen this man?" he demanded at once. The constable winced, but was forthcoming. "Harvey Heaton from the inn, it be, and some of his lads."

"Need more be said?" The doctor spoke between his teeth, struggling to control the anger that welled up in him. He turned to the usually gentle potter whose eyes were blazing now. "Charlie, I pray you to use your senses and think this thing through. Consider the parties involved—consider the circumstances: Adam here doesn't even own a horse that could have brought him into the village and carried him back with the spoils that he is supposed to have then taken the trouble to dig and bury—right within easy reach at the front of his house."

He saw a twitch of hesitation pass over Charlie Bates's face and lowered his voice.

"Drop charges and go home. I'll send a party over to help you clean up the place—and I shall make good all damages. Come, what do you say?"

Everyone liked the doctor; his good offices hung like an aura around him, and he had proven himself to be trusted in all things. The maddened potter let out his breath and lowered his head. "Isn't fair for you to have to do that—"

"This has nothing to do with *fair* from start to finish, but I shall be more than glad to do my part and put things right again." He held out his hand. After a bit of shuffling and mumbling his antagonist took it, and to Archibald's relief the conditions were sealed. He glanced at Adam, standing mute and miserable. There were tears in his eyes.

"Get back to Rose, lad," he urged gently. "I'll see to things here." He put his hand on the young man's shoulder and gave him a mild shove. "We don't want to cause Rose unnecessary uneasiness."

Adam took a few steps and the doctor followed. When they had put a little distance between themselves and the others, Archibald spoke in a lower tone. "It is a pity that you were singled out for their plaguing this time. But it won't be the last."

These words caught Adam's attention, and he returned a look that was struggling for comprehension. "Persecuted for the truth's sake," he breathed.

"It has always been thus, I fear, my young friend, since this old world began."

"I am all right then," Adam said. "I shall be all right, sir." He paused. "God bless you, doctor. Rose and I shall pray for you."

"Thank you for that, Adam. Give my best to Rosie."

He watched the young farmer walk away before turning back to the others. There was a terrible heaviness inside him that nearly made him feel ill, nearly made him feel hopeless. *What have I done bringing the Church of Jesus Christ to this quiet, ordinary village? To these people who are struggling to understand it—or to permit it among them—what have I done to their lives?*

"Sorry to have kept you, gentlemen," he said, with as much life and lilt to his voice as he could muster. "Let us see now what all must be done."

Rose scarcely had time to become concerned when she looked up and saw Adam walk in the door. He came over and put his arms round her. She could feel he was trembling. "Sit down, Rosie," he said, and then told her, in as few words as possible, all that he had been through.

He hated to see her face go pale and her eyes fill with misery. He hastened to finish his narrative, and then drew her into his arms again. "We must remember what the doctor said," he soothed. "God is with us; I have no doubt of it."

Rose smiled through her tears. "Nor do I."

"Then we shall trust in His care and not fear, my lovely girl. We can do that." She said nothing, and he pressed on, with a need to know. "Do you regret what we've done, Rosie? The decision we've made?"

"Joining with the Mormons? Being baptized?"

He nodded. He was watching her closely, though he did not want her to know. "I do not, Adam. I know the fire that burned within me, and I know its source. I feel that God has touched me with His finger since I was baptized. When I read from the Book of Mormon I feel light pouring into my soul."

Adam nodded. There was a lump in his throat, and he could not speak.

Later that same morning he returned to town, the several intact pieces of pottery which had been secreted in his yard wrapped up in a stretch of cotton toweling, and presented himself at the potter's door.

"I am truly sorry for what you have suffered, Charlie," he said.

"And what of yourself?" came the begrudging return.

"What I suffered was none of your fault." Adam glanced around him. "Busy as a beehive here, Charlie. Looks like the place is nearly back in order again."

Charlie smiled, despite himself. "That Doctor Sterne is a wonderment when he wants to be," he admitted. "I'm most grateful to him." He knew, uncomfortably, what he feared Adam knew also, that most of the willing workers putting his kiln works to rights were of the number who had been baptized as Mormons at the river that day.

"You deserve his help," Adam said humbly. "You know as well as I do that it satisfies him to be of service."

"He's gotten too far into the habit, being a doctor and all." Charlie grinned.

The two men shook hands, and Adam walked away with the little yellow pitcher tucked under his arm, a present from the potter for Rose.

Later in the day Harvey Heaton appeared on the constable's doorstep and began to harass him in an ugly way about how he had handled things.

"I ought to have been called in," he snarled. "I'm a legitimate witness—don't you consider me trustworthy?" He knew his question would rankle the lawman yet further.

"Charlie Bates and Doctor Sterne came to terms; it is their business, not mine."

"These Mormons are become *everybody's business.* Don't you think, constable?"

"No, I do not. And I am well aware, Heaton, of your penchant *and* your reputation for stirring things up. I've my eye on you, that's who I have my eye on, and don't you forget!"

Harvey gave it up, but he left in a sour mood. "At least we've started," he consoled himself. "Least we've stirred them up, hurt them, made them uncomfortable." He took pleasure in the thought. "More's to come," he muttered under his breath as he drove along. "More's to come."

Chapter Eight

Summer was a time of gentle days and languid mellow evenings, but of long working hours as well. Harvey Heaton was hard-pressed to stir up the trouble he wanted, especially since the next Mormon baptism had been postponed indefinitely. Things seemed to hover like a cloud of insects, misty and still, just above his reach, suspended right now for weightier matters closer at hand.

Squire Feather was aware of the Mormon complaints in only a vague way. He had stated his case to the pastor and left it at that. If truth were known, he tended to put little store in what the villagers said when they took it upon themselves to complain. He had learned by experience and through the instincts of at least fifty generations before him to let well enough alone: once he started interfering with the ups and downs of the village—once he stuck his ladle into the pot and stirred with the rest—it was likely to end up costing him money, and no end of woe. Let them be. They had a way of sorting out their own affairs. He was content with that comfortable conviction, which had also been long handed down.

He liked the time of turning the soil and sowing the seed, of watching the crops green in a blush across the long fields. He liked the smell of the heat and the turned earth, he liked the ruddy, sun-bronzed faces of the workers as they tramped home, laughing and bantering with one another. He liked knowing that his eldest son, Jonathan, his namesake, was coming into his own, that he was a good worker, fair with those placed under him, and beginning to be respected by all. Life was good, and each day of the summer's moist growing season held more promise than the last. He had two pretty daughters, whom he was in hopes of marrying off soon, perhaps extending his property or prominence thereby. He had fathered four sons, healthy and lusty, capable of carrying on his good name. Well, perhaps all but one. That second son of his was a throwback of sorts from his wife's side; lamentable result, he was convinced, of too much Scottish blood. He'd gone off to explore the dubious mysteries of his seafaring kinfolk along the rough Solway coast, and perhaps that was just as well. Things ordered as they ought to be—sometimes as they had to be—but ordered to the squire's will, nonetheless.

The Mormon meetings were well attended, by many who were interested as well as by those who had been baptized. They had outgrown the doctor's parlor and met regularly in the mill house now. Elders and deacons administered the sacrament and saw to other priesthood duties; the men were learning slowly but surely how to govern themselves according to the laws of the gospel set out by the Prophet in far-off Nauvoo. And they taught and helped one another as they learned proper order and organization, they read from the scriptures often together, and also united in prayer. The missionaries who had first come to them returned periodically, to guide and assist, to strengthen and encourage, and the days and the weeks went by.

The women met among themselves when need required, and helped one another with children, with sewing and quilting, with sickness when it came, and in harvesting and preserving the ripening fruits of the season. It could not be said that they kept to themselves; they had no such intention. Yet a sympathy, a depth of comprehension and unity, now existed between them which had not been there before. The Spirit of the Holy Ghost moved among them and illumined their path, and they were free to discuss the beauties of the kingdom and express their gratitude and wonder, knowing that all ears that heard them would understand.

Paul Pritchard had emerged quite naturally as one of the leaders; it was in his nature to serve as such. He enjoyed the position of host to his friends. If truth be known, he enjoyed hearing the hymns sung in his own house, music soaring to the rafters and hovering there. It was an idle image, as if he could hear the strains of music tremble long after they were still. He marveled at the difference it made to call men and women he had known most of his life *brother* and *sister.* It had never felt awkward to him, as it did to some of the others. Even Paisley had giggled like a girl at first and gone red in the face when she tried to call the blustery black-smith *brother,* or stern Dorothea Whitely *sister.* But very soon it began to grow sweet and familiar to address one another that way. *The voices from the dust that speak with a familiar spirit . . . so much that felt known and famil-iar, as though already part of oneself.* Paul murmured the words out loud as he straightened the meeting room for tomorrow's workday.

Then he heard it. The music he had half-listened for, half-recognized, unembodied and faint. He stood still, so that his ear might catch more of it. And as he listened, he knew. 'Twas that lad of his playing his flute again, playing alone in the dimness that sets in at sunset. Paul contrived some excuse to go out where Daniel sat, leaning against the wide trunk of the elm tree, his dog at his side.

A picture you two make, he wanted to say, but he didn't. Without look-ing up Daniel spoke excitedly. "I've figured out most of the notes, Father. 'The Spirit of God like a fire is burning'—could you tell?"

"I only recognized it vaguely," Paul said, honestly. "But then, I was not paying much mind."

"I've got half a dozen hymns put together now," Daniel went on. He glanced up and saw his father's expression. "You don't mind?"

"Mind? Whyever should I mind, son?" Paul's throat had gone thick. "You do your work, you tend to what I tell you, you respect your mother—why should I mind what you do with the time God gives you?"

He could feel Daniel smile. "Give me your hand, we'd best go in by the light, boy." His voice had gone husky, and he coughed to cover the awkwardness. He watched his son go before, walking with the painful uneven gait that required both patience and care. He wanted to reach out his strong arm to help him, but he did not. He could remember, before the fall from the big tree, the scampering lad who could run circles around the lot of them, who could jump like a faun, who could—Paul coughed again into his cold hands. "We need a storm to settle this dust and to cool things down." It was but an idle comment he made for himself. The boy by now had entered the mill and was going through to the house. Paul had already framed his desire into words, into the words of a prayer. *It was bold to come before God for such favors. Did he dare?*

"He is your Father, He is your loving Father," the elders had taught. "The power of the priesthood, the power to *act in God's name*—"

"What is it for but to use?" Paul muttered. "To use with faith—to use to His glory—why else did He give it to us, but to use?"

❦

"Another baptism, another baptism! I do not wish to hear of such things, Andrew, especially from you!" Esther frowned; she could feel the unkind expression settle over her face.

"My father's mad as a hornet. It's some of *his* people who will go this time."

"And what is that to you and me?"

"Esther! What's gotten into you? I thought you were—well, even *interested yourself* in all this Mormon nonsense."

"If I were interested, I would not speak to *you* of it, Andrew; you have made yourself plain on this point. Other than that, what can you or I do about it, but watch your father fuss and watch my father be hurt—"

"That's a bit unfair, I'd say—"

"No you wouldn't, not if you are honest."

"Esther, what's come over you?"

Esther sighed. She had driven things now to a standstill. Andrew was as unaware of what she was truly trying to say to him as if she had not spoken at all.

"Never mind. Is that what you came to tell me?"

"No, I came to see you."

"See me."

"There you go again."

"Yes. Sorry. Shall we walk? It should be cooler under the trees than it is out here." Andrew fell in with her, and she bit at her lip and tried hard to think of something pleasant to say. She knew she was out-of-sorts; she knew dimly what forces were behind it. But all was beyond her power, all that mattered right now. She glanced at Andrew—*was he part of what mattered? Was he part anymore?*

He was prattling on about something inane that did not interest her at all. She tried to divert the conversation. "What will you do in the fall? I know you plan to help your father through the summer and hire out to the squire for farmwork. But what after that?"

"School, I am sure."

"Divinity school, like your father?"

"You know I do not want that."

"What, then?"

Andrew reached for her hand and she let him take it. "It's Father who wants me educated, wants it for his own pride. I'd like to apprentice myself to the blacksmith, but he's got a passel of sons."

"They're young yet, they won't be much help for a long while. Have you spoken to him?"

"I do not dare. You know what my father would do to me if I step out of line."

"What line, *whose* line? Andrew, it is your own life you must live."

"Would you be content to be wife to a blacksmith, Esther?" He spoke the words lightly, but she knew that he meant them with real intent.

"I will be content to marry a man I love, a man I can *wholly respect.* Nothing else matters, I think."

"Living matters. Feeding and clothing your family, and making your way a bit."

It seems he refuses to understand, Esther fumed. *We used to understand each other, we used to think the same thoughts—want the same things—laugh and be happy together.*

"Look, there's a meadowlark's nest."

She stooped to see where he pointed. "Leave it be the while, 'til the eggs hatch."

"I'll not hurt it," he said.

"You've crushed many when you were a lad—"

"Looking for eggs for you! And berries, and other treasures—"

"I know, I know." Esther smoothed the firm skin of the hand she held. "Speak to the blacksmith; surely that could not harm."

"Zachie Kilburn's become one of those Mormons now, don't you know?"

"Yes, I know. But what difference can that make? He's still a man, perhaps a bit better man, if there is to be a difference."

"No, Esther, I can't. Not now, not in the face of my father."

"It is your decision. I cannot force you to it—" *Or beguile you*, she thought. *I used to beguile you with my girlish ways and be glad when I saw the tenderness I had teased forth leap into your eyes.*

She roused herself at the remembrance, and drew her friend out a little, and brought a smile to his face. He left her contented enough, but she walked into the house feeling angry with herself for even this little deceit, feeling frightened because things were changing, because she knew that Andrew was blind to what lay at the core of her being, and that blindness was beginning to separate them, and she was alone—more and more alone and confused and angry as every day passed.

Sallie Brigman had stacked the dried osiers in piles, out under her apple tree, with her hives not far off. She liked to work with the gentle sounds of the bees in her ears; with an awareness of their comings and goings. People smiled at her indulgently when she said she could smell the honey as soon as she got near the hives, but so, though she spoke of it little, she could. 'Twas a blending of flower scents, mingled with the cleanness of grasses slippery with dew. 'Twas the mustiness of sun that had beat on thin petals for so many hours that it penetrated the skin of them, stored as it were, and still pulsing there.

In a deep tub she had set a large batch of reeds to soaking. Mary and Martha, old Peter's granddaughters, were coming along to make baskets with her. She would teach them the skills she had acquired, especially with the twining, where she used the weft strands in pairs, and the herringbone weave, at which she was especially adept. Aye, Sallie would teach them gladly enough. They were good girls, especially Martha, who liked to work in the way of women who ennoble the efforts of their fingers with the fine senses of their heart. They would work well and help her get this next batch out to sell at the county market. But she could not settle down to the usually pleasant task with gladness in her heart.

"We are losing the lass, and that is the truth of it," she said to the bees. "I asked her to come, my own little Esther, and she made some excuse—an awkward excuse, to my thinking." Her voice had dropped low, like a croon. "She isn't up to dissembling, our Esther, it does not come natural to her." She paused and splashed about in the tub with an impatient hand, testing the pliancy of the wet reeds. "She *wanted* to be with me. I could hear it in her voice, you see. The girl is so lonely these days. Ought to be with us—her spirit be hungering, hungering—"

She paused midsentence because Mary and Martha were rounding the corner of the fence and might hear. She rearranged the lines of her face and looked up with a smile. "Ready, young missies?" she called. "Be you ready to stretch those young fingers—make them supple as the reeds they must work with—"

Martha smiled in return and led her sister back to the cool bower under the branches where the old lady huddled and her bees wove lazy circles about her head.

The sweet warmth held, the grains burgeoned daily, and the berries grew thick on their vines. And a second baptism was held at the calm pool beneath the bridge. This time it was evening, and Constable Johns had half a dozen deputized assistants prowling every inch of the ground. He had gone so far as to have notices printed and stuck up all over the village, notices that actually listed the names of the converts and warned that any harm or mischief that came to them or theirs, seemingly by way of an accident of nature, would be rather taken as an act of unlawful violence, and the perpetrators would be tracked down.

Some thought to laugh off the extremity of the law agent's zeal, but when he read the notice aloud, word for word, before the sacred services, no one could be in doubt as to the earnestness of his intentions.

Esther did not attend the service, and she found out too late that her father had gone to the river himself. He had stood close by the little group, so that all eyes could attest to his being there. He had taken the hands of the newly baptized and been kindly with them. Within a few hours the entire village was full of it, wearing themselves out with wondering and conjecturing just what their pastor might have in mind.

Archibald Sterne knew, and only he guessed the cost of it to his friend. But the minister's presence had the desired effect of calming down the naysayers and of giving the idle and curious something else to get up in arms about.

Nicholas Sheppard sent his son to count heads for him. There were seven in number who had deserted his fold; seven men and women, not to count the children, the upcoming generation they dragged to the devil with them. He did not possess Christian Grey's forbearance, but sat right down at his desk, roaring for a tall glass of ale to be brought in to him, and began to compose a fiery sermon for the upcoming Sabbath.

"I have done with what Christian is pleased to call 'a Christlike acceptance.' He's got no spine, that one; have I not always known it? That's all right—" He was working himself up a bit, and had already downed half the ale. "I shall fight on my own; better that way in the long run. Those who are duped by these Mormons will at least squirm for their penance, aye, and suffer, too, if I've aught to say." In such manner he fumed the night away, and grew heavy with the effects of the drink and of the cold meat and cheese that he had his housekeeper bring in.

❦

His wife, Rhoda, knew what her husband was like when he was in one of these moods, and she went up to bed. She had long ago abandoned her efforts to change the man. Nothing worked on him; she had tried to shame him, to entreat him, to appeal to his sense of nobility and fair play. At such times he had none. She had once thought it a fine thing to be the wife of a clergyman and had liked the idea of ministering to the wants and needs of her neighbors, of assisting in God's goodly work.

It had not turned out that way. Most men, she had come to learn, took what vocation life's circumstances offered them; very few responded to a calling from within, though Rhoda believed that in the church it should be different—a man who chose the church should harbor a dedication, a spirit of—well, all of that was long past. All her hopeful desires, all her disappointments; she had been forced to let all of them go.

At least Nicholas's office was far removed from the room where they slept. She would not hear him pacing back and forth until all hours, nor bellowing out his frustration and sense of impotency. She drew the light summer coverlet up over her shoulders and slept.

Christian took a long route back to the rectory, and he walked in long strides, trying to tire his active body if he could not wear down his mind. He did not want to think, thinking got him nowhere; there were no answers to the dilemmas that stalked his soul like so many demons. There were no answers, and there was no peace.

He came in the back way, so as not to disturb the household, for the shadows had lengthened and Pearl would most probably be making ready for bed. He saw that bread and cheese and cold meat had been set out for him, and he saw that Esther, huddled on the chair beside the cold hearth, her head cradled at an awkward angle against the hard wood, had fallen asleep while she waited for him.

She stirred at once, as soon as she heard his footfall; she sat up and rubbed at her eyes. "It is late, Father."

He said nothing.

"You were walking. Here—there is food waiting for you."

She pulled a chair back and it scraped with a jarring sound along the uneven stones of the kitchen flooring. "Please eat," she urged, as he sat down woodenly. Then she drew an audible breath. "Why did you go, Father? And why did you not tell me?"

Christian did not look up at his daughter, but fell to his food, as she'd asked.

"You went for *their sakes,* didn't you? To help avoid further trouble." She stood expectant and trembling beside him. At last, with reluctance, he lifted his eyes.

"I cannot explain in words, Esther. You ought to understand that."

"I understand nothing at all! Nothing at all—less and less every day!" She sucked in her breath. He could see the racing of her pulse at her throat. "And, what's more, Father, you are not talking to me!"

"Whatever do you mean?" He took another mouthful of bread and cheese.

"You know what I mean. We two have always talked, talked everything through, ever since I was little, ever since Mother died!"

She had said it out loud. The silence that followed was audible, it was as thick as the shadows in the old room that the light from the one candle had no power to touch.

"Esther, please. This is of no good to either of us."

"It has to be, Father!" Her trembling increased, so that she had to steady herself by grasping a hold on the chair. "You have never shut me out like this before."

The words sat in the air between them. "I am not shutting you out now, my dear daughter. I just—I—I simply have nothing to share."

The silence vibrated for a few seconds, then Esther sighed, sighed and moved forward to kiss her father's forehead. *I am right,* she thought, as through a haze of gray shadows. *Oh, dearest God, I am right!*

"I'll leave you now, then, Father," she said as she kissed him. But walking up the stairs, feeling the cold drafts bite at her ankles and a colder chill clutch at her heart, the tortured thought ran through her head, over and over: *He does not know what to do. He can never be happy again; the Mormon teachings have forever spoiled that. Yet, he has not the courage, he has not the courage!—the courage to do what?* Esther had not the courage herself to form, to face, an answer to the tormenting thought.

Chapter Nine

The storms came unexpectedly, without the usual warning signs in earth, cattle, and sky. The clouds stole in like a thief in the night, and when the rains came, they came with a terrible vengeance; some said, like the vengeance of God.

"'Tis to teach those who have gone over to the Mormons," many whispered. "'Tis to give them a lesson, like the preacher promised; 'tis to open their eyes."

Nicholas Sheppard had delivered his scathing sermon—pointing his thick finger down from the pulpit and naming names. He had gone a step further and denounced the deserters and instructed his flock (good, comely, obedient people) to shut them out, to refuse to give them custom, to do all they could to stamp out their offensive heresies—oh, much was carefully couched in those words!

Various of the minister's worthy hearers were shocked into a more tolerant attitude toward the sinners in reaction to his very hardness, while others rubbed their hands in smugly approving accord. The Latter-day Saints, both the newly-baptized and those somewhat seasoned, kept themselves watchful and spent much time on their knees in prayer.

The storms raged, one following on the heels of another, beating the grain into the ground, flooding gardens and meadowlands, dripping through the thatch of the cottages, wilting and drowning, felling trees and sickening animals, and when they were through—when they had passed and taken the breath of destruction with them—and folks looked around, not one of the people who now called themselves Mormons had suffered any losses at all. Hard to stomach, it was, as the news got round, as the facts settled in. Not so much as a bag of the miller's flour had been wetted, nor his grain barrels burst. Even the kitchen gardens seemed to bounce back, their fields to go dry before the fields of the other farmers. Over and over again things were noted that seemed to bespeak divine favor. But, how could that be? How, under the heaven the villagers thought they trusted, could these Mormons who were conniving and deceitful, who were strangers to them in every way, how could they have found favor with God above?

The magpie, free of his cage, preened his long sleek feathers, perched himself on the settle, and rapped out a series of sharp, happy cries. Hannah, kneading her bread into loaves, paused to admire him for a moment, calling into the next room, "This bird is the only company and conversation I get of late."

Her husband heard her and came out. "Can I read this to you, Hannah, while you work with the bread?"

She nodded. What was it this time? A pamphlet written by Parley P. Pratt. Brother Pratt had come to be one of her favorites, for he had a fiery way with words that at times was almost poetic. She had come to know these Mormon writers by name, and had pictures of them all in her mind, imagining their looks and expressions as Michael read their words out to her.

Michael had devoured every bit of Mormon literature he could get his hands on, and he had traveled twice now with the doctor and Elders Hascall and Walker to the Church conferences held in Preston. That was a long way for him. But he had come back each time with a glow that concentrated in his face and his eyes.

"I feel myself expand, Hannah," he tried to explain. "I don't know any other way to explain it. The more I learn, the more I *am*. Does that make any sense?"

"It makes sense to me." Hannah thought, watching him, *We have never been in greater harmony, one with another. I have never loved him more, nor longed for his happiness as I now do.* She had no doubt that this religion of love and revelation was a precious gift, and she marveled that heaven had sent it to her, that God had stretched forth His arms and drawn the two of them in. Nothing seemed the same; everything was new, everything was colored with knowledge, with happiness, with hope.

The storms took the shine off summer, reducing things to a limp and bedraggled state. And in their aftermath came the thing more dreaded than flood or crop failure; in their aftermath came fevers and sickness that would level not the golden heads of wheat but the golden heads of children, and the gray heads of the old.

Doctor Sterne began his bleak rounds with a heavy heart.

Colds could develop into pneumonia, and pneumonia could weaken a patient so that he was much more likely to succumb to the deadly consumption. Fevers could mean the just-as-dreaded cholera, which seemed to attack children often in the summer and could strike even the strongest man down. The doctor was at his rounds day and night until his own eyes became bleary and ringed with shadows as dark as those on his heart.

One little girl in particular he had labored and labored over and was determined to save. Jane was the daughter of a local cooper, and her family was not one of those who had joined the Church. She had been with other children in the fields, drinking water from the ditches, full after the rains. But there were cattle kept in those fields, and the water was tainted. Unfit drinking water was one of the surest sources of the disease. The doctor had wished from the beginning that he might kneel in prayer with the distraught family, but knowing the general temper in the valley toward the Mormons, he had not dared.

It was a sultry evening, heavy with unshed rain and shades of the gathering night, when Archibald Sterne was called from his late supper to attend to the child. He left reluctantly, knowing that the disease had reached its crisis and he had gone the full length of his knowledge and skills in knowing how to save her—like a rope uncoiled and stretched long and taut—straining, straining for just a little length more. He sat on one side of the bed, and Jane's parents sat on the other. How gray and drawn their faces looked in the fading light. He marveled, as he often marveled, at the power of pain to drain vitality from us, to leave scars on our outward appearance as well as in our hearts.

The little girl stirred, hot and restless upon her pillows, and the sound was like the hollow rustling of dry cornstalks with the wind wheezing through. He had tried to get her to drink even a few sips, get a little liquid down into her thin body, emaciated now by lack of nourishment, limp as the rag doll that lay curled at her side. He rested his head in his hands, closed his eyes, and prayed—knowing that this was by far the best resort left to him now.

He heard nothing until he started at the touch of a hand on his shoulder and saw, through blurred eyes, the gentle, pain-filled face of his friend.

"Millicent asked me—well, we both thought it best to send for the parson." The father's voice was raspy with dread, and he cleared his throat painfully. "I didn't suppose—you don't mind, do you, doctor?"

It has come to that, then, Archibald thought, blinking back at him. *Everyone is resigned to this child's death but I.*

Christian walked close to the bed and lifted Jane's hand from the coverlet, cradling it in both of his own. His eyes sought Archibald's, saying as clear as day, *Are the parents right? Have you declared that the end is in sight, and there is no longer hope?*

Archibald rose and drew his chair forward. "Sit here, sir," he said.

A slight frown marred the calm of the clergyman's countenance, but he bent his head over the still form. The father reached for his wife's hand, and they bent their heads in prayer, too.

Christian Grey opened the small *Book of Common Prayer* on his knees and began:

> O Almighty God and merciful Father, to whom alone belong the issues of life and death: Look down from heaven, we humbly beseech thee, with the eyes of mercy upon this child now lying upon the bed of sickness . . . visit her, O Lord, with thy salvation; deliver her in thy good appointed time from her bodily pain, and save her soul for thy mercy's sake . . .

Archibald knew the form prayer Christian was reading; he had heard it often before. It was a prayer of resignation, a prayer acknowledging mystery and the will of a god whom man did not understand.

> . . . or else receive her into those holy habitations where the souls of them that sleep in the Lord Jesus enjoy perpetual rest and felicity . . .

Both parents were weeping quietly now. Archibald arose and took the vital signs of the sick girl. His eyes were shrouded, and he felt the stillness of death surrounding them; he felt the weight of eternity pressing on his own breast.

Let me be an instrument in Thy hands, he had prayed earlier. For well he knew that this matter, all matters, were not about the Mormons and how they were received by their neighbors. It was about the dissemination of truth, *the saving of souls.* He was aware of the sobering statistics that had recently come to light, that only seven million out of eighteen million people in Great Britain attended church—*any church.* He was aware of the godlessness of the practices of a large portion of mankind, of how the 1819 Factory Act allowed children over nine to labor twelve hours—from the gray darkness of early morning until the dim darkness of early night—for the benefit and profit of men who regarded them as less than their animals. *Man's inhumanity to man,* he thought, drawing in his breath. He felt his whole frame shudder, and the others in the small room looked up.

I know, too, that Heavenly Father loves His children, loves them dearly. Each word, as he thought it, was like a small piercing light in his brain. *I know He loves this little family, huddled in misery here.*

"Mr. Lumley," he said, moving so as to stand close beside the grieving father. "Your daughter lies, indeed, at the point of death." The man looked at him, eyes moist, with a trusting sorrow and resignation. He nodded his head.

"I have exhausted all the skill and knowledge I have as a physician," Archibald continued. "But I possess another power, a power I reverence, a power in which I have faith." The father and mother both stared at him, willing his miraculous words to continue.

"As an ordained minister for Jesus Christ, hands have been laid upon my head and I have been given the authority to use the power of the Savior—to act in His name."

"What does he mean?" Millicent Lumley muttered. "What is he talking about?"

"He is talking about healing your daughter," Christian Grey answered. And, with her minister's affirmation, the woman heaved a sigh of relief.

"Nothing strange in this?" the father asked bluntly.

"Nothing strange," Christian said. But his words were a whisper, and Archibald felt the pain that each one must have drawn from him.

"Have I your permission to give your daughter a priesthood blessing?"

"We have always trusted you, Doctor Sterne." *The eyes again: dull with pain, not daring to be hopeful.* "You go ahead."

"I will be the mouthpiece," Archibald attempted to explain. "The blessing shall come from Jane's Father in Heaven to her."

He placed his hands upon the head, covering the moist, tangled curls with the strength of his fingers and the strength of his faith. He closed his eyes. He invoked, by the authority of the holy Melchizedek Priesthood, a blessing of healing upon the suffering child.

Before he began to speak he knew that the Spirit was with him, for the blessings he promised and the words that he said came from outside himself, and had not yet been formulated in his own mind. One promise in particular stood out in his mind, and remained with him vividly, almost word for word as it had been given: "You shall recover your health completely and go on to live a long and useful life. You will receive protection whenever it is needed, and guidance in all righteous endeavors you undertake to accomplish."

When he pronounced his "amen" and opened his eyes, Jane was gazing upon him, like a solemn-eyed angel come back to life. She reached out for his hand. "Did you hear what I spoke, Jane?" he asked in a low voice.

"Yes, doctor, I heard every word. You came to the beautiful place where I waited and spoke to me and brought me home again."

Her mother fell upon her with kisses and caresses and Archibald stepped aside. "Will you go and arrange for a little warm broth to be brought to her?" he asked the father. Then with reluctance he met the gaze of the pastor, the gaze that had been penetrating like a hot poker, searing his vitals. He had been thinking to make a kindly apology, but the words died on his lips.

"I felt strongly impressed by the Holy Ghost that Jane would be healed, or I would never have attempted, never have presumed—"

Christian waved him aside. "It is no matter. I wish I'd have known you would be here."

"You will say nothing of this matter—Christian, please—" Archibald placed his hand with some urgency upon his friend's arm.

"Doctor Sterne, *I say nothing!* What of these parents who have had their child given back to them? What of the kitchen maid who has taken all of this in?"

"I did this for her sake, for their sakes—"

"Not for show, you mean?" There was an edge to the minister's voice that he did not attempt to control. "All will work out, one way or another, Archibald." He ran his hand through his hair. "This is most singular," he muttered, "and it is late and I am tired. I think I shall take my leave of you now."

Doctor Sterne's heart felt constricted in his chest. He was aware of the battle his dear friend was fighting, he was aware of the man's fear and his pride. Tonight's events might have drawn him, but they did not, for they revealed too starkly his own sense of inadequacy and powerlessness when he had lived a lifetime believing in the sanctity and power of the church that he served. And yet . . . it was he who had said, in accents incontestable, "He is talking about healing your daughter." He had known his words would help Archibald's efforts. And yet he was torn, so painfully torn!

Doctor Sterne stayed awhile longer, to make sure Jane's condition had stabilized, to be with the little family who did not yet know what had happened to them.

"I shall return in the morning," he assured them, "to see to Jane, and to answer any questions you two might have."

They smiled, they grasped his hands in theirs, they thanked him and thanked him, and let him go. He rode home in a stillness that whispered of unheard harmonies just out of his reach. A steady wind had come in on the curtains of night and cleared the hot air. He breathed in the unexpected coolness with gratitude, and he realized that he no longer felt tired, nor did he sense the elation that often came when he had sweat and labored to outdo death and had won.

This was different altogether. It was as pure as the lights in the heavens or the supple grasses under his feet as he slid from his mare and led her back to the stables.

God moving through me—God within me—myself a part of God, a true child, a true son—

This night had given him a testimony, and he possessed through experience a surety that nothing could shake. His eyes were drawn to Janet sitting in the shadows by the burned-out hearth, curled up in her favorite chair. He held out his arms to her and she rose and came to him.

"Something wonderful has happened tonight, hasn't it?"

He nodded.

"Somehow I sensed it; I know you can understand that. And I can see the light of it now in your face. Come, you can tell me everything while we get ready for bed."

Archibald did not question the goodness of God to him, though he felt it like sap to a tree in his cells and his bones. But he rejoiced, and did not forget, even when a terrible tiredness at last came upon him, to sink to his knees in gratitude such as he had never felt since he had grown to a man.

Chapter Ten

‿⊶⊙⊙⊶‿

*E*sther knew she was unhappy. She knew that everything in her life had changed, and nothing for the better. She was on the outside looking in; no one needed her or would come close to her, from her father to Andrew, from Janet Sterne to Sallie Brigman, for it seemed all the friends who were dearest to her had joined with the Mormons: they had one another, and did not think of her.

As always when she felt truly alone or neglected, the cry went up from the core of her being: *I want my mother.* Her soul was tender, much as her body would feel if every part of it were bruised and hurting. *I want my mother,* she cried voicelessly as she fed the cats, as she helped Pearl clear up the tea things, as she set vases of fresh flowers in the parlor and the dining room, as she mended her father's collars and darned his socks.

Nothing answered. No one took note of her. She seemed to exist in a void. At last she knew her state had reached critical proportions when she was no longer able to concentrate on the books she was reading. And that meant, in short, that there was *no* comfort, no help.

She prayed. And in her mind she began to talk to her mother, the way she had done as a child. *I know you are concerned for Father, if you are looking down upon us,* she said. *I know that you expect me to take care of him. But if you were here, you would know what to do, Mother, I know that you would! I feel myself an ignorant child in both age and experience. I feel I fail you—as well as Father—as well as everyone!* She had traced her familiar way in the still night to the place where her mother's young body rested, where it had been put away from her. She remembered the day, but only as a dim, half-real sensation of things she could not understand, of everyone crying, even her temperate, submissive father, of everyone taking her hand, until it felt like a hot stinging pulp of mashed strawberries, and she snatched it away.

She remembered the scent of the sun on the thin greening grass, and the sound of swifts, screaming and swooping in narrow circles just above her, anxious to get on with the business of building their nests. Little things, inconsequential and unrelated. Her mother had lain ill for weeks, but Esther had been brought into her room not only each morning but every evening. And during those thin gentle hours when the light of day stretches to gossamer and darkness seeps in like spilled ink, they had sung hymns together, their voices mere whispers in the listening stillness, their hands touching, her mother's fingers like the stems of white flowers atop the coverlet.

Together they said evening prayers and read out favorite passages of scripture, with no rhyme nor reason at all. These were moments when time held its breath for their sakes, when nothing in the world was real but what took place in that room.

"Am I like you, Mother?" she would ask.

"You are better than I am, Esther. You will do bright, wondrous things with your life."

"But am I like you?"

"Look at our hands, look at the shape of the nails and the fingers. See how like each other they are." Esther would look, and nod her head most solemnly. "Look at the shape of our mouths—look at the deep way our eyes are set—"

Then at last Esther had summoned courage to say, "But am I *like* you—are we the same *inside,* Mother?"

When she asked this, her mother had cried, rested her head against her daughter's much brighter one, and under her breath murmured the words, "Heart of my heart are you, daughter, skin of my skin; I cannot say where you end off and where I begin. Your thoughts are my thoughts, and what you surmise, I can see written right there in your eyes."

They both had giggled then, through tears, and a few days later she had found the pretty words on her pillow, written carefully out for her in her mother's own hand. Days later. Fragile day following fragile day. Then suddenly the door of life had slammed in her face, and they took her mother away.

Her thoughts and memories were undoing her! She paced in front of the narrow space of earth that was the low humble home of her mother's remains.

I am unhappy, she confessed. *And I am so confused. Above all, I wish I knew what you would think of these Mormons if you were here right now, Mother. Would you denounce them as opportunists, as disturbers of the peace? What would you see in their faces, what would you read in their eyes? Would the pages of their Book of Mormon speak to you as they have spoken to me, as truth calling out from the ground?*

"Mother!" Esther spoke the word aloud and the sound of it trembled like a night wind through the grasses, then rose to tangle itself in the swaying arms of the trees. "Mother, I do not know what to do about all of this! And I can find no one to help."

She paused in her wild questioning and pacing and hugged her arms to her sides. At once there was silence, silence that seemed to spread out from the spot where she was standing to rise into the trees, to settle over the ground, to *engulf* all the abrasion of noise and emotion that had jarred her soul. Esther, too, sank to the ground and gave way to the stillness until she felt it enter her soul. She closed her eyes and listened, empty and waiting, and one thought, one image came to her mind. *Oliver Morris, the shepherd on Windy Strath.* Oliver, who had once known her mother and who, Esther believed, cared for her memory still.

"I will go to him," she said aloud. "He will talk to me, he will answer my questions, and perhaps I shall find something to help."

The decision pleased her. It seemed at least the beginning of what she had been looking for, and with that she would be content. Two days passed before she could arrange to leave the rectory unattended. She could not choose too early an hour, for her father would miss her at the breakfast table and question her absence. But on this particular day he was feeling unwell and told Pearl he would take his midday meal in his office, where he would be working on his sermon when he was not resting on his couch.

Esther seized her chance, telling Pearl she had errands to run and people to see in the village. She went a roundabout way, so that no one happening to catch sight of her might recognize where she was heading nor discern her intent. A girlish precaution, she knew, for there was nothing unseemly nor even uncommon in a walk along the river or into the hills, or even in a chance meeting with the shepherd. It was her own thoughts, and the purport of her intentions, that brought her unease.

The morning was cool for late summer. The tall, uncut grasses were laced with rock roses, wild thyme, and wild mint. Blackberries on the bushes that hugged the rock walls were fattening, though white and unripe still. The meadowlarks sang their trill of pleasure, boldly stated, repeated over and over again, and the thrushes darted about her like tiny bright arrows of living sunlight. Unconsciously, Esther's pace slowed; she shed her light shawl and removed her hat from her head so that the sun could warm her skin and her hair as she walked.

She reached a stretch where the slant of the earth steepened and broke into waves, broad and smooth-peaked, the uneven stretches of them speckled with bracken ferns, uncurling in the hot sun like soft fairy fans that would whisper and bend with the merest touch of the wind's breath. Harebells surprised her, tucked here and there amid the thick grasses, like tiny specks of blue heaven shaken down from the clouds.

Thus it was that Oliver came upon *her* and startled her, for she had not heard his approach nor even been aware of the sheep and their soft sounds as they grazed the sweet grass. "You've come to see me, then, have you, Miss Esther?"

"Yes." It seemed natural for the shepherd to state her purpose, and for her to acknowledge it, simply, with no questions either way.

He led her to a seat on a smooth flat stone, moss covered and cool. He dropped to the earth and sat cross-legged before her, his long shepherd's staff at his side. "There is no one else," Esther stated simply. "I knew you would"—she hesitated—"talk to me. I knew you would tell me the truth."

Oliver did not bother to nod. It was his gaze that reassured her. "You wish me to tell you of your mother," he said, pulling up a long, slick grass blade and sucking it between his strong teeth.

"Yes. You knew her—I believe that once you . . . cared for her . . ."

"The follies of youth ought to pass into the hidden vaults of memory with decorum and not plague us the rest of our lives." He spoke the words out loud, but to himself; Esther could see that by the look on his face. "I loved your mother as a light-headed lad who is drawn to beauty and virtue loves the trees and the sun—as he loves the thrush that rises above the spring meadow, and the newly-birthed lambs."

"My mother was like that?" she breathed.

"Brushed with beauty," Oliver continued to muse, "as the Creator paints His loveliest landscapes and works of art."

"Oh." Esther could feel herself slump on the backless stone, and she cast her eyes to the ground. "Did others see her that way?" she asked at length, when the shepherd made no further effort at talk.

"Many did. Many saw something unusual in her, even if they could not say what it was."

"So my mother was patient and lovely, childlike, yet wise, making a heaven on earth for my father, bringing happiness to everyone—" Esther was aware that her taut voice was rising in pitch and intensity, but it seemed beyond her control.

"It is all right, lass, for you to resent her for dying and leaving you." Oliver placed his rough, warm hand over hers for a moment. As he took it away, he rose in one smooth, easy motion, then perched on the edge of a rock close by Esther's so that their eyes were now on a level. "She was as human as the rest of us, Esther. There were things she failed to see, things she failed to do. There were times when she was selfish and willful, tired and dull." Esther nodded, feeling suddenly hot and miserable.

"Yes, of course. But she was extraordinary in her own quiet way. That is what *really* matters." She was silent. One of the ewes, straying close, pushed her nose against Esther's hand and bleated inquisitively. Esther buried her fingers in the thick tangled wool.

"Did she feel as my father felt—about—well, religion—about how to live life—" She paused, straining for expression. "I suppose what I mean is, did she love the things of the Spirit as my father, or did she simply support what he did?"

"You believe I can answer that?"

"Yes, I believe you can answer that. I believe that she *talked* to you, Oliver. That you knew some of the things she was thinking and feeling." The shepherd pierced her with the gaze of his quiet, deep-set eyes, but she went relentlessly on. "And if she did that, it means that she trusted you."

Oliver made a small sound of acquiescence that was very much like a sigh. "You are more like her than I realized," he said, "not really knowing you at all, miss, until this moment, that is."

His words made Esther smile, and the kindness of her smile cleared the atmosphere between them. He leaned forward and squinted his eyes, but never took them from off her face.

"I can tell you that she had doubts. There were practices of the church that seemed cold to her, things they taught with which she did not agree. 'I have questions,' she said. More than once. 'I feel weak and unfaithful having questions, Oliver, and I do not know what to do.'"

The warmth of the sun seemed to be stifling Esther. She covered her face with her hands. "She had questions!" She mumbled the words in an undertone, but each one felt like a burning stone in her mouth.

"'Man is not perfect,' I used to tell her. 'He takes what God has given him and bends and stretches and changes it, because he is human and imperfect, and he wants comfort, Mary, as well as truth.'"

"Yes, I see that," Esther replied eagerly.

"You see it because you want to, Miss Esther. Your mother struggled with it, because she did not want to see."

"Yes. Of course. Of course not. Poor Mother." Esther sighed, then straightened her shoulders against the slight ache in the small of her back. "Oliver, do you know if my father realized that my mother had questions and doubts?"

The shepherd shrugged his thin, straight shoulders. "She never spoke to me of that, lass. But husband and wife—together—in harmony as she and your father were . . ." He let the words trail out and finish themselves.

Esther nodded and sighed. "Have you heard of the doctor's healing of little Jane Lumley?"

"Aye, even I have heard that."

"My father was there, in the room."

Oliver frowned and leaned forward. "That must have been sore hard for your father; terrible hard indeed."

"My father is a gentleman—my father is so painfully honorable!" The words tumbled out of Esther. "But what must he have gone through!"

"Your father is a true shepherd, Esther." Oliver rubbed his cheek thoughtfully. "I always believed that was a large part of why your mother trusted me; she saw the similarity, too."

"The shepherd would lay down his life for his lambs," Esther mused, almost bitterly.

"The shepherd knows how to pace his inner life with the flow of the flock," Oliver began, very quietly. "Their needs not only become paramount, they somehow become his own. He is part of them—they are not part of him; there is a difference, you know."

"Yes, as Christ is a part of us in His unfailing love and forgiveness. But we—we struggle, we complain, we never seem like Him enough to enter in where He is." Esther spoke the words with a passion that surprised her. She was steeling her mind against thoughts that rose within her unbidden. *The Book of Mormon prophets taught how to do that. They loved the Savior. All they did, all they suffered, was to bring their people closer to Him!*

"Esther?"

She drew in her breath and swiped at her stinging eyes. "I did not know I was crying."

Oliver said nothing. He sat back, at ease with the richness of life around him, the life of the earth and its creatures, as filled for him with the sacred and the eternal as a cathedral could be.

Esther stirred, and the shepherd seemed to awaken. "I wish I could be of more help to you, Esther; I know you have come to me for help. I know you are torn by what you feel for this new religion and the deep love you have for you father."

She turned hollow and tortured eyes to him. "I cannot choose nor decide. I am his little lamb, the lamb of his heart—I am all my father possesses!" The last word caught on a sob, but she gulped for air and went relentlessly on. "If I drew away, if I left"—a shudder went through her—"left him in emptiness and humiliation." She shook her head; her whole body sagged and she covered her face again. "I have no choice, *I have no choice.* I must go where my Shepherd calls me. I must stay by His side."

She was not even aware that Oliver Morris had come up beside her, wrapped his strong arms round her shivering body and drawn her head to his chest. She cried into his warmth until her tears began to choke her and she lifted her face to draw in big gulps of air.

❦

There was much the shepherd wanted to say to her, but he merely pushed back her hair, rose, and walked to the trickle of water that had found its way from the streambed. Here he knelt and wetted the large handkerchief he drew from his pocket. With this he bathed her face very gently, until she smiled at him with a small grateful smile. "You are a good lass. I have no doubt you shall make the best sense of things,

Esther, and come out all right." He gave his hand to lift her off the rock. She stood, smoothed her skirts and hair, and looked up at him as a child would, guileless, with gratitude and trust.

"Aye, come whenever you've need of—" he hesitated. "Whenever you have need of a friend."

Esther smiled, or tried to, and bent down to caress the head of the collie that had come close to her and now leaned his warm lean body against her leg.

"Thank you, Oliver. I think I shall be going now."

The shepherd nodded. The girl turned and began to descend the long valley. The stillness closed in around her and she let herself give way to it. *These were your hills, your ways, Mother,* she thought. *How many times did you walk them, in weariness, in grief, or in gladness, before I even opened my eyes on this world?* Just the idea of her spirit communicating with her mother's soothed the churning emotions within Esther's breast and gave her a sense of oneness with all that lived, with all that loved—and, with that sensation, an uplifting of hope. Oliver had not offered her any answers, any solutions, but she had learned more of her mother and, indeed, more of her own self in those moments she had spent on the quiet hill.

Chapter Eleven

*H*umans are a strange lot, always looking to the ways of their neighbors more than they look to themselves, some in idle curiosity, others with a penchant for mischief, or even for malice. And this interesting range of humankind was well represented in the inhabitants of Throstleford.

So, of course, the fact that Doctor Sterne had healed the Lumley child—*no, not by his doctoring, not with the use of medicine*—ran like quick-fire through the village. *He healed her with Mormon magic, putting his hands on her head and saying prayers over her.*

"Mormon magic" had a nice ring to it. *Doctor, good as he is, always has held himself a bit above the rest of us. . . . Yes, and who knows what these strange doings will come to . . . next thing . . .*

People talk, they believe there is no harm in it; they think, surely, all is done in goodwill, for in truth it is nearly impossible for most of them not to give in to discussing the affairs of their neighbors and passing innocuous judgment upon their behavior. Some few souls act as corks to the bubbling cauldrons of speculation and inference, and do their best to put a stop to speculations, or in the least to get others to modify what they speak.

Parson himself was there, you know, when Doctor Sterne healed the child.

Best to remember that. Nothing too unseemly could have taken place under his nose. If 'twere done wrong, we'd have heard of it, right from Parson himself.

Harmless, and soon blown over—except in this case the little family who had experienced such a phenomenon decided to take it one step further: they began attending Mormon meetings; they began showing a decided interest in being baptized themselves.

Most folk, though pretending more astonishment than they actually felt, would have left it at that. But there was an element in the village that kept the low embers rousing, feeding in sticks of discontent and mock indignation—anything to stir up contention and annoyance for those whom they had marked out.

At the Stragglers' Inn, Harvey Heaton rubbed his hands together. "I think we need to start keeping a count," he told his mate, Monk Smedley. "Matthew Lumley's a cooper—skilled craftsman—valuable member of our little community."

"So, Harvey, he's joinin' himself to the Mormons. That doesn't mean he's unable to work anymore."

"Doesn't it?" Harvey leaned forward and scratched at his chin whiskers with a blunt, unclean fingernail. "That might be exactly what it means, my friend."

Monk took a swig of his ale and shook his head. "Doesn't make sense. We need the cooper and the miller and the green grocer and the blacksmith as much as they need us."

Harvey scowled. He did not want those men who listened to him, who followed him, thinking this far on their own. "That's well and good." He leaned even closer, so that his elbow knocked against Monk's mug and the dark liquid sloshed over the sides. "We want to scare the Mormonism out of 'em, comrade. And we want to send the perpetrators packing—so they'll never think of finding their way back to our village again."

Monk drummed his fingers against the stained table in a nervous tattoo. "Put the fools back in their places again"—he grinned stolidly—"make 'em eat a bit of humble pie."

"Aye—a good portion of it!" Harvey thrust his fist into his friend's ribs and laughed low in his throat. "You've got the gist of things now, lad."

He topped Monk's glass, then went his rounds of the other tables, speaking in a friendly manner to all, and in the same friendly manner expressing amazement at what had happened over at the young cooper's house last week—carefully tucking little seeds of distrust and misgiving in the fertile soil of the mind, just under the thin surface layer that he had scratched open with his words.

Sam Weatherall, unaware of the hidden currents beneath the surface of Throstleford, had made arrangements to leave his grocery establishment in the hands of his reliable young apprentice for one day and drive with Meg to the neighboring village of Bristlebury, where three of his five brothers lived. He carried with him an extra copy of the Book of Mormon, which Doctor Sterne had procured for him when he attended the last conference in Preston. Sam also carried high hopes. He was fond of his brothers, and he knew they were fond of him. Half a dozen times a year they made occasion to take company one with another and share bits and snatches of the happenings of their lives. This would be an unanticipated visit, but he hoped a welcome one; he hoped to open his heart to his brothers and share the treasures of the Spirit that had come into his life.

Meg was happy for the chance of an outing, especially seeing that the day turned out fine. She packed up some of her herbs in small burlap bags to bring along as gifts: a goodly bunch of borage as a garnish for summer salads and cold summer dishes; coriander, which she had just harvested and which was particularly good for indigestion or, sweetened with honey, beneficial in the curing of worms; a little dill; a little fennel; and a generous bunch of lemon balm to flavor chilled summer drinks. And, of course, thyme, which made into a refreshing drink for hot summer and was good for coughs and stuffy noses when the cold weather came on again. Thyme was a plant Meg favored, for it was said to be one of the herbs that made up the bed of the Virgin Mary, and it was also known as a favorite of the fairies! She was bustling about so that Sam had to take her by the hand and tug her gently out of the cool, fragrant room at the back of the kitchen where she stored and prepared her herbs.

"Enough, woman, enough," he said in a kindly manner. "'Tis well past time already to be on our way." He helped her stow her treasures, then handed her up into the wagon. "Walk on," he said to the horses, who were as eager for the road as was he.

Meg was fond of Sam's family, the sisters-in-law as well as the brothers, and she enjoyed the anticipation of a good thorough visit about everything from chickens to children, from spun goods to the latest in women's hats.

The day was pleasant, the heat no longer bearing down like it did in July. Bracken grew alongside the roadway in bright clusters. The hedges sheltered foxgloves and wild roses, honeysuckle, and ferns. Meg drew the fragrance of them into her lungs; it seemed the very air itself partook of the sweetness that thrived all around. Soon it would be time for the harvest and there would be work in plenty for all hands. These were the last weeks when summer held her breath against change, and it seemed as though nothing cold or bitter could ever live and survive.

"The boys are bound to see it as you do," Meg encouraged, noting a little pocket of wrinkles between Sam's eyes.

"I've prayed about it," he replied. "I've taken it to God."

"Then it is in His hands," she said.

They drove on, past the small outlying farms that marked the countryside between the two villages. Down a lane to the north of them sat a tiny hamlet, set like a jewel amid the green fields that sheltered it in. Sam felt at times that his village was getting a bit beyond him: too many people shoving and pushing for their own advantage against their neighbor. He eyed the quiet cluster of houses with a sharp sense of longing. *Nothing there that the world could tussel over,* he thought. Yet, since embracing this restored gospel, he knew that much would be expected of him in assisting and instructing others, and he was in a good way of it, his trade being that of greengrocer, which brought him into contact daily with all the village people and all of their various needs.

He took up the pannikin of milk that Meg had stowed beneath the wagon seat, tilted his head back and drank deeply, enjoying the coolness of the liquid as it poured down his throat. Life was good. He had nothing to complain of, and much to be grateful for.

Thomas was the first to greet them as they pulled into the yard of the old family house. They had a routine that they followed: Sam would settle into his grandfather's sagging, cane-bottomed rocker that sat in the corner of the parlor, Meg would scurry into the kitchen to greet Thomas's wife, Miriam, and to set the kettle to boil, while Thomas, himself, went next door to inform Lucy, who would send her oldest son into the fields to fetch Mark, even as Thomas crossed the street and down two blocks to Herman's tidy shop, for he was a greengrocer as well. Herman and Helen would come along in good time, carrying something fresh to be cooked for supper, and Lucy was a great hand at stirring up a pudding while the women were busy over their talk. Thus at length all were gathered, and Meg forgot her husband's errand in the enjoyment of the moments as they spun their lazy threads through the warm summer kitchen.

Sam, on the other hand, was intent on igniting his brothers' interest. While the women were at work he told them in detail of the visit of two strangers to Throstleford, of the book they had brought, of the new religion it contained. He did his best to portray the joy and hope of it in face of the harsh doctrine they had grown accustomed to since their youth. His enthusiasm shone in his face and trembled in his voice, and he thought it must be all but contagious to those who listened to him. Surely the Spirit he felt with such gentle power must be manifesting to them.

To his astonishment, each of his brothers drew visibly back. Herman coughed into his hand, and Mark got up to stir the embers in the low fire, and then walked round the room with his hands at his back. Sam paused. He drew the book out of his big coat pocket and set it on the table that had stood beside his grandfather's rocker for over three generations. "Please," he said, confusion thick in his voice, "will you not give it a chance? You have always trusted my judgment—we have always stood fast by each other."

"Indeed, indeed we have, little brother," Thomas nodded, and there was a tone to his voice that let Sam know this was difficult for him. "But you take us by surprise—that is all—"

"No, it isn't." Sam could not keep the sadness he felt from his voice. "You are afraid of something—is it the opinion of your friends and neighbors? Have you heard ill things of the Mormons here?"

"I fear we have." Mark picked up the dark thread of discussion and held it uncomfortably. "As we've been brought to understand, brother, these Mormons are a strange lot, with outlandish ways. They cause trouble and division with the people they go among, snatching one from a family, two from another—" He drew closer, though he still, Sam noted, did not meet his eyes. "It has even been said that they intend to ship the people who join with them to America, to swell the ranks of menial workers who are made to serve upon their leaders, who are—"

"Enough!" Sam held up a firm hand. "And you believe such non-sense?"

All three brothers blinked at him while their thoughts ran, like ran-dom thread, through the uncharted channels of their minds. "How could we know different?" Mark defended. "We can only know what we hear."

"Hearing is not knowing," Sam replied. His voice had grown quiet and he leaned back in his chair. "If I tell you I am one of them, does that not make you realize that what you hear of them cannot be true?"

He paused. A silence, heavy as a wet night, folded its wings above them. At last Sam drew a shuddering breath. "Ye have no interest, then?"

"'Twould bring trouble and censure upon our heads in these parts," Herman protested. "Upon us and our livelihood—upon us and our families—" He reached forward to lay his hand upon his brother's arm. "Surely you can understand that."

"No, I cannot. For if this matters enough to me that it has changed my life—that I have brought it to you in love and expectation—"

As the devil would have it, Lucy entered the room just then and announced that the food was ready to be put on their plates. At once, with an obvious relief, Herman and Thomas rose to follow Mark, who was already on his feet. They made a beeline for the large kitchen table, so cheerily laid, never more grateful for the company of the women than they were at this moment.

Sam closed his eyes in a brief prayer before he rose to join them. He must make it through the meal set before him, somehow. Meg was ignorant of what had passed, but she sensed something and gave his hand a squeeze as she walked past him to take her seat. Good food, good company, a harmonious blending of spirits—all this Sam had rightfully thought to meet. Now he had the taste of ashes in his mouth, a disappointment that pressed upon his frame and tightened his innards so that he scarcely could swallow his food. Nevertheless, he attempted to smile and be pleasant, to join in the small talk that always graced these occasions. After what seemed an interminable time, they pushed their chairs back and retired into the parlor, where Thomas went in search of his pipe. Herman coughed into his hand again. "I'd best get back to see how the shop is faring without me." He muttered the words, and his wife looked up in surprise.

"So soon?" she complained. "We've only just started, the girls and I."

That brought a few kindly laughs and broke through the tightness that seemed to be closing around the four men.

"Meg and I haven't as long to stay as usual," Sam said, "so it is of no matter. We must be on our way, too, as it is."

"I'll ask my boy, Roger, to harness the wagon," Thomas offered, and Sam nodded in assent.

There were flurried good-byes then, the women sensing the strain and wondering at its cause, though Meg was the only one among them who might have guessed. As Sam rose to leave, he drew the book again from his pocket. "I b'lieve I'll leave this here, anyway, Thomas, if you don't object. That's what I brought it to do."

Thomas nodded in his turn. There was a sadness in his eyes that smote Sam's heart. He knew his brother well; he knew the sadness was saying, *it grieves me to hurt you and disappoint you, and well you know that, but I shall not change my mind.*

The brothers embraced, as was their wont before parting. Not until

Sam was settled in the wagon did he look back at the house. Thomas had closed the door behind them; he did not stand at the open entrance waving his usual friendly farewell.

"Walk on," Meg told the horses, clucking her tongue at them as she slipped her hand into her husband's. She had no need to ask any questions, but simply leaned close to him and whispered, "I'm so sorry, love," into his ear.

He drove half a mile before responding in a broken way, "I don't understand. If I could just understand—"

"Hush, dearie," Meg murmured. "Remember, you put the matter into God's hands."

"But, what if—"

"What if? Well, we shall worry about facing all the 'what ifs' as they come around."

Her voice was so rational and normal that it lifted Sam's spirits a little and he smiled over at her. Her own heart ached for him, but she would not let him know it, at least not yet. The day had cooled into the first grays of evening, grainy tonight as bits of sand and pebble left by the long streaks of gold and crimson, pebbles that scoured the glittering curve of colors away. The two rode in silence, and there was nothing to disturb them, only the harmonious sounds of the earth's creatures making their various settlings in preparation for night.

Back at the family house in Bristlebury, all the rooms had been lighted save one. Thomas sat alone amid the gray shadows of the parlor. He sat straight as a ramrod, straining to think, to reason, but his mind would take him nowhere at all. Glancing up once, for the space of a heartbeat, he thought he saw Sam still sitting opposite him in their great-grandfather's chair. It stunned and frightened him. He was unused to grappling with matters of deep import; he was an honorable and straightforward man, and he had lived his life fairly and kindly. And that was all he wanted to give or to glean from life now.

He did not know how long it was that he sat alone there, but he began to realize dimly that the chill of the room had crept into his bones. He rose heavily, stared down for a few moments at the book his brother had left, then snatched it up with every intent of hurling it into the fire. But there were only embers in the grate, not enough flame to do the business. He must be rid of it! Yet, simply throwing it away might be a risky affair. No one must find it, not even a fragment of it, and suspect what had taken place.

Annoyed now, and aware of how tired he was, Thomas paced the floor. At last a thought came, the only one he had had all evening, so he acted on it. He let himself out through the kitchen door and walked to the barn. There was an old feed box in one of the empty stalls that had not been used for many a year. Under the dusty leavings of straw and snippets of wood and leather and other debris he thrust the offending book until it was well out of sight. *It will rot here,* he thought, *and no one will ever hear of it, and we can rest easy again.*

As he stumbled back across the empty yard he heard a night plover cry in sudden alarm right over his head, and a shudder passed through his frame. Once inside again, with the door latched behind him, he drew a deep breath. The old dog, Queenie, lifted herself from her comfortable resting place to greet him, but Roger, his farmhand, had gone home to help his mother with the milking because his father was ailing. He would not be back until morning, and Thomas was grateful for that.

Poor Sam. It shocked him to see what had happened to this once-favorite brother of his. He had never seen Sam as the kind of man who could be taken in and used by others for aims of their own. *Sam. Perhaps the kindest of all of them. What would become of him now?*

The question was too disturbing for him to entertain. He knew he must get some sleep, so he moved with a cautious tread up the creaky stairs, undressed in the hall, then felt his way to the big four-poster bed he shared with his wife. He hoped Miriam wouldn't bother him with questions about this unpleasant affair. Tomorrow was baking day; perhaps she would have too much on her mind to think about it at all. There was no peace for him as he slid back the covers, and that disturbed him, causing a prick of anger at his brother for bringing this day's proceedings to pass. He was tired. He hoped he could close his eyes and sleep now, and put the whole lamentable unpleasantness behind.

Chapter Twelve

arjorie Poole knew the squire's son, Jonathan Feather, was in the back room drinking with Heaton's sons, Spencer and Alan. She knew their boisterous high spirits had turned to a thunderous, desperate sort of rudeness spilling out of the space that was meant to contain it. Soon they would draw the attention of Heaton's foreman, Monk Smedley, and then the feathers would fly. She was glad her duties of the night kept her far removed from the powder keg that might at any moment ignite.

She turned her attentions away from the jarring disturbance and began to sing over her work. She didn't mind dishes, and one of her assets was that she enjoyed peeling mounds of potatoes, a task most servants loathed. *Hard work never hurt anyone,* her mother used to say to her when she was a girl living at home. Now she was eighteen and had been out in service for nearly six years. She being one of the youngest of seven, her mother could spare her, and she expected her to work for wages to help the family along. For the first year and a half she used to cry herself to sleep nights, not really because she was homesick—for what was home but a dank, crowded cottage with never enough to eat, babies crying, older brothers shouting and teasing, and her mother's worried voice raised above it all? It was more for sheer loneliness, she expected, belonging to no one and having no one who really cared about her.

For two years she had been scullery maid in the house of a mean-spirited woman up Bloomsfield way. Never a kind word, never an extra scrap of meat or dumpling, not even on Sundays or the occasional feast holiday. Mean and slovenly the woman was, but Marjorie kept her kitchens spanking clean, so that you could eat off the floor of them if you had a mind.

Mr. Heaton had caught sight of her one day at the market, and she knew he had looked twice because she was a comely lass. It was her hair more than anything, long golden mounds of it that she could never keep under control. When Mrs. Booth made an appearance, bawling loudly for Marjorie and yanking her thin arm roughly, Harvey Heaton had stepped in her way. One of his serving girls had gotten in the family way and he had need of immediate help. Mrs. Booth swore a blue streak at him until she gathered that there would be some little coin for her in the transaction that was being proposed.

Marjorie never liked Harvey Heaton. She remembered staring hard at him that day. His hair was thinning on the top and he brushed long strands of it across his bald crown, creating a curious streaky effect. His face was long and angular and wore a resigned, hungry expression as though he never had enough of anything he liked.

But he offered her a much fairer wage and the prospect of advancement and, for some reason, she believed him. He might prove a hard taskmaster, but he was no fool. He would not abuse her and undermine his own interests, Marjorie had a conviction of that.

So she collected her few belongings, and when he saw that she had little more than the clothes on her back, Heaton bought a bolt of good cloth for her to make two new dresses with, and another more coarse, gray fabric for her to cut working aprons from.

"We're a rough lot, me and my sons," he told her plainly. "Haven't had a woman's influence—at least not in any decent way"—and he had thrown her a grim, lopsided smirk—"for a sorry long while. But you do your work honestly, keep out of my way, and keep your mouth shut, and I'll play fairly with you."

He shook her hand on it, and somehow she knew that he had stated a code of some sort, a code he honored, and she put her vague fears aside.

That was over three years ago. Beyond doing dishes, scrubbing pans, and polishing silver, she had learned to wait tables, cook stews, bake puddings, churn cream into butter, and milk the cow first, if need be; she had learned to iron lace cuffs, polish boots when Heaton's man was too drunk to do it, mull the master's hot cider just the way he wanted it, trim his pipes as he liked, deal with gentlemen callers whom Heaton wished to avoid, and keep a roomful of men, hot under the collar and calling for drink, so involved with their food that they didn't have time to be at each other's throats.

Marjorie felt she had grown up here in this grim, wild place, with scarcely a friend save an adopted kitten from a litter that was to be put in the river, one who was allowed instead to curl up, a little spot of warmth, at the foot of her bed. Now Cobweb, with his long whiskers that poked into everyone's business, had grown into the tallest, longest gray tom folks had ever seen. His prowess subjugated the countryside for twenty miles round, and Heaton boasted that every litter of kittens in the village was fathered by him.

Marjorie had one other friend, and he had come quite by accident into her life.

She had not meant to befriend the youngest son of the master of the house. At just rising fifteen, she'd had her hands full learning her duties and holding her own. But one night, coming out of the scullery, she had heard a sound that froze her in her tracks, for at first it seemed to be the wild keening of some hurt animal. She paused, her heart pounding, and listened again. It seemed to be coming from behind the storehouse, a large stone building, all gloomy recesses and shadows now that the sun had set and the moon rode behind clouds.

She approached timidly, feeling the hairs on the back of her neck rise, expecting at any moment some unknown and unimaginable apparition to jump out at her. When nothing happened, and the pounding of her heart ceased to take her breath away, she decided that the creature was a little hurt thing—a cat or a hare or a raccoon—and she might be able to help.

Turning a corner, she saw something huddled there and dropped down on her knees before what looked like a heap of old clothes someone had tossed aside. Then a whimper came from out of it, and the shadow of a head moved, and Marjorie reached out a hand to feel hair, lank and cold, then the shape of a forehead, a cheek, before she snatched her searching fingers away.

"Who is it?" she hissed low. When no reply came she added, "Here, give me a hand, let me help you."

"Go away—get away from me." The words were muttered so she scarcely could catch them, but they were choked by an unexpected sob, then a curse.

She suspected then; rather, she knew, by some inner sense. "Your brothers did this, aye? Big brave men that they are. Come to the kitchen with me, lad. I can at least clean up your wounds."

He came, though he rose slowly and kept his face from her, his body half hunched and protected as he followed her through the murkiness and down the stone stairwell to the kitchen entrance. Lighting only a single candle, she worked in the dim kitchen to cleanse the boy's cuts and bruises. He sat silently under her ministrations, only wincing once or twice when the pain surprised him. Marjorie was not at ease. She had seen precious little nurturing in her life and experienced less. But the boy's gratitude was mute and, therefore, nothing to embarrass her. It was only when she looked into his upturned eyes and saw the expression written there that she felt like shying away.

Later, in her own cramped room, getting ready for bed, the realization came over the lonely girl that all she had done was to meet with another creature as lonely and misplaced, and in truth more misused, than herself. After that she ceased to concern herself about it, but did what she could to assist the youngest son of the house whenever he came to her for help. It was little enough she could offer him, but she offered it willingly, for his older brothers picked on him often, aware of his vulnerable sensitivity. Benjamin became her friend, and Cobweb's friend as well, without a thing being said. A friend. He was the only human one Marjorie had in that place.

Tonight she caught sight of the squire's son stumbling into the courtyard. He was not one of the usual young men who drank until their feet would no longer support them and someone from the inn had to help them up onto their horses and, from time to time, tie them in place so that the animals, who knew their way, might carry them successfully home.

This was different, and something within Marjorie sensed it. She remained in the cold of the doorway, screened from sight, and watched Jonathan Feather being helped to his horse by Heaton's two oldest sons. The lad seemed insensible to what was happening around him. She could hear, like echoes, the murmur of conversation between Alan and Spencer, then the three disappeared—long shadows that lost their way in the thick darkness behind the stables. At last, still feeling uneasy, she turned away, dog tired and eager to seek her own bed and the renewing relief of sleep.

The night was a long one for Doctor Sterne and, though he was used to moving through the solemnity of night from house to house, from need to need, he was growing weary and anxious for the season of summer fevers to end, snuffed out by the frosts of autumn as surely as a flame is snuffed out by a gust of fresh wind.

He was riding slowly down one of the narrow country lanes, letting his mare feel her way. He saw nothing at first. The night was too dark and the shadows thick and indistinct beneath a moon that was a cloudy recreant and gave little light. It was his horse that alerted him to the fact that someone or something living was near. With not a little uncertainty he dismounted and took a cautious look round.

Nothing, save a growing sense of uneasiness. He searched with the toe of his boot; at length he lifted his voice and asked the old question, words flung into silence: "Who is there? Is anyone there?"

No reply, but a sound almost too faint to register. The doctor knelt down and felt along the ground with his gloved hands. Ah! clothes; something soft and giving beneath them. He explored the length of the body until his hands met the head. There was blood flowing freely from a cut or two, that much he could tell. No groan, no response at all, the man was in a dead faint. Whatever shuddering sound he had heard a moment ago must have come from the wind scudding through the underbrush, the very vaguest of warnings if one's ears were pricked up to hear.

He clicked under his tongue to call Honeysuckle to him. "We'll have to hoist him aboard, old girl," he said, "and take him to Janet's kitchen before we can see who he is, and what services he may be in need of at our hands."

The little gray mare came close and stood stolid and patient while the doctor did what was needful. This routine was not new to her. The moon rocked in the unsettled sky and the earth remained mute, as though the heavy darkness had smothered all warmth in her and driven all life underground.

Squire Feather had his eye on the grandfather clock in the hall. He had seen his wife and all of the servants to bed, except for old Betts. Betts had been in the house since his father's time; he understood things, he had become part of the rhythm of life in this place. If there was anything to be done . . .

The squire was no longer a young man himself; he had not married until his late thirties. Now his eldest son, named Jonathan after his father and after a distinguished line of Jonathans at least ten generations back, had failed to return at the usual time. Inane to worry: a man in his late twenties who did not show up for the evening meal—it was just that the lad was so regular in his habits, easy to rely upon, decent in his ways. But the hours had dragged slowly, and now it was after midnight and the squire, fussing and fuming, blamed himself for not sending someone to look for him—but how would that seem? He and his heir would be the laughing stock of the county; no, he couldn't have that.

What then? Waiting it out like this while the fire burned low and the wind fretted in the chimney and the silence became a presence that clutched at his heart with a cold, pitiless hand?

What could have happened? Was the boy in trouble—or worse, in some terrible need? His younger sons, James and Nathan, were spirited boys, feisty enough to get into scrapes every now and again. But Johnny, his Johnny—he heard the approach of a wagon, he must have heard it as it emerged from the last cluster of young ash trees at the end of the grove— he *felt* the sound before it became palpable to his ears. By the time the doctor drew into the drive, the squire was out in front with Betts, both of them swinging lanterns. Then the worst had befallen, his worst fears were realized. That was all he could think. "God and highlanders," he muttered under his breath. "God and highlanders, this is a bad business!"

Together they got Jonathan into the house and laid him out on the daybed in the smoking room. His father stood over him with his hands to his head at the look of the lad, plastered here and there in bandages, and inert as a corpse.

"Don't trouble yourself, squire," Doctor Sterne soothed. "Your lad's had a rough time of it, but I think he'll pull through."

Together the doctor and the old servant got the squire to take a chair and a brandy while the doctor filled in the details, at least those few he had been able to surmise.

"He's been drinking, but I believe it's more than that—too much spilled on his clothing, which is mussed up in a way that indicates there may have been a struggle—look, here's a nasty purple bump on his head."

The squire drew close again, muttering under his breath.

"Yet," the doctor continued, "I see indications that he's been drugged—just enough to complete the effects of the drinking and make others think he has drunk himself senseless—"

"My lad is not a carouser—he can hold his liquor and he's never had too much to drink 'cept at a wedding or on a Christmas night."

Doctor Sterne nodded. "All the more reason for the administration of something to help things along."

"Has he been robbed, then?"

"Indeed, it appears that way." Sterne rubbed at his eyes, which were beginning to sting with exhaustion and the effect of riding for hours through the moist night air.

"Shall I put him in his bed?"

"No, cover him and leave him here, sir. This will do nicely for the time being. Keep him warm—that is essential, for he has been deeply chilled and we do not wish the cold to settle into his lungs. If he wakes before I arrive back in the morning, give him a little warmed milk to drink, nothing stronger."

"I think, doctor, you had best stay the night."

Archibald smiled wanly. "I'll sleep better beside Janet, thanks, if it's all the same to you."

This drew a reluctant smile from his listener. "Ah, you young men so in love with your wives still that you can't see straight—that will fade in time, that will fade—"

"I hope not," the doctor grinned. "See you in the morning, gentlemen."

Both master and servant followed their visitor out and saw him safely settled atop the light wagon. The night air stung them, and they stumbled a little, cold and unsteady.

"I must say—" Archibald gathered up the reins and spoke with reluctance. "I do believe the mischief makers who left your son did not expect anyone to come along and find him—especially not me."

The squire's brow darkened, and he muttered imprecations under his breath until the old retainer, with a significant cough, poked him in the ribs and he sputtered to a stop.

The doctor rode off, and the sound of the horse's hoofs along the gravel of the drive appeared hollow and out of place in the deepness of night. The squire felt suddenly weary and wished he had something to lean upon as he walked back into the house. He could not imagine who would wish ill to his eldest son, who was a genial fellow, and patient to a fault as husbandman, landlord, or friend.

He turned to see Betts dragging Jonathan's saddlebags through the hall, scraping them in an annoying way along the surface of the wood. "Too heavy to lift properly, sir," he explained as he caught the squire watching his efforts with beetled brow.

"Leave them for now and get to your bed, man," the squire growled. "God and highlanders, this is a bad business, is it not?"

Betts shuffled off, but Squire Feather knew he would be back in two or three hours to take his turn at the watch. He thought of waking his wife—who would want to help—or one of the younger lads. But something stopped him; perhaps the thought of the sheer energy of will and body it would take to explain, to comfort, to go through the agony with each one over again.

He was shaken and exhausted, but not sleepy. As he reached the doorway of the room where his son lay he noticed close by a book, toppled out of Jonathan's open saddlebag and lying splayed and spine up. With a dull curiosity he scooped it into his hands. "What have we here?" he muttered aloud. He carried it into the room and sat down with it. "The Book of Mormon," he read on the title page as he opened it up. *What the deuce?* This couldn't be one of those Mormon books; Jonathan was a great one for reading, he knew that, but he would have nothing to do with strange sects and ideas that threw disrespect on the church, the squire was certain of that. He pinched his spectacles onto his broad nose and examined more closely. There was a name written on one of the end pages: *Zacharias E. Kilburn*, he read. *The blacksmith! What business was this, then?*

The squire scratched at his head, alert now. In his mind, in ever-increasing clarity, the possibilities ran—dark possibilities, every one, as he explored them—his eyes drawn from time to time to the pale helpless form on the chaise lounge. *Evil times*, he thought, *evil times! But who would wish to hurt a lad as good as my lad?*

None of it made any sense to him, and he knew he was too weary to think clearly. Sleep would solve that. He'd do well enough in the chair here beside Jonathan, and in the morning he'd put the pieces of the puzzle together. But, somehow, his resolve brought him no peace, and he dozed fitfully as the hours grew tight and silent around him; cold and troubled, he muttered and moaned more than his son did as the night wore away.

Chapter Thirteen

*L*ucius Bidford was making his first attempt, all decked out for courting, with a glow about him that no discouragement could dampen. He had made up his mind. He was a changed man since accepting the gospel, and he was now aware of his worth—not only as a farmer who was well off, well set up for life, but as a *man* who possessed much he was willing to offer to the right worthy maid. And that "right maid" was none other than the fair Martha Goodall, old Peter's granddaughter. Aye, she was a proper maid, well mannered, and as hard a worker as ever they came. That other gal, Mary, her sister, was more capricious in nature, not fashioned to be reliable and comfortable to a man the way Martha was. He hummed under his breath as he walked along to the cottage, not looking to left nor right, seeing only, in his mind, a wedding at Christmastime, and a woman making pies in his kitchen of a morning and resting her feet in his parlor at night.

He knocked with a resounding rap of his knuckles and, sure enough, Martha herself opened the door to him, smiling ever so brightly.

"What may I do for you, Brother Bidford? My grandfather is out gathering windfall from our apple tree, but I can call him in, if you'd like."

Lucius raised his head and drew in his breath, aware of the dignity of his station and calling. "It is you I have come to see, lass."

"I?" Martha stared at him, wide-eyed. He only nodded his head and said no more, but stood beaming upon her, so that she felt she had to ask him inside. "Mary," she called, when they had both sat down stiffly and were staring at one another, "would you please bring some tea for Mr. Bidford?"

Mary caught the note of alarm in her sister's voice and was quick to comply. Lucius sat, still beaming, until the tea came and Mary poured out a cup for him. He appeared in no hurry at all, but Martha felt a growing annoyance that she had difficulty concealing.

"What might your business be, Mr. Bidford?" she asked as soon as he had swallowed his first mouthful. "I am sorry to hurry you, but I have duties to see to and—" She left the sentence unfinished, hoping to indicate the necessity of some sort of action being taken, in courtesy's sake.

Lucius sucked the last of his tea from the cup, but Martha did not offer to pour him another. He leaned forward in his chair, the grin still wide on his face.

"Lass, my business is pleasure, actually; aye, pleasure for the both of us, as is my hope."

The jumble of words made little sense, yet Martha felt an anxiety creep over her like a chill, and she responded a bit sharply. "I have no idea what you are talking about, sir."

"I've come to court, Martha. You be fair and wise and clever in all the ways that recommend a woman to a man's admiration." He cleared his throat importantly, not seeing that Martha shrank back. "It is time you had the appreciation of a husband—a man who can provide you a home of your own to take care of—some status within the community— a place for your—"

"Stop! Please, sir, stop!" Martha had shot to her feet unbidden, and stood over her visitor, trembling and white. Lucius Bidford paused. He stared at her, his own face blank and surprised.

"I do not mean to disturb you, my girl. I *have* been hasty. Perhaps I ought to have spoken to your grandfather first."

"Most definitely." Martha was struggling to control the pitch of her voice, though she knew her face must look as though she had just seen a ghost. She drew in her breath and attempted to face her visitor squarely. "In truth, sir, I have given no thought yet to the notion of marrying, of leaving my sister and my grandfather—" She hesitated. "You honor me with the compliment, Brother Bidford, and yet you are—well, a good deal—" Her pale face was growing red and she knew she was stammering stupidly.

"Older than yourself—I know that is what you be thinking."

Martha had hoped he might speak those words with a disheartened sigh, but the grin had returned to his face.

"A mature man, not a twit of a lad who has nothing to offer you. Why, I have house and barns and livestock and lands. A woman such as yourself needs a house to run, work for her hands to do, responsibilities to bring out the best in her. Think how you would shine among the housewives of Throstleford, Martha. Think how proud you would be."

Martha sighed. "Please, Brother Bidford, please do not speak to me of it again."

"Aye, you be a proper modest maid. I shall speak to your grandfather instead."

Somehow he rose, took his leave with much fine speaking, and was at last out of the house. Martha collapsed onto the settle, trembling still, but when Mary came in from the kitchen, wiping tears of laughter from her eyes, she sat up straight and indignant.

"'Tis a laughing matter to you, perhaps. It isn't to you that he spoke—it is not you that he wants!"

She groaned and Mary took up her hand comfortingly. "Martha, how could he possibly think of it—he is old enough to be our father—what would you say, fifty at least?"

Martha nodded, her eyes miserable still. "But he *is* serious, Mary."

"Grandfather will put him straight."

"Will he?" A vague fear was fretting at the corners of Martha's mind.

"Do not be a willy-nil. Of course he will, dear. Now, come and help me with the bread. You know you shape the loaves more round and plump than I can."

Martha rose reluctantly, trying to rid her mind of the unpleasant sensations that clung to it.

"Don't fret. Don't spoil the fine morning," Mary coaxed.

"Yes, yes, of course." Martha smiled thinly. "That would be silly of me. Surely he wasn't in earnest. It was only a foolish idea he got into his head."

❁

"I tell you, I leave the book here, on that high shelf, and bring it down to read for a spell when I'm taking my midday meal or when the work of the day is slow."

Zachie Kilburn spoke with a measured solemnity that had the ring of truth to it. The squire scratched at his head.

"I am inclined to believe you, my man," he said bluntly. "But how did this book of yours get into my Jonathan's saddlebags—give me a believable explanation for that!"

"It was stolen, obviously. Every man in the village knows I keep my Book of Mormon up there." He glanced toward the empty shelf, then fixed his eyes on the squire's. "Harvey Heaton or his lads, I would guess. They've stirred up trouble against us more than once already—and what's more, their interference can be proven—their attempts to implicate those of us who have aligned ourselves with the Mormon Church—"

The squire sighed and scowled darkly. "'Tis a shame this whole thing had to blow up."

"This 'whole thing,' sir, meaning the Mormon religion coming to Throstleford?"

"Precisely, my good man, precisely that."

Zachie closed his mouth in a tight line and answered nothing at all.

"As a matter of fact," the squire continued, a bit reluctantly, "I've spoken with Harvey Heaton this very morning—" When Zachie glanced up sharply he added, "just by happenstance, really, meeting him on the road."

"And, of course, he had heard what has happened."

"Well, yes, I believe that he had. Said you and my lad fell out over the price of a gelding and parted with angry words."

Zachie met the squire's gaze. "There's some truth to that, squire, but nothing ugly nor angry about it. If there had been, would he have taken my book, or would I have offered it to him?"

The squire winced. "Were you trying to convert the lad, and put the book into his saddlebags before the quarrel started, then—"

"Ye're snatching at straws now, ye are, sir, and well you must know."

The squire nodded heavily. "I can make no sense of it."

"Well, it makes sense to me!"

"Sense or no, 'tis a bad, bad business, and my son lying broken at the root of it—and Heaton or no Harvey Heaton, 'tis the fault of these wretched religious zealots for blundering in where they've no business to be." The squire was working himself up, and the skin at the root of his raven-dark hair was mottled and red.

Zachie Kilburn knew the importance of the moment, and felt helpless as to how best to proceed. "I am sorry about your son," he said at length. "'Tis a shame, sir." He wanted to add, he was itching to add, *And who did he drink with last night, squire? And who sent him, drugged, on his way?* He thought it strange that Heaton had picked out this son of the squire's as a target for his dirty work. Jonathan was as good and fair and unspoiled a lad as ever was born to the gentry. Was this the very thing that tantalized Heaton's wickedness? Zachie shuddered at the thought.

"Doc Sterne is concerned about the condition of his lungs and is hovering over him like a meddlesome old wife."

"Course he would," Zachie mumbled.

"Well!" the squire shook his head and seemed to rouse himself. "You've not heard the end of this, Kilburn, there shall be more to account for—more for the lot of you! I can promise you that."

The great man had to end with a threat, shaking his finger and glaring in that icy, imperious way that made Zachie's blood boil. "Ah, 'tis a shame such things come to pass, a shame that men such as Heaton should walk God's green earth with the rest of us!" Zachie muttered the words to himself as the squire marched off. He did not want to give way to fear. Louisa would feel that in him; she would feel anger, too. "There be certain disadvantages," he muttered to himself, "in having a deep understanding with a woman." The jesting nature of his complaint eased things a little. He could leave the matter in God's hands; he must. But not the least of the frustrations of the situation was the loss of his book. He would sorely miss the reading of the scriptures, night and morning. And Louisa would notice that, too.

He sighed. *I shall pick up another copy at Preston when I go to conference with Doctor Sterne and the others*, he determined. *But perhaps he has an extra about the place that I might borrow or buy from him. It would be worth the asking, it would.*

He went about his business, but the day seemed clouded. When it came time for his midday meal, he was forced to eat it alone, with no company but his thoughts. Troubled as they were, he faced head-on the question that had sat like a stone all morning at the back of his mind.

This Mormonism is a thorn in the side of the flesh, that's for certain. It has brought trouble and trial and uncertainty. Are you sorry, Zachie Kilburn, that this is where you've cast in your lot?

He considered the question coldly, from many angles, as he chewed at his cold meat and bread. The answer came quietly, as sunrise eases light into the sky of a morning, as the embers of fire in a forge stir and build into power and life.

No, he told himself. *I do not regret it and, God willing, I never shall. I know what I know, and the testimony is strong in me and grows more precious each day.*

He knew it, and he had reinforced that knowledge by making room for any doubts that had a mind to enter, learning thereby that they had no power to trouble him.

He found himself whistling as he went back to his work; he found his mind cleared and his spirit at peace. When the smithy was empty during a spell midafternoon, he closed his eyes for a moment and uttered a prayer of gratitude to that God who had found him and blessed him. And then he went on with the work of his hands.

❧

Doctor Sterne entered the cool refuge of his house, sank into a chair, put his hands to his head, and closed his dull, stinging eyes. Janet found him there a quarter of an hour later, and the sight of him caused a chill to creep over her heart.

"What is it, Archie? Someone has died; something quite terrible has happened." Her husband never came home midday. He was punctual for meals (which needed to be punctual for him), unless an emergency claimed him, for he could mold his schedule around the certainty that necessities would be there when he required them, and then he could be on his way.

She went to him and massaged the back of his neck with her thin, cool fingers. He moaned, but said nothing. She continued, moving to the tight line of his shoulders. It grieved her sometimes that this work her husband had chosen, the work he loved, demanded so much more of him than other people supposed. The strain, the constant presence of it, the spiritual demands. Besides, if a horse threw a shoe it was a matter of inconvenience; the same if a pot broke, or if a loaf of bread was not properly raised. But if a person failed to be healed, if he was left invalid or impaired, if he happened to *die* following a doctor's ministrations, it was much easier and more plausible to blame the flesh-and-blood man who surely could have worked the magic, worked the miracle that would save a loved human life!

"The squire's son has pneumonia, I fear. All the signs are there: pain in the upper back, labored breathing, chills and a high fever which I cannot bring down, and the telltale prune-colored sputum—and, of course, pain in his chest. Janet, I've done all I know how to prevent it!" Archibald's voice came thin and hollow from somewhere deep down in his chest. Janet moaned softly. "He's sent for his second son, the one who's somewhere off in Scotland."

"Is it that crucial, then?"

"I'm not certain. Jonathan is young and has lived a healthier life than most men his age. There is still a fair chance that we might contain it and he'll pull through."

Pull through. A simple phrase for a great many complications, all beyond his control.

"Let me get you a cool drink," Janet suggested.

"Yes, I should like that. But first—" He raised his tired eyes to her and reached for her hand. "First, would you kneel and pray for the boy with me, Janet? That is why I've come home."

A terrible tenderness of love for him made her sway on her feet. She nodded and slipped down to kneel beside him, her head in his lap. They remained that way for many minutes before he moved to kneel also, with her hand cradled in his.

It was a chill day in the borders, with a wet wind blowing in from the sea. The Firth of Clyde was lashed by a late summer storm that spilled onto the land. The squire's man had to ride the tedious route from Carlile to Gretna Green through Dumphries and on to Ayr before he could leave the main road—a loosely used term in the rough terrain of Scotland—and head north a little way inland, approaching Kilmarnock, to the manor of the squire's lady where Tempest Feather could be found. By then the shadows of a restless night had stretched long quivering fingers across the lengths of stark, uneven land.

He had not relished the journey nor the errand, but being an old retainer of the family, he set his will to the task. When he appeared at the door, slump-shouldered and dripping wet, he was drawn in by the fire quickly enough and generously received. But when he announced his purpose he felt his listeners stiffen. The tall lad who had been listening intently made a sound deep in his throat and glowered upon him. The lights from the fire playing in red and gold upon his auburn hair made him appear somewhat like a surly beast. Rufus Sims recalled then, with a bit of a shock, that the boy, Tempest, had been here, among his mother's people, for well over two years. He had been weaned away from the softer life of his English village and trained to ways certainly more undisciplined and primitive.

"They think Jonathan will die? My father wants me back because I am the next in line—" The boy paced as he spoke the words, his shadow, long and dark, keeping stride with him.

"Your father *fears* he will die. I believe he simply wants you with him in these difficult circumstances—it *has* been a long time."

Tempest shook his head and the russet curls, loose and long, shimmered golden. "If this accident had not happened, I would have been left here in peace."

Only silence greeted his statement; Rufus was not foolish enough to attempt to argue him out of an obvious fact.

"He sent me here—my father." The strident voice paused and a slight laugh escaped the long, thin mouth. "It was natural to want to get rid of me, place me where there was scope for my desires and passions. He did not understand me, and I cannot fault him for that." His voice was dropping in volume and growing softer, more reflective.

"Course I've missed Mother and home—missed the lot of them." He leaned forward, his whole body, thin and supple as a young tree, expressing the emotion he felt. "The devil take it, man, *I've been happy here!* I've no desire to go back."

He paused. Sympathy for the lad seemed to rise up in Rufus like a warmth to surround him. These people of his mother's knew little of the squire, his ways and his needs. Rufus Sims swallowed. He must bide his time, that was all, for the lad had to give in to his father's will at the last.

"I've done and learned all Father hoped for and more—much more."

The frustration in Tempest's words brought out an involuntary word of praise from his uncle. "Like one of my own lads he's been, Sims, and twice as quick and hardworking as some of them."

"You have other brothers. Whatever happens to Jonathan, you have other brothers at home. In time you will have a choice—in time you will be given the freedom and opportunity to live whatever way of life that you choose to live." The soft voice of his aunt wrapped itself inside their eardrums, whispering comfort like an old lullaby, half remembered. And her words turned the tide.

"Of course. Of course, you are right!" Tempest cried. "It is my duty. I must go now—I *must* leave you!"

He glanced about the room a bit wildly, his eyes raking every known detail, every loved face.

Rufus coughed into his hand and the shipbuilder, master of the household, picked up his hint smoothly. "Ewan, would you kindly take Mr. Sims down to the kitchens and instruct them to feed him until he's had his fill—hot food *and* a tankard of warm ale, son."

The boy rose to his feet and Rufus followed gratefully after him. He had seen more than he wished he had seen. There would be a good bed here, heaven be praised, and he ought to rest well and be ready by first light to begin their long ride.

I'm taking a prisoner back, he thought. *I had not expected that. Like a wild stag driven, or a wild dog chained.*

He shook the gloomy thought from him and followed young Ewan toward the tantalizing smells that drew them both on.

Back in the great room, Tempest renewed his pacing until he felt his aunt's hand on his arm. "I shall send Margaret to help you pack. No— on second thought, we shall both come."

He looked at her a bit desperately, with less resignation than he had expressed a moment before.

"To keep you company," she murmured.

Tempest nodded miserably. "Yes, bless your heart. You know I could not do it without you," he said.

Chapter Fourteen

*S*allie had sent word to Esther by one of the Pritchard children. Esther now stood with the note in her hand while the little girl sat in the grass playing with the kittens Silky, the white cat, had given birth to six weeks before.

"Would you like to take one home with you?" Esther asked, watching her.

"That would be rare kind of you, miss!" Kathryn's eyes lit up and her pretty mouth trembled into a timid smile. "Any one that I'd like?"

"Any one that you'd like. I'm sure there's always a place and work for another cat to do at your father's mill."

She left the child to concentrate on the terrible task at hand and went indoors to compose a reply to Sallie's request. She could not conceal from herself the girlish pleasure she felt to know that Sallie wanted her, needed her—that there could be a reason for her to enter into some sort of fellowship with her old friend again. Since the day of those first Mormon baptisms Esther's whole world had changed, and this included the well-loved pattern of common days. True, she still paid visits to her father's parishioners and, on such excursions, sought for a viable excuse to drop in on Janet or Sallie or the Goodall sisters, but such excuses were

not easy to find. When she did call, there seemed always an awkwardness in the atmosphere that was to Esther as choking as fog. They
struggled for things to talk about, for they could not feel comfortable
asking about her father nor the affairs of the parish, and she was dimly
aware that their daily lives evolved around their new church activities:
Thursday fast days, prayer meetings, Sabbath meetings, afternoons of
quilting and sewing together, visiting the needy and sick. All this in a different way, and for different ends and purposes, it seemed to Esther, than
what used to be. What could they talk about without regret casting a
shadow over every expression and every attempt?

I will come, she wrote. Surely, this was important if Sallie sent a fixed
time and an undisguised urging. *This afternoon at three will be convenient
for me, and I shall be there.*

Esther hummed to herself as she watched Kathryn Pritchard scurry
off with her note in one fist and a gray-and-white kitten cradled under
her arm. Her father was busy; she would slip out at three and he would
not even notice. And yet, she knew that he would not object to her going
to Sallie's, no matter how often nor for how long. *These were his people.
They had been his father's people before him. He had not stopped loving them.*
Esther knew that. And the knowledge prickled under her skin like the
stinging of a dozen of Sallie's bees.

Tempest left Scotland reluctantly, wrapped in a silence more thick
than the sea fog that circled them round. Rufus Sims was inclined to
grumble at the boy, but kept his silence, and they rode along together,
stopping only briefly to rest the horses and stretch their own legs. They
could cover the distance in two days and nights if they pressed, but
Tempest appeared to be content to plod along, his unexpressed gloom a
general condemnation that spread to take in his companion. At length
Rufus could endure it no more.

"I say, Tempest, rouse yourself like a man; you'll be of no use to your
father this way."

Again the boy seemed to start out of an almost dream state and shake his great mane of hair. "What a fool you must think me!" he cried. "I've been a miserable companion and, of course, you are right."

He perked up a bit after that and the rate of their going increased and they had made what Rufus considered good time when darkness fell.

They secured a room in an inn, but he noticed that his companion slept fitfully and in the morning was again mute with gloom. "I'll leave you to it then," Rufus muttered to himself as the young master mounted, "and let your father deal with you. Hopefully he'll do it better than I."

It was a world of such sweetness and serenity that Esther felt her spirit sink into it, as her feet might sink into a deep cooling pool. "How could I have forgotten the pleasures of your garden?" she murmured to Sallie.

"How could you, indeed! Comes of stubbornness and silliness on both our parts," she fussed. "Why, my dear, I've taken to talking to the bees about you—you realize that they wonder where ye have gone."

Esther nodded. She understood enough concerning these tiny creatures and their amazing ways that she took Sallie at her word. She remembered that when she was a little girl Sallie had taught her how to train her bees to "visit" Esther at the parsonage at the very same time every day. It was a simple procedure of putting out a feeding post at the same time and place, then removing it one hour later. After a week or so of this careful schedule, the clever bees, equipped with their own internal clocks, would show up at exactly the same time, day following day.

How delighted she had been! For, even as a small child, Esther had never felt afraid of the bees. "They know you for what you are. They can sense and smell you," Sallie would say. "They're fussy about a lot of things, and can tell the flavor of something as sour or salty, or bitter or sweet." She would screw up her face and her cheeks would be round as a chipmunk's and her eyes as sparkly blue as flowers, set amid the fine smile wrinkles that spread out from them like a network of vines. "Where people are concerned, when a man is bad the bees know it quick as a shot! They can smell meanness, and haven't a bit of mercy for it."

Esther smiled at the memory. For the old woman's words had been a comfort to her, really, giving her the assurance that there were other forces, as well as God and her father, who were keeping evil in check.

" . . . Now then, dearie," Sallie was saying, "young squire is not getting better, though doctor has done all that he can." Her eyes grew gentle with concern, like a stream that had stilled and was sitting in a spot of shade, breathless and waiting. "He's near distraction, poor man," she murmured. "But—we can do something, I believe, to help him. And that is why you are here."

Esther did not yet understand, but she never would have said so; she bided her time.

"I've something very precious here that will help, if anything beyond medicine and God can." Sallie breathed the words as she busied herself among the flowers, straightening one here, snipping another there. "And, of course, old ways *are* best ways, many of them proven almost before time began."

She turned and smiled upon Esther benignly. "Did you know, my dear, that honey is said to be the first and the last food that Jesus Christ ate on the earth?"

Esther stared back at her, calmed within herself and happy. "Is it honey you are giving him, then?"

"No, no, dear, not honey *as such*, but the queen's *royal jelly*. Do you know what that is?"

Esther shook her head, her eyes as wide in her face as when she had been a child.

"The worker bees secrete it from their glands and feed it to the queen bee throughout her life. It stimulates the body's natural defenses, especially during convalescence, it restores vitality and energy—" Her voice was as rich with delight as the stream, awake again and tumbling merrily over stones and rocks as it found its way. "Many believe it is almost magical in its properties, for man has observed that the royal larva increase two thousand times in size in a matter of five days—all from eating it, we can surmise."

Esther was impressed. "Will the squire accept it—will he let us give it to Jonathan, or will he brush it off as a bit of old wifery?"

"That is where you come in." Sallie fixed her determined gaze on the girl. "Oh, I think, truly, the squire would try anything at this point but, all the same, 'twill be better coming from you."

"From me?"

"Why, I've never been up to the manor house on my own, dearie, these long—" She paused and laughed. "Seventy years and more."

Esther smiled in return. "All right. I shall be willing to help."

"Of course. I knew that you would."

"You'll tell me what to do?"

"I've instructions all written out for him. You simply go and be your own pretty self, Esther. Beauty used to be called a charm, for it has restorative powers of its own, my dear."

Once that was settled they sat together for awhile in the sun, sipping tea and speaking of simple things, until Sallie said, "We must stop this nonsense, you know, dear. We must bridge the gap somehow, and go back to old ways."

Esther knew what she meant, and was grateful that Sallie, in her old, forthright manner, had stated it clearly for them both.

"Your father, to begin with. We all love him as we used to—how could we not, Esther?"

"Yes." Esther was growing a bit uneasy, but she drew a deep breath. "Yes, I know what you mean. And, of course, you know that—of course, well, you know how much he still cares—about all of you—"

Sallie sighed and placed her soft hand over Esther's. "We miss his companionship and his wisdom. It pains us to have withdrawn from him, to have in any way *diminished him* in his own eyes, or in the eyes of others."

Esther nodded. "I think he understands that. But he cannot help feeling the loss." She longed to add, *and the confusion within him.* But perhaps her eyes said as much; she felt, gazing into the old lady's eyes, that, yes, they had.

"We must help him and return our love to him. I've ideas abrewing."

Sallie's whole soft face crinkled into a smile again. "And you, dear Esther, you have had a difficult time of your own, I know."

Of course Sallie knew! Of course her heart was with Esther! Why had she doubted that?

"I have been lonely and confused. I have missed all of you—and I have worried about my father."

There. She had tipped the whole barrel and all the fine truth spilled out!

"Yes, I know this. And more. I have prayed day and night for you, child. We all have."

I need your prayers! Esther wanted to say. But, instead, to her horror, she found herself gulping out very different words. "I need all of you—back in my life—I can't get along, somehow, on my own."

The pain in Sallie's eyes reached out like a balm to her, for it was pain for *her* sake: pain and tenderness and understanding.

"We shall do something about that, my precious girl, I promise ye."

Esther realized that her whole body was trembling, but she gulped again and nodded, and clung a few minutes longer to the soft, plump hand.

"Can you get up to squire's house soon, then?" Sallie prompted gently.

"First thing tomorrow morning; will that suffice?"

"Yes, dear, yes. And you will bring a report to me?"

"Of course! As soon as I return."

Sallie nodded. "That is well, Esther, and I shall have some warm honey cakes for you; a new receipt I've concocted myself. I cannot wait to see what you think of it."

Esther smiled. There was a lightening within her breast, as though she had been laced into tight corsets and someone had loosened the strings. Even her feet trod more lightly as she walked through the village streets, and she found herself smiling at everything and nothing that crossed her path.

She sensed dimly that it was *love* that made the difference. She had been deprived of associating with those who loved her, and whom she loved in return. Perhaps the feeling for her had still been there, but it had not been *with her.* Now it was back again, and without seeing the hows or the wherefores, she knew the flow of that sustenance would never again be cut off from her. *Nothing,* she thought, in a simple, childlike conviction, *should ever be allowed to interfere with love.*

Tempest had not expected to feel any sensations of pleasure when he topped the hill beyond Windy Crest and looked off past the stream and fields to where the ash grove drew a lush green border, like a protecting wall, in a sweep along one extended side of the old manor house. Memories that were little more than a mottled rush of vague impressions crowded upon his consciousness, so that when a half dozen crows rose suddenly out of the old ash they had stopped beside, the movement startled him so that he rose in the saddle and wanted to cry a curse at them, raucous creatures tousling like black rags in the currents of the gray skies. It was to his interest to cover the awkward moment lest his canny companion observe any of the emotion he wished so fervently to conceal.

Home. He wasn't certain what the word meant to him any longer. As a lad it had been a rich and secure place in which to grow up, with the cushioning of his position as one of the squire's sons, and all the privileges that station allowed. He had a gentle, indulgent mother who, though perhaps lacking in a perceptive wisdom that might have helped her understand and control her young sons, yet possessed a sincere love of them and interest in their welfare. And his two sisters. Were they growing into silly, giddy girls, he wondered? They had once been excellent playmates, adding a dimension to make-believe adventures that the boys conjured up, always game to attempt any role their brothers might challenge them with. Sarah, in particular, was more skilled and fearless at fencing matches than either of his younger brothers, Nathan and James.

He rode on, scarcely noticing the landscape now, immersed in his thoughts. For they had led him to his older brother, Jonathan, heir to the lands and title, the only one before him in line.

He was a good elder brother, fair and kindly, with everything in his nature fashioned for leadership and responsibility. There was nothing petty in his makeup, therefore he drew others to him and easily obtained their trust. *Steady, he's a steady lad, that one,* the squire always used to say of him, looking on with an admiring eye. No foolish escapades for Jonathan; he was always aware of responsibility and duty, and his desires to please and be worthy tempered all that he did. Yet this did not make him a dull, uninteresting fellow; not at all. He was the best rider among them, and could catch a longer string of trout in an hour than the rest of his brothers put together.

Tempest knit his brow, for he felt a darkness well up within him at the thought of Jonathan lying sick and inert. It seemed an affront to all that made sense in life. *He must take his place! No one else could do it half so well—and how should any of us get on without him?* His thoughts bristled like the fine hairs of new wool against his skin. *What will they want of me?* he wondered. *When they have me back among them will they remember what a trial I once was? Will the contrast between me and the dying son be a greater contrast than ever, and even harder to bear?*

And yet, he had found himself there in the harsh Scottish lowlands. The expectations placed upon him suited with his own innate skills and interests, and he soon proved himself clever and capable. *Why?* Why the difference? There was a tussle of cousins to contend with, but they accepted, aye, even admired him. Was it the old family sense of competition and place? At home he had been looked upon as the instigator of trouble, with his younger brothers eager to tumble after him—not looking to Jonathan's "steady example" but craving Tempest's wild, willful ways. Tempest Feather—a name that ought naturally to have brought teasing, even derision, but none of his friends had ever mocked or laughed at *him*—none of them dared.

He ofttimes wondered if the fact that he was named after his mother's great-grandfather had set a curse or a mark on him, dropping him into the channel of a path already carved out and bespoken for him long before he was born.

The original Tempest had been a smuggler and an adventurer along the Solway coast, with the heart of a saint, they said, and the spirit of a daemon. Afraid of nothing, but fair in his ways, he was able to mould others to his wishes, wild and willful as they might be. He rode the waves to places where no man could follow, coming back safely each time with magnificent prizes, only to venture into dangers and hardships—again, and again.

There were stories in plenty to illuminate and fire any boy's youth! Especially since they did not end in loss and disgrace, nor the hangman's noose. Rather, Tempest had succumbed to the one temptation that few men can resist: the love of a virtuous woman. At the age of thirty-eight he had married, built a grand house set safely inland, and raised up a passel of strong, lusty sons. He had turned responsible citizen in every way he could think of, constructing a school for the village children, rebuilding the mill when fire destroyed the old one, funding apprenticeships for worthy lads, generously loaning money to any of his neighbors who had need of assistance, and then conveniently forgetting the matter as being of no consequence to any involved. This behavior quickly endeared him to the other members of his community and, to a man, they defended his honor, and would have defended his person and property if so called upon.

A happy ending. And when Tempest was born with his forebear's red hair, rather than the raven locks of the Feathers, his mother's desires won out. Perhaps the fact that she had nearly lost her life in the birthing of him had something to do with it, too. Nevertheless, here he was, living up to the name and the blood that ran through his veins. *Or was he?* And if he had to step into Jonathan's shoes—*God forbid it!*—what would become of him then?

Ah! Here was the clean-swept gravel drive widening into the courtyard, approaching all too soon the front door, broad but unpretentious, set back into the gray-colored limestone of the sixteenth-century manor house. Tempest dismounted slowly, scarcely aware of the stable boy who stepped up beside him and took Phantom's reins. He was too overcome to feel anything; it was all he could do to take one step after another, walk into a world he had left—but a world which was obviously altered and changed now—and face, in his mind and spirit, what he would find waiting there.

Chapter Fifteen

Was it no more than happenstance that Doctor Sterne should be stepping out of his house at the precise moment that Esther was passing it? She did not think so. Her father had always said, *Everything in life happens for a reason, even if at times those reasons are known only to God.*

As she met his clear gaze and saw the warm welcome in the smile he gave her, an errant thought ran through her mind: *If Father is right, then why did Doctor Sterne come to Throstleford and, through him, why did Mormonism find its way here? And why did a Book of Mormon find its way into both my hands and my father's?*

"Esther, are you all right, my dear?"

She started at the sound of the strong, gentle voice that gave her a sense of confidence and well-being every time she heard it.

"No—sorry. Yes—I am fine. I was just—thinking of something, that's all."

"That is a lovely hat you're wearing, Esther! You are a treat to my eyes."

"Not every man would notice a girl's hat," she responded. "But then,

I am sure Janet's flair at wearing pretty things has given you an eye for them."

Archibald smiled. "I shan't deny it. How is your father doing?"

"Well enough—I suppose. He talks less to me now than he used to." Esther started at the words she had spoken, but she could see instant concern come into the doctor's face.

"Oh, how I miss the two of you!" He spoke the words with a sigh, in a tone so dismal that Esther fought the urge to reach out to him. "I miss your father's wisdom," he continued. "His wisdom and—" he hesitated. "His love for me." He ran thin, tired fingers through his hair. "I am in need of it now, you know."

"Yes," Esther replied, sighing, too. "Especially with this business of the squire's son, I suppose."

She told him then of her visit with Sallie and the errand that had been set for her, glad to see approval light his eyes as he nodded his head. "Well done!" he murmured. "Trust that woman; trust Sallie!"

Esther smiled and confided, again, without meaning to, "I am a bit anxious about going up there, sir. Do you suppose they'll resent my coming, see it as an interference?"

"No, not a bit. I agree with Sallie, that they shall be glad of anything that might make a difference and prove helpful. I'm going there tonight, and I shall mention to them that you might be coming along."

"I shall believe you are right, then!" She smiled and began to walk on, but the doctor placed his hand over her arm.

"Will you give my love to your father?"

"Yes. Yes, of course I will."

"And yourself, Esther—how are you doing—really? Are you faring all right?"

She tried to avoid looking into those lovely tender eyes as she answered him, but found she could not. And the words of truth tumbled out from somewhere deep within her, where it must be they were anxious to escape and break forth.

"I am having a difficult time of it, truly. So many of my dearest friends left with you and Janet to—" she hesitated.

"Yes, yes, so many, my dear." He spoke the words as sadly as she, herself, might have. "And we *did* leave. We deserted you and your father, and all that we used to support and be part of."

"Why?" The word came as a cry, of its own accord.

"*You know why*, Esther. You have read the Book of Mormon, you have felt the same feelings I have felt—"

"Do not say that, oh, do not, Doctor, *please.*"

"The last thing in the world I would want to do is to distress you, child—but I must answer truthfully when you ask. I have seen in your eyes what it would be wrong for either of us to deny."

Esther hung her head, feeling her whole body go limp, and the doctor's next words took her by surprise.

"Do not allow yourself to be downcast, Esther—to what purpose is that? Your Heavenly Father is watching over you, and He loves you. He will lead you aright." He moved his hand from her arm and took up her hand, patting it in a fatherly way. "He will bless your father, who all his life has been a bright, noble servant of his."

"But—"

"No buts, Esther. Love and trust—and be happy."

"That sounds too simple."

"But it is not. It might not appear to answer any of the questions that distress you, but be patient, Esther. Be patient—and pray. Never, never neglect your prayers, nor lose faith in them."

He gave her hand a squeeze before releasing it and sending her on her way. But he stood watching after, a bit baffled himself at the words he had spoken to her. Yet, since the priesthood of God had been bestowed upon him, such things had happened, enough times that he could not overlook circumstances, could not deny the power that blessed and enabled and, at times, inspired him. He went on his way thinking deeply, renewed in strength and spirit by the gratitude that surged through him as he thought of a Heavenly Father who would so abundantly love and direct and ennoble his earthly sons.

Esther decided to inform her father of what she would be doing; she felt it would be better that way. She knew the discomfort and shame of "being found out" when an action was discovered later, and there appeared no plausible reason for it to have been covered over or lied about. Besides, she could not bear the thought of anything that might mar what remained of the confidence between them that to her was so dear.

If he was surprised when she told him, he gave no visible sign. He seemed pleased to hear about Sallie, information Esther volunteered in as natural a way as she could. She also mentioned her encounter with the doctor, but did not give every detail. The time would come when she might—but that time was not now; she would bide yet awhile.

When the morning came she made special preparation, feeling she must both look and feel her best for this enterprise. She was glad that the day promised mild, for that meant she could walk and enjoy the freedom of being on the moors and along the water, which ran cool and yet full at this time of year.

She was pleased to leave the village behind and skirt the edge of the fields, many of which had tall fragrant grasses growing along their fringe. She drank in the mingled fragrance of soil and sun, of green things growing in their last strength and splendor, before autumn drew the sap from them and laid her silencing finger upon the land. The hedgerows sagged with their abundance of thistles, burdock, and woundwort, all purple and pink. The dew was still drying from the spiderwebs, all tangled in with ferns and climbing bittersweet, which nearly reached the top of the hedge. Painted Lady and Peacock butterflies clustered like bits of colored glass, and Esther found herself reaching out to touch them with eager fingers, as she had when she was a child.

There was a path winding through the ash grove that she had taken before, but once or twice only, when she was a little girl and had tagged along with her mother, holding her hand. The few times she had gone with her father, or others. After that, they had made the journey in a carriage or on horseback, so she had not walked this way for years.

In the dim undisturbed recesses she could almost remember the feel of her mother's slim fingers and hear the sound of her voice. It grieved her to be going on an errand into a household where death hovered; for its presence seemed close here among the old trees that knew and remembered so well.

She found herself moving quickly and no longer dreading the approach to the squire's door, opened by the old retainer, Betts, who ushered her in.

"Wait here a moment, miss," he instructed, so she stood in the dark hallway, resting her eyes on the paneling carved generations ago and the portraits of ancestors, mute and stiff save for their eyes, the only alive part about them; some languid and concealing, others burning with a passion or a temper which the artist had captured and which death could not still.

Death. Esther shuddered and found a place to sit on the bench under the stairwell, her legs feeling suddenly weak.

"Hiding, are you then?" The voice that accosted her was vibrant with a life that dispelled the shadows that had crawled into her mind. "You've come on some errand, I understand."

It was not a question, but a statement he spoke. Esther rose to her feet and looked upon the tall, russet-haired stranger who gazed intently at her. She held out her offering like a child, and explained how it was to be used. But before she had finished the young man brushed her aside.

"Who sent you with this nonsense? Good heavens, girl, you are wasting our time."

Esther paled and took a step away instinctively, so that the back of her knees pressed against the hard wood of the bench.

"It may not cure, surely, but it will help; I know that." She was surprised at how boldly she answered him, despite the weak shaking inside. "Doctor Sterne knows I am come, and he approved of it," she added, aware that she had raised her chin and was facing his gaze more squarely.

"Oh, he did? Well, that does not impress me. Who did you say that you were?"

"I did *not* say." Esther sighed; she was always sighing without being aware. But this and her little-girl stance, perhaps, made her antagonist pause.

"Tell me now, then—if you please."

She wished she could study this stranger; he had an interesting face and a bright restlessness to his eyes, reminding her of a wild animal who had somehow roamed into a caged area where he could pace and wander, but could not get out.

"I am Esther Grey, daughter of the vicar," she answered, her chin still jutting at a defiant angle.

"I see. Well, come with me, Esther Grey, into the sick room and we'll find out what Jonathan has to say."

Odd words. She followed the young man, finding it difficult to keep up with his long strides. They found the patient awake, propped against pillows, his breathing shallow and labored, his face as white as the sheets that covered him. Esther would have drawn back if not for the imperious watchful expectation of her companion.

She was not acquainted with the young squire, for he was several years older than she, and the ways of his life far removed from her own. She had seen him now and again at various public functions and on occasion at a Sunday meeting, and from what she could tell she shared the general opinion concerning his goodness and gentleness. She liked the look in his eyes. Once she had met those eyes and smiled, her tense fears fell from her, and she spoke to him easily. The other gentleman stood at the foot of the bed, darkly watching, his arms crossed over his chest.

At length, when she had finished, and set the precious royal jelly upon the bedside table, clearing her throat in the sudden silence, the stranger stepped in.

"You have tired him."

Another statement, bluntly given. She glanced down at the sick man, whose eyelids, weakly closed after a fit of terrible coughing, were as blue-veined and thin as a child's.

"Yes, I have. I shall leave now."

"Will you come to see me again?" The question issued hollowly from the thin chest, and Esther could feel the pain in it.

"Yes. Yes, I shall, if you'd like."

"I should, thank you." The thin voice answered her, but the eyes remained shut, and the tall man, brimful of life and energy, moved to the door while motioning her to do the same.

She followed him down the long hall in silence. As they neared the entry enclosure she drew a deep breath and spoke to him. "Is he in earnest? Shall I come again—and if so, when would be right?"

"Devil if I can tell you, Miss Grey." The strident voice sounded annoyed. "I do not know him of late well enough to give answer." He paused, and the silence was strangling. "Suit yourself in the matter. Come, if you'd like."

He opened the door. Sunlight poured in; Esther felt she could gulp it, and she stepped gratefully onto the small recessed porch. She wanted to say, *This house is an amazing structure. Does it speak to your spirit the way it does mine?* She wanted to ask, *Who in heaven's name are you?* But she could not. She clutched at her shawl, her fingers trembling again.

Was he watching her as she walked away from him? She would not turn to see; nothing in the world could cause her to turn and catch his cold gaze on her, see the impertinent stance of his body, at ease in its use, yet at the same time restless and uncomfortable, in the same way as his eyes. She walked slowly, careful not to stumble over any unexpected stone or bulge of earth in her path. When at last the green-leafed haven of the grove closed over her, she paused with a sigh of relief. "I will not look back," she said, stomping her foot on the ground and startling half a dozen small birds into flight. "I will not give him the satisfaction, even in my own mind."

Feeling better after that, she walked more swiftly, in order to be home by teatime. And when her father asked her about the visit, she omitted any mention of the fractious stranger, telling him only of the plight of the sick man and his unusual request that she come to see him again.

∞

Evaline Sowerby, through one means and another, contrived to attend every third meeting or so. It was not enough. She had gained her own testimony of Mormonism, as firm and as bright as that of any of those who were both privileged and faithful in attending all their meetings and in helping one another: she wished to do both.

The harvests were beginning, and Edwin had hired himself either by crop or by the work week to some of the neighbors, as he did every year, earning welcome payment, in money or kind, to see them through the long winter months. Then, in the cold quiet days when labor out of doors had abated, he could cut and sew clothes for his neighbors that the harvest work had worn out.

Edwin would be in the fields many a Sunday, and every time he was out, Evaline walked boldly to meeting, though her heart pounded painfully within her tight breast. Each time was worth it, though, and she returned home more resolute than when she had left.

The first time he heard of it he merely growled and threatened, and she had felt a grateful sense of relief until the next Sabbath came and she saw that her Sunday-best gown was missing, and nowhere to be found. She hunted everywhere for it, at last seeing a bit of the material sticking out from under her bed. She dropped to her knees and tugged triumphantly at it, only to let out a small cry, for she pulled out only a handful of small, raw pieces cut and stripped by Edwin's tailoring scissors, entirely ruined and past repair.

She sat on her heels and rocked back and forth, hurt and shame as harsh on her as though someone had dashed a barrel of scalding water over her head. As soon as she could she choked back the tears that remained, washed her face in cold water, and went off to church in her second-best. No one minded; no one would think to censure her, especially when they saw her red eyes and face. And, though she said not a word to anyone, it seemed by the next week that the whole village knew what had happened to Evaline's Sunday frock.

She said nothing to Edwin, nor did he bring it up to her. Meanwhile she bided her time, and did her best to be agreeable and kind to him, not allowing herself to think about what he might come up with next.

∞

When Martha Goodall told her grandfather about Lucius Bidford's visit, he had thrown his old gnarled head back and laughed aloud. She thought that unfeeling of him, and said so, but he brushed her objections away.

"You could do worse, lass," he teased. "You'd be a woman of property and could lord it over the rest."

He was laughing still, but she wanted sympathy, not mirth at her expense and at the expense of the poor man who came round the following week to speak to her grandfather, as he had said that he would.

She was too horrified to believe her ears when she heard what transpired—for the old scoundrel laughed at Lucius, too, and told him bluntly, "If you cannot win the lass on your own merits, Brother Bidford, do not expect me to do it for you." Then, leaning close, with a twinkle in his eye, he had added, "Ill-won and ill-kept is a wife wooed for a man by another." And he had ended his torment with a grin and a wink.

Lucius had retreated to lick his wounds, but was back before long. The girls had seen him skulking around the gardens, loitering at the edge of the barn, watching to catch Martha's eye. When he was unable to catch her, he resorted to standing outside her window, gazing up at the lighted square, sometimes calling her name. In the morning there were gifts of ripe vegetables, finely-ground wheat, or one of Janet Sterne's newly-baked pies. One morning there was a cunning yellow and blue butter crock from Charlie Bates's pottery; another time a fine full-brush broom. In the afternoon flowers would festoon the doorstep, or bowls of blackberries, blue-black and ripe. *This could not go on!* In horror the sisters flew for aid to Sallie, and Martha cried on her kind, ample breast.

Sallie checked the urge to laugh at it all in her turn, and gave the most gentle advice she could find. "Be kind to him, Martha, he has no power to hurt you."

"Sallie!" she cried. "You cannot know what it's like! I want to shout at him when he looks at me all drippy and moony-eyed."

"Yes, my dear, I understand that." Sallie spread honey thick on her newly-baked scones. "Eat this; it will soothe you," she instructed. "Yes, we must think of something," she agreed firmly, "and I have an idea already. Just give me a day or two to let it stew up in my head."

Mary was willing, but Martha agreed more reluctantly, and for the next two days she did not step out-of-doors one time. Mary was forced to attend to all the outside chores, though Martha more than made up for it by working up a veritable hurricane of cleaning and cooking and mending—anything to keep her fingers in motion and her thoughts occupied.

When at last Sallie sent for them, Martha threw a long dark shawl over her bright hair and slipped through back yards and alleyways that she might not be seen.

"Dear, oh, dear," Sallie comforted, "is it that bad for you, Martha? Well, we shall see what we can do."

When she told the girls what she had in mind, even Martha, the more skeptical of the two, had to give way to approval and hope.

"I've the first note right here for you," Sallie whispered, drawing a sheet out of her ample pocket, a sheet of fine writing paper sealed very neatly with wax.

"What does it say?" Mary asked.

"You do not need to know that; in fact, it is best you should not." Sallie was firm, and her very firmness gave her actions a stamp of authority and lent Martha a sense of safety she snatched at gratefully.

"I shall drop it at her doorstep myself tomorrow morning when I know she will be out at the shops, and then we shall have to just wait and see."

Mary was excited, and Martha was willing, and for the first time she felt a lovely relief. "Whoever would have thought that kindness could be a burden," she mused to Mary as they walked, hand in hand, home.

"Kindness with a purpose behind it," Mary reminded her sister.

"Yes, I know, but it still seems a shame." Now that she was even beginning to imagine herself out of harm's way, Martha felt an unexpected sympathy arise in her for the hapless man, whose determination was, after all, admirable, whose hopes and fears to his own heart must be—

She felt her sister shaking her. "No, you don't, Martha," she scolded. "I can see that soft look in your eye, the same that you get when you see a stray dog or a lost kitten."

Martha nodded in quick agreement. "You are right. I just—well, I just felt sorry for him."

"You need not," Mary replied. "If we are *all* lucky, Sallie's plan will work well, and Lucius Bidford will be a happy man after all."

They both laughed gently at that, and hurried home to put their bread into the oven before the loaves rose too high and spoiled.

Chapter Sixteen

Harvey Heaton was pleased. Things were brewing slowly, 'twas true, but they were still going his way. When he saw Tempest Feather stride into his common room, sit down and order a drink, he felt an elation it was difficult for him to disguise.

He sent Marjorie Poole over with a tall mug of ale brewed in the highlands of Scotland and a message, which he knew she would deliver prettily enough.

"Master gives ye this with his compliments and asks after the welfare of young squire."

"Young squire is in a bad way," Tempest growled, grabbing the mug handle roughly so that the liquid spilled out. "I understand he was drinking *here* that night, with Heaton's own lads. Is that not the way of it?"

Marjorie's eyes went wide and she nodded. This young man had fierce ways. *But then*, she thought, *I would be angered if 'twere my brother sent home drunk to lie by the roadside in the night and catch his death.*

"Tell me, miss, do you know if my brother drank here often?"

Tempest was watching Marjorie closely and saw her hesitate before she leaned close.

"He *never* drank here. He was not the drinking sort."

"Then why was he drinking here with the likes of the Heatons?" Tempest roared.

"He was drinking here with *my lads* because they were discussing the Mormon problem." Harvey Heaton had come up behind Marjorie and pushed her roughly away.

Tempest glowered still. He was of a humor to thrash the insolent man before him. "What are you talking about, Heaton? Just what problem might that be?"

Heaton scraped back a chair, sat down with ceremony, and answered the question at length. Tempest listened, though his eyes darkened beneath his beetled brow and he scarcely touched the ale Heaton would have liked to get down him and replenish.

"Enough!" Tempest said suddenly, pushing a strand of dark gold hair from his forehead. "Your story is too smooth, innkeeper, not to have *something* concealed behind it."

Heaton growled under his breath. "Are you calling me a liar, then, lad?"

Tempest threw his head back and laughed contemptuously. "Even I, a boy when I left here, knew certain *realities*, Heaton." A merriment had crept into his eyes, but behind it the steel gray power in his gaze held the older man. "The fact is, my brother drank here, and you are trying to make me believe that he rode away merrily and was waylaid on the back roads, dragged from his horse, forced to take more drink—that was drugged—and left on the cold ground to die?"

Heaton spread out his hands and shrugged his shoulders. "The blacksmith's book was found in his saddlebags; believe what you like."

"*I shall!*" Tempest pushed his chair away and rose, towering over the other man. "Zachie Kilburn couldn't hurt a fly, and you know it!"

Heaton growled again. "Religion does strange things to people!"

Tempest dug in his pocket for coins and threw them with a resounding clink on the hard surface of the table.

Heaton was agape; he had not expected this from the intemperate boy he thought he had known. Before he could conjure something clever to say in return, the squire's son had turned his back on him and was halfway across the room. He went to the window and watched Tempest head back to the stables, where he knew he would collect and saddle his own horse.

Well, he thought, *the devil take him and all his kind!* Out loud he said, under his breath, "I'm not through with you yet, my fine young fellow. Cocksure are you, better man than when you left us—too good for the likes of us now?" He scratched at a sore spot on his cheek where a horse-fly had bitten him, and was suddenly aware that the bunion on his left foot hurt. Cursing everything he could think of that tormented or taunted him, he went off in search of Marjorie, a black mood settling fast, determined to scold her roundly for her part in the travesty of the day.

∞

Her father was ill, just ill enough to take to his bed and need a little fussing over. Esther welcomed the opportunity to make the old rounds next morning, with a basket over her arm, and stop to request some little dainty for her father wherever she could. Sallie sent a honey and lemon concoction for his throat; Meg Weatherall an angelica mixture to ease the hoarseness and sore throat he was suffering, and a bag of lemon balm for tea, in case his cold became feverish. Dorothea Whitely, who appeared especially bright-eyed and pleased with herself in the chill dullness of the September morning, sent a marigold infusion she said she swore by to sweat out a fever, and which should also be used to bathe the vicar's hot, tired eyes.

The sisters, Martha and Mary, were more practical. They sent a loaf of newly-baked cinnamon bread, and Janet Sterne, seeing Esther pass, ran out after her with a bouquet of autumn chrysanthemums and marigolds, white starched daisies, and small yellow roses, all sun-bright and fragrant, seeming to belie the colorless sky that sat over them.

"Sallie told me a bit about your visit to the squire's—it sounded as though Tempest was quite beastly to you, when he should have—"

"Tempest?" Esther stared stupidly, understanding coming very slowly. "Of course . . . I ought to have known . . . the other brother who was sent to Scotland—"

"You were only a slip of a girl at that time, come to think of it," Janet mused, then added, with a pleasing smile, "You're hardly more than that now."

"That is why he was unhappy—as well as the concern for his brother, I don't think he wants to be here at all."

"I find that understandable," Janet replied. "I have heard from several sources that he has done well among his uncles and cousins, and he loved the wild coastal weather and the sea."

Esther nodded, thoughtful still, remembering suddenly that she had not returned to visit the sick man as she had promised.

"Oh, I have missed you, Esther—I have missed both you and your father very much."

"Yes. Yes, I know," Esther responded, clasping the small warm hands held out to her. "I feel the same—you and the doctor—I know Father misses you—" She blinked back tears she had not expected.

"You will take our love with the flowers?" Janet's eyes were dark with misery, too.

Esther nodded.

"And tomorrow I shall make a blackberry pie for him—and bring it over myself."

So, Esther's little venture went well, but it left her feeling strangely alone and deflated as she walked back to the vicarage. They could all make efforts and try, but things were still not the same. These people she loved would still not be there next Sunday morning, nor the next, nor the next—nor at prayer meetings or workday socials. *The doctor, himself, saw to that!* she thought a bit wickedly, and then felt sorry at once.

She hated for things to be "spoiled"; she always had, since she was a young child. *The poor thing—her young life spoiled by her mother's death—* Someone had said that on the day of the funeral, but she could not recall who. Pity; pity and tenderness for her, but just as now, it did not *restore* anything; it did not make things right again.

She put on a brave face for her father. After feeding the cats and giving instructions for her own simple supper to be kept warm, she took her little accumulation of treasures up to her father's room.

"It is chilly in here," she complained as she stooped to stir up the fire.

"It must be this fever." He coughed into his hand. "I feel almost uncomfortably warm."

She sat beside him and explained who had sent what, and remembered the words each had used when he or she asked about him, repeating them as nearly as she could. He was pleased. He nodded his head thoughtfully several times. Once he muttered under his breath, "'Tis a shame, Esther, 'tis a pity and a shame."

She knew what he meant and shook her own head woefully. She could see the tired pain in his eyes. *This will never do!* "I shall come back in a quarter of an hour," she cried, jumping up suddenly, "and read out loud to you—any book you choose, for as long as you'd like—that ought to help you to grow drowsy and sleep."

"That and a large cup of Pearl's steeped peppermint tea."

"As you will, sir—I shall bring a whole pot full." Esther laughed.

We have each other, she thought as she flew down the stairs, suddenly overwhelmed with a sense of gratitude. *We are surrounded by beauty, from the trees in the churchyard to the birds that nest in them, to the clouds in the sky, to the grain in the fields, and the rain on the gravel paths, and the roses blooming clear until harvest time, and—*

"Bless me, Miss Esther, you near to run me right over!" Pearl moved aside indignantly, while Esther's flying elbow struck at the pile of linens she carried and scattered them over the stairs.

Esther laughed, undisturbed. "I shall take care of these, Pearl," she offered, feeling that nothing on earth could ruffle the sense of well-being she had right now. *Strange how life does that,* she thought idly as she refolded the sheets and pillow slips. *Sorts things out for us when we least expect it—when we cannot even figure out how!*

She walked on into the kitchen, humming under her breath. Tomorrow morning she would help Pearl make a pot of soup with the ham bone they had in the larder, adding fresh carrots and cabbage, onions, turnips and parsnips from the garden, and if the afternoon promised fair she would take a bowl of it up to the squire's house for the sick man to eat.

Thus resolved, she bolted her own meal much as she used to do when she was a child and in a hurry to get back to her little girl pleasures. She felt the same now: as though simply being alive and having someone to love and to love her was reason enough to be hopeful and happy and grateful with all of her heart.

⟨∞⟩

Holding his own—what a limp, dodgy answer. Tempest, provoked, glowered at the doctor, who arched an eyebrow but answered him calmly.

"Your brother has survived the crisis, and is out of the woods for the time being, but he has contracted consumption, a much more severe condition—" Doctor Sterne watched the angry young man closely. "It is often the case that a patient, weakened by pneumonia, cannot fight off the infection, and consumption, ever present at this time of year, worms its way in—"

"How can you tell for certain?"

How impatient the angry brother was. "All the signs are there, Tempest: weight loss, continuing hoarseness and lack of appetite, night sweats, and the most sure indication—" He paused, and Tempest raised tortured eyes to meet his. "Coughing up blood."

"Can he be cured?"

Doctor Sterne held the questioning gaze and answered the straightforward question in like manner. "With a person as young as your brother the disease can often be controlled and contained, and go on that way for years—"

"While he lives a normal life?"

"Not entirely, but nearly."

Tempest ran rough fingers through his untidy hair and swore under his breath. "Have you told my father?"

"No, I have not. You were in the sickroom, you followed me out; perhaps it is best that you know first."

"Best for whom?" He grabbed the doctor's arm and steered him out of the front door onto the cramped, sunless portico, scant protection from the spitting rain that was sweeping across the drive. He leaned close and, though they two appeared to be alone together, lowered his voice. "My father *loves this son*—more than all the rest of us put together!"

Doctor Sterne did not try to gainsay him, but listened carefully, while the boy still held his tight grip on his arm.

"I was sent for, but only halfheartedly. I cannot fill Jonathan's shoes."

"Nor can any of your brothers. I know that." Doctor Sterne spoke calmly, rationally; he gave the truth in answer to the boy's truth, and saw astonishment flash in Tempest's eyes. "Do not anticipate, lad. You *came* halfheartedly—"

"Yes; I admit freely to that."

"Well, be patient, lad, and give circumstances a chance to work themselves out. Do your best for your father and your brother—and, by the way, how do you think your mother is?"

"She has the girls to comfort her; I have little idea what goes on in her head."

Doctor Sterne nodded. "Well, make yourself available to her, Tempest. Give her a chance to ask you for help if she wants it."

Tempest chaffed at the doctor's words, and a hot displeasure with himself rose like a bile. *Selfish brute that I am!* he chided himself, but not out loud. For the doctor's eyes and ears he did what was expected. But he had to relent in the end, drop his gaze and plead, as a raw boy might, "I do not think I can tell the old man that his son may be dying—that his useful life, at least, may be at an end."

"I agree. It might be hardest of all coming from you."

"Aye—braw and healthy as an ox as I am!" Tempest attempted a grin, but his generous mouth only went awry into a strange, unhappy shape above his jutting chin. "You will tell him, then?"

"Yes. And I think I ought to go back inside and do it right now."

But the doctor did not have to return and search the big silent rooms for the squire; he came striding across the fields toward them, his boots muddied from the wet fields, his cheeks bright with the tang of the autumn air. "Much more pleasant," he called, "much more pleasant to be out and about now that things have cooled down a bit." He took his hat off and shook the moisture from it. "We can do with this rain."

He stopped on the porch where the other two stood. "Are you coming or going, Sterne?" he asked in a friendly manner. Then he looked into the doctor's eyes. "Ah—news of Jonathan—you have bad news for me, Doctor?"

Sterne swallowed, but said nothing.

"Well, you had better come back inside."

The two men passed together through the narrow entrance into the wide ancient hall. Tempest watched them, then melted away—ran away, he would call it, if he had any starch to his backbone to be honest with himself. "Be patient, the good doctor says. Be patient and wait your time out!" He mumbled the words like a curse. *Serve and stand by, and then live the life others want for you.* That terrible sense of panic began to choke and narrow his breath again. He knew such a life would kill something vital within him—he knew it, but what could he do?

Stomping out to the barn, feeling caged in and cornered as he looked out at the curtain of rain, he recalled Harvey Heaton's words. *It's all the doing of the Mormons. There weren't any trouble, any division in this village until they came. They don't belong here.*

The words were like a burning coal tumbling against the sides of his brain. *Heaton's right,* he fumed. *They do not belong here any more than I do. And if they had not come, I would be safely back in Scotland where I belong.*

Resentment ate at his energy, so that he felt weak and enervated by the time he headed back to the house. The doctor's horse was no longer tied to the front post, which meant that his father must know. He couldn't bear to see the old man slumped and shaken, with that wounded look in his eyes. What of his mother, his sisters? Would they weep and carry on? He dearly hoped not. *My father will send for me,* he thought with a weariness that frightened him, *and he'll be as miserable and unhappy as I am, and awkward about what in the world it is that we ought to do next.*

Who would need him, who would demand things of him when he went through that door, things he did not want to provide? He squared his shoulders; he steeled his heart for whatever might be coming to him, and walked quickly inside.

Hannah Bingham was happy. It was raining, and she liked the rain, the scent of it and the sound of it. Her pet magpie, Waif, perched by the open window and preened his long glossy feathers, drinking in the rain in the same way she did, through his very pores.

Michael had several commissions he was working on right now, including a long dining table that was wanted up at the mill. A "party table" Paul Pritchard called it, for now that his home and the overflow of the mill rooms themselves had become the unofficial center of the little Mormon community, he felt a personal, rather fatherly responsibility for every last one. *We are well nurtured,* Hannah thought. *Between Paul and the doctor we are given the instruction and organization we need.*

She never ceased to marvel at the way the priesthood worked, at how her own husband had grown into the responsibilities his callings had placed upon him. Within their modest group they functioned with chorister and choir, with the sacrament administered each week and the meetings that followed, where ordinary men and women, *lay members,* took part. It still felt new and sometimes strange to her, but it had also felt *right,* from the beginning.

Michael, she knew, was interested in the organization of Saints across the ocean, in the place called Nauvoo, Illinois.

"They have built a temple," he was always reminding her, with a tone of awe in his voice. "Since the days of the ancient Israelites there have not been temples on the face of the earth in which men can worship—in which sacred rites can take place."

She agreed. The joy in his spirit reached out to her like a live current. He read everything he could about ancient temples and about the short history of the restored gospel of Jesus Christ. He devoured the issues of the *Times and Seasons* and every pamphlet or teaching tract that might come his way. Especially he was drawn to the modern revelation that had come to the Church through this young Prophet who had restored it under the direction of God.

His testimony of the Restoration was so strong and sure that Hannah drank from that, too—for it was not that her own convictions wavered, but that she froze at the thought of change, of the almost-horror of *leaving. Gathering with the Saints!* There were Saints here, and she was among them, and this was her *home.* This village had been the home of her people for ten generations, and time had folded itself around them, accepted their hearts and the labors of their hands, had enfolded their bones and flesh when the breath of life went from them, and here, in this rich soil, with the protecting arms of ancient trees bending above them, they all lay at rest. *America* was nothing but a word to her, and a word that struck fear to her heart.

So she listened to Michael talk of Zion and the Prophet, and his longing to work on the new temple that would be built in Nauvoo. But "a new way of life" sounded foreign, even sinister, and she could extract no comforting details from the haze that surrounded the almost meaningless words.

But this morning she was happy, and would be content with that, as the blessing it was. Waif fluttered to her shoulder and she stroked his glossy head with her finger. "What have you to say, my pretty one?" she crooned. The bird cocked his head and repeated the words she had spoken: "pretty one, pretty one." Michael had found him in a broken, abandoned nest when he was only a fledgling, and they had nursed him around the clock for weeks, keeping his new nest in a box beside the stove warm and clean, hand feeding him until he was able to fend for himself. Hannah had thought he would leave them, fly off to his own kind once they let him go out-of-doors. But he always returned to them, so Michael built a large cage of narrow wooden slats—ten times as spacious as an ordinary cage—and the bird settled himself there. The hinged door was usually left open, and Waif's chatter and mischief became an accepted—at some times delightful, at some times annoying—part of their everyday life.

Children would be nice. Children would be better than ten birds. Hannah prayed every day for this blessing, and she felt that God was mindful of her—her *Father* in heaven; she had begun to think of Him, the great, fierce, overpowering God of the universe, in this gentle intimate way ever since she had joined the Church. Surely He would so bless her! Little Rose Dubberly was with child now and, even deep in her heart, Hannah was happy for her.

She must "wait upon the Lord" as many righteous women had through all recorded history and probably long, long before. Surely in time He would make His will manifest to her, and give her cause to rejoice.

Esther did not complete her plans. Her father was little better the following morning, and besides, it was raining miserably, with clouds and mists hanging low, and the moisture making the coldness bite deeper. She was not good at biding her time, and it was difficult to maintain the mood of the previous day. Her father spent many hours sleeping, and she felt she was treading water again. Nothing was happening; her life was going nowhere. *What have I to look forward to?* she asked her own image as it gazed back from the mirror. Her eyes were dull, the lovely streaks, golden and luminous, were gone from them, and even her hair looked lusterless in the wan, hindered light. "Oh, Mother," she moaned softly, "how did you know it was right to love and marry my father? Would you have been different—would your life have been longer, if you had done other things and chosen another way?"

The questions sat like rocks in the clouded, shallow pool of her consciousness. She realized dimly that she did not know what she really wanted—and if she had any ideas, she was holding them at arm's length away from herself. She sighed. Surely life was not meant to be this confusing, and this infernally *slow.*

Chapter Seventeen

❦

*T*he desire was gone from her, but Esther felt she must keep her word to herself and take her soup to the squire's house, and pay the visit she had promised the sick young man. The day wore a coat of freshness following the cleansing rain, as though the whole earth had been newly baptized. She felt the beauty and renewal calling to her, giving her the courage she needed to go again to that place.

She had not lost her reluctance when she reached the squire's and knocked tentatively on the door. She felt it odd that she, a mere girl and largely unknown to the family, should be bold enough to visit the young squire, who was a man more than a boy, and of a rank and position in life that would have entirely excluded her had not this strange accident and Sallie's urgings brought her to his attention.

The old retainer, stooped yet sharp-eyed, seemed not in the least surprised to see her but ushered her into the sick room, announced her most formally, then took the soup, rather gently, from her hands.

"I shall have cook prepare a bowl of this for you, young master," he suggested.

"That would be splendid," Jonathan replied, and he smiled at Esther before adding, with a chagrin that looked ill suited to his features, "I did not really believe you would come again."

"I told you I would, didn't I?" Esther chimed back.

"Ah, and you are the vicar's daughter and therefore prize yourself on keeping your word."

"I do not know if being the vicar's daughter has much to do with it. My mother was the one who taught me to be honest, and 'tis for her sake that I am."

"Your mother died, did she not? Several years ago?"

Esther nodded and dropped her gaze, uncomfortably, to her lap.

"How difficult for you, a slip of a girl then," the sick man mused. "I never considered death much—before now, never thought that I'd have to." A rueful expression flitted over his features. "Son and heir, you know, spending my time hunting and riding, young and robust, with the world ripe before me—" His last words trailed off and ended in a fit of coughing that drew Esther to her feet.

"Shall I call for a nurse—someone to help, sir?"

He shook his head at her and indicated a glass of water that stood on the bedside table. She hurried to bring it to him and helped him take a drink. He drank slowly, and his whole frame shuddered as the last of the coughing passed.

"'Tis a shame," Esther cried out. "And you the kindest and the best of them!"

Jonathan attempted to grin, but made a sorry affair of it. "You mean my brothers, I take it? Ah, well, the first is always more steady than those that follow. Have you brothers and sisters yourself?"

She shook her head. "None that lived. All born and buried before I came."

"You are close to your father, I'll warrant." Jonathan tried to sit up in his bed, pointing at the same time to a bookshelf that stood in one of the corners of the square room. "See over there—on the top shelf, lying cover up on top of the others."

"Shall I get it for you?"

"Yes, it is something I would like to show you."

As Esther rose to do his bidding, a servant came in carrying a tray bearing Esther's soup and some thin slices of bread. The young squire waved her away with a touch of his old imperiousness. "Not now, after the young lady has concluded her visit I shall have time in plenty to eat."

Without a word the woman left them, and Esther approached the bed. She was clutching the book a bit tightly and the muscles of her face had tightened into a wariness, too. "Where did you get this?" she asked.

"Ah, that is a long story." He saw that she looked on with interest. "It was found in my saddlebags that night. Has the blacksmith's name in it, and Heaton claims he is the one that assailed me—"

"I do not believe that!"

"Neither do I, miss." Jonathan was watching her closely. "But he *is* one of these Mormonites, and frankly—" He paused. "Have you ever seen one of these books before?" He paused again, watching her.

"Actually, yes, I have. Doctor Sterne gave a copy to my father."

"Your father?"

"And I have read part of it—much of it—"

"Your father knew of your reading?"

Esther nodded her head, feeling both daunted and confused by this sudden turn in their conversation.

"Tell me, please, *what did you think?*"

It was her turn to hesitate.

"Please, Esther. Frankly—I find myself interested in it. You see, it was left in my bed that first day when they dragged out the contents of my satchel. I found it tangled in the coverlet, actually, and hid it under the mattress." He arched an eyebrow thoughtfully. "I am afraid I could not tell you why. But, I've had a chance to look through it now and then over the past days."

"Who took it to the bookshelf?" Esther asked.

"My brother. I believe he would have destroyed it had I not appealed to him, so he grudgingly agreed to return it to its rightful owner instead. Though, of course, he hasn't quite gotten round to that."

Esther nodded and sighed. "Yes. Well, you see, you see—my father was drawn to it, despite himself, and, in truth, so was I."

A warmth spread over the pallid face. "This fascinates me. Gives me an added respect for your father." He laughed weakly. "And I see I am in good company."

"Sir, did you happen to read anything about King Mosiah and his sons and the high priest's son, the young Alma, and how they—"

"What in the deuce is this?" The vibrant voice reached out to them with the strength of a lash, and both recoiled a bit as Tempest came into the room. "I see our fair visitor has returned." He lifted an eyebrow sardonically, and Jonathan attempted to slide the offending book under his covers, but Tempest's long arm seized it. "How did you get hold of this? What's addled your brain, brother, that you—"

"Stop it! Leave the poor man alone!" Esther's voice came clear as a ray of sunlight, slanted and concentrated. "He is your elder brother, and he's had an exceedingly hard time." She snatched the book from Tempest's loosened grasp. "Surely, he's a right to his own opinions. He may be ill, but he's a right to do what he has a mind to—especially now!"

"Here, here, missy! I see we've a cheeky little maid before us, a regular vixen couching under the surface."

Esther chaffed at the teasing tone. Did he mean to provoke her? She bit her lip; she would not take up his bait. Instead she slid the Book of Mormon under the crook of the sick man's arm, gave him the warmest smile she could muster, and stepped away from the bed.

"I have enjoyed our visit. I shall come again, if you'd like."

"Please do, Esther. They say good rest might mend me in the end—that is, if the lethargy and boredom of it doesn't do me in first."

A spasm of sympathy passed over Tempest's rough features.

"Good-bye, then, sir," Esther murmured as she left the room, feeling that she was scurrying, as a little trapped mouse might, and she berated herself for this terrible timidity that played games with her boldness; light and shadow, always struggling within.

She had cleared the porch and was several feet down the drive before she became aware of footsteps following after her. She paused, fighting the urge to glance behind, instead struggling to lengthen her pace.

"Hold up, will you, lass?" a strong voice boomed. "You make it almighty hard for a fellow to have a word with you, much less to apologize."

She stood stock still then, feeling her breath catch in her throat. Why did this Tempest disconcert her so terribly? He must not see it in her! For that reason alone she must face him down.

As he approached, she turned to meet him, holding her head purposefully a bit higher, yet attempting a pleasant expression, so that he would not guess at her discomfiture.

"I come to you as a repentant. Bad manners are beastly things."

"So your elder brother told you to come?" Esther clutched her hands behind her, wondering what in the world had brought that retort to her lips.

Tempest laughed, a deep sound that burst forth like the bubbling of a freshlet of water on the hillside in spring. "So he did, so he did. But I am sincere, ne'ertheless."

Esther gave him a bit of a smile. "Then I shall accept your apology, for the present."

"For the present. What in the deuce does that mean?"

The sparkle was still in his eye; she had not offended him. Yet she felt he was toying with her. "I suppose I mean when you go back. Will you defer to your brother, make things easier for him, rather than—"

"If you refer to that Mormon book, no! He's being foolish about it, for some obstinate reason." Tempest stood back on his heels, yet at the same time moved his expressive face closer to hers. "That book started all his troubles, you know."

"That is nonsense. Harvey Heaton started Jonathan's troubles. His sons planned the whole escapade, caring neither one way or the other what befell your brother—"

"Yes—but if these blasted Mormons were not in the neighborhood, stirring things up like a mad hornet's nest, nothing like this would have happened. You must grant me that."

The impish eyes, blue and wide, gazed into Esther's, the long expressive mouth curved.

"They've as much right to be here as you and I."

"And this from the minister's daughter!"

Esther felt an uncomfortable color begin to crawl up her face. "There is nothing bad in them. They do no harm, only good—only the best of people are drawn to them—certainly not riff-raff like Heaton and his lot."

"You are quite an advocate, but you will not win me to your cause, lass, so do not waste your breath."

"I want your word, nevertheless, that you will leave your brother alone."

"In this matter?"

Esther's breath caught in her throat. "In this matter."

"I shall give it some thought." Tempest's eyes had clouded over with a perplexity or concern that Esther could perceive but was not able to identify. "That is the best I can do."

Esther sighed. "I suppose, then, I must be content with it. Good day to you, sir."

She turned on her heel; she did not want him to detain her further, to speak out again, to taunt her. She felt a wave of relief when he did not stop her nor follow after. Once she was away from the park and into the darkened safety of the woods, she slowed her steps and attempted to control her rapid breathing and the agitation that had caused it. *A pox on him!* she thought angrily, kicking at the thick carpet of leaves before her, marking a long, crackling path as she walked, from which the fragrance of the crushed leaves sifted up, a heady perfume that calmed her senses. And she found, as she went on, that her thoughts reverted to the pale man she had left lying, weak and bewildered, at what life had suddenly done to him—struggling for what? Animation and health again? Hope for the future that perhaps had been snatched from him?

Cruel, cruel life was, she pondered, without some understanding of what it may all be about. *I wish I could have taken that book with me,* she thought suddenly. *It would have helped me to read in it now. It would have—* No. She must stop such thoughts and desires. She knew that she must.

When she neared the house she saw her father sitting on a bench beneath one of the large yew trees, a book lying unopened on his lap, his eyes gazing ahead, seeing nothing.

"Daughter," he said, holding out his hand to her. "Did you have a nice visit then?"

Oh, how she longed to unburden her heart to him as she always had! Standing there she perceived her childhood drop away from her, and she felt alone and exposed.

"Yes, Father," she murmured, taking a seat beside him, still holding his hand.

"I know it can be an oppressive thing visiting the sick, Esther. How is the lad?"

She proceeded to tell him, struggling foolishly with tears, angry with herself because of the strength of these feelings she could not suppress.

Too much sadness lay on her heart as she rose to leave him, not least among them his own. She felt a weariness of soul greater than any weariness of body, and wondered dimly how one made it through a long life and carried the burdens of living clear through to the end. She bent to stroke one of the cats that had curled itself round her ankle, then slipped into the welcome warmth and silence of the house.

Dorothea Whitely sat with the post in her lap, her fingers idly sifting through the papers 'til at length they drew out one slim sheet that must have been hand delivered, for it bore no stamps or markings of any kind. Her name was written in a fine, sure hand that she did not recognize. Slitting the seal with the tip of her finger, she pressed out the sheet upon which were written words that seemed foreign to her, words the like of which she had never read before, even in books. She sucked her breath in and laughed defensively, then pushed the paper from her so that it slid to the floor.

"Nonsense," she said aloud. "What in the world is he thinking to say such shameful things to *me*, even on paper!" Something in her bristled, and the bristling felt comfortable and safe to her, nothing like the strange weakness that had risen within her when she first read the words.

"Can't be true," she muttered, bending to swoop up the paper. "Must be some kind of mistake." She hesitated, then with a sudden resolved motion crushed the paper into a crumpled ball and flung it into the kitchen fire, where it went up with a small puff and disappeared from her eyes. "There, that's done." She wiped her hands along her apron and went back to the table where her sewing was spread out waiting for her, unable to accept as reality the possibility that Lucius Bidford, or any man, for that matter, would write tender, silly words of courtship to such as her.

Lucius, at much the same time, was fingering a paper that was becoming worn in the places where he had grasped it already dozens of times. It was a note with no signature on it, and very few words. It stated merely, *Dorothea Whitely thinks highly of you, Master Bidford, and would, many believe, welcome any advances on your part to gain her favor.*

He had not been able to stop himself from thinking on it after the first time he had read it and got it into his head. Then, strange as it may seem, during the next Sabbath meeting of the members he heard Dorothea praised by no fewer than three people. Was that a coincidence? It could hardly be so! He had studied her features more carefully as she sat singing with the others. A handsome woman, she might be called, not running to too much flesh, nor dried up and prunelike, as some women got when they aged. A fine-looking woman; he must have known that before but had simply paid it no mind.

The more he thought on it, the more he liked the idea. The more he was sure that he had been foolish to imagine he wanted a young chit of a thing in his house; not half grown up yet and given to fits of fancy and girlish emotion. While Sister Whitely, on the other hand, knew well how to behave. Come to think of it, she carried herself with a pleasing dignity; Lucius could picture a man walking down the street with the likes of her on his arm.

After a few more days had passed, he trembled at his narrow escape, and determined to waste no more time. He penned the note that Dorothea read with such consternation. Then, losing his nerve a bit as he went home to wait out the results of what he had done, he brought out the odd note that had started this whole thing, smoothed it with his hands, and wondered how he would be able to wait this matter out, and just what his next move ought to be.

❧

Esther came upon Andrew unexpectedly, walking back from Sallie's, where she had vividly reported her last visit to the sick young squire. She had been honest and had not left out the part about the Book of Mormon, Jonathan's interest, and the questions he asked. She knew Sallie would think on it all and come up with something, even if she first had to talk it out with her bees.

She was not particularly pleased to see Andrew, nor, she noticed, did his face light up when he caught sight of her. Rather, he seemed to droop and turn surly as he approached and called out with a sidelong glance, "Still administering to the parishioners, are we? I'd heard you had better things to do with your time."

"Whatever are you talking about?" she retorted, though trying to keep her voice friendly and matter-of-fact.

He fell into step with her, and this enhanced her displeasure. "Ministering angel up at the squire's, no less; young squire himself preferring your company and sending especially for you."

She shook her head. "This is not worthy of you, Andrew. Only stupid and petty people behave so when—"

"Ah, you insult me on top of it!"

She stopped and lifted her face to him. "On top of what, Andrew?"

He fidgeted then. "It isn't unheard of. Young squire has never shown the least interest in any girl hereabouts. Now, suddenly he's asking for you—"

Esther took a step back. "You cannot tell me people are thinking—thinking—such utter nonsense!"

"'Tisn't utter nonsense."

"The boy is probably dying, Andrew!" She hissed the words at him. She was beginning to feel ill inside. "I have befriended him—and that at

old Sallie's insistence—when others have left him bored and neglected."
Andrew was still fuming; she could see. "It was no more than that."

They began to walk again. "Have you met that insolent brother of
his? The one come back from Scotland as crude as any highlander."

"I have met Tempest, yes."

"Rude blighter, isn't he? It was a mistake for the old squire to send
for him."

"Is that what everyone says?"

It was Andrew who paused now, and looked at her closely. "Are you
going to stand up for him, too?"

Yes, she was. She could feel it coming. "He isn't at all what you think.
And you've no right to condemn him when you know next to nothing
and do not intend to give him a chance."

"I don't understand you, Esther. I don't understand you anymore."

"I do not know what you mean."

"I don't know either!" Andrew nearly shouted the words. "Ever since
that first night when the Mormons came, remember, and you and I
talked in the woods?"

She nodded her head.

"You've been different, somehow, Esther, and I think it started back
then."

They had reached the parsonage, and, feeling suddenly tired, she
sank down on the bench. "You have changed, too," she said.

"Perhaps I have. I've reached the age where my father is making me
think about my future: 'long past it,' he says. Says he's allowed my
mother to coddle me long enough."

"That isn't fair."

"Fair or not, I've got to choose what school to go to, or what profession to enter."

"Oh, Andrew." Her heart went out to him. "Have you thought what
it might be?"

"Finding something that pleases *him* enough so that he'll see his way
to support me, and at the same time be a thing I want and can see myself
doing—"

"Have you prayed about it?"

"That's no answer, Esther."

"I think it is."

"Anyway, I shall probably go to London and stay with my mother's brother. He is in the law, you know, and in need of clerks and apprentices."

She nodded. "I think you might do well at the law."

"I shall be gone, then—does that not mean a thing to you, Esther?"

She leaned back against the cool wood and sighed.

"It would have at one time." He spoke almost bitterly.

"It still does."

"But not in the same way."

"Andrew, you're being unfair. I *happened upon you* today; it is not as if you came to see me. You have not come here for a very long while."

"Yes, that's true."

"And what am I to think of it?"

"My father did not want me to come. And, somehow, I wanted you to miss me and send for me, and—"

Esther turned and looked hard at him, this boy who had been her childhood companion, who had always been able to win or cajole or inveigle her because of his handsome face and the natural charm of his ways. He still smiled like a little boy, and it still struck a chord in her, spilling her childhood like bits of stored sunlight. She reached for his hand, aware for perhaps the first time of the weakness in him, which was part of the many things that were coming between them. "Our lives have changed, and we've both changed inside in ways we didn't expect, perhaps did not even choose."

"So, that is that. And I'll go my way, and you'll—"

"I shall still be here."

"You believe so?"

She laughed out loud. "Where else *shall* I go, silly? I'll be here with my father."

"Here to come back to?" He looked at her darkly. "No, Esther, you did not say that."

"I *cannot*, and you know it." She sighed and, as if that were a signal, he let go of her hand, stumbled to his feet, and stood before her awkwardly.

"Will you come again? Will you let me know what is happening? You will not just—go away?"

"No, I do not think I could go away without saying good-bye to you, Esther."

His eyes were so miserable that she trembled and fought an urge to draw him close to her. It was Andrew she had always run to for comfort, since she was a child. But now, in a woman's way, she wanted to comfort him, kiss his lips, smooth his hair back, and whisper encouragement that might take that haunted look out of his eyes.

"Farewell for now, then, Esther," he was saying. He had already turned and was walking away from her. And, although she wished it, she knew she could not call him back. She could not really give him the things he desired; not any more. *Without us even knowing,* she thought, *childhood has deserted us, and dropped us in this unfamiliar, unfriendly place.* That sense of aloneness which had surprised her so often these past months settled over her now, as chill as the silent settling of twilight, which nothing in heaven or earth could hold back.

What will happen to me? The question became a cry in her, and she realized, from the depths of that awful aloneness, that there were no arms she could run to that possessed the power to hold her tomorrows at bay.

Chapter Eighteen

*H*annah knew for a certainty now that she would be having a baby, and that he would be born in the spring. Michael laughed at her because she was so certain it would be a boy child.

"I cannot explain it," she told him. "I see him very clearly in my mind's eye, and that is enough for me."

It was enough for Michael, too. He wanted to begin work right away on a cradle for his son, but she held him off. "You *must* complete the little one for Rose Dubberly," she urged. "Rose will need it before the snow flies, and everyone's helping, because they're poor as church mice; some knitting and sewing, some weaving blankets to warm her."

"Oh, this one, I see, is a girl."

Hannah laughed. "So we have all decided."

"Well, then, I believe, it shall be so."

There were servants from the squire's house who brought wheat to the mill and collected the flour in bags after it had been duly ground. Paul Pritchard wished he had occasion to visit the squire in person, but he could think of no viable excuse. After much frustration, an idea came to him; a little bold, by his reckoning, but he decided to take a chance.

He put it before the brethren on the following Sunday. Ought they to organize their efforts and take gifts to young squire, things that would cheer and help him? Or, even more, offer their services to the squire outright, who might appreciate having things taken care of that he had not the heart for himself.

Much discussion ensued. Some were fearful. "Any attention we draw to ourselves right now is bad attention," Sam Weatherall pointed out. "Zachie and Adam can vouch for what happens when eyes get trained in our particular direction."

The others knew this was true. "Leave well enough alone," Lucius growled. "If we stir up another hornet's nest, we'll have ourselves to blame."

"Could be anonymous," Michael Bingham suggested softly. "No one needs to know it is us."

"Might work," the doctor conceded thoughtfully. "We shall need to find some trustworthy person, unattached to us, to act as courier."

Zachie Kilburn bolted forward, nearly upsetting an inkwell and brushing half a dozen sheets of paper off onto the sawdust of the mill floor. "*Constable Johns!* What think ye? I b'lieve he would do it. He's time enough in a day's work, and his comings and goings would be suspected by none."

"But, so much for the idea of impressing the squire with our goodwill," Peter Goodall muttered. "I still think we need the powerful man's favor just a little right now."

"Peter is right, of course," the doctor interjected, "and yet I feel that blessings will come to us if we do good to others, no matter how."

Back and forth they went, until at last it was decided that Doctor Sterne would approach the constable, and Adam, working as he was on one of the squire's farms, would feel out the squire's foreman every few days during the coming weeks of harvest to learn of any need that may develop for extra hands to complete a field or bundle a harvest safely to barn. Bit by bit they would grasp what opportunity presented itself, and leave the rest to the Lord.

"He *will* sustain us in this matter, and guide us," Paul assured them, for he felt it deep down in his bones in a way that left in him no doubt. "I'll begin with a sack of flour so finely ground it will seem like a lady's face powder," he offered. "I've a method I'm working on, tedious, but effective, and the bread it makes will be easy for the lad to digest."

They called the women in then, and made out a list and a schedule so that all would be in order when Constable Johns agreed to begin on his rounds. Ideas came easily, for what the sick boy could not manage, the rest of the household could. So any picked fruit or choice garden vegetables or baked goods they felt would be welcome. And, of course, there were some who offered to weave a blanket for master Jonathan, piece together a quilt, or make a warm bed shirt or knit slippers for the cold nights to come. Dorothea had a new set of bedsheets that she had just made of finely spun cotton, beautifully finished, which she stepped forward to volunteer, keeping her eyes purposefully and discreetly away from the chair where Lucius Bidford was sitting beside Sam Weatherall. But Lucius saw her, and the hum of admiration and approval that swept through the gathered group at her generous offer was not lost upon him.

They ended the meeting singing hymns, whichever of their favorites that were suggested. Young Daniel accompanied the singing on his flute, and it seemed he knew the tunes to them all. It appeared to Paul, as he watched his son, that the lad had grown, that even his shriveled leg seemed to drag at him less, and that the rest of his body had filled out and was more sturdy and straight. He *wanted* it to be so. He wanted the boy to lead a full life, to be able to work as a man and provide as a man.

"Fiddlesticks," Paisley would scold him. "Education is the answer, Paul. We'll send him to school. You work with your hands and your brawn; well, Daniel can work with his head just as easily. There'll be a place for him, husband, just wait and see."

Daniel looked up and, seeing his father's eyes on him, smiled and missed a beat, but no one paid it mind. They wound up, as always, with "The Spirit of God Like a Fire Is Burning," and if anyone had begun to forget why he joined this Church, any hint of a doubt was burned out of him after that song had been sung. They went to their homes with grateful hearts that were softened into a willingness to do what the Lord would require of them.

What a catch that woman would be, Lucius marveled over and over again. He went home from meeting and thanked God on his knees for leading him aright in this matter, and saving him from the machinations of a thoughtless lass whom, in his foolishness and pride, he had sought. "Time to move forward. With haste," he told himself, speaking the words out loud. There was no one to hear them but, with God's help, in the future—in the near future—there would be. Ah, then he would watch his tongue, to be sure, and say only the sweetest and kindest things that even the most exacting of ladies would find it pleasant to hear. He sat in the gathering dusk and planned his strategy, anxious and uncertain as he had never been when he courted Martha Goodall, who—*thank Him who knows all*—had rejected his suite.

Roger had fed and watered the horses and completed the small tasks that his master had set him, such as running a needle and skein of thread to a neighbor three doors down for the missus, and taking tomorrow's order to his brother, Herman, the greengrocer, two blocks away. He had shined the boots and polished the master's best saddle and the second-best bridle, which he preferred. The late light still slanted into the barn and made the dust motes dance like bits of flint, hundreds of them, floating beside one another yet somehow not bumping heads. The barn was heady with the clean smells of straw and grain and fresh hay in the feed boxes. He liked living here in his own room. Though small and tucked away in the rafters, it seemed spacious and private compared to the cramped space he had come from, with a mother and father, four brothers and three sisters crowded into two rooms and a loft.

He wondered if he dare take out the book from its secret hiding place. He had found it only ten days ago, when Thomas Weatherall had told him he thought he had dropped his pocketknife whilst in the barn, and asked Roger would he mind looking about for it. He had not minded at all but, rather, had remembered, as he searched, a pair of gloves he'd misplaced last winter. Knowing he might have need of them soon, he began in more earnest, not leaving one corner of the old place untouched. The master's dog, Queenie, had a way about her of dragging off things she took a shine to and depositing them heaven knows where.

In one of the back stalls, drooping with cobwebs, busted boards, and the rubbish of the past year or two, he had taken a stick and poked through the damp straw on the floor and in the sagging feed box. He had found it there; a bump against the tip of the poker. When he first began to draw it out he had thought eagerly of a box of money concealed by a miserly ancestor, long forgotten and lost. When he realized it was a book, his thoughts ran to family histories containing terrible hidden secrets, or money still—bank notes stuck in the pages.

It was none of these things. As soon as he took a good close look at it, he knew what it was. So the master had not burned the book, but only hidden it here. He thought that a bit strange. He had opened it gingerly, feeling that surely eyes must be upon him, or the voice of the master would call out from the rafters and catch him out.

The Book of Mormon. He remembered the look on the face of that brother, Sam, when he had driven away that day. Must have left the book here, and this is what master did with the gift.

Now the spotlight of concentrated sunlight had faded from the sky and the dust sparkles with it, and the dove gray of early evening was settling into the barn. Roger lit a lamp and settled down with an early, crisp apple in his lap and the book open in his hands. He had begun at the beginning, and found it an amazing story from the very first page. This family of brothers spoke to his imagination as well as his mind. He had four brothers, and at times he could picture them in the places of Nephi, Laman and Lemuel, and Sam. He seemed able to *feel* what they went through, returning to Jerusalem to obtain the records, wandering in the desert and breaking their bows so that the whole group of them had to go hungry. He knew what it was like to go hungry; he knew what it was like to work to the point of bone weariness, whether you felt like it or not. He wondered if he would have supported a visionary father and been as Nephi, wanting the same kind of knowledge and power. Could he forgive his brothers, the way Nephi did when they hurt him and humiliated him? He could so vividly imagine what it must have been like. He read the vision of the tree of life four times over, so that he could get it all straight. And when Nephi built a boat by the side of the great ocean—at the edge of his known world—he felt the excitement of it as though he were there by his side.

Bit by bit the beauty of the doctrine, the wisdom and power of what Lehi and Nephi taught, began to seep through. The story made it easy and enjoyable, but the spiritual teachings began to surface in Roger's conscious awareness and hold their own. When Lehi was getting old and aware that death would soon be upon him, he spoke to his sons about their stubbornness in rejecting truth, and about their cruelty to Nephi. The words seared into Roger, as no other words he had read before:

> And I exceedingly fear and tremble because of you, lest he shall suffer again; for behold, ye have accused him that he sought power and authority over you; but I know . . . he hath sought the glory of God, and your own eternal welfare. . . . His sharpness was the sharpness of the power of the word of God, which was in him; and that which ye call anger was the truth, according to that which is in God, which he could not restrain. . . . It was not he, but it was the Spirit of the Lord which was in him, which opened his mouth to utterance that he could not shut it.

His evenings were not long, and he had read every night since he found the book, so that, though he knew he was a plodding reader, he was now in the part called *Jacob*. It seemed the more he read, the more he wanted. And the more he read, the more he learned and the greater differences he began to be aware of within his own soul.

He sat now, leaning a bit forward, forgetting the apple and the seeping chill, and the annoying flicker of the lantern, immersed in the amazement of the world he had entered, the world he held in his two hands.

⟨∞⟩

"I'll go for you, sir, if you'd like. I can find out what the trouble is, and even set the men to working, if you're ready for that."

The squire regarded his second son with a pleasant but quizzical expression; the boy was still inscrutable to him. Tempest appeared respectful, willing to work, willing to do anything of any nature that his father asked him, but it seemed he was somehow detached. *He doesn't like it here.* That was the thought that kept coming to the squire. And he had read more than once a panic in his son's eyes when anyone spoke of the possibility of Jonathan dying and Tempest stepping into his place. That made no sense. By and large, the boy made no sense to him, but he was waiting for an answer right now.

"Thank you, son, I *would* appreciate that. Means I can check out the drainage works in the far meadow with Sims. And see to your mother's horse, will you; I fear he's gone lame."

They walked out together, and he gave his son instructions concerning the cottage roof that had collapsed and asked him to examine some of the others while he was at it, to see what repairs might be wanting before winter set in.

Tempest mounted his horse and turned down the lane that led to his father's farm cottages, strewn in clusters here and there in the midst of fields or along a sluggish tributary of the river, paying no mind to any pattern or order. Most, he reckoned, had stood where they were from time immemorial, perhaps since the first Feathers had established themselves here, over seven hundred years before. *What stories they could tell,* he thought, as he approached the first of them—that of old man Weatherstaff, whose roof had caved in on him while he was sleeping the night before.

Tempest knew he would have to smooth ruffled feathers and make promises to atone for the indignity, and he believed he could manage that well enough. *Tame work,* he complained to himself. There was more passion for life in the Scottish lowlands; a roughness, perhaps even a coarseness, he would admit, but a lithesomeness, a sense of *awareness*— och, he didn't know what name to put to it. He knew only that he was restless and bored here among these slow meadows and hills. To think that he might have to press and contort his own fierce spirit into the confining mold his father would expect him to step into—the notion unnerved him.

He dismounted, dropping the reins and telling his horse to stand, knowing that he would, and walked toward the low entrance, sagging and misshapen now by the partial collapse of the roof. He expected to be here and in the adjoining vicinity for several hours, but would probably make it back just in time for late tea. That did not particularly please him. His mother and sisters would be full of questions, petty questions about the petty things that interested them and were of no concern to himself.

Och, man, he scolded himself. *Aren't you the cocky and vain one!* He drew a deep breath. The tenant he would soon be talking to was a man every bit as much as himself. He must put all other thoughts and considerations from his mind and see to his needs. He could not call himself a gentleman if he did less.

Lucius still hesitated. He had been rejected, aye, even laughed at before, and he felt himself shrink from it now. So he resorted to the old tack of leaving gifts to sweeten the way for him. He selected a time when he was certain Dorothea would be safely and soundly abed. Nearing midnight, it was, and the darkness ink black when he found his way to her house. A bit of a wind scuttled leaves at his feet and the hairs on his neck rose at the sudden screech of a cat. At length he stood trembling on her porch, feeling as foolish as a schoolboy and very nearly determined to take the fine basket of new apples and fresh vegetables back with him and never resort to such measures again.

Just as he wavered, the door in front of him swung open, to his horror, and the maiden lady stood there staring at him, her mouth agape, her hands clinging to the sides of her dressing gown.

"I do not know what in the world you are doing here, Brother Bidford," she said sternly, "but perhaps you are heaven-sent. Come in, come in quickly!"

She pulled at his arm and he felt himself propelled into the too-sudden light of her immaculate sitting room. "Quick, please, back here in the kitchen. My little terrier is trying to deliver her first batch of pups— neither she nor I have done it before. I don't think—well—" She wrung her hands in front of her. "I believe something might be wrong."

Lucius followed more quickly then. "Boil some water, Dorothea," he said firmly, "and gather a handful of clean rags for me. I shall see to the rest."

And so he did. In less than an hour three puppies were safely delivered; only the runt of the litter was sacrificed to the circumstances at hand, awkwardness of the birth process this first time, when the little dog's body had been slow to respond. Lucius wrapped him into a little bundle and took him quickly outside, so that Dorothea scarcely saw him at all.

They both were radiant as the mother dog curled herself round her babies. "Shall I do anything else for them?" Dorothea asked anxiously.

"Not for the time being. But you may do something for me."

"A cup of tea; I know you would like something hot to drink after the fine work you have done." She smiled at him and he realized what fine, intelligent eyes she had. "I've a large wedge of one of Janet's pies left in the cupboard," she called over her shoulder. "Put your feet up by the fire and relax for a moment, I'll be right back."

Lucius Bidford did as she had tempted him, and closed his eyes into the bargain, and imagined that this was what heaven itself must be like. He had not truly believed that there were women who knew how to take care of a man; that was why he had never married before. But the gospel, this Mormon religion, had changed all that. He could *see* something in this business of a man and wife together, and had convinced himself it was worth taking the chance.

Dorothea returned and set out a tea before him that made his mouth water. He sat up and smiled, wishing he could thank her more properly.

She returned his smile warmly. "I wish I could thank you more properly," she said. And when the amazing words were out of her mouth he choked on his tea and replied, "You can do that. You can give me leave to come courting you."

He held his breath; the cup and saucer in his hand nearly started to clatter. He looked into her eyes. "It would be an honor, Dorothea Whitely," he added softly. "It would be an honor to court a woman like you."

She nodded slowly. "Well, let us give it a chance, Lucius; by all means, let us give it a chance."

Constable Johns took his role of deliveryman with due solemnity and respect. During the following weeks, despite the press of the harvest being upon them, the Saints kept their word, and every three days or so the constable—laden with everything from tea and honey to vinegar ointments and iron pills, to meat pasties and fruit pasties and bread by the bushelful—found his way to the squire's big square house.

At first the family, not knowing what to think of such beneficence, expressed a degree of reluctance. But the good-natured, blustery constable was indeed the right man for the job.

"Can't deny your own folk from giving back to you, squire," he insisted. "Not a man or woman in the village but thinks well of your son. This be one of the few ways folk have of showing their respect and concern, sir."

The squire hesitated and the constable pushed his advantage.

"You would not want the whole lot of 'em lined up at your door now, would ye? The women flustering and blustering." He pushed his basket of offerings closer. "Isn't this by far the best way?"

At length his argument was admitted to and, as time passed, the squire's family began to look forward to the gifts and offerings as they came, the girls' anticipation like that of children at Christmastime.

Though he would never have admitted it, the squire's rough heart was touched.

Esther had fallen into a pattern of coming to read to the young squire twice weekly, usually on Tuesdays and Thursdays. At first the rest of the house was uneasy at the young girl's presence, but her quiet, easy ways won their confidence, and even Jonathan's mother could see the beneficial influence Esther had on her son.

"I read to you often," his sister, Sarah, complained, "but you don't get that light in your eye when *I* walk into the room." The two sisters giggled, but Jonathan paid no heed to them. Girls, he knew, had their own little ways. He often marveled that it was this calamity that had befallen him which had brought Esther into his life. He would never have sought her out on his own, not when he was the posh young master with an array of brilliant choices before him. She, quiet and chaste as a little moor hen; he would probably not have noticed her presence at all. But her spirit spoke to his spirit, she was becoming part of things that mattered to him, new things he had discovered after his accident, much as he had discovered her.

Part of a new life, he liked to tell himself. *When I get up from this sickbed I shall be a different man, and life shall be dearer to me. I shall make something of it that I never dreamed of before.*

But he knew the words were a lie. He had heard the doctor talk with his father; he had seen the expression in both their faces, the pain in their eyes. There was a chance; aye, there is always a *chance at life* until Death pronounces the last word and shuts everything down. And he knew what no one else knew, that the weakness within him was spreading, that the pain in his chest seemed deeper, that at times he felt he would scream if he could not open his mouth and *breathe,* gulping great draughts of clean air deep within him, air that would drive out the terrifying weakness.

"Master Jonathan, Miss Esther is here. I sat her in the parlor to wait for you."

Good old Betts. Worth his weight in gold. "Would you wheel my chair in to her, Betts? I feel I should like being out of this room for an hour or so."

Esther rose to her feet and smiled when he entered. All the sunlight of the day seemed cupped in that smile, and all the hope of youth. He had the Book of Mormon on his lap, tucked under the rug that covered his legs. He smiled back at her. "Have you time for a good read today?"

"Long as you'd like." She inclined her head slightly. "Your pleasure, sir."

He did his best to grin back, but a tightness in his chest prevented him. Everything in him was crying out for the chance to *live!*

She took the book from him and thumbed through the pages. They were midway through Mosiah. He closed his eyes and waited for the sound of her voice.

Esther read slowly, savoring the words as she suspected the young squire was. She refused to let herself think what she was really doing in reading this scripture to him; refused to consider her offering to the desolate young man as a betrayal of her father. What would he say if he knew? Would he understand and urge her to continue, or would he consider it a deception, and turn those disappointed, almost haunted eyes of his on her face?

She *would* not think of it. Jonathan's need had become her first consideration; she knew that instinctively. All else she would have to sort out some other way, at some other time.

Chapter Nineteen

*T*he harvest went forward in earnest now, and the serene late summer days seemed to hold their breath for the people's sake, soothing the foreheads of the burdened workers with cool winds that carried the tangy sweetness of apples, the muskiness of squash and pumpkin, the clean fragrance of the soil, itself, upturned and rich with the yield it had granted them.

When the harvest was abundant, life was also abundant, and hope soared like the throstles that spun and glided above the ripe fields where the golden corn rustled, and against the intense blue of the sky, settling for the night in nests of fresh soft hay hung among the rafters, where they might breathe in the garnered fragrance of earth and sun.

A good year because the Mormon missionaries came to us. That is what the converts would say. At least, by the by, there was, for the time being, nothing the disgruntled or bitter could lay against them, and for a spell there was peace.

Everyone felt it; even Marjorie, stuck at the Stragglers' Inn. Everything seemed to sag, to relax. She could see the difference in the face of the youngest Heaton, who was not walking on pins and needles as he was usually required to do. Work for the hands and work for the heart;

autumn had power to mellow people, draw them close to the source of
things, calm away the sharp edges of working and struggling in a few
weeks of abundance and the sense of satisfaction that comes from seeing the fruit of one's labors; the reaping of what one has sown.

❧

There was to be a baptism the beginning of October; they'd discussed it at last Sunday's meeting. Elder Hascall and Elder Turner were
to come out from Preston, where they were headquartered. Levi Walker
had left last month to go back to Nauvoo. Back to a place where a living
Prophet awaited him, and where, if the enticing murmurs held truth,
some among them, some of their very own selves, would soon have the
chance to go.

Evaline spoke to no one, said nothing of what she intended. But she
had made up her mind. She was going to be one of those baptized
before winter set in on them. She would not go through another year
without the blessings she saw in the lives of those who had entered the
waters, who had the glow of the Spirit upon their countenances, who
spoke of the Holy Ghost as one who comforted them, warned them,
instructed them, even kept them in line. She wanted fiercely to be one
with this people; she would allow nothing to stand in her way.

❧

The women had not forgotten the pastor, but the needs of the young
squire had pushed his needs out of their minds. Now Sallie rallied the
women and they made a list of Brother Grey's favorites—for so they
called him in their minds, and out loud sometimes.

"I'll do the takin' myself," she stated bluntly. "I've been missing our
Esther something awful. I'll find my way up there, just don't make the
basket too heavy this time."

As luck would have it, Sallie came upon Pearl alone in the kitchen,
and Pearl turned a sour face on her. "Miss Esther's gone up to the big
house readin' to the young squire, as she does twice a week."

"Is that so?" Sallie mulled the information over in her mind. "I shall speak to your master then."

Pearl's long face arranged itself into one scowl and she stood her place at the stove side and did not move.

"You go and announce me or I'll go myself," Sallie snapped, her hands on her hips.

Pearl glared at her. "He doesn't like being disturbed this time o' morning."

Sallie, clicking her tongue in annoyance, swept past the startled servant, through the kitchen, and into the hall and was on the fourth stair before Pearl came from behind her and grabbed a fistful of her skirts. "You can't go up there!"

"I'm going, aren't I?" Sallie called back without slackening her pace.

"What in the world is happening here, Pearl?" The pastor had come out of his office and, leaning over the banister, fixed his eyes on the two women. "Did Mrs. Brigman call to see me, Pearl?"

Pearl blanched. "Said she meant to talk to you, and I says you don't fancy being disturbed—"

"Pearl." Her name, spoken softly but firmly, was the worst kind of rebuke; the old servant stopped dead in her tracks. Christian held his hands out to the visitor, who was laboring up the steep stairs to reach him. "Sallie, come in, come in and sit a spell. It has been much too long since I've set eyes on you."

"That's a fact, Pastor, it is," she wheezed, following him into the study. Before he closed the door behind them he called out to Pearl, who still stood frozen halfway up, halfway down. "Would you bring us a spot of tea, say in fifteen minutes, Pearl?"

His command seemed to release her. She bobbed her head and darted into the safety of her kitchen. Christian smiled sadly; he could almost feel her relief. As he entered his office and sat down beside his old friend, he determined to enjoy her company as he always had. So he asked questions about how various people were doing, and enjoyed her full and colorful replies. Sallie had been a godsend when his wife died, she'd had a way with Esther and could calm her more easily, he remembered, than anyone else. He asked after her bees, he asked after her health. When Pearl came with the tea she leaned her head back and sighed before lifting a slice of bread to her mouth.

"You've plumb worn me out. I haven't talked so much in a month of Sundays."

"Oh, Sallie, I do not believe that."

She laughed and reached for her cup. "Well, I've not heard a word yet about yourself and Esther."

She could see the minister go stiff a bit. "Oh, there is not much to tell."

"Nonsense. That's no answer, and you know it, sir." Sallie sucked at the hot tea. "I miss that girl something fierce."

"Yes." Sallie glanced up to see Christian's sad eyes watching her. "Yes, well, that is how it is now. Things change, and we cannot do anything about it."

"I beg to disagree with you there. Did we come up with the plague out of the waters of baptism, Pastor?"

He blanched at her blunt words. "Sallie—"

"Well, really, sir. 'Tis a pity, and I know it, that religion gets in the way of friendship, that we came to hurting you and her to do what we felt we had to." She had kept her eyes on his face, her cup in her lap.

He tried to respond to her, but every time his thoughts began to form into words and sentences in his mind he discarded them.

"We were yours, sir, and 'tis a cruel thing to be torn away from you, to think of anyone putting blame or censure or pity upon *you* because of what we have done."

He rose and stood above her; he could not say any of the things that he felt in his heart.

She was watching him closely. She sighed and set her cup on the table. "Heaven knows I didn't come here to make things worse—sir—" She lowered her head and sat silent. Christian clutched his hands behind him and walked back and forth in front of her. At length, with a long sigh of defeat, he sat down.

"There is nothing for it, dear old friend. It is because we still love one another that this separation can hurt." *Nothing can separate us from the love of Christ.* The line ran through his mind.

Sallie sniffled, impatient with herself for showing emotion that might discomfort the minister. "I know that, sir; yes, you are right." She tried to take a sip from her tea, but the liquid stuck in her throat, and she set the cup down. "We just plain miss you. I suppose that's the long and short of it."

Christian nodded his head.

"I've a basket of goodies down in the kitchen," she said as if remembering. "From all of us—things we remembered—that you especially like—"

There were tears in Christian's eyes as he nodded again. "I thank you, Sallie. How can I thank you?" he said.

With some effort Sallie eased herself out of the chair. "You will give my love to Esther. Tell her to please come and visit me. 'Tis a sore thing to miss her today."

"I shall certainly do that." They both took a few steps toward the door. The pastor reached for the knob and opened it. "Will you give my thanks to the others, Sallie—to each one separately?"

"Course I will, Pastor. Faithfully." They looked squarely at each other for a minute. She had forgotten how kind his eyes were, and how sad. "And I shall tell them how much you still love them."

They stood on the landing now. Silence had fallen between them. "I shall see you down," Christian muttered.

"No, please, sir, no. I can find my way out."

As soon as she had made it to the bottom of the stairs he retreated to his room, closing the door, ignoring an urge to lock it. He was trembling all over. There was a tightness constricting his heart, constricting his breathing. From the window he watched her figure retreating, slowly, painfully. His mind was dull; he struggled vainly to hold all thought out.

Then suddenly, with a meanness that startled him, a deliberate impression took form. *I wonder if Doctor Sterne sent Sallie here to do the talking. I don't doubt that they could have discussed me, thinking I might get the gist of things, find my way to their side.* He could almost hear it: *You are a good man, Minister. You could come with us, enjoy the fellowship again that we once knew. We could never come back where you are.*

Sterne had pretty well said as much to him on more than one occasion. He sank into his chair; he felt sick inside. *You are a wretch!* he cried to himself. He knew these allegations were unworthy of him. He hid his face in his arms. He had never been more unhappy, not since Mary died. He felt as if he were failing everyone he cared for and everything he held dear. *Yet he was doing nothing, nothing at all!* He knew that Esther was both confused and disappointed. He knew he had cut her off from the tender concourse they once had shared, and he had not meant to do that. But what counsel could he give her? How could he talk of what stood between them? How could he unburden his thoughts: thoughts and desires and fears all frightfully mingled together? He had not confessed them to himself. He was facing nothing, deciding nothing; he was of no good, as he stood right now, to anyone at all.

"Come early spring we can get you out of all this. I've arranged a place for you in London. A place with your uncle." There were both pride and frustration in Nicholas Sheppard's voice. "Well, have you nothing to say to me, lad?"

"Thank you, Father. I know you have gone to great efforts on my behalf." Andrew attempted a smile to go along with his words, for his father was watching him closely.

"If you're thinking to moon over that girl of Christian's, don't waste your time."

"Her name is Esther, Father. And she and I have been friends, you may remember, from before the time we could walk."

"That is as may be, but times have changed, Andrew, and that spunky miss has changed, too."

"What do you mean by that?"

"Nothing but truth, lad; more than hearsay, if that's what you mean. She's friendly to those Mormon sots, has been from the beginning. Do you know what she is doing right now?"

Andrew shook his head and prayed he could keep his temper, no matter what his father had to say.

"She's reading that devil book to the young squire up at the big house."

"Reading the Book of Mormon to Jonathan Feather? I do not believe it."

"You will *have* to believe it, because it's God's truth."

"Does squire know?" As soon as he asked the question, Andrew regretted it.

"'Tis a good question, that, son, and I am not certain of the answer." Nicholas Sheppard's small eyes had constricted and brightened; Andrew could see the purpose growing in them and shuddered.

"Leave well enough alone, Father," he ventured.

"What in the world do you mean?" his father growled, turning on him.

"I mean, if you were to be the one to tell squire, well . . . the bearer of bad tidings is seldom thanked for them."

The minister grunted under his breath. "Fancy words, but they mean little; you do not understand these things, son."

"I understand them better than you think," Andrew mumbled. His father had already turned away. *Why does my father have such power to provoke me?* he fumed.

"See you get Farmer Petty to pay you in coin for your days at harvest," he warned his son. "You'll be needing coach fare for London, and there will be clothes your mother will have to make up for you; perhaps new gloves and collars, I suppose smart spring boots, a hat fit for London . . ."

His voice droned on and on. Andrew was not listening. He was seeing Esther's face as she said to him, "I have befriended him, and that at Sallie's insistence," or some nonsense like that. *Sallie.* Sallie had been baptized into the Mormons. Perhaps his father was right. He had felt rejected before, but now he felt entirely betrayed. *She doesn't know what she is doing!* he thought. *What in the world is she doing?*

He fought a powerful urge to run straight to Esther and confront her, but he hadn't the heart for that now. He knew also that he was afraid of what it was she might reveal to him.

"Ah, what difference does it make?" he muttered under his breath. "'Tis nothing to me now what Esther does or does not do. I'm out of it, far as she and this place are concerned."

He tried to growl away his pain and insecurity, the way his father did. But it did not come to him naturally to behave in that way. Wretched still, he sought out his mother, and they talked quietly and naturally of the details of life in London, and of the preparations that would have to be made for his going. She told him how much she would miss him, yet at the same time assuring him of how well she believed he would do. As he was leaving her room she called him back, and he stood still in the doorway, half turned for her words.

"I know it will be difficult for you to leave Esther, Andrew. I know what a rare girl she is, and how long you two have been fond of one another."

Her words set his pulse to racing, and he swallowed at a sudden constriction in his throat. She did not seem to require a reply from him but continued. "You shall have to trust this matter to God, son. He knows what we want, and He knows what is best for us. It will all work out right in the end."

"I wish I could believe that, but, thank you, Mother." His answer was swift and muffled, and he was out of her sight by the time his words ended. She sat watching after him, her hands idle in her lap, her eyes clouded. She murmured aloud, "I wish I could believe, too, Andrew. I can only hope and pray it is so."

"Come, Martha, come and see. Come quickly!" Mary tugged at her sister, who wiped her wet hands on her apron and followed her to the front window. Right there, bigger than life, walked Dorothea and her suitor, Lucius, arms linked, heads close together, strolling straight down the center of the village thoroughfare for all eyes to see.

"Bless Sallie," Martha murmured. "'Twould be good to see them both happy. Will you look at her face?"

It was true; the old maid of Throstleford was beaming like a school-girl, and the whiskery farmer gazing at her the while as if she were a heavenly vision planted in front of his eyes.

"She *is* a handsome woman, Dorothea is; I've always thought so," Mary offered.

"Yes, she is," Martha agreed. "And worthy of someone to love and look after her."

"Aw, yon woman is well capable of looking after herself! And that is good, for I fear 'twill be the other way round." Their grandfather hob-bled into the room, exerting himself into their conversation. "Did you not know the marriage date has been fixed? No grass grows under their feet."

He was greeted with howls and titters of amazement, and a barrage of questions: precisely what he had wanted. There was a sparkle in his eyes when he said, "Brother Bidford states he's of no humor to spend another cold winter alone, without companionship and comfort—of a cold night." He was teasing them now. "But 'tis true. When the elders come for the baptism, there'll be a wedding as well."

All who heard were glad of it. Even Esther, up at the parsonage, shared a kindly laugh with Pearl over the matter. *Love is an odd commodity,* she thought privately. *Who can say what it is or what it means, or what can blow the flames of it into life? Andrew and I loved each other; I am certain we did. We shared something precious that grew from our childhood, altering itself and changing as we changed and grew. So, what blew the flame out? What source said, "Oh, so sorry, I do not believe this will work anymore?"*

Was she bitter? She hoped not. Merely confused and tired. She had her tasks at the parsonage; Pearl could not take care of everything. And there were the errands she went for her father; she *must* help him, must minister to the needs of his people, since there was no wife to take her place, to stand at his side. Then these last weeks her sessions at the squire's had grown longer and longer. So it was only natural that she be tired. Yet she knew it was more than just that. She was longing, yes, longing, and she could not have told anyone—even her father, even her own self, for what.

∽

Roger was reading furiously, burning each night's candle into nothing but a thin film of hot wax shining over the surface of the metal before the soft flame went out. The baptism was only three weeks away. He wanted to finish the Book of Mormon before he presented himself as a candidate for the honor of baptism. He had read only two other books all the way through in his life; it would be a mighty accomplishment if he made it to the end of this one.

I've got Master Thomas to thank for it, he said to himself. *The master always told me I should be grateful to him someday that he taught me to read, and insisted I practice—and practice, and practice, whether I felt like it or not!* He thought it an odd show of how life goes. For the very person who had hidden his brother's book from the sight of man, who had condemned it to high heaven, was the means of opening up the joys and wonders of it to the boy who had learned how to read at his hands.

"So God works, we've been told more than once," Roger mumbled as he mucked out the stables and prepared feed for the pigs and the poultry. *He did it for my sake!* The thought was a wonder, that God in heaven could be mindful of him. Made no sense, no sense at all. But he meant to be there, nonetheless; present himself able and willing to be baptized into any church that could produce men like Nephi and Ammon and Moroni—men like this Prophet Joseph somewhere in America who had brought this wondrous book into life.

∽

The timing was unfortunate. Parson Sheppard was ushered into the parlor to await the appearance of the squire a scant fifteen minutes after Esther Grey had settled herself in the small sitting room with the young master positioning his couch and her chair just where the afternoon light played through the tall mullioned windows. Sun-warmed by the morning, the room was pleasant and comfortable for them both.

Sheppard took his time and built his case carefully, so as not to offend. He knew the stubbornness of Squire Feather; everyone did. He recognized, too, that the squire was not part of *his* flock, and may not look kindly on counsel coming from a source for which he held only a tenuous regard.

Touchy business, and he nearly lost it a time or two, for the squire got caught up in the fact that the parson's daughter may be duped by these imposters, and this seemed to concern him as much as the state of his son. He was scowling when Sheppard rose to take his leave. And, as ill luck would have it, the younger son, Tempest, walked in just then and his father turned to him, growling out his displeasure at the news the pastor had brought him. "We trusted the little vixen," he growled, his shoulders hunched against his frustration. "I wonder if Grey knows of this, knows of his own daughter's—"

"Hold, Father." The son spoke emphatically, with a tone almost of authority that silenced the older man. "I believe Mr. Sheppard is on his way out; let me see him to the door."

Nicholas fumed. There was more to this lad than met the eye, then, and he was after protecting his own and their privacy. Considered Nicholas an intruder; he could see that in the boy's cool eyes.

But there was nothing for it. The door closed firmly behind him, and though he stood a moment in frustration, he had to go on his way. Back inside, Tempest had returned to his father, whose temper was still rising as his thoughts churned.

"You mustn't blame the lass," he said bluntly. "She is doing what Jonathan bid her."

His father sputtered at these words. "What do you mean by that? You had better explain yourself, Tempest."

"Let us go ask them and find out for ourselves." Tempest took his father's arm and led him into the room where he knew the two were sequestered. Both looked up as they entered. "What have we here?" the squire barked. He saw the book open in Esther's hands; he read the title. "Caught in the act?"

Neither protested, nor offered explanation, though Tempest noticed that Esther's face blanched, and her knuckles turned white where she now clutched the book.

"What in the world, Father? Esther is reading to me, as I asked her. What is this to-do about?" The young squire leaned up on an elbow and fixed his eyes on his father.

❧

He knows how to handle the old blusterer, Tempest thought, watching. *He has had years of experience in it, which I lack.*

"Reading *what*, I ask you?" The squire snatched the book from Esther's hand and waved it aloft.

"'Twas found in *my* saddlebag. I have a right to peruse it." There was almost a sparkle in the sick man's eye, but then he lowered his voice and added, "Perhaps it was put there for a purpose."

"Without this book, and all that stands behind it, you would not *be in this bed!*" The squire's voice rose to a bellow now. Esther began to move toward the door.

"Do not leave, Esther. Please." Jonathan turned beseeching eyes on her.

"Very well, if you desire me to stay, I shall wait just outside."

The young squire drew a ragged breath and turned to his father. "That which *is* cannot be remedied or changed, Father, nor is that the issue right now. The issue is whether I, as a reasoning adult, have a right to read whatever I like."

"Fiddlesticks! You know very well it is more than that. *As a reasoning adult!* What about as my heir?"

Jonathan sank back against his pillows. Tempest detected a grayness in his face which suddenly alarmed him. He thought it was time to step in, but then his brother began to speak slowly. "I do not think we can consider that as a viable factor any longer, Father. You need an heir, surely. But I do not believe it will turn out to be me."

His words seemed to burn all life from the atmosphere; no one spoke, there was no sound made. Tempest glanced at his father's face and wondered if his own looked as stricken.

"Come, Father, you know what the doctor has told you."

"There is hope—you will not give up the fight?"

"No, I shall not give up the fight, nor have I given up hope."

The elder Jonathan was getting his feet beneath him again. "Then, son, why are you squandering your strength on nonsense like this?" He brandished the book again and, with the motion, Tempest stepped forward.

"I do not understand nor like it any more than you do, Father, but I believe you should respect his wishes in the matter."

"Oh, you do, you young pup!" The growl was back in the old voice again, his father's trusty shield against opposition or disappointment of any kind.

"Father—"

Tempest could see by his brother's face that Jonathan was going to attempt to explain himself. He made a sound in his throat and shook his head warningly. "Let's be off then, shall we? We can speak more of the matter later. Esther is still waiting outside."

Grumbling under his breath, the squire suffered his son to lead him out of the room, not raising his eyes to the anxious girl whose skirts brushed his coat as he passed. Tempest nodded, and she slipped through the open door and shut it behind her.

Once within she met Jonathan's eyes. He did his best to smile, but the attempt did not deceive her.

"Has he forbidden you?" she asked.

"No, strangely, he hasn't. Thanks to my brother."

Esther sighed. "'Tis a pity that it has brought you to quarrel with your father."

"You are right. It grieves me to distress him."

"Ought we to—"

"*No!*" The word was almost a cry. There was a flush over the white face. "No, Esther, I may not have very much time. Winter is setting in, and the cold damp air will do its worst on me—"

"Do not speak so, Jonathan, please!"

Esther, on her feet still, had moved close to the bed and now laid her hand on the coverlet, over where his own lay.

"I believe that is the first time you have called me by my name." He smiled weakly at her, but she felt her cheeks go warm at his words.

"I should leave now. You are upset and tired."

"Yes, but read just a few verses, will you, little one, just a few words to calm me."

She did as he asked. During the reading his eyes were closed, and when she shut the book and handed it back to him, he nodded and said, "Good-bye, little one. Will you return at the usual time?"

"Yes, of course," she replied, and let herself out as quietly as she could. She felt weak and trembly inside, and she knew she was shrinking from meeting the thoughts that were all achurn in her head.

She had walked but a yard or two from the house when she heard a rustling in the low bushes to the right of her and turned to face the second son of the household as he stepped out of the protection of the shrubbery and the screen of thin young saplings.

"May I walk with you for a short way?" he asked.

She nodded, instantly uncomfortable and on her guard at the sight of him.

"Could you tell me something," he continued, "to help me understand what my brother is doing?"

They moved a few steps into the grove, where the fragrant trees bent their arms to them. "I do not believe so. Why don't you ask him yourself?"

Tempest smiled, and Esther realized that his eyes became softened and quite beautiful when they were lit up that way. "Because I want *your* version first, nor do I wish to disturb him just now."

She knew his words were reasonable. But how in the world could she unfold to him the intimate and conflicting thoughts of her heart?

"You ask much," she began, "because it involves my *own* feelings as well as your brother's."

To her surprise, he reached for her hand. "I will be discreet," he promised. "I respect that kind of privacy, because I have once had it myself. What you say will go no further than what these trees can whisper for the breezes to carry away."

Was he making light of her? His eyes did not seem to say so. She sighed and sat down on one of the benches placed here at the end of the walk through the ash grove, at the approach to the house.

"He simply asked me to read to him," she began, "and I said that I would. Then he brought out the Book of Mormon and explained how he came by it and asked me if I knew what it was."

"And did you?"

"Yes. Doctor Sterne had given a copy to my father—"

"*Your father!*"

"Hush! I shall never get through this!" Esther breathed the words as a sort of entreaty and Tempest nodded, his eyes warm on her face.

"It will further amaze you to learn that my father asked me to read in the book and tell him what my thoughts of it were." With a side glance she added, "He has always esteemed my opinion, ever since my mother died, and I was all that he had."

Tempest looked away. He could not bear the agony of watching her. Her voice, her presence, was having a devastating effect on him. He tried to concentrate as she went on.

"I did not read much, not as much as I should have preferred to, for I *liked* what I read. When your brother asked me what I thought, I told him, so I suppose he felt he had a kind of ally in me."

"Would you have read it to him anyway?"

"Yes, I believe I would have, unless my father had forbidden it."

"Does your father know what you do?"

Ah, it had come to that, all of a sudden! Esther felt herself jump, as if startled. She was glad that Tempest was avoiding her eyes.

"He does not know. He has never asked for details concerning my visits, and I have never offered them." She sighed again, unconscious of it, but the sadness in the sound touched Tempest's heart.

"This is more than I thought," he muttered. "This Mormon business is—"

"Why do you call it that?" There was annoyance in Esther's voice as she turned on him. "They are a religion of intelligent, educated people, with a way of life and belief that would astound you if you explored it."

"Is that so?"

Esther smiled. "You sound just like your father." She could see that the comparison did not please him, but she went on. "What they teach is much the same as those things my father teaches—only better—and more—"

Speaking those words out loud seemed a struggle for her. "Why do you defend them?" he cried.

"I am sorry, but it angers me to see people ignorantly persecute others—"

"Have these Mormons been *persecuted* in Throstleford?"

"Yes, they have! If you should like to hear—"

Of a sudden Tempest rose to his feet. "No, I should *not* like to hear! For isn't that what happened to my brother—he unwittingly stepped into the way—"

"The way of whom?" Esther was on her feet, too, glaring at him. "You would blame the Mormons, peaceful and innocent, rather than the perpetrators—the stupid, ignorant villains—"

Tempest waved his hand at her. "Stop, Miss Grey! I told you I do not wish to hear any more."

She drew a deep breath. Her gaze had grown cool and appraising. "Very well, sir. Blame the tree for being in the forest. For when the willful, runaway horse ran headlong into it, it was certainly the fault of the tree."

She turned on her heel and began to walk away from him. He uttered a sharp cry of exclamation, but did not attempt to pursue her nor draw her into an exchange of words again; he had too much pride. She had stung him, even though he detested admitting it! But it went far deeper than that. She had—moved him in some essential way that had taken him entirely by surprise. "Sprite of a lass," he muttered under his breath, "you may as well have come at me out of a highland mist to bewitch me this way."

He walked back to the house. He did not go in to his father, but found work for his hands to do, work that could wear out his energies and claim his attentions entirely, so that he had no room left for thought.

Chapter Twenty

꧁ ❧꧂

*P*aisley had sent her son, Daniel, to the village that afternoon to get him out of her way. It was a terrible thing to admit, but, with his energy and his constant ideas, well, he gave her no peace. When he was underfoot she could scarcely bear to say no to him and see that sparkle of hope go out of his eyes, for his plucky ways at times made his handicap stand out all the stronger to her. She knew the lad accepted his limitations as a part of his day-to-day life. Yet she knew there was pain, for of an evening she would rub his leg for him, and he would screw up his face and blink back the tears that filled his eyes. "Just smarts a little, Mam," he would say.

She thought of a simple errand or two, adding, almost as an afterthought, "Will you go by the rectory and see if Esther is there? Give her this note from me and Sallie. Don't forget, now."

Daniel obeyed her cheerfully enough and did her bidding in the village, but with that tension that always accompanied him when he went out among other folk, the fear older boys might take it into their minds to plague him; it had happened so often before. But today he seemed to go on his way unnoticed, and by the time he reached the parsonage he felt hungry and his lame foot was sore. No one came when he knocked on the kitchen door, so he sat down to play with the cats, then tried the door again. When there was still no answer, he wondered what he should do. He had sensed that his mother wanted to clear off the bairns and have a bit of peace for herself, for she had sent his sister to play with a neighbor girl, and he thought he ought not to hurry back.

He had tucked his flute into the pocket of his jacket, and he remembered it now as he looked out on the trees in the churchyard and the shadows they cast, and the thought came to him that it might not hurt for him to find a sheltered spot in one of the corners and play a few tunes, passing the time pleasantly until Esther returned.

Once settled beneath the long, sweeping branches that drooped with leaves, Daniel felt shielded from the whole world, as though no one could see him or discern his presence at all, and he played with the abandon of one who enjoys what he is doing and takes pride in doing it well.

It was the parson, walking back from his chapel, who heard the clear music and stopped in his tracks. The notes sounded thin and unembodied in the still, undisturbed air of the burial ground. He leaned against a sycamore, closed his eyes, and was reminded of faces and voices that were never far beneath the surface of his mind.

He recognized dimly that the notes he was hearing were the strains of hymns, as familiar to his spirit as were his own thoughts. He walked forward to see if he might discern their direction and source. When he saw the boy curled beneath one of the plane trees, he recognized him at once as the miller's son. He remembered the accident that had lamed the boy. He remembered the eyes that looked into his so trustingly when he had tried to comfort the lad. He listened for a few moments longer, reluctant to disturb the performance. This last was a tune he did not recognize, so he leaned forward to ask. "And what is that you are playing, young Daniel?"

The boy looked up with a smile as the notes tumbled into one another in a short surprised breath. "'Tis my favorite," he chirped back. "'The Spirit of God Like a Fire Is Burning.' Would you like me to sing the words?"

Guileless with the innocence of childhood. Christian felt a shudder pass over his frame. He had heard that hymn at the Mormon baptism; he remembered some of the words. "Something else, if you would, please. I'll sit down here by you for a spell."

The boy asked no questions, nor did he seem to mind the presence of the parson. His music came forth, as naturally as the flow of air through the branches, the flow of water in the stream. He was good with his fingers. Christian allowed himself to lean back and close his eyes.

He had no idea how much time had passed when the boy placed a hand on his arm and shook him gently. "Sorry, sir, but your daughter is come, and that is what I'm doing here. I've got a message for Esther from my mam."

Christian rubbed at his eyes. "You play exceeding well," he said. "I thank you for the concert."

"I practice out with Sallie's bees. They don't seem to mind, nor do they scold me for wasting my time, the way Mother does. I will come again, if 'twould please you, sir."

"Yes—I would be glad of that," Christian said slowly. "Any time, Daniel."

The boy moved with remarkable alacrity, calling out to Esther as he ducked beneath branches and came out on the path. Christian walked more slowly, watching the two heads together: the boy's bright face and Esther's gentle one, observing the beauty in each.

So much in the commonplace things of life to bless us, he thought. *Those things that seem the most simple, I believe, are really the hardest to understand.*

Esther waved her hand to him. "Father, come sit with me a minute. I've sent Daniel to the kitchen with orders that Pearl give him a slice of bread and meat and a glass of buttermilk." Her sensitive mouth lifted in a wistful expression. "But I've found you alone, and I hope you do not need to go into the house or your study just yet."

A stab of remorse, sharp as a pain, caught at him. She must be lonely, this quiet daughter of his, and he realized with a start that he knew little lately of her needs; he had allowed himself to become so immersed in his own.

He held out his hand. "I acquiesce gladly. Make room for me and I shall sit as long as you'd like while you tell me all you've been doing and thinking about."

She smiled happily, yet at the same time he sensed a reticence in her that had never been there before. *I have thrown her back upon her own resources,* he realized, *and she cannot return to me what I have relinquished.*

With a woeful sadness upon his spirit he returned her smile, drew up her slim hand into his, and prepared for the pleasure of her company and the somehow reassuring sound of her low, lyrical voice.

Constable Johns had been notified that another Mormon baptism was in the offing. He did not know what the protestors expected him to do. He was enjoying more and more his role of village deliveryman, and these people who constituted the Mormon flock, whom he had known his whole life, seemed only better and brighter and happier now that this change of religion had come to them.

He chewed on the matter; like a dog with a bone, he could not leave it alone. He had thoughts that disturbed him, thoughts he had ignored for a long time. But he took them out and looked at them now, and considered them slowly, slowly and very carefully as the gleaning days waned.

Harvest Home, held in the miller's yard by the light of lanterns and a lazy full moon, had an air of timelessness about it, though it was really a break with tradition for the Mormons to hold their own feast. They had deemed it best, having received hints here and there that their presence would not be welcomed at the squire's, where the rest of the village would meet. If truth be known, they preferred it this way, for they had freedom to speak their minds and feelings openly. They were grateful this year for more than the harvest of wheat and potatoes, of fruit from the hedgerows and vegetables from the gardens; they had other harvests in mind.

Following the mowing, reaping, and binding came the busiest of the labours, the carrying time when the corn was stacked and thatched before wet weather set in. For days, far into the twilight, the men and wagons had passed and repassed, with the load of sheaves built as high as the weary men dared. There was the merriment of relief and satisfaction when the last load was brought in, and the men and boys sang out as they walked, "Harvest home! Harvest home! Merry, merry, merry harvest home!" The women at the cottages they passed left their own work to come out and wave, and the squire with his daughters and maids were waiting to honor the laborers with jugs of drink, which they handed liberally all round. It was then that he invited the men to the Harvest Home dinner, and the days of preparation had begun.

The first of all the ancient customs came with the procession of villagers walking to the parish church, bearing with them not only the fruits of their harvest but the various implements of their trades: ploughs, hay rakes, and forks to be blessed by their pastor while they, all together, gave thanks. There were enough to fill the ranks, despite obvious omissions, faces that had marched in the procession since they were boys, faces that bore the marks of fathers and grandfathers and great-grandfathers on their features; faces that were missed from their time-honored place.

In this way the small group at the miller's felt their loss, though in other matters they did not miss out; rather, the large group had not the advantage of some of the best cooks the village could boast. Puddings and loaves were baked in abundance, with huge sides of beef and ham and a leg of mutton as mainstays, along with a liberal smattering of vegetable dishes and apple and plum dishes, with baskets of fresh bread and butter and newly-made jams.

The celebration at the big house began in the afternoon, so that the eating would go in two waves and the drinking all night. The Mormons confined themselves to fresh cider and hot tea, but the beer jugs were filled and refilled at the squire's house.

The squire himself carved at the principle table and his lady served at the large tea urn, and after the dinner there were to be sports and games until dark, when the eating would commence once more, with dancing to look forward to at twilight.

The lane to the squire's park was choked with wagons and carts filled with freshly-scrubbed children, women dressed in their Sunday best, and men so washed and clean that Esther had trouble recognizing some of them.

She walked beside her father, but her eyes were constantly roving: was that Andrew with his mother and sisters? Perhaps not. Would he come and, if he came, would he speak with her, and what would she have to say? Was that the doctor; no, perhaps the rumor she had heard was true, that nary a Mormon would show his face. She hoped it wasn't true; she wanted some of Sallie's honey cakes and Janet's plump pies. Would the shepherd come down from the hills? She hoped that he would.

As they grew close she could not believe how many flower-decked tables were spread on the lawns. Her eyes searched for Jonathan. He had said he meant for his chair to be carried out among them; the feasting and the merriment would do him good.

She was not so confident as he, for she was aware of how easily he tired. She also feared that it would be harder for him than he realized to see other men, their bodies straight and well-muscled, walking, running, laughing and boasting, sparring with one another, and playing at love making with the young women, too.

He was there, sitting in the shelter of a weeping birch, a blanket spread over his knees. But that was not his mother standing beside him; of course not, she would have duties elsewhere. The tall shape must be that of his brother, Tempest. For some reason it made her feel better that he was there.

She turned to greet friends who were pressing close and asking questions. With some effort she pulled her mind back. *Forget everything, for just a few hours,* she urged herself. *Simply enjoy the cool air and the taste of food and the blessings of life that surround you here.*

At first it seemed awkward for the miller and the blacksmith, for the mason and the shopkeepers, and especially for the farmers, to be gathered in such a quiet place, around such a small board. They were accustomed to the boisterousness of dozens and dozens of sturdy men released from their labors and bent on enjoying themselves. They were used to laughter and congratulations, to rude jokes and back-slapping, to talk over horses and livestock, to flirting with women and organizing troops of feisty young boys into games they had themselves played as lads. They felt a bit of the sting of rejection—*Mormons, outcasts*—yet they had all agreed to the decision unitedly.

It took a while for the spirit of festivity to enter into them, for their bodies as well as their minds to relax, for that sense of plenty and well-being, which was harvest, to take hold. The air itself seemed imbued with the satisfying reality that their work for the year had come to an end, that the harvest the men had brought in was sufficient to see them through the harshest winter Nature could come up with. To know that life would be snug and safe for their wives and children until spring arrived, and that it would be time for another planting again, brought a peace to the men that they did not experience any other time of the year.

Esther had purposefully delayed a visit to the chair beneath the birch, though she was watching carefully as others came forth to greet the pale young squire and shake his hand, then to stand awkwardly with their own hands clasped behind their broad backs, coughing and staring, and wondering just what to say. *He sees enough of me,* she thought, *let him spend time with others whom he may not see again.*

With a gasp she put her hand to her mouth. Why in the world had that thought come so easily through? Was she reconciled, then, to his dying? She had seen consumption before. She had heard the doctor's reports, gently given, but containing little of encouragement. And she had watched, week after week, the flesh and vitality of the young squire fade.

She glanced around. Near the nucleus of the rough male games she saw Monk Smedley, Harvey Heaton, and some of his sons. Her stomach turned as though something sour had been poured into it. She could scarcely bear the sight of them, and turned her head away.

Andrew had come; she had caught his eye once across the yard. But he remained in the cluster of his mother and sisters, while his father stalked the perimeter of the large group like a big watchful bear. It grieved her to see Andrew like this, docile and dispirited, for, in a sense, he had given up. *Given me up*, she thought, *among other things.* But that was not entirely fair. Would she have had him, if it really came to that? She felt rather sure she would not. Life was pulling each of them away from the path of their childhood, the path they had shared. They desired different things; they even saw life differently. She supposed that was natural enough. But it grieved her, it grieved her to gaze at him from across this distance of a few yards and know that it was really the stretching distance of a lifetime that she could never cross over again.

She shook her head. *Morbid thoughts!* She must not indulge in them now. "I believe I shall go and pay my respects to Jonathan," she told her father as she stood and shook out her frock and straightened the tendrils of hair that kept spilling from the tidy rim of her bonnet. "I shan't be long."

She tried to smile at the faces that greeted her as she passed through, but was relieved to reach the shelter of the tree's shade and see the now-familiar face raised to greet her approach.

"I thought you had forgotten me, now that more pleasant company could claim you," Jonathan cried.

"I have remained away purposefully," Esther replied in a soft undertone, "thinking you have perhaps had your fill of me and would be glad to mingle with the others."

He laughed lightly. "Not so, and you ought to know it!" He put his hand to his mouth and pressed the handkerchief it held against the coughing that suddenly tore through him and shook his frame.

"The day has worn you out, I fear." She glanced up and realized that Tempest still stood at the side of his brother. Had he been in this spot all the time?

"Can you talk him into going inside?" she asked.

"Not a chance of it," he replied at once. "But you might."

She could not discern the meaning in his tone, but there *was* meaning in it beyond a mere pleasantry, that much she knew.

She dropped down so that she rested on her heels and her face was level with Jonathan's. "Please," she entreated. "Your eyes look so tired, and a coughing fit in the midst of all these people—" She moved her head as if to indicate the watchful villagers behind them. "A coughing fit would not be seemly, nor certainly pleasant in front of them."

He was looking at her strangely; she turned away from the terrible sadness she saw in his eyes. "You are right, of course." He reached out to touch her, something he had not done before. He rested his long fingers on her arm, and the feel of them was hot on her skin.

He lifted his eyes to Tempest, who had moved a step closer. "Will you find Sarah to take me? I want you two to stay out here."

"I shall go in with you; we can read for a little while."

His fingers slid from her arm. "It would not be seemly, Esther, in front of all these people." His tone was light; he was teasing her, but she also knew he was right. She found the long fingers again and pressed them for a moment before she rose and stood back.

"I'm taking him myself," Tempest told her. "I shall come back and report to you."

There was levity in his tone as well, and a stronger lacing of the Scottish burr, which she had noted in his voice from the beginning. She liked the sound of that voice. It was low and richly modulated, and his words were always distinct and measured. And the richness—was that the proper word for it?—held a strain of passion, always ardor in what he was saying, never the commonplace.

She walked away; she did not want to watch Jonathan's leaving, but she saw the old squire pause in what he was doing to gaze at his son being wheeled back to the house, an invalid who could not do the simplest things for himself. Squire's black hair had streaks of gray running through it and his shoulders sagged, as if at this moment the weight of his head was too heavy for them to support. She understood the weight he was carrying; she felt some of it, too.

The remainder of the afternoon seemed to go yet more slowly, and Esther was grateful when the sun melted into a pool of crimson laced with bright yellow ribbons, diaphanous with light. Servants were spreading platters of food on the long tables, and she realized that she was hungry again.

"Let us have a bite to eat, Father, but I do not wish to stay for the dancing, do you?"

He gave her a very tentative smile, but his lips never parted and his eyes were dark with memories, so that Esther wished she could shake him and cry, "Tell me what it was like, Father, when you danced with my mother, when you held her close in your arms!"

She did not see Tempest approaching because she was lost in her churning feelings, and one of her father's parishioners had drawn him away.

"I've made up a plate for you, Esther, piled it high. Come eat with me—"

She raised her head and blinked blankly.

"I have discovered a place a bit protected, a bit apart."

He was not mocking her now. He turned, and she walked beside him, feeling happy to do so. He had never called her by her Christian name before and, as with every other word, it sounded more lyrical and alive on his lips. He seated her at a small table set in a square of dim, cool shade, and for the first few moments they ate in silence, but when she glanced up she found he was staring at her.

"Were ye starved then, lass?"

She colored, but could not help laughing a little. "I must have been. Is Jonathan all right?"

"He is settled, well covered, with a drink and a book at hand, if that is what you mean, but he is not all right."

She nodded.

"You've gone white at my words," he said, bending over the table as if to observe her more closely. "I did not mean to distress you; I know how deeply you care."

Esther sighed and leaned back, dropping her own gaze.

"Precious little enjoyment ye get in life, I'll warrant," Tempest said thoughtfully.

"You are lapsing into the Scottish," she told him. "I like it."

He smiled a real smile that nearly took her breath away. "I dinna realize I felt at ease enough in your company to do so." He cocked his head thoughtfully. "Harvest Home in Scotland is an entirely different affair. They call it the *Hairst*, and when the grain is all in and the workers drink a toast to the farmer he lays his bonnet on the ground, lifts his sickle and faces the sun, then cuts a small handful of corn. He moves sunwise three times, with the grain held above his head, and chants a blessing upon the harvest."

"I like that."

"I thought you might."

Esther was feeling strange. "Do they feast and celebrate otherwise much as we do?"

"Yes and no. They have food and drink at the Kirn, a brew that knocks the socks off the strongest of men, but they've lots of old homey traditions as well." He looked at her, considering whether to tell her further; she could see the hesitation in his eyes.

"When a special sheaf, called the 'hare,' is cut, they race to win a special dram from the squire. Or, in some parts, they race to the house and the winner, they believe, will be the first to marry."

Esther smiled, and her expression encouraged him to continue.

"The last sheaf they call a maiden, and they often dress her up like one with ribbons and finery. They make corn dollies, too, which the young men give to their sweethearts. Have you ever had a corn dolly?"

She shook her head.

"Ah, that's a pity which shall have to be remedied." He lifted his head. "Is that a fiddle warming up, and a mouth organ?" He pushed back his seat and stood. His face was angular, his nose long and straight, the shape of his mouth soft as a woman's, but more full. She knew she was staring at him, but she could not take her eyes away.

"Will you dance with me, Esther? Will you do me the honor?"

He reached for her hand. It felt small against the hard, cool fingers that wrapped around hers. She let him lead her out, walking purposefully, gracefully across the long stretch of grass to the cleared circle where lanterns were being lit and the village musicians were tuning their instruments. Eyes were watching them, and she knew that she dare not let herself think about that. Too late she remembered that Tempest was next in line as the squire's heir, was most likely considered by some to be in the position of young squire already. Had it meaning, then, that he was leading the first dance with the minister's daughter? With her?

The music began. From the first notes Esther heard the haunting quality, felt it inside her head. Old as time, old as pain, old as longing, it brought tears to her eyes.

"I requested a Scottish air for the first tune." He was watching her closely, his eyes burning into her. "It is making you cry."

"Yes. It hurts deep inside, this music."

Tempest swung her away from him in a fluid arc, then drew her close in again. "It is making you cry, lass." He breathed the words out a second time, and she could hear his astonishment, she could hear his pleasure. She looked at him in wonder. There were tears in his eyes, as well.

The Mormon revelry lasted full as late as that at the squire's, but it settled into a more intimate pattern as the dancers fell away or paired off, Lucius Bidford and Dorothea Whitely among them. The little ones slept, rolled in blankets beside their mothers, and the chill of the night began to make itself felt. They had eaten for a second time, they had danced, they had lit a large fire and, sitting in a circle together, raised their voices in song. As they prepared to break off and go to their separate houses, Paul Pritchard stood, as the doctor had asked him, and raised his voice in a prayer. Now truly the gratitude of their full hearts could be expressed. Many *amens* were whispered when he concluded, and Louisa Kilburn, herding her children round her, said to Zachie, "I've naught known as prayin' a people as these Mormons be."

"These Mormons?" He laughed gently.

"Aye, I know that I'm one. And, what's more, I've never really known what praying to God was until I learned it from them."

The moon was shy this night, shy and soft, like a young girl's first lover, and her light was a dipping veil, a benediction that sifted over them. The harvest was gathered, they were safe and well cared for, and life was good. Every heart felt it as they put out the fire, gathered their families, and went home to their beds.

Chapter Twenty-One

*H*arvest Home marked certain endings and certain beginnings. Or perhaps it was merely a point of pausing, looking around, and seeing what had been happening steadily all along.

The rooks were raucous, picking over the leavings of the harvest. Esther liked their sound, the piercing yet hollow cry that had the same feelings in it as Tempest's Scottish music. Loneliness, all the loneliness of the world was in that one sound, and a longing more wild than the gray churning of the sky against which the blackbirds tumbled and dipped and soared. A longing that tore her, lifted her, and left her unsatisfied.

She was thinking such thoughts one morning when she went out of doors, stood on the porch, and listened while she breathed the cool air deeply into her lungs. It was but three days since Harvest Home at the squire's. She looked down at the cats, weaving moving circles of fur around her ankles, and there on the ground was a small box wrapped in brown paper. She picked it up, ran to the wooden bench under the plane tree, and pulled back the wrappings. Within was a small wooden box of exquisite design, a pattern of birds and thistles carved by someone's sure hand. The grain bid her fingers reach out to stroke it. She opened the lid, and gasped. Within, cradled in a layer of soft cotton, lay a small corn dolly. She sat holding it, frozen and wondering. What could this mean? *"They make corn dollies, too, which the young men give to their sweethearts."* That is what Tempest had said. Was he just being kind to give her a present, a token of the life he had come from? Or did he mean something more by it? And if so, oh, if so, *what* did he mean? And *why?* And what ought she to do about it?

At last she lifted the doll, stiff and crinkly, and examined the face, pulled tight with a stiff cap atop it. It wore a long stiff gown with an apron smoothed over the front of it. It had such billowy sleeves, and what looked like a necklace of kernels wound round the small throat.

She had never seen anything like it. She placed it back in the box. Ought she to return it? No, that would wound Tempest's feelings, bring that angry, tortured expression into his eyes. Whatever his meaning, he had meant well by it; of that she was sure. Ought she to tell her father? Not yet, not for a while yet. She carried it into her room and placed it in a protected nook where, nevertheless, her eyes could see the box and the dollie's head and shoulders just poking out.

She stood a long time in the silence of this space in which she had lived for the whole of her life. Without actually thinking, she had impressions of all that was dear to her since her memory could serve; tender visions that mingled and whispered, that had brought her to this very day. *Much has passed and left me that I once loved,* she thought painfully. *My mother, of course. Various friends from my childhood, dogs and kittens.* She smiled to herself. But *now?* Now there was greater loss. *Andrew*—she had never thought he could possibly pass out of her life! And many of her dearest friends, lost to her because they had chosen to see God differently from her father, and worship away from his friendship and care.

What of Jonathan? *Life becomes too complex and intricate,* she realized, *and the losses not simple, not black and white.* What had the squire's son been to her brief months ago? Nothing; not even a shadow or an idea upon her days. What was he now? *Dare she ask that question? Dare she search for the answer to it?*

And what of this other son, this enigmatic stranger? Would her encounters with him come to nothing, or was he meant to become her friend? She was not entirely at ease with him; she did not understand him at all. Too many strands, too many threads tangled together. She put her hand to her forehead; she could feel her pulse pounding. "Be calm, Esther," she said aloud. What would her father tell her? What would the shepherd say? This is *life*. Take it into your hands and cherish it. Do not pick it apart with your doubts and your wonderings.

She sighed. She smoothed her skirt and took a deep breath, then forced herself to do something as mundane as going down to see what Pearl was cooking for supper tonight.

While she was in the kitchen, young Daniel Pritchard remembered the promise he had made to the minister. He showed up at the door with his flute tucked under his arm and a grin on his face. Christian was there; he came down from his study, though Pearl scolded and frowned. The two wandered out into the churchyard together and found a tree to sit under. "I should like to close my eyes while you play, if that is all right. I can feel the music that way."

"Oh, sir, I know what you mean! I close my eyes, too, especially when I first try to learn a piece; I can hear it inside me better that way."

Christian paid no mind to where the music was drawn from. He did not try to identify each refrain. He let the melodies do the work for which they were created. Neither did he let himself think of why the boy had come, the young boy who was drawing the music forth, both from the slender instrument his fingers played over and from his own heart.

The entire village knew when Andrew Sheppard took the train to London. *Then it is true,* they whispered. *The lad be going to work for his people who live in the city. He'll never come back. No, not to stay, he won't. . . . And what of Miss Grey, do you think? What will become of the likes of her now?*

Esther heard, but she had received no word from Andrew himself. Was he pleased and excited to be going? Would the new life mapped out by his parents fit him? Would he wear it with honor and ease? Would he forget about her easily?

She was playing with such thoughts, like the kittens played with the old cat's tail, as she walked to the squire's house. It was scarcely more than a week after the Harvest Home celebration, and a note had been delivered to her father requesting her attendance upon the young squire. She was experiencing an uncomfortable amount of concern for him, yet at the same time, a terrible sense of anticipation of a different kind. Would Tempest be there? Would he seek her out? What would his manner toward her be, after the gift left on the porch?

Betts came to the door to answer her knock. "Young squire is worse today," he told her, head lowered. "Has been ever since the doings out in the park, and he is asking for you."

She entered the sickroom with a growing sense of unease, almost fearful to look on his face. He called out her name before the door closed behind her. "I have missed you, Esther," he complained. "I am better already, just at the sight of you."

She moved slowly until she came to stand close beside the bed.

"Am I that dreadful, then?" His eyes were watching her closely.

She knew he wanted honesty from her. She swallowed at the sudden dryness in her throat. "There are shadows under your eyes and you look thin as a wraith."

"Oh, is that all?" His eyes laughed, but he did not attempt to bring any sound up from his chest that might set off a cough. "Before we read, tell me what has been going on in your life, Esther, and what's happening down in the village."

She thought a moment, keeping her face impassive. The biggest thing of late was the gift of the corn dolly from his brother; he would not want to hear about that. Her thoughts were a jumble; she sighed, and made an attempt at arranging them.

"In my own life things are quiet enough," she began. "And I know little of the affairs of the village."

"I do not believe it! Do you live a nun's life?"

She smiled. "Yes, I suppose that I do. Andrew Sheppard, who has been my unofficial intended since I was a child, has gone off to London this week to arrange his apprenticeship with an uncle there." She hurried on, for she did not wish him to question her about this. "Dorothea Whitely, the most delightful old maid one could imagine, is to wed Lucius Bidford. Crusty as he may be, he is dotty with love for her."

He smiled at her description.

"Let me see. There is to be another Mormon baptism before long, and the wedding will correspond with that."

As soon as the words were out of her mouth, Esther knew she had made a mistake. Jonathan's eyes widened. A light she had never seen there before made them beautiful. "Do not even think about it," she entreated. "It is impossible, you know."

"Why impossible? You and I know the magnificence of what is written here!" He touched the Book of Mormon that lay beside him with his fingertips. Then, lowering his weak voice even further, he added, "We know the truth of it, Esther. That is the power that has united our spirits, which no one can understand."

She nodded. An errant thought came: *he cares nothing for me. I have been but the vehicle to bring truths to him, truths whose beauties spill over onto me.*

Somehow that thought gave her courage to say what she had to say. "I doubt the doctor would endorse it. Your father would never permit it, and you would break his heart if you pressed him. *And—*" Her words tripped over one another so that he would not interrupt. "And you very well might not survive the experience—in cold water on a brisk autumn morning." She shook her head, but he groped for her hand.

"This is what I want, Esther! Is *all* I desire to be denied me?" His gaze burned into hers, intensified by fever, but also by a longing that brought tears to her eyes. "I can never say what I feel for you, Esther. I have no right." He drew a deep shuddering breath before he was able to continue. "If I had only known—if I had only learned, only discovered all this when it would have made a difference, when I still had a life left to live!"

Esther pressed her fingers against her mouth to hold back a sob. He shook his head at the expression on her face. "I do not want your pity, my dear. I have come to grips with it, most days, but every now and again—"

She sat leaning forward to rest her head on the pillow beside his. "You are so full of light and goodness. You are"—she stumbled—"everything a woman is attracted to, everything she desires, but never believes she will find. It is cruel, too cruel to think of *your* life ending!" She buried her face; she was saying nothing the way she wanted to.

He touched her hair, his fingers stroked the lustrous folds gently. "The joy," he whispered, "the joy that shall never come to me."

They both fell silent. She could hear his labored breathing. His breath was cold against her cheek and she thought that her heart would break.

Some time later, before she was ready to close the book and leave him, Betts entered the room. "Young master is to rest now," he announced, and she knew immediately whence these orders had come. She looked at Jonathan and he met her gaze steadily, as if to say, *You are right. Yes, my father is interfering already, checking this Mormon business as much as he feels he can.*

"Thursday, then?" he said.

"Thursday," she repeated. She walked out into the hall, her eyes searching as discreetly as they could for a glimpse of the tall lowlander, or a trace of his voice from somewhere in the house. *He was not here to greet me. He always watches, he is always somewhere near!* With a sense of disappointment she could not ignore, she started her walk through the ash grove, entering the gloom of the tunneled path with a deeper sense of gloom on her heart.

"*Esther!*" The hissed whisper startled her ear and for a moment she froze. After the first few heartbeats she knew the voice did not belong to Tempest, and as she was wondering what was happening, Sarah Feather stepped out from behind a protecting thicket, her black hair drawn back from her head, as glossy as the wings of the ravens that fluttered above.

The two girls did not really know one another, and for a few moments they stood, each taking the other's measure. Then Sarah scuttled forward in an almost furtive manner, pulled Esther to the side of the path with her, and said in a still-lowered voice, "I have come to explain." Esther stared at her. "My brother—Tempest—asked me to."

"Is he all right?" Esther asked.

"Oh, yes, Father sent him off for the day because he knew you would be here."

"But, why?" Esther could not resist the question.

"'Tis not that he *disapproves* of you." She stressed the last words. "It is your sympathy toward those Mormons. It is the fact that you read their book to Jonathan."

"Does he abhor it so much?"

Sarah nodded her head. "More now, since the Harvest Home when not one of them came here to honor him and celebrate at his house."

Esther sighed. Of course! They had not looked at it that way, she was sure; they had not considered what the squire would think.

"I believe they were trying to avoid trouble—for his sake."

"That is not how he sees it at all. He's gone thundering around the house about how they have insulted him, spurned his good graces, shamed him in front of the villagers—'*Don't think they need me any more, is it?*'" She attempted to imitate his voice, which made both girls smile, and Sarah drew even closer. "He did not want to allow the reading to continue, yet he does not wish to distress Jonathan and risk any—further damage."

Esther nodded. There was a question she must ask. "Will this blow over, or shall we encounter trouble from here on out?"

"I fear the latter, knowing Father."

"Why did he not want Tempest to see me?" Esther's heart was pounding when she spoke the words, and she set the muscles of her face to betray nothing.

Sarah grinned in an almost conspiratorial way. "I think he knows Tempest admires you. He does not want any more"—she hesitated—"what he calls 'involvement.'"

"I understand. He certainly would not want my influence to widen."

"That is right. And he cannot punish Jonathan—but he can punish you."

A lightheartedness had crept into their conversation, and it cheered Esther, except that in her heart, deep in the core, she experienced a terrible sadness that Sarah's words had brought forth.

"What shall we do?" Esther spoke the words out loud before realizing it.

"Carry on. Tempest will figure out his own ways of seeing you. And Father will not deny Jonathan your company *or* your reading. Not now."

Her words brought their eyes together, the sorrow in their gazes mingling so that, on a sudden tender impulse, Esther drew the girl into her arms. "I have become very fond of your brother," she murmured, "in this short time I have known him. He is so good and gentle. Loving him as you must, as a sister, I can imagine your pain."

Sarah clung to Esther for a moment. "Thank you," she whispered. "Have you a brother of your own?"

Esther shook her head. "No brothers, no sisters, save little ones who died before I was born."

"And your mother died when you were still young."

"Yes."

"It must be hard for you—still."

"Yes . . . it is . . ." Esther's gaze softened. "No one seems to understand that."

Sarah leaned forward and brushed a kiss over Esther's cheek. "I'm back to the house before Father discovers my absence." She began to scuttle off, but stopped and turned. "I shall try to see you on Thursday."

"I should like that. Very much." Esther's eyes were stinging with unshed tears. "Thank you, Sarah."

Sarah flashed a smile and was gone.

Esther stood still where she was, drew deep breaths, and tried to sort out the painful thoughts that vied with one another for her attention. She wished she could sit down and cry. She wished her father were here and she could weep into his arms. She wished Tempest's figure would emerge, tall and dark astride a dark horse in the distance, to carry her out of this place. She wished she would have known Jonathan, "the goodly young squire," when he was full of vigor and life. She wished he had loved her back then.

Rain came day after day to weep at the failing of the autumn, the slow drying and decay that preceded the hard frosts that winter would bring. The baptism would be in two days. The presiding elders would ride in from Preston to perform the ordinances of baptism and confirmation—and a marriage, as well.

All the sisters were in a dither of preparation, all but Dorothea herself. She knew exactly what she wanted, and she had prepared the essentials to her satisfaction, so that anything beyond these she considered as frosting on the cake. She possessed drawers filled with fine sheeting and linens that she had carefully washed and folded. She had polished her grandmother's silver, packed the china in straw-lined boxes, cleaned Lucius's house as well as her own, made new curtains for the windows, which he had obligingly cleaned—dozens of tasks which she knew were important, and which she wanted done right.

Without much ado or mention to the other women, she had sewn at night, by candlelight, half a dozen fine nightdresses in patterns she had dreamed over long ago when she was a slip of a girl. She felt almost grateful that those painful, undeveloped and untried longings had evolved into something deeper, something with dignity in it. Dignity and a desire to create fulfillment for another would serve her now. *It is happiness of a different kind I will be experiencing,* she told herself, *for I cannot say I have been unhappy in the life I have lived.* But this happiness would possess elements she had never known before: protection, companionship, *admiration.* And perhaps most important of all, the dying of loneliness, that loneliness of the solitary which stares out of vacant eye sockets on a frozen night in winter, that loneliness which mocks the birdsong and the sweet-scented blossoms that spill over the gate, that loneliness which garners the sweet fruits of autumn into empty hands. Lucius liked her little dog, and her dog had decided that she liked him. *All will be well,* she told herself, *because we will make it so.* And watching this man in his humble efforts to please her, she knew that what she felt would be true.

⚬

Roger was ready. He had written a note that explained everything to his master. He had written it two weeks ago, and rewritten it half a dozen times, burning each previous draft. He had a pretty good idea that Thomas would not take him back on again when he found out what had happened. But he had to face his now-uncertain future with faith. He figured God had wanted him to find that Book of Mormon where it was hidden. He figured God had wanted him to read it, to believe it, to align himself with others who believed it, and to never look back. He was young, he knew how to work hard, he could make his way. He had no fears for himself, only gratitude to this God who had become so real to him, who cared about a simple stable boy in Yorkshire and what happened to him.

⚬

With the return of the elders, with this baptism, there would be changes; Archibald was certain of that. "It is time," he told himself. "We are ready; we are seasoned enough." He could only hope it was true. He was fearful, and so was Janet, in her own way. But she had, with her woman's wisdom, quieted him.

"Change is a walk into the unknown, Archie. And we are happy here, with our lives. We know the changes we are contemplating will be wrenching and have far-reaching results . . . into the lives of our children and grandchildren . . . in times and places, in circumstances we cannot even imagine right now . . ."

She had smiled at him and touched his cheek with her fingertips. Her words, bravely spoken, had given her own heart courage as they had his.

I know too much, he thought, *I know these people I have tended and nursed too intimately, so that I worry too much about them.*

Too much. Perhaps just such a deep love was needed for what they all wanted to do. He sat late with his scriptures, night after night, seeking answers and strength. At length he concluded that love *was* the answer, the simple answer he sought. Love and faith; two eternal sources of power that would serve the obedient, no matter how weak or how frightened they felt. *Thy will be done, Father.* He wanted to be able to say it with all of his heart. *Prepare me to serve thee.* As a doctor, he knew much about service. He was prepared to learn more. He knew he could utter this prayer with a true desire, and he knew his prayers would be heard.

Chapter Twenty-Two

It was the same outworn complaint it had always been. The constable rubbed his chin while Harvey Heaton went on. Heaton *did* have one new tack.

"Squire is angry himself. He's getting fed up as the rest of us are."

"Stirred up, is he?"

"He feels shamed by these Mormons' lack of respect for him."

"I'd like to hear it from his own lips before I start in worrying overmuch." The constable saw rage in Heaton's eyes after he said that. "I'll be there, and I will be watchful," he concluded. "You may be certain of that."

When the detestable man had taken himself off, still dark-visaged and grumbling, Constable Johns sat alone on the bench at his doorstep and pondered long. Then he took himself into the house, calling out for his wife. He had certain matters he had better discuss with her.

The baptism was set for midday so that the business of the morning could all be done. The wedding would not take place until the day

225

following, when the merrymakers would not be wet and bedraggled from being dunked in the stream.

Jonathan had spoken to the doctor, though he entertained no real hope. Archibald frowned as he had never seen him do. "Your father has warned me," he said, "and I am treading on thin ice already."

Jonathan nodded. "I know. He would have dismissed you with the keenest of pleasures if not for me." He attempted a grin, which made his face appear boyish. "He knows what I will do if he tries."

Something about his tone kept the doctor from questioning further.

"I shall die without anything then," Jonathan continued.

Doctor Sterne met his eyes. "If you die, you will die with all that you are, mind and spirit, intact. If you die, those who have loved and watched over you will be waiting, my lad. And God will accept you, and all your righteous desires, whatever may or may not have been performed in this life."

After a long moment of silence Jonathan nodded. "I believe you. But it is not much with which to be contented."

"It is more than you know." Archibald's spirit was aching, and his mind was groping for what he could give to this lad. Knowledge so new to him that he hardly knew how to explain it—keys and powers and possibilities—all ringing inside his head. He wished he could get him to just one of their meetings, let him hear one of their sermons and one of their prayers. But the infection was deeply settled in the lungs, and the lungs were weak, and he feared the young squire's time was even shorter than he had judged.

"I shall come following the baptism and report to you," he promised.

"Will Esther be there?"

"Esther?" Archibald was surprised by the question. "I hardly think so."

Jonathan lay back against the pillows. "It does not matter," he said.

But Doctor Sterne knew then that in some way it mattered, mattered as deeply to the sick man as the things he had talked of before.

Few people knew for certain who all the new candidates for baptism were to be. Some were aware of one, some of another. An entire family from the Methodist congregation had already been coming to church, for their minister, when he learned of their sympathies, had stood at the very pulpit and asked them to leave his congregation. The family of the potter, Charlie Bates, was also being baptized. Their numbers were increasing. Their meetings were filled with richness and diversity and an amazing unity, part of the glue that kept them together no matter what challenges they faced.

∞

Zachie Kilburn, watching Louisa fancy herself up for the occasion, thought back to those few months ago when he and she had gone into the water, come up, and had hands laid on their heads, and how this had altered their lives. He had learned what it meant to rely on the Holy Ghost during that rough spell when the old squire accused him of doing harm to his oldest son. At first he had railed inwardly at the injustice of it, but he had learned of depths and strengths he possessed that he had not dreamed of before. He could be grateful now for what he had suffered and what he had learned. And his Louisa had softened, there was no doubt about it. She was more patient and wise, with both him and the children, and she did not snap and fret and criticize in the way that she had before.

She looked over at him now. "You've got your eyes on me, Zach," she said. "What are you thinking about?"

"I am thinking how pretty you are, and how lucky I am."

∞

Adam and Rose left for the baptism early so they could walk at a leisurely pace. The throstles were going wild in the hedgerows, flitting and rising in wide, graceful arcs, like so many sprites of the airy world, unmindful and uncaring about what went on below. It was a matter of mere weeks now, less than two months before their child would be born, but Rose felt well and strong, and she had not put on very much weight. Indeed, the roundness of her stomach was still that, not a protrusion that made her appear out of proportion, or walk unbalanced. The harvest had been good, so Adam had been able to work all the hours he wanted, and they had a bit of coin put aside. A child of their own, just in time to celebrate the birth of the Christ child. Holiness had begun to take on a new meaning for them. They felt they were the luckiest people in all the village that autumn day.

Sam Weatherall had been struggling with his disappointment these many days. The closer the approach of this baptism, the more gloomy he became. Finally Meg, with her hands set on her wide hips, took him to task.

"Honestly, Samuel, you're mooning about like a sick calf, and it makes me ashamed."

"Ashamed?" That was a strong word to use on him, but it got his attention as she thought it would. "I considered you, at least, would understand, Meg, what a bitter disappointment my brothers have been."

"Stuff and nonsense. You gave 'em a chance and they wanted no part in it. You can't do more than that."

"But now I have lost them, because this comes between us, and they cannot or will not understand."

"'Tis a pity, I know." Her voice became more gentle. "But you must have faith. The good Lord can only do so much with people, but he'll bless you, Sam. He'll find other ways to bless you, I know he will."

"What would I do without you, Meg?" He gulped out the words.

"You've got sons," she reminded him, gentle still. "They'll grow up to give you this spiritual brotherhood you're wanting."

She could not fully understand what he felt, being a woman, but their conversation had helped. He was grateful that *he* had been given eyes to see and accept this light. Not for one minute had he ever regretted the decision he'd made. Now there would be others, and he, for one, meant to help them along. Good effort that would be, effort to heal some of the pain in his heart.

◆

Michael had finished the cradle for Rose's baby. Hannah was grateful to him, for she knew how many hours of painstaking effort had gone into the task. They meant to present it to Rose and Adam after the wedding tomorrow. And she knew, though he had not told her, that he had already begun work on theirs. The child within her was beginning to make himself manifest, and she was no longer too sick to feel the presence of a spirit abiding and dwelling alongside her own. She lived with the miracle of it daily: this child who was not only part of the woman whose body sustained it but part of the man; woven together, two bodies, two spirits, two lines of living people that stretched back to the very beginnings of time. Another link, yet another entirely new and distinct individual. It pressed her understanding to the limits and beyond. The winter that was coming would end, as all winters do, and with the coming of spring and new life, she and Michael would be part of the miracle and part of the bringing of renewal and joy.

First Rosie, Hannah thought. *I'll watch her and help her and perhaps learn a little about what it shall be like for me . . . a natural thing. . . .* She drew a breath. *Every person walking along here to the baptism began in the very same way. Every man and woman who stands on the face of the earth! And so we accept the miracle as commonplace.* She smiled inwardly. *Until it happens to us,* she thought, *until it happens to us.*

◆

Old Grandfather Goodall, as they called Peter, felt the power of harvest much as a farmer feels it when he picks up a handful of living earth and holds it close to his face, to drink in the fragrance and texture of it, before it sifts through his hand. This harvest of souls was as real and powerful a matter, and it would go on past the thousands of uncounted harvests the earth had known. These souls had planted the seeds of truth within them, and truth would thrive and produce harvests mortals could not dream of, long after this life, long after the useful seasons of Mother Earth.

It pleased him so to contemplate. And it pleased him that Martha was here, walking alongside him with her sister; and it pleased him that, for a wife, Brother Bidford had chosen a woman more fitting and left his own household unchanged.

Things had been quiet at the vicarage that morning. Esther had kept to her room, wondering whether her father might happen to send for her. When at length he did not, she went down to the kitchen and helped Pearl with the midday meal. The thoughts in her mind were at war with each other. She could not find an even, untrammeled ground to stand upon. Her first concerns were for her father and, mingled with those, the deep compassion she felt for Jonathan, unable to help himself, unable to act, as a man acts, on his own. She dared not dwell upon their miseries lest she start weeping, lest she elicit questions she had no way to answer. How wretched she felt!

Because she wanted to see her old friends, she had asked her father about the wedding tomorrow, and he had granted her permission to go. She must be content with that. Her presence at another Mormon baptism would in no way be wise. Nor loyal. Nor even kind.

She stepped out into the sunshine, warm on her skin, yet not with the burning penetration of summer. Low in the sky a pair of throstles wove patterns around one another, back and forth, back and forth, as though nothing in the world existed beyond the beauty they made. They must be the pair who had built the deep cup of a nest in the tall grasses at the protected back corner of the churchyard. She had counted three sets of sea-green eggs spotted with black before the summer was through. Now their notes, more clear and full than any other bird, floated down to her like small piercing arrows of song. Now that October had come, these white-throated thrushes would disappear, not to be seen again until after the snows of January had passed. *Everyone is going, in one way or another,* she thought, *flying away into a silence where I cannot follow.* She watched the birds until her eyes stung with tears, then she went back into the house.

❧

"Go for me, Tempest."

"You must be mad, brother! I shall do no such thing."

Jonathan gazed at him and he glared back.

"To what purpose, I ask?" demanded Tempest.

"I want to see what it is like, through your eyes. I want you to bring me all of the details, tell me who was there, and what happened, what it all felt like. Even tell me the songs they sing, and the words they speak."

"No chance of that!" he snapped. "You should have asked Esther to go."

The words were out; a stupid thing to say, and both brothers knew it. "What good would come of it?" Tempest pressed, more kindly. "You would submit me to the humiliation? And besides"—his eyes lit with a purpose remembered—"what would Father say?"

Again he cursed himself for his thoughtlessness. Jonathan's face had begun to sink into itself, as though a clenched fist had struck the white flesh. "I thought he need never know, but of course that is foolish. He would find out in one of a dozen ways; I see that now."

Tempest trembled with the fury of his impotence. Love for this brother raged through him as strong as did his anger. But Jonathan was shaking his head. "Do not fret yourself, brother." He lifted a hand, then let it fall weakly to the bed again. "Wishful thinking, that's all."

"But you ought to be able—you ought to—"

"*Yes, yes, I ought to!*" There was vehemence in Jonathan's voice, despite the haggardness of his features. "*God knows I am weary enough of this dying!*" He spat the words out and they froze Tempest, like small pinions of ice.

"Do you know what the worst is?" Jonathan was saying.

Tempest shook his head.

"The worst is that I've learned so much since this happened. I am ten times the man I was before. And I have Esther in my life. And *I long to live!* I long to use what I've gained—not lay it down in the grave with me."

Tempest let out a cry, a mighty cry that tore through him against his will.

Jonathan's sallow face went even whiter. His features, too, were distorted with emotion. "You must possess all Mother's Scottish blood, Tempest. You sound like a wild hie'land lad, kilted and ready for battle." Both brothers attempted to smile. "Come to think of it, *you* are another thing I have gained, brother. If this had not happened, you would still be in the borderlands of Scotland, growing further and further away from me."

"I do not know if I deserve a brother like you," Tempest cried.

Jonathan began to reply, but his words were choked in a fit of coughing, a coughing so violent that Tempest hurried to the bed and lifted up the laborer's head, holding to his mouth a handkerchief, which came away spotted with blood. "Can you breathe now?" he asked when the spate had ended.

Jonathan nodded, but his eyes were closed, and the blue veins stood out in bold pattern against the thin skin of the lids that covered them. *He looks as fragile as a newly hatched bird*, Tempest thought. A sudden desire came upon him to gather the suffering man into his arms, to carry him bodily away from here. Perhaps to the sea, to the bleak quiet of the Scottish coastlands, where surely the very air and the music that vibrated through it would be able to heal. Surely there existed, somewhere, some power to succor this young man—some power to *save him!*

Tempest shuddered as Jonathan's breath, harsh as sandpaper, lifted his wasted breast in spasms. *I cannot endure this!* he cried, though only inwardly. He held a cool cloth to his brother's forehead and sat by his side until his sister, Sarah, came to relieve him. Even then he refused to leave the room until she urged him with the caution, "Father is waiting for you. He grows impatient when he does not see you for hours"—she smiled wanly—"nor know what you may be 'up to,' as he puts it. You know how he is."

Tempest knew, more and more all the time. But things were different now. Of a sudden things were different. Inside himself he knew this was true. He had discovered—*oh, there was no way that he could put words to it*—but what he had learned, what he had felt back in that room with his brother had changed everything. Everything. Now he just had to figure out what that would mean.

Several presiding elders from Preston came to officiate at the baptism, and there was an air of authority that most everyone who gathered there felt. Curious onlookers hung on the fringes, while relatives and well-wishers hazarded a closer approach. The group of Saints, expanded to nearly thirty adults, many with large families of children, stood or sat in a half circle together. The candidates, those who had put themselves forward for baptism, collected themselves a little apart, and many curious eyes examined them. Sallie thought there would be some surprises, because she had heard rumors by way of Meg, who was the greatest gossip among them all. The rumors sounded promising to her ears. She had shared her hopes with her bees only that morning, and felt that she would not be disappointed.

Following a prayer and a song, a short talk was delivered by Elder Turner, taken largely from Mosiah:

> *As ye are desirous to come into the fold of God, and to be called his people, and are willing to bear one another's burdens, that they might be light; yea, and are willing to mourn with those that mourn; yea, and comfort those that stand in need of comfort, and to stand as witnesses of God at all times and in all things, and in all places that ye may be in . . . if this be the desire of your hearts, what have you against being baptized in the name of the Lord, as a witness before him that ye have entered into a covenant with him . . . ? And now*

when the people had heard these words, they clapped their
hands for joy, and exclaimed: This is the desire of our hearts.

The candidates lined up and, one by one, were taken into the water. The potter, Charlie Bates, his wife, and his two oldest children were first in the line. The cluster parted and young Daniel Pritchard came forward, limping, but with a heavenly smile on his face. He was old enough; he had requested baptism on his own accord, been interviewed and accepted. The waters, darker in autumn and bearing clumps of leaves—sodden and colorless, floating here and there—closed around his small form, but a sudden shaft of sunlight, refracted through the tree limbs and concentrated, lit the boy and his companion and, as if from its depth, the dull stream shone, too.

People smiled; Daniel's joy, after all, was contagious. When he came up out of the water there were tears in his eyes, but he wiped them away with the droplets of water and walked with a grace before unknown to him onto the bank. His mother covered his wet shoulders with a blanket. He grinned up at her, but kept his place, watching the others who were moving forward.

The next to come forth was a stranger to almost everyone present. He was a boy, not much older than Daniel, and his face, though not shining like the miller's son, was set with a resoluteness that none who looked at it could deny.

"Where be he from?" several whispered behind their hands. "What is he doing here amongst us?"

"I recognize that lad!" Samuel turned to Meg and shook her arm. "Look at him. Does he not look familiar to you?"

Meg squinted and pondered, then shook her head. "I cannot place him, Sam."

The stranger walked down into the water with Elder Hascall, who raised his right arm to the square. But even his name, spoken out loud, held no familiarity for Samuel. However, when the boy came out of the water and walked, dripping, to shore, he came right up to the astonished Samuel and held out his hand.

"I've you to thank for this, sir."

Samuel shook his hand. "What do you mean, lad?"

"The Book of Mormon you left with your brother in Bristlebury; he never threw it away, just hid it in a far disused feed bin in the barn." He shook water from his thick mop of hair and grinned. "Left it there for me, without knowing. I've been reading it these past months and gained a testimony of its truth for myself."

Samuel wrapped his long arm around the boy's shoulders and drew him close in a man's bear hug of pleasure. "And all this time I've been praying," he said under his breath.

"Never know what will show up in the harvest," Roger laughed.

Meg tugged at her husband's arm. "Look who's here, bless her heart."

There were several gasps among the watchers as Evaline Sowerby, her hand lightly resting on Elder Turner's arm, waded into the water. Everyone there knew how her husband felt about the Mormons; many knew of his threats and his unkind treatment of her. A skiff of wind blew up and lifted her hair about her white face. Many thought she looked like an angel, standing radiant and determined as the sacred ordinance began.

She, herself, was thinking little, for the warmth of the Spirit was as both a protection and strength to her. She had prayed and fasted before coming; she desired to be worthy of this blessing she had longed for: the comforting and guiding presence of the Holy Ghost in her life. As her thin body slipped into the water she felt a weightlessness, lifted up, somehow held by unseen hands. Standing on her feet again, the water running from her, she was aware of nothing but light. Light within her, and light around her, and beyond, a circle of faces smiling love and encouragement to her.

As she stepped onto the bank, gentle hands reached out, drawing her into the protection of the trees, wrapping a warming blanket around her. With tears in their eyes, her sisters brushed her hair back and kissed her cheek. And the light did not diminish. The light, she understood, would never leave her again.

∝⌘

Harvey Heaton noted that some of his mates had slipped off. The proceedings were tiresome to them, and the instructions he had given had not been definite enough to induce them to stay. He found Jem Irons and collared him. "Do not you desert me as well, Jem," he grunted. "There may still be work here for you."

He glanced round in search of the constable, only to find that Johns was walking, hand in hand with his wife, toward the river's edge—that others, speechless as himself, were making way for them. *What's this!* His mind was sputtering like a guttered candle. He could not make sense of what his eyes saw.

Tempest saw too, from his seat atop his gray gelding, for he had just arrived upon the scene a few minutes before. He could feel the tension, though he did not understand it. So he backed up cautiously to a spot where he could survey nearly everything before him, and kept his careful gaze constantly moving, constantly taking things in.

"Gettin' himself baptized, is he?" Heaton's son, Spencer, chuckled under his breath. "You going to let him get away with that, Father?"

Heaton's eyes were dark, his mouth drawn tight, but he made no answer. Wilford Johns came up out of the water, and his wife, Hilda, looking timorous as a sparrow beside the thorn-rough figure of her husband, moved forward to take his place.

Heaton signaled to his sons and, with Jem's collar still stuffed into his fist, moved apart to a small clump of stunted hawthorns. He pushed the others inside and began bluntly, "Can't do anything here, boys. Too many watching too closely. But"—he paused for effect, treating each with the searing fever of his gaze—"we can certainly give the good constable a fitting reception to come home to!" The sound that followed was like a rattle in his throat, deep and ominous.

He leaned closer and barked out detailed instructions. Tempest, who had inched as close to the tangle of hawthorns as he dared, could not make out his words. But he made sure that the men did not observe him as they left stealthily, one at a time, each heading in a slightly different direction, shoulders hunched, heads down. Watching them, Tempest's skin crawled. He had a pretty sure hunch what they would do. He headed out himself, in a tight loop that nevertheless avoided the well-traveled foot trails the men would be using.

He knew the trails well and, after a few moments, cut back into the brush so that he would cross the path of the most secluded of them—best to start there. Sure enough, he spied a figure coming toward him. He spurred Phantom and moved toward the boy like a madman; he could see it was one of Heaton's sons. He would run him down if he had to, but he wished only to give that impression. As he came close the lad let out a cry and put his hand to his throat, half-frozen before the hurtling mass of horse and rider. Tempest pulled his gray up short and jumped from the saddle, grabbed the boy by the throat and let out a shout that would have made his smuggler grandsire proud.

"I know what your father is up to, boy," he snarled, his face nearly touching Alan's. "The game is up. You get yourself home, you hear, while I've a mind to let you." He was breathing a bit heavily and he knew his face appeared wild. The boy nodded. "I am in earnest," Tempest pressed. "I am the squire's son, if you happen to not know it, and if I find any trouble—*anything amiss at the constable's*—I shall have you before the county sheriff before the week's out. Do you understand?"

The boy nodded again. Tempest gave him a shove that sent him sprawling and was back on his horse before the lad had got to his feet again. He did not look behind but rode a few yards farther, veering away from the river into the open meadowland. The man walking here, pitiably exposed, had nowhere to hide from the ghostly horse that bore down on him. Being older and more seasoned in shifty dealing, he attempted a pretense of innocence. "Just goin' home. Drank too much last night, and I've got the collie wobbles—besides—"

Tempest did not permit him to continue. He pounced on him, and with a knee, held him pinned to the ground. "I know what you and Heaton are up to. I heard your conversation back in the hawthorns." The man's face went white. Tempest dug his knee in harder. "It's the magistrate for you this time if so much as a hair on the constable's head is disturbed, if so much as a clod of dirt or a pebble on his property is found out of place."

Jem Irons gulped. Tempest lifted him to his feet, then off the ground a little, so that his legs dangled down. "You have that straight then?"

Jem nodded. Tempest did not realize that his tongue, loosened in this manner, took on the cadence of the Scots, and that this added to the effect he was trying to create.

In one easy movement he mounted, turned and moved away, leaving the startled man gaping at his dust. As he caught his breath he blessed the uncle and cousins who had taught him the skills, the confidence and pluck, that he was now drawing upon. One more—two more? He wondered about Heaton. Something primal within him itched to get his hands on the man, but a cautioning voice warned him to hold back and not reveal his whole hand. He knew where the constable lived, and he headed there now, coming upon the other son within yards of the holding, with the cottage and outbuildings sitting tidy and quiet beneath the slanting afternoon sun.

This boy, Spencer, was more insolent than his brother, and Tempest was tempted to rough him up a bit, when that same caution, like a force, made him draw back and only repeat the same kind of warning he had given to the others. When the boy turned and left he was still sullen, and Tempest could feel his resentment as palpably as he could feel a cloud moving over and blotting the sun.

I had better bide here for a while and keep watch, he told himself. But there was no need—Heaton had observed the last performance from behind a gentle rise in the meadow where he had secreted himself. Trembling with anger, cursing under his breath, he had stomped back to the inn, too aggravated to even take his rage out on his accomplices. He took to the bottle instead, bellowing for Marjorie Poole every ten minutes until at last, spent with running up and down stairs at his bidding while her work piled higher and higher, she brought half a dozen bottles and lined them up on the table in front of him. Then, with her hands on her hips, she growled back, "Drink yourself to purgatory, if I care. But don't drag me from me work again. I'll come back when I'm done, and if you're still alive, I'll get you into your bed."

Her spunk appealed to him. He wished his sons possessed a little more of her high spirit, and he let her go.

It was getting well on to twilight; shadows streaked the dirty surface of his table, but Heaton paid them no heed. Tempest did, though, at his hideout. As the shadows lengthened and his horse danced in place, eager for the stable and his evening oats, he felt a restlessness, too.

Pity that Esther was not able to show up for the baptism, he thought. *Jonathan will be disappointed when I tell him.* He watched the sky for a few minutes longer, then turned his horse's head. His mother would worry if he did not show up for the evening meal, and Jonathan would wear out his slim store of strength in waiting and watching. *Well, at least I shall have a story to tell*, he thought to himself with some satisfaction. *It is too bad about Esther, though.*

He rode close by the parsonage before he veered away from the village toward open country and the line of the darkening grove. There was a light in the kitchen, scarcely more than a halo in the half gloom. Was Esther there, friendless and lonely? But, wait, another dim glow from an upper window. He slowed for a moment. Yes, surely, there was a slight girlish figure moving there; the curtains were disturbed. He was certain he saw a brush of bright hair.

He turned away, himself feeling a loneliness for which he could not account, save that twilight—or the *gloamin'*, as the Scots called it—placed a spell on a man; breathing, as it did, the voices of all who had ever lived, ever loved, ever suffered, and crowding the air around with the energy of lives long gone but that were, somehow, a part of life still. *Longing.* Oh, that dark, ceaseless longing for he knew not what.

He rode with it, unable to quell or dismiss it, unable to face it down. He passed into the shadowy grove beyond which his father's house awaited him with all the responsibilities it held, all the suffering and grief.

Chapter Twenty-Three

There was to be no business conducted that night, only celebrating. But Doctor Sterne had already been informed by the visiting brethren that he would be set apart as the presiding elder before they left on the morrow. He was not certain in his understanding what all this implied. He *was* sure of the responsibility of it, and of the honor that God, not man, was conferring upon him.

He did not sleep much that night but spent a long while either bent over his scriptures or on his knees. Many thoughts came to him, many perceptions that seemed startling and new. "Lead me, Father," he prayed over and over again. "Show me what you want me to do." How different the Lord's will could be from his own; he understood *that*. He understood that everything this restored gospel exacted of them involved change—major changes both within and without. For his people, these Throstleford natives, he was not sure which would be the most difficult: changing the inner man, or changing an outward way of life that was written into their very structure from long generations past.

As he pondered, his thoughts turned now and again to the young squire up at the house on the rise. He knew Jonathan Feather was dying; it was only a matter of time. He felt cruelly robbed himself, for if the boy had been spared, he would have been a strong force amongst this little flock of converts. Sad to say, he would have added a sense of validity to their existence and, more than that, a protective safety that someone of his stature and social standing would command.

As a doctor he ought to be inured to death by now, but he knew he was not. It always bit deeply to see a young life, a life with promise, taken. The emptiness left, the lack, could never be filled by another; life did not work that way. Yet now he understood for the first time the hope of what life after this life might be, the *quality*, the nature of existence once mankind had returned from this place. Sons and daughters of God, empowered by the experiences, the learning received here, able to progress following mortality to become more and more like Him, to fulfill the stature of their own divine natures.

Simple words; beautiful simple concepts with all the glory and intelligence of the Maker of the universe behind them.

Doubt not, fear not. Those words were becoming his watchword. He repeated them over in his head as, at last in his weariness, he made ready for bed.

There was a little fear nagging at the back of Wilford Johns's mind as he rode homeward with his family. He had declined to attend the festivities at Pritchard's mill, for he had seen Heaton and Jem Irons take their covert leave. Being familiar with the nature of such men, as he was, he steeled his mind for the worst, at the same time berating himself.

I should have left one of my lads to guard the old place, he chastised himself. *I'm a fool not to have done.* As he approached his house he craned his neck and then squinted his eyes; he could identify nothing amiss.

"Worried, aren't you?" Hilda put her hand over his hand that held the reins. "I admit I've had a few qualms myself."

He pulled up the team, but left them standing, and entered the house before Hilda and the children. By the light of his most powerful lantern he went carefully through each room. He did not know exactly what he was looking for, but he feared that even a trap of some kind had been laid, a trap that might harm one of his children. Yet he could find nothing, sense nothing—absolutely nothing at all.

Once he came to the door and gave them the nod, his children scurried into the house, and he left Hilda to take care of them while he went out to the barn, unharnessed the team and put them into their stalls, then searched with the same painstaking care he had used in the house. The longer he searched, the more amazed his mind grew. This did not make any sense. Heaton would have been here. Heaton would have left his mark somewhere; he was certain of that.

At length, when he felt he had been over every inch of his property, and his back and feet were telling it, he stood with his hands on his hips. "I'll be sniggered," he muttered out loud. "What stopped Heaton and his boys? I should give my eyeteeth to find out."

Roger was invited to stay and celebrate with the others, urged in particular by Meg and Sam.

"I left a note for your brother," he explained. "So I suppose I could hitch a ride in the morning and it would not do much harm."

"Will he have you back?"

Roger shrugged his shoulders. "Your guess is as good as mine on that, sir! Truth is, I've saved up every bit I can, for I would not bet on him wanting me around the place after this." He grinned, his happiness still stronger than any other thing. "I figure I'll stay and work as long as he wants, though, until he can find someone else."

Sam nodded. "Good man." As they walked along, he added, "We'll work out something to help you keep yourself, lad, never fear."

There was no fear in Roger's heart, and no uncertainty. He was thoroughly happy, and he had never before had more than a vague inkling of what happiness might be about. He was also grateful. "I will not forget," he told God in his prayers that night, "what you've done for me. 'The least of these, my brethren,' that's how I've always counted myself. But you took notice of me. I'll not forget, Lord, and if you'll still help me, I intend never in my life to let you down."

❧

Evaline went with the rest out to the Pritchards'. She was determined to have this one day, if nothing else, and to have it all, to its full. The Spirit remained with her, a steady warmth deep inside her own being, and she knew her prayers had been answered: if she remained worthy of this presence, she would never again be alone.

She was surprised that she was able to put her fears aside and join in the celebrating, and truly feel the joy that the others felt. When she wrapped her shawl around her head and shoulders and got ready to make her good-byes, she saw Louisa give Zachie Kilburn a light shove, and he came up to her, his eyes smiling in an open, friendly way. "I'll be taking you home, Evaline. And I'll poke my head in and give Edwin a word or two if I must."

She shook her head and tears came to her eyes. "I thank you—but 'twould only make matters worse."

Zachie stood firm. "I will not send you back there alone."

"Please, you mustn't."

Zachie put his hand on her shoulder. "Look, my dear, if he's of a mind to mistreat you, he'll do it with or without me. But this way—" He fixed his eyes on hers and smiled so kindly that she had to blink back her tears. "This way he shall be warned, and he'll know that everyone's watching, and he'll have to make an accounting, for once."

Evaline nodded. Her body felt limp, like a willow sapling that a slight breath of wind could make to tremble and wave. As she rode with Zachie she closed her eyes, concentrating on the light within and the warmth that it gave.

Edwin was waiting, pacing the floor, tight and angry. When Zachie Kilburn pushed the door open, Edwin's hands were clenched into fists at his sides.

Zachie tipped his hat to him. "I'm bringing your wife home safe to you, Sowerby. She's been with the rest of us at the baptism—"

"I know where she's been. And I know what she's done." Edwin reached for Evaline, but Zachie moved out to block him.

"Listen here, man. I said I've brought your wife home safe to you, and I expect you to *keep her that way.*"

Edwin glared at him.

"I expect to find her *unharmed* the next time I see her." Zachie fixed his eyes on the man opposite him until his clear gaze stared him down. It was all he could do to close the door on the two of them and leave her that way. He prayed in his heart as he drove back to the mill, but he knew one could pray for the good Lord to soften a man's heart all night and all day, and it would come to little account if the man was deaf and blind altogether, determined to have his own way.

Evaline knew Edwin would first exhaust himself with raving and ranting at her, calling her names, trying to shame and degrade her. His words had no effect on her at all. She was still wound safely in the shelter of what had been given her, and what she had given herself to.

When he had worn himself out a bit and she thought it safe to walk past him and enter their room, he followed behind. She could feel his breath on her neck and hair, she could feel his malice. He wanted to hurt her, he had to hurt her to restore something within himself. But tonight he did not know how. Zachie's words had stopped him, made him reconsider. Perhaps the words would buy her some time. He had been drinking. Perhaps he would sleep it off and not touch her. She took off her dress and stays and reached for her nightgown. He did not move, did not speak.

"I suppose you think this makes a difference, that you can do what you want now?"

She stood still. She did not know how to reply.

"Starting with the wedding tomorrow. You expect you'll get all dressed up and go to the wedding—you expect *I'll let you!*"

What should she do? She could not use reason with him. Whatever she opened her mouth to say he would use against her. But she knew she must try. "We can live together in peace. In most every way I am a good wife to you. This does not have to come between us, Edwin, if—"

He moved quickly then and came to stand beside her, his breath ragged with anger. "Clever of Kilburn. Doesn't want to see that I've put a mark on you." He was too drunk to think clearly. She knew his mind was searching around for something cruel he might do.

She didn't mean to give him an excuse. She simply moved her arm and with her fingers brushed back the hair from her face. But he snatched her hand and held it in a vise that made her cry out.

"Won't show much, swollen fingers, small broken bones." He took one of her fingers and, in a swift movement, snapped it. Evaline heard the bone crack. She struggled and moaned, but he was holding her body helpless with his shoulder pressed against her. He wrenched one more before letting her fall into a heap on the floor. He tottered out of the room, closed the door behind him, and slammed his way out to his tailor's shop. She heard him muttering imprecations under his breath, and knew he would sleep the night there, as he so often had.

After a time she raised herself to her knees, sat for a while breathing heavily, then, with the aid of a chair to hold onto, stood on her feet. It seemed her whole hand was on fire in a deep throbbing way, so that it felt the very skin might explode. She sank into the chair and tried to think. She could hear the pulse of her heart in her head like a rushing of water. She must, before all things, calm down. Her brown eyes were open wide, staring into the dimness of the room lit only by one guttering candle Edwin had left behind. She tried to pray to that Being who had placed her here, who held her life in his hands.

At length she comprehended what she must do, though she felt herself shrink from it. Of course she had contemplated the idea before. But now it was here, staring back at her from the shadows.

But where to go? She should have spoken to someone beforehand. Most anyone, she felt, would be willing to take her in. Yet, who would be strong enough to withstand her husband if he decided to make trouble? The doctor, of course. But the doctor had much too much on his hands already.

She put her hand to her mouth. Tomorrow was the wedding! She dare not spoil it in any way, dampen the spirit of the occasion—some people would be prone to think that sorrow brought upon that day would jinx the couple. She shuddered. Could she bear to spend the night here with Edwin? If he were as drunk as he had seemed, he would sleep late. She could pack a few things now and . . . ? Yes, hide them. She would have to do it now, by candlelight, for the place that she had in mind to hide them was a little way off, in a hollow depression beneath a large oak tree that stood nearly half a mile away.

She rose to her feet again and moved about the room slowly. Pain shot through her fingers every time she tried to move them and she wished she had someone to help her wrap and bind them. The doctor— no; she would not distress him! He could treat her injury, true, but he would fret about the other, and that would be the first inroad to spoiling the day.

She had no awareness of time as she folded and packed her few belongings as neatly as her hurt hand would allow. She moved in a sort of trance, and even the push of fresh air, tingling cold against her cheeks when she walked outdoors, failed to rouse her. She carried the case in her good hand, stopping every few yards to rest. She wished she had a light, though she knew the way well, and she would not have been able to carry one nor willing to risk discovery in any case. After awhile the night wind cooled her cheeks and cleared her head a little.

When she reached the oak tree, the pattern of branches, tangled across the moon like so many entreating arms reaching out, sent a thrill of fear down her spine. She glanced around on all sides. There were sounds she could not identify, there were shadows that seemed to come from nowhere and reflect nothing at all. Quickly she covered her things with the layer of leaves and mulch she had pushed back to admit them. She could only hope that no one would notice a disturbance or happen upon what she had hidden.

At last she made her way back, the wind scudding behind her, pushing her along with a cold hand, but she was grateful for that. Once she was safely inside the house again she bolted the door, then washed her face and neck, her hands and arms, with the tepid water that was left in the bowl. There was only silence, a thick, heavy silence, from the rest of the house. She lay on the bed, fully clothed, and the pain in her fingers throbbed so terribly that she had to roll up her nightgown and rest her hand upon it. The last thought she had was not of the man who lay asleep in the silence, but of the wedding next day, and of how in the world she was going to dress and groom herself, hurt and maimed as she was.

∞

Dorothea awoke on the morning of her wedding feeling a pleasant sense of anticipation. She harbored no illusions about perfect beauty and ideal happiness. But she knew, as well as she could before the fact, that Lucius would be good to her, and that his company was something for which she would be grateful as the years before her lengthened into age, and then old age. She also knew that *she* would be good to him, that she would be able to make him happy. That realization was one of the pleasant things she felt as she dressed for the day. Mary and Martha would be coming soon to help, to put on the finishing touches. She had not had the heart to deny their eager entreaties; after all, marriage to a young girl was still fraught with dreams and desires over which they were able to exercise very little control. And there had not been a marriage in Throstleford these past two years or more.

When she opened the door to them, Martha drew in her breath. "You look lovely, truly lovely," she cried. Dorothea knew the girl meant it; she could see the truth of it in her eyes, so she drew both sisters into her arms and they wept a few tears together. "I have ribbons," Mary beamed, "and the most heavenly scent that Janet Sterne sent along with us."

"Lots of lovely little surprises," Martha added, "so we had best hurry up."

Not far away Lucius rose from a bed that had granted him very little rest that night. He had slept in the spare room on purpose, as *his* room, cleaned and partly redecorated by the ingenious Mary and Martha, was prepared for his bride. It all seemed a dream to him still. He only realized the truth of it by the performing of outward things, and he was grateful for all the tasks that his hands had to do. A few months ago he would have been terrified at the prospect of being left alone with a woman as accomplished and formidable as Dorothea Whitely, but now he knew her too well. He knew her heart, her ready wit, her reticence to speak ill of another, her tender overlooking of his little oddities and faults. They talked easily together of subjects he had never given much thought to before, and that part of their growing relationship was like coming upon a whole garden of roses right in the midst of a desert. He knew he loved her, if love was what you called this magnificent thing that had driven out doubt and boredom and complacency, had even driven out self-interest, and placed her image, instead, in its place.

He went to his bureau and drew out the wedding clothes she had sewn for him, with seam upon seam of small even stitches. He could smell the faint scent of lavender on the fabric. He drew the shirt close and stood for long minutes with his face buried in its folds.

Esther arose early, and was pleased to see that the morning was fair and that the bride and groom would likely enjoy the benediction of sun. She prepared to go to the wedding with anticipation. She had vague memories of attending weddings in her father's chapel as a child; the music, the flowers, the colors of the bride's frocks all blent into one. This ceremony would be performed on the green by one of the Mormon preachers, who was authorized as an official clergyman, but she knew the form and words would be different from those which her father would speak.

She had not discussed the matter with him; it felt as though he had given her his permission without speaking a word. She would not let herself think of *his* feelings on this occasion, or of anything unhappy at all. If she did it would spoil her own enjoyment, and she wanted awfully to feel young and joyous for just this one day.

She went about the room humming under her breath, and from her perch atop the dresser the corn dolly blinked back at her, but Esther paid her no mind. Her very presence was a puzzle to Esther, and she did not wish to be puzzled today, nor distressed, nor worried, nor discontented in any way. She continued to hum and sing snatches of little ditties, and the late October sun, forgetting it was not August, sent streamers of light, as golden and warm as a day in summer, over the fields and houses of Throstleford.

〜

The bees were disturbed. As soon as Sallie opened her eyes she could tell it. But why? She knew of nothing offhand that might have distressed them. She made the rounds of the various hives, checking to see if they were set far enough off the ground. They were placed well apart from one another, away from the wind, several in protective niches in the old wall that surrounded her garden. And, since it was October, she had placed little shallow troughs filled with fresh spring water near the hives. Later she would add honey boiled with rosemary for them to eat.

Perhaps they were offended to have been left out of the marriage ceremonies. They certainly remembered the bee's place of honor in royal bedchambers, kings anointed with honey before their coronation, infants fed honey as the first food after their births, and solemn deaths in Egypt, where the pharaohs were embalmed in honey; all through the world's history men were blessed by the honeybee.

"I've the gifts all ready," she reminded them. "A dozen large beeswax candles, a pot of salve, and a large crock of pure honey that ought to last those two through the winter and into the spring."

She had not gathered honey from her hives since the last part of August. If a fine scattering of snow did not come soon, she would cover the hives over herself. For now she walked, chattered to herself, and wondered. Then, of a sudden, it came.

The wedding. Happiness and promise. *Discord.* Why a sensation of discord? An image of Evaline's face, wide-eyed and frightened, came to her. Sallie never questioned or doubted such things. "I must go and fetch her," she said aloud. "Something is wrong, dreadfully wrong, my lovelies. I must go to her at once."

So it was that Evaline awoke to a light tapping on her door and an urgent whisper. Tears of relief streamed down her face as she saw who was there. Sallie brisked her about and out of there before she knew what was happening.

"Your things concealed by the old oak, are they? I'll send one of the men for them later. For now, we must bathe you in soothing lavender water, dress your hair, and I have just the frock for ye to wear."

Evaline stared back at her. "I do not understand."

"You will." She went to catch up the younger woman's hand, but when Evaline winced and drew it away from her, her own button eyes darkened. "I see we have much to talk about, we two," she declared.

Evaline gave way; she had no energy with which to struggle. The sound of Sallie's voice was as balm to both body and spirit. It was such a long time since anyone had fussed over and cared for her.

"The bees never lie." Sallie spoke the words under her breath, but Evaline heard. "The bees know more of men's hearts and men's doings than we could dream of," she went on. "And they will be a protection against that man, now that you are coming to live with me."

"You should attend yourself, Father, but if not, then someone must go and stand in for you—squire's family, and all."

"You think so, missy?" Squire Feather bent over his eggs and kidneys, his face a misery. "God and highlanders! I'll send Tempest, as a token, all right?"

"I intend to go with him myself." Sarah said the words calmly, turning away from her father as she spoke, so that he could not catch her eye nor suggest any way to detain her. She had her mother's support. She, poor woman, was afraid of going against her husband's wishes, but she thought this Mormon business nonsense. The people were still *their* villagers; what difference did religion make? Her mother liked the idea of having a feminine representation as well as her tall, rather broody, rather unfriendly son.

Sarah had planned ahead. She'd sent word the day before to have the pretty little palfrey groomed and ready to mount. "I could drive you in the carriage, in style," Tempest offered, but she knew how he liked to ride, and she was itching for a good canter herself. "I hope to see Esther there," she said, as they mounted.

"You and Esther are friends?"

"Oh yes, little brother. You and Jonathan are not the only people in this family who admire the parson's daughter."

Saucy wench! Tempest followed after her, with her mocking laughter still in his ears. He could not remember seeing the two of them together, so what did his sister mean? If it were true that they were friends, so much the better. But he could not say so much the better for what.

Chapter Twenty-Four

*I*t was a lovely ceremony. The bride and groom were as radiant as though she were eighteen and he twenty-one. Yet they possessed also that dignity borne of experience, even of suffering, that drew strong lines in their faces beneath the surface expressions of joy.

Sallie had called Doctor Sterne in, against Evaline's wishes, but because of it her fingers were spread with honey ointment and carefully bound in white cotton, then concealed within Sallie's gloves, which were a size or two larger than Evaline's and so worked very well.

Many of the marriage customs were deleted, due to Dorothea's insistence, for she knew they would embarrass the groom to the point of mortification. But her wedding cake, all five tiers of it, was set on a board in the old way, festooned with flowers and ribbons, and carried around the company while the men cheered and the children sang. Coins were tossed as the marriage couple walked hand in hand to the head of the wedding table, and well-wishers left a kiss on the bride's flushed cheek and a wish in her ear.

Esther watched with a sense of delight mingled with a longing that was as sharp and distracting as a toothache. She did not see Tempest approach, though Sarah ran ahead and held out her hands to her. "We meet again, my young friend."

Esther was pleased by the greeting, but smiled and colored when she saw Tempest come up behind, eyeing them with one of those enigmatic expressions that frustrated her so. "Pay no mind to my brother," Sarah advised, aware, too, of his scrutiny. "For a few moments I want you all to myself."

Sarah knew she was tantalizing both her friend and her brother, but it could not be helped. This frustration would make him all the more determined, and for reasons she could not quite understand herself, she did not mind that. Besides, she *was* in need of a friend, a friend besides her sister and the county girls whom she saw only occasionally. She liked Esther Grey. She would like to spend more time with her, find out more about her.

They strolled through the crowds and spoke in kindly terms of the people they passed by or stopped to greet.

"You possess a large array of friends, Esther. I envy you the treasure."

Esther gave her a gentle glance. "They have been there since my childhood, simply part of my life. Since my mother died, I have grown closer to many—"

"Like the bee woman?"

"Yes." Esther smiled. "Like Sallie. She is, you know, very wise."

"I have no doubt of it. She certainly breeds a superior strain of honey; my father praises it every time it is brought to the table."

"It would please her to know that. May I tell her?"

"Of course."

Tempest watched them, walking arm in arm, weaving in and out of the assemblage, appearing flowerlike in their beauty and the grace of their step. He waited as long as he could bear, then set out after them.

"Here he comes!" Sarah cried.

"Away with you, 'tis my turn now, sister."

Sarah took a step back and, with a mock bow, dropped Esther's arm, whispering in her ear at the same time, "Will you come to see me some afternoon, if I send for you?"

"Yes," Esther blushed. "Of course. Yes."

Tempest made no attempts to disguise his interest. He drew her aside, brought cider and cakes, then sat down beside her. "Did you think this a nice wedding?" he asked.

"I believe so, yes." Her eyes looked questions into his. "I thought the bride and groom beautiful, I suppose because I know them both and love them."

"I thought it a flaccid affair compared to the weddings I have witnessed in Scotland."

"Oh, I've no doubt of it." Esther smiled. "Please tell me all."

"You are teasing, you are humoring me!"

"No. I am sincere in my interest. I enjoy hearing you talk of the happy times you spent there."

He regarded her for a moment. How intense was the blue of her eyes. He could hardly bear to look into them. "All right." A sparkle leapt into his own eyes; he was nearly laughing. "If you insist."

He relaxed and began with a shake of his head. "I do not rightly know where to start."

"Begin with the bride herself."

"Well, as I remember, she would dress in a new-made frock of any color but green. Green is considered unlucky because it is the choice of the fairies. And the women would always leave one stitch undone, but do not ask me why. And a silver coin in her shoe, but salt in the pocket of the groom, for luck. And she must always approach the church from right to left, though the groom arrives with her bridesmaids and is accompanied by a piper." He grinned like a boy. "So much more comes to me as I get going. After the knot is tied, there is always a rush to be the first one to kiss the bride, and the canny minister is often the winner of that prize. The bells are rung to keep away evil spirits, and rose petals are thrown over the couple as a symbol of fertility. And that's only the beginning; we have not even got to the celebration part yet."

"Much enchantment in their ways," Esther sighed. "When you marry, would you like a Scottish wedding?"

"Indeed, I would." His eyes as well as his voice were dreamy.

"And a Scottish bride." Esther added the words tartly, for his demeanor had grown disturbing. He gazed at her now with an expression that thrilled through her. "Not necessarily, Esther, that is not what I was thinking at all."

She liked to hear him call her by name, for he spoke it with a lilt and a little trill in the middle, drawing the syllables out so that they sounded musical rather than ordinary.

Yet all this was making her exceedingly uncomfortable, and she was relieved to see Janet Sterne approaching her with Mary and Martha in tow. Tempest rose as the ladies approached and acted in every part the gentleman as he excused himself and left them, but Esther was intensely aware of his disappointment; was she coming to know him so well?

The sisters were bubbling over with pleasure at the happy occasion, but when Martha mumbled something about a close call and Mary pinched her arm warningly, Esther glanced at Janet for explanation.

"My lips are sealed," Janet chuckled. "Suffice it to say 'all is well that ends well.' Right, girls?"

Esther wondered, but the conversation veered off in other directions; indeed, due to the nature and youth of the sisters, in half a dozen directions at once.

"Tempest Feather is as handsome a man as I've ever set eyes on," Martha piped up, lifting her eyebrows as she looked pointedly in Esther's direction.

These are dangerous waters, Esther thought, but attempted to respond to the curiosity in as natural a way as she could.

"Do you think so? 'Handsome is as handsome does,' I always say."

As soon as the words were out she wondered why in the world she had said them. Martha knit her brow in displeasure. "He seems quite a gentleman from what I have observed."

"And so he is," Esther hastened. "I was only teasing, you know. But he is quite a changeable creature, and not entirely happy here." Both girls were still staring at her, so she continued, though her discomfort was mounting. "His brother's illness is a source of great sadness to him, and I think he misses the home he had in Scotland with his uncle and aunt."

"He appears most devoted to you." Mary spoke the words guilelessly; she was a good little creature. Somehow the innocence of her interest made Esther relax.

"He needs a friend, I think. And since I have been going up to the manor house to read to young Jonathan, Tempest and I have also become acquainted."

"The young squire is not doing well, is he, Esther dear?"

Bless Janet for the question and the shift in conversation. Esther responded, and then another question followed, and the girls wandered away. After they had left, Janet placed her hand on her friend's arm. "It has been difficult for you, Esther, I know. It is easy to grow fond of Jonathan, for he is a remarkable young man."

"And easy to resent and grieve over the destruction of so much life and goodness," Esther replied.

"Not destruction, dear." Janet's face had grown as soft and entreating as her lovely voice. "We who desire the boy's presence and are denied feel the loss of it, but *he will live on* in a happier state. You know that as well as I."

Do I? Esther wanted to cry, but she only nodded her head.

"Come say hello to Sallie and Evaline, will you? They have been asking for you."

How good it was to greet these women, young and old, who had been her friends since childhood. It strengthened Esther to see true affection for her in their faces and eyes. She remembered suddenly that she had meant to be happy this whole day long. She took their hands, she returned their smiles, she hugged the radiant bride. She promised kittens to half the children who crowded round her, and ate her fill of sweet breads and pastries and Janet's rich pies. And for the most part it worked, she held all the shadows at bay. But the desires that chaffed at her mind were not so easy to tame. Her own desires and others she had felt were like gleams through the tenuous tapestry of a spiderweb on a morning in May: gossamer things of little substance, and yet more strong than the mightiest oak that stood rooted against wind and rain.

∾

Rose and Adam enjoyed their own little celebration with the cradle Michael Bingham had made for them, a gift wondered at and exclaimed over far into the night. Such kindness warmed their young hearts and spiced their anticipation of the child who would come to lie in it and listen to her mother's lullabies and her father's proud praise.

"'Tis a girl you carry," Hannah had assured Rose. "And this tiny one within me"—touching the rounding of her stomach tenderly—"will be a son."

Rose was content with that, and Adam also. He wanted a daughter like Rose, a wee delicate bit of beauty. There would be time for sons to come who would grow up to help him in the farming. Perhaps with sons, in time, he could buy a spot of land of his own. A dream only right now, but perhaps someday . . .

The bees were quiet. After the sun set, the night grew cold, and no one had sighted Edwin Sowerby once during the day. Doctor Sterne, however, had alerted the constable to what had happened and asked him to post lookouts for a week or more outside Sallie's house.

"The women don't need to hear about it," the doctor had cautioned. "But you know the disposition of Sowerby." The corners of his mouth lifted in a rueful expression.

"Aye, he cannot come to me and complain about his wife and the Mormons. So you and I know where he'll go."

"Yes, and all Heaton needs is an excuse like this to reignite him."

"We shall do what we can, to be sure, and trust the rest to Him," the constable replied, lifting his eyes.

For some reason that made the doctor feel better and he went to his home with a sense of peace he was grateful for.

⟨∞⟩

The next day, the visiting elders called a meeting and set the doctor apart to preside over the congregation of Throstleford Saints, henceforward to be known as a branch. Paul Pritchard and Zacharias Kilburn were selected as his assistants or counselors, all three being sustained by the solemn raising of the right hand of all present. Regular worship services were to be held on the Sabbath and prayer meetings on Thursday, and the brethren were all admonished to preach only the first principles of the gospel, and not to contend with their neighbors.

The first British mission conference had been held on Christmas Day in the "Cockpit" in Preston nearly three years ago. The work was moving forward; it was a new decade, and the calendar in January would turn to 1841.

"Last summer at the beginning of June, the first company of emigrants was organized and sent forth by Brigham Young. Forty Saints headed by Elder John Moon sailed in the ship *Britannia* from Liverpool to New York," Elder Turner happily informed them. "We are pleased with the progress since then. You would be interested to know of the reception the gospel is receiving in other parts of the land. Brother Kimball and Brother Fielding baptized one hundred and two people in a matter of days and organized branches in Downham, Chatburn, and Waddington. Many approached them begging for baptism, and a group of forty young people took hold of their clothing, grasped their hands, and walked with them to the next village, singing the songs of Zion."

There were tears in some of the listeners' eyes; others were shaking their heads in wonder at such a scene taking place.

"The Brethren are organizing passage on half a dozen other vessels," Elder Turner continued, "and there soon will be room for all who wish to go to Zion."

The very words sent a thrill through Michael Bingham's spirit that made his flesh tingle. He knew he must be one of those who left England and followed this unknown path across the wastes of ocean and a continent of wilderness to the place called Zion, where prophets dwelt and a temple was to be built.

Hannah, watching his face, knew of the strong emotions with which he grappled. She was less certain than he, more attached to the land and people of this village in which she had lived, in which she had first drawn breath, and in which her own child, yet safe in her womb, would first taste of life. Change held a certain terror for her, but she would never reveal that to the man she loved. Some sort of vision of this new life promised them had been given to him. To labor on the temple of the Lord. *Such things have not been since ancient times,* he would say to her. *And, Hannah, I know—I know I can do work with my hands and heart that will be worthy of it.*

What could she do against such as that? She would borrow a portion of his faith, lean on it until she was able to develop a strong enough faith of her own.

"There are many less fortunate than yourselves," Elder Turner was saying. "We have seen them in the streets of Birmingham and Preston: women and children begging on the streets without shoes or stockings, or any covering to shield them from the elements. Why, I have even beheld—" His voice dropped and his face went ashen, "I have seen delicate females gathering up animal refuse from the streets and carrying it to places where they might sell it for a penny or a hae'penny. It wrenches our hearts." He sighed, lifted his head, and tried to look cheerful though his eyes were dark with compassion. "We are so fortunate, every one in this room, and the Lord will continue to bless and uphold us . . ."

Zachie Kilburn knew it was true. He reached for Louisa's hand and enjoyed the cool feel of it resting lightly against his own. He felt humbled by the words he was listening to and, at the same time, exalted. *Truth exalts,* he thought. *Truth gives a man power, real power that nothing in this uncertain existence can touch.*

Paul Pritchard was troubled as he listened. Ought he to uproot his family and go to this Zion? Had they need of mill builders and millers there? He was able to provide a good steady living for Paisley and his children here in Throstleford. But nothing could be certain in a place of which he had no understanding, which he could not imagine. Even when he closed his eyes, no picture would come.

He wondered what Paisley was thinking. Pert and feisty little thing when he married her, she still had much of that spirit left. Enough to do what these men were asking—or offering? He glanced over his children, letting his eyes rest on each in turn. Would a new life necessarily be a better life for them? What of Daniel? A long journey, new challenges, living among strangers—all would be hard going for him.

He knit his brow, and as he shifted his gaze his eyes rested on old Peter Goodall. *Surely, if some of us go,* he thought, *there are others who, of necessity, will be left behind. What if his granddaughters leave him? Would that break his heart, or would he be comforted by the blessings and advantages that awaited them?* He wished he had answers to the seething questions that were as busy as a swarm of Sallie's bees in his mind.

Louisa Kilburn, riding home in the wagon beside her husband, felt a dull spirit overtake her. She knew in her heart that her feelings for this new religion did not match Zachie's. She did not love it as he did, and she had watched a bit disconcertedly as it had grown to fill a more and more important role in his everyday life.

She had always known that she did not have much ardor for matters of religion. She had always believed that religion was well in its place, but she had not the *hunger* inside for it that her husband had. That was all right, given normal circumstances; she could still do her part. But now Zachie had been placed in a position of leadership, and now there was this talk of emigrating to *America!* They may call it Zion, but it was America still. And she had not the least desire to go to that heathen, uncivilized place: Mormonism or no Mormonism; truth or no truth.

She glanced at his profile. He had a gruff exterior, it was true, a stocky body and large hands with long flat fingers; a blacksmith's hands. She liked his looks, the dark, solid presence of him. She liked his gentle ways that touched his common features with a kind of grace. She had always felt she would do anything for him, but after today—after today . . . well, it may not come to that, and she would not fret about it, at least not yet.

On the other hand, Rose and Adam held hands like children sharing a secret. The dream they had scarcely ever put words to stood before them, clothed in common phrases: "ships will be ready" . . ."there will be enough room for all." These Mormon elders spoke of a community where men built their own little houses on land of their own, where every man helped his brother, and progress was inevitable. Commonplace realities, as they saw it. Could Adam believe in them, too? It seemed *possible,* even for the humblest, like himself. He would speak to the doctor tomorrow and see if he knew of work anywhere in the village, *any* work he could do, that would earn him a few more shillings here and there, and Rose would husband their scanty means carefully, so that they could put money aside and, God willing, be able to take passage on one of those ships and find their way to a place in the world where these things were possible.

∞

"Would you go?" Evaline asked Sallie that evening as they sat sipping tea. "Would you leave your bees?"

Sallie did not answer at once. A hard question that. "I'm getting on," she remarked. "A change of that scope would take some thought."

They sat in silence for a few minutes. Sallie thought the wind was getting noisy; she could feel the cold edge on it, even inside the house. "You would like to go, Evaline, wouldn't you?"

"Yes, I would, yes."

"It would be an answer of sorts." Sallie sighed. "An escape for you; we may as well call it that."

"I am a good worker, they must have need of good workers in such a place."

Sallie nodded her head. "Indeed. Indeed . . . I believe it will come to that, if it comes to anything at all."

Evaline sensed what she meant. They fell silent again, but in her heart Evaline felt a great surge of gratitude for this small, kindly woman, and for the men who were calmly holding out salvation for her to grasp.

∞

Edwin waited. He was not sure where his wife *was*, first of all. Besides, the men like Zachie Kilburn and Paul Pritchard, men who could fell an ox, let alone a man, would be watching him now. *And* men like Sam Weatherall and the doctor would be on the lookout as well. He'd give it a few days, maybe a week, maybe longer. See what happened, see if Evie came home. He had work in plenty to do, and he could drink of a night without his wife nagging at him. Yes, he supposed that he would give it awhile.

Chapter Twenty-Five

C hristian could not say he had not been expecting something of the sort to occur. He knew he was being watched, he had felt it in his bones, the way one feels random pains with a weather change. He had been at this post a long while, and the archdeacon who was his local superior generally left him alone, only paying the perfunctory periodic visits required, sharing a cup of tea, and making out his usual report.

Now a missive came in the post with the official letterhead announcing day and time that the archdeacon would arrive to visit the parson. He sat with the sheet in his hand, tapping it lightly against his leg, trying to think, trying to assess his situation. He certainly knew that he was up against challenges he had never dreamed of before. Could he be honest? *Should* he be honest? What should he say?

He stood, letting the sheet of paper drop to the floor. It was not *that* at all. He could be courageous enough, if he had to, to take a stand. The problem, the real dilemma, was: what *did* he think? What were his feelings, his opinions, his understandings? These would be probed by the man of the cloth who had authority to do just that. Now he *must* face what he had been avoiding these many months. He could not speak for himself, could not make decisions that would affect the rest of his life, until he knew things inside, things he was running away from just now.

Ought he to call Esther to him, tell her what was to happen, give her warning? *Give her warning of what?* No, he had best desist until he knew what was happening; there was a little time yet. If Esther was in any way aware of the struggle he was going through she would make it both easier and harder for him. He must do this on his own, plain and simply, between himself and his God.

It was time for Evensong, a service he attended to with the greatest pleasure. His little choir, sadly depleted by the departure of some of his best singers, still performed the solemn old hymns with a loving air. The congregation sang in their turn and he, their leader and shepherd, sang along in his heart. But a snatch of melody and the words that went with it kept getting in Christian's way, quietly, unobtrusively implanting themselves over every other refrain that the organist was attempting to play. *The Spirit of God like a fire is burning, the latter-day glory begins to come forth.*

His smile became a fixture, not a reality. He prayed with his eyes open, prayed for himself and for those he loved, with all of his heart.

Winter came suddenly, overnight, with the advent of a single gray morning. The sky stretched above the village was gray. The birds that flew against the sky, with no sun on their wings, appeared themselves as spots and streaks of a darker gray. The landscape had grown drained and colorless, there were no greens on the hillsides, no red, no gold. Even the water in the river was a slate gray, not shadings of white and blue. On such a day the archdeacon came to examine his rector, with some definite ideas and recommendations firm in his mind.

Christian sent Esther to the squire's on some pretext.

"You wish to get rid of me, Father," she protested stoutly. "You are distressed about something; you have been these past weeks."

"That is of no matter to you," he replied firmly. "Please do as you are told. That is the best way you can help me, Esther."

He spoke the words with such earnestness that she nodded miserably, determined to do as he bid. Perhaps Jonathan would not mind her
showing up a day early and she might spend some hours with him.
Perhaps . . . She allowed no thoughts, no expectations in that direction,
but put on her muff and bonnet and headed out of the house.

She *could* ride, and Father insisted she take his little mare lest the
weather take a bad turn. The air in the ash grove, as she entered, felt
heavy, and she wondered what it was until she realized that it was the
absence of birdsong she was feeling, the stillness of beauty withdrawn.

Life seemed to hover in a state of suspension, Esther thought, and,
sensing it, everything in the village slowed down. Snow would come one
day soon to shake loose the apathy, Christmas crowding close after that.
Mischief and malice had no place in the frozen dark days that would
follow, brief bitter days that made men want to scurry in by the hearth-
side, where the wind could not find them and the darkness could not
follow. There would be no more trouble until spring, there would be
nothing really happening in their little world at all. Or so she concluded,
not realizing how terribly amiss she could be.

Betts was at the door, looking as ancient as the hall itself and register-
ing no surprise. He took the parcel her father had sent with her, murmuring thanks, and began to ask if young miss would like to wait, but
before he got the sentence out, Sarah flew down the stairs, her face alight,
holding her hands out to Esther. "What a perfect surprise!"

Within moments she was tugged up the stairs and into the room that
Sarah shared with her sister. Esther had never been on this floor, where
the family rooms were, and she felt herself an intruder, despite her host-
ess's friendliness. How grand the furnishings were. She looked with wistful interest at the ivory-handled combs and brushes, the row of bottles
holding exotic scents and perfume waters. She had a peek at the gowns,
some flounces and some deep embroidered silks, all of costlier fabrics
than Esther had ever seen in the Throstleford shops.

Sarah brushed all compliments aside and asked after Esther's father,
and after the newlyweds, and after the cats and their remaining kittens.

At last Esther had to laugh at her and entreat her to stop. "What of yourself?" she asked, and that started Sarah off again, telling how her mama was bothered with sick headaches, her sister off visiting a cousin, her father like an old toad full of foul moods, and Tempest, struggling against the general moodiness, always busying himself out of doors.

"And Jonathan?"

Sarah shook her head. "He is not doing well. But he will be happy to see you!" She stood up suddenly and tugged at Esther again. "I'll take you to him, then go tell cook we need tea, and come to join you again."

So it was that she stood outside the closed door and the whole world went silent again. "Let us surprise him," Sarah suggested.

"No. Announce me, Sarah. Please."

But she had already pushed open the door for Esther and turned to race back down the hall. Esther sighed as she slid through the half-opening, blinking her eyes.

"Sarah?" The voice that spoke was so altered, so laden with pain that Esther drew her breath in and clenched her hands at her sides.

"No, I am sorry, it is Esther—I tried to get Sarah to announce me, but—" She swallowed. She felt suddenly hot.

"It is no matter." He lifted his head and tried to smile at her, and she realized with a sudden shock that he had purposefully never allowed her to see him like this before. He had always known the day and time of her coming and had prepared himself for it, determined that she not know the extent of his illness, the extent of his suffering . . .

"Esther." He lifted one hand and held it out to her. She flew to the bed, dropped to her knees, and buried her face in the folds of the coverlet, blinking madly against the tears that she did not wish him to see.

After a few moments she raised her head and hazarded a question. "Would you like me to read?"

His eyes were dull and sunken into his skull a little, and, like everything else, they were rimmed with gray. "I *should* like that, but Sarah is coming with tea, isn't she?"

"Yes, she is. I forgot."

Jonathan knew what that meant; he knew the extent of this girl's devotion to him. The realization went like a flame through his body, burning him empty and breathless. Of what good was this marvelous creature to him?

"Shall Sarah and I take the tea elsewhere?"

"No, I should like to have you both near me."

Her eyes asked, *Will it overtire you?* But they agreed, without speaking, to ignore that tormenting question for once.

Nevertheless, it was one of the most difficult quarter hours Esther had ever spent. As soon as she could she thanked Sarah and excused herself. "I will come back tomorrow," she promised, "and read to you at the usual hour."

She walked up to the bed, reached out her ungloved hand, and brushed a lock of hair back from the fevered forehead. Then she bent slowly and pressed a light kiss against his hot skin before turning away. She had never done that before, and she did not think of it now, for it seemed the most natural and necessary thing for her to do.

She liked Sarah and, under different circumstances, would have taken delight in the friendship and the enthusiastic affection her better bestowed on her. But not now, not today. Not while—her mind had leapt ahead to say, *Not as long as Jonathan lives.*

Once out of doors she drew the cold air into her hot body in grateful gulps. She felt a terrible compulsion to put that house at a distance, away from her sight and her thoughts.

It was cooler beneath the trees and quiet still. Esther put her heels to the mare just ready to urge her to a faster gait when a horseman came out from nowhere. "May I ride beside you, Miss Grey?"

"Where did you come from?" she asked bluntly.

Tempest grinned like a schoolboy. "See there?" He pointed through the thick boughs. "One of the secret trails that Jonathan and I plotted and hacked out when we were young. It winds madly back and forth like a serpent, but comes out at the house eventually. Truth is—" he hesitated, "I've been repairing it, cutting away the areas that are choked and overgrown—thinking about the past."

Esther dropped her gaze. His looks were so bold, so arresting; she feared her eyes would reveal the interest she felt.

"I would have been sorry to miss you," he said as their horses fell in together. "Why have you come here today?"

"I am not certain. My father sent me on an errand, but I think, really, he wanted me out of the house."

"For what reason?"

"Right now I have no idea." There was distress as well as perplexity in her voice. She half turned in the saddle to face him. "Sarah took me in to see Jonathan. He was not expecting me." A kind of vehemence crept into her tone. He looked at her quizzically.

"Do you not understand?" she cried. Her eyes were dark now, almost colorless with what he could only call pain. "I never knew before, I never realized that he *prepared himself* to see me the other times I have come, purposefully concealing—concealing—" She could not go on.

Tempest put out his hand and brushed it along her coat sleeve in a clumsy gesture of comfort. "He does appear bad, doesn't he? Tears one's heart apart to look on so helplessly. That is why I came out here—had to do something to work out the pent-up energy that I cannot use for his sake."

Esther looked full into his eyes and saw therein the same depth of feeling she had so often seen in her father's. It startled her. "I do not know how you can bear it." She murmured the words without thinking. He reached for her hand, then checked himself and drew what seemed a protective blind over those deep things he had almost allowed himself to express.

"Yes, well, one does what one has to. And pain, you know, never kills us, though we wish that it might."

"I must hurry," she pleaded, suddenly overwhelmed again. "But I shall be back tomorrow, at my regular time."

"Ah, then I also shall have something to look forward to." He moved his horse away from the path and let her go past. She did not turn, though she felt his gaze burn into her. But she would have been surprised to know that he sat at that spot a long time, and she would have been more than surprised to have known his thoughts.

∽

The archdeacon came straight to the point, as Christian had known that he would. He was a man in his sixties, in the prime of his own hard-won power. He was not in the habit of giving quarter where concerns of the church were at stake.

"You have sworn an Oath of Allegiance to Her Majesty," he was now saying, in sonorous tones, "as well as the Oath of Canonical Obedience." He leaned forward, his hands planted square on his knees. "And yet, you have allowed *your flock* to be deceived by these *Mormons!*" He spat the word out. Christian kept his face as impassive as possible.

"Do I understand aright that you have allowed these people to have baptisms in the village, that *you* attended one of these travesties yourself? That you stood by while a once-respected doctor claimed to heal a sick child by spiritual authority—and you did not denounce him?"

The words and the images they conjured were greatly unsettling the archdeacon as he called them forth, and Christian knew there were more to come. "You allow those who have betrayed you and the church the freedom of your home, the freedom of your association!" He trembled visibly. "My good man, have you any idea what these people teach? They blaspheme heaven. This man they call their prophet they have set up as a god."

Christian said nothing, though he realized silence was as injurious to his cause as the incorrect answer would be.

"They have concocted a gold bible of their own and teach their blasphemies from out of it, deceiving the innocent and unwary—"

"Not so, sir, you criticize in ignorance there."

The archdeacon drew his breath in sharply and sat back in his chair, astonishment like a shock on his features. "You have seen this book, Christian?"

"I have *read* much of it, sir. It is what it claims to be; a second witness for Jesus Christ."

"Revelation then?" The archdeacon's voice had become a low rasp. "You *accept what they claim!* You dirty your hands and your mind with their infamies! This is disgraceful, Christian, for a man of the cloth!

There is no revelation in our day and we *must* safeguard the church and the traditions of our fathers from such heresies."

His statement seemed to draw up all the energy in the room. The two men sat facing each other with no sound at all, save the archdeacon's heavy breathing. At last, with some effort, he roused himself.

"You have done nothing to win your parishioners back to the church? To warn them of the deceit that has been practiced upon them—to redeem them for Christ again?"

"I may have tried if I had not known it would be futile."

"What do you mean by that, man?" The question was a growl; the archdeacon's patience was wearing thin.

"They have been converted—by powerful means—I have no influence with them—" Christian paused, then added ineffectually, "save to pray for their welfare, as I always have."

The archdeacon waved an imperious hand. "I am astonished—I know not what to think of the matter. I know not what to think of *you*, Christian. What have you to say for yourself?"

This was a moment of truth; yet, faced with it, Christian could not bring himself to deny before this man all the things he had stood for, with the integrity of his whole being, these many years.

"I regret that I have caused you and those who serve with you concern and distress. I regret that I have failed in certain aspects of my stewardship, your grace."

Another silence ensued while the archdeacon drummed his fingers on his knees. "Insufficient, a mere apology, insufficient." He muttered the words. "I shall have to give this matter further prayer and consideration, I see. But action of some sort must be taken." He rose to his feet. "For the time being I shall draft an official reprimand from the church." He reached for his hat. "Which will become part of your record henceforward, you know."

Christian said nothing, made no move of acquiescence or dissent.

"Bad business, this, Christian. Sorry for it, very sorry, indeed."

Christian lifted the bell and rang for Pearl. When she arrived, he asked her to please see the archdeacon to the door.

"Thank you, sir, for coming to counsel with me," he said very formally as he extended his hand.

The archdeacon touched it only briefly. "A sad duty, I will tell you, one of the saddest duties I have been asked to perform."

He was gone. Christian listened to the sound of his steps descending the stairs, heard the blessed sound of the door being opened and shut again, heard the silence of his own home close round him. And yet he felt more hurt and exposed than if he had been left alone on the windswept moorlands to starve and die.

He sank down into his chair and covered his face with his hands. Tears came, then sobs that shook his body. There was no peace. It was not meant for him to have peace ever again in this life.

Chapter Twenty-Six

꩜

The entire village knew. How did the entire village know what he scarcely knew himself? Christian, for the moment, was overwhelmed more than angry, his only concern being for Esther's well-being. He called her in to his room and attempted to lay the matter before her without telling too much. The attempt was a failure. When at length he dismissed her and she went her way, he thought, *I have lost Esther. And it is my own fault.*

The villagers, in truth, knew less than he realized, only the vague shameful awareness that the parson had been reprimanded by the church. Of course, the official letter had come through ordinary channels and been duly noted by the postmistress, but beyond that there was nothing but angry conjecture as to the details. Almost to a man the folk of the village were fond of Christian. Even the Methodist flock, under the didactic eye of Nicholas Sheppard, respected the gentle Church of England minister.

It was nearly December and the holiday season would be upon them, then the icy restraints of the winter months. The letter had said that Parson Grey would be granted six months' probation. At the end of that time his conduct and status would be reevaluated and a decision made.

Esther was angry. And she turned her anger, for the first time, against her old friends. *This is all the doctor's fault,* she stewed, *from beginning to end.* He and the strangers, on that day that now seemed a lifetime ago, had rung a death knell to all that Esther held dear. Not only were the best of her friends snatched away from her but *now* she had heard that there was excited talk amongst the Mormons of leaving their outworn past behind and emigrating to Zion. *Whatever that means!* she stormed inwardly. How nice for them! They would be leaving behind the ruination of a village and of a noble man's life.

A sob choked at her unexpectedly and she put her hand to her throat. *I will not cry,* she vowed, *I will not cry!* But the look on her father's face as he had tried to explain his disgrace to her—she would never get it out of her mind. *You wreak ruination and heartache,* she stormed to the faces that came up before her mind, *and then walk away from it all. And why?*

What was left for her father? And, for that matter, what for her? She had no friends, she had no place, even Andrew was estranged from her. The chances were real that she and her father would be set adrift, with no way to make a living nor a home to live in. *I will never see my mother's grave again,* she thought bitterly. *We will become wanderers on the face of the land. Perhaps the shepherd will take us into his hut and the far hills fold around us to hide our shame.*

So darted her distraught thoughts, but the one strain that ran through them all was the cry: *I wish I had never heard the word "Mormon" in my life.*

Esther's distraught mood had not lifted as the days before Christmas arrived. The Latter-day Saints, on the other hand, were enjoying each moment they had, wondering, with mixed feelings, if this might be their last Christmas celebration in this loved place. Much of the talk and conjecture had died away; people simply had too much to do. Sam Weatherall's store boasted a window display of handmade toys for the children and the special hard barley candies that Meg concocted for the holidays in shapes of mice and kittens, which were their special delight.

Esther resented the little time they had left, but nonetheless, there was still a congregation for her father to preach to every week, and she had helped the ladies festoon the chapel with greens and berries, and wreaths for the door. But the light had gone out of living for Esther; she struggled through the motions, but little more. Her father watched her anxiously, and she watched her father, but neither knew what to do.

The Advent Sabbaths were Esther's favorite. She had taken note of the squire and his family attending each of these weeks, much more regularly than was their wont before Tempest arrived. Or—as she realized with an inward blush—before she began going to the house and making the acquaintance of both of the squire's sons.

She and Sarah usually snatched a brief conversation at the service's end. And occasionally Tempest would find an excuse to speak with her for a moment or two. He cut a fine figure in his Sabbath clothes. The green frock coat, tailored to his long torso and longer legs, set off his fair skin and the red lights in his hair. His vitality was evident in all his movements, but in his eyes the real truths of his spirit resided; he could not hide them from her. Others may have thought him only a vainglorious, privileged young man, but she knew *more* because he had revealed it—some of his own accord, some unwittingly.

He also knew that *she* was disturbed, wounded and angry. On her days at the house she had been unable to disguise her moods from him, yet when he questioned her about them, she was adamant. She would disclose nothing to him that might compromise her father. And besides, how could he understand her feelings and struggles in such a matter as this?

With Jonathan it was different. She was most careful with him, reading from the Book of Mormon still when he asked her to. But there had been a subtle alteration in her visits of late. He could not endure a lengthy reading any longer, so most of the time she sat and talked to him, drawing his mind from the burden of pain and dissolution that pressed it down.

They spoke no more of living and dying and the larger issues of life. He had passed some kind of a threshold where she could not go. At times she was stretching her hands out to him from across a great distance. At times she knew there was a presence in the room more than mortal, an *atmosphere* that seemed to hallow the very air that the two of them breathed.

Christmas week Esther helped Pearl with the baking of breads and puddings and mince pies. They brought fresh greens into the parlor and up into her father's study as well, draped mistletoe from the chandelier in the ancient hall, and made balls of cloves and other sweet-smelling spices to distribute along with the doilies they had tatted all year. But her mind was still blank and desolate beneath it all.

Then on Christmas morning she dressed carefully in her best frock and her dove-gray gloves, and a gray hat festooned with grouse feathers. Her furnishings matched her mood. She walked the long yew path to the front of the old church, dark against the dun sky and the field of gray headstones that seemed to stretch back before memory, before time. It was beginning to snow, and the flakes sparkled in brief diamond shapes that blurred her sight. If she blinked they were gone, in a heartbeat. But more filled their place, more and more pushing steadily forward to blot the sky. The sight made her think of the souls lying silent in the graveyard whose lives had been replaced, with more and more coming after them. And for what? What purpose held life and its brief, intense sorrows and joys?

She walked to her place at the front of the chapel, her heels making sharp little tappings against the stones. Discreetly her eyes roved here and there through the aisles in search of certain faces, but none were there. She felt keenly aware of the absence of her old friends. What were they doing right now? Holding some makeshift service in the big room at the dusty mill, crowded together and sitting on makeshift pews? Did the doctor do the preaching, and what in the world qualified him?

Other faces were missing also. Where was the shepherd? Where the squire's household? Why would they not be in attendance this day? She felt tinklings of hopelessness, much like the pricking of the snowflakes, and she thought life very drear on this solemn Christmas morning.

Her father began the Collect. He had a very nice voice; it was clear as a boy's and yet full and resonant so that even the old people at the back of the chapel could hear every word.

> Almighty God, who hast given us thy only-begotten
> Son to take our nature upon him, and as at this time to
> be born of a pure Virgin: Grant that we, being regenerate,
> and made thy children by adoption and grace, may daily
> be renewed by thy Holy Spirit; through the same our
> Lord Jesus Christ, who liveth and reigneth with thee . . .

The words possessed their own power. They tugged at her sorrowfulness so that her spirit could not help but respond. The carols lifted above the ancient walls of the church with such purity that Esther thought angel voices must be joined to their own.

> *Oh, come, all ye faithful, joyful and triumphant!*
> *Oh, come ye, oh, come ye to Bethlehem.*
> *Come and behold him, born the King of angels;*
> *Oh, come, let us adore him;*
> *Oh, come, let us adore him;*
> *Oh, come, let us adore him, Christ, the Lord.*

There was a contented settling all around and behind her. The music went on, into the strains of "Hark, the Herald Angels Sing." Esther felt cold air at her back as the door opened wide and, half-turning, she saw from the corner of her eye the shepherd entering like one of the ancient ones on that sacred night. *Perhaps there was heavy snow in the hills, or a sick lamb to detain him,* Esther thought, not at first hearing the hushed whispers of wonder as the shepherd kept on walking up to the front of the church.

Everything stopped. There was no sound but a shuffling and a breathing. The pastor leaned down and the shaggy man spoke into his ear, then turned aside, just a little way, to come to stand beside Esther and hold out his hand.

"Child," he said, "there is a carriage from the squire's house waiting outdoors. They have sent it for you."

"Jonathan is dying."

"He has asked for you, Esther."

She bowed her head. Her eyes were burning with the pain of her heart spilling over, but there were no tears. She stood slowly, took the shepherd's hand gratefully, and walked the long aisle with him, glancing neither to left nor right. The words in her head were one prayer, repeated over and over, "Please, God, let me arrive in time. Let me be of some little good to him before he comes back to You."

"How is it that you are here?" she asked Oliver as he handed her into the carriage. The man from the house, she thought his name was Rufus, tucked the rugs around her with a tenderness that nearly made the tears come.

"I was walking down from the hills, a bit late because I had some sick ewes to attend to. This man spied me and asked me to ride along with him and break the news to you," Oliver said.

She nodded. She had forgotten to pull on her gloves. Oliver's fingers pressed hers with a warm strength that was reassuring. "Are you going into the church?" she asked.

"Aye, that is what I came for."

"Will you say a prayer for—us—then?"

His eyes answered, and she felt the last pressure of his hand over hers. Then he stood away. "Walk on," the driver called to the horses, and the carriage lurched into movement across the uneven ground.

The snow was coming more heavily now, but not blinding. Esther leaned back against the seat and tried to think, tried to concentrate on what she ought to say and do once she arrived. But her mind remained as blank as the faded sky through which the snow swirled and battered and steadily fell.

❧

Esther realized too late that no one else wanted her there besides Jonathan himself. Even Sarah stood at the foot of the bed with her arms wrapped around her sister, Diana, and did not look up when Esther entered the room. The younger brothers—Esther had scarcely ever seen them—stood awkwardly to the side of their sisters, their hands clasped tightly at their backs.

The squire's lady sat in a chair at one side of the bed, her hands up to her face, weeping bitterly. Squire Feather stood behind her, his hands clenched white over the edge of the chair.

Where was Tempest? She did not see him until she came to stand on the other side of the sick bed. He was there, on his knees, his hands and arms cradling the head of his brother, his face white and tear-stained.

"*Jonathan.*" Esther whispered the word, then she, too, dropped instinctively down. "I have come. I have come to be with you." She touched his hand. The flesh was cold and rigid, not supple to her touch anymore.

"I was certain you would." His voice came from a distance. "I have taken farewell of everyone but you, dear girl." He opened his eyes and she saw nothing and everything in them. "I can even do that, though I wish you were coming with me . . ."

She must have let out a cry, for he attempted to lift his hand to her, but it fell back on the bed. His eyes stayed on hers, a smile trembled on his lips, then his face went still. The lines of pain relaxed out of his noble features and there rested a peace on his face like a glow of benediction over the emptiness there.

Esther did not realize she was weeping. She turned and went from the room, though with each step she thought her legs might collapse under her. Rufus Sims stood by the doorway. "Will you take me back now?" she asked.

"So soon, miss?"

She shook her head. "This poor family is grieving. They do not need the presence of an outsider." She sighed. "They were kind to let me come at all."

"'Twas because young master asked. Because he insisted."

Esther bit into her lip. "He is gone now. I have done what I came to do. Please, sir, will you please take me back?"

He helped her on with her cape and they walked out into the snow. She felt no warmth at all, only a growing coldness, within and with out. She shut her eyes and rode through the cold waste in silence. *He is dead. He is dead.* The words were like frozen pebbles pressing against her mind. *He is dead. Everything good is dying, and I do not know what to do.*

At the manor house the mourning was bitter and wild. Mistress would not stop crying and the master would not speak a word. Diana, constantly dabbing at her eyes, would not leave her mother's side. When at length he arose, stiff-limbed and bleary, and assessed the situation, Tempest realized that he must take over, in some way take command. It was like a splash of cold water in his face. He was "young master" now, every person in this room had need of him, and arrangements—God help him!—*arrangements* for the funeral and for the care of his brother's body must be made.

He blinked his eyes against the enormity of it. Where to begin? He glanced from face to face, then made a decision. "Sarah." He addressed his eldest sister. "Would you come out into the hall with me, please?"

Once free of the room he gave her a few simple instructions to carry out. "There must be food prepared; we must make Father and Mother eat something to keep up their strength. And someone must speak with the servants; the stock have not been fed nor cared for. And then we—"

She put her hand on his arm. "It is Christmas, Tempest. There is food prepared in plenty. All the rest can wait for one day."

He blinked again. "Very well. Make sure a good fire is laid in the parlor. We'll get Mother and Father in there. And I still must send Sims into the village to find the doctor, and to talk to the minister and sexton to make preliminary arrangements—"

"Sims is not here. I believe he has left to take Esther back home."

Tempest blanched. "Did you even speak with her, Sarah?"

"No, no—"

"Of course not."

"She understands. That is why she had your man take her out of here."

Tempest nodded. Suddenly he was miserable. He could see her small, pinched face, her lips set, but trembling. *We snatched her out of meeting,* he thought. *What a shock it must have been to her. No warning, only Jonathan's words, Jonathan's terrible eyes. Then he was gone, and she was running away from—*

"Tempest!" Sarah was shaking him. He came to his senses and smiled. "Yes. I am sorry. Will you see to the fire and the tea, then? I will see to the rest."

And so he did, through every interminable hour of the interminable day. Weeks later his father was to say he did not know how they would have made it without him, and his mother told all her female acquaintances, "One can never tell about one's children. Tempest has grown up much better than we expected, and that day he was a strength to us all."

He did not see it, did not feel it. He simply lived from moment to moment, allowing no distracting thoughts, and certainly no feelings, to get in his way. In some vague sense he was aware that it was Christmas and that Christmas had been brushed aside for the ultimate tragedy that faced them. If Christ had been born to raise mortals from death, that would certainly happen at some future time that men's minds could not comprehend, and it was of no use to them now. Indeed, the whole celebration seemed a mockery of this reality that stared them all in the face.

Sims returned with a message of condolence from the minister and an assurance that he would see to all that was under his province to do. Two hours later Doctor Sterne arrived, having heard the sad news from his friend. He asked few questions, save when death had actually taken place, nor did he need to be instructed, but took at once to the task of laying out the body for burial, doing whatever such men do to prepare the dead for their last life's journey.

In sight of the spirit? Tempest wondered. *Jonathan's spirit lingering and watching somewhere close by?* He wondered with the intense, powerless abandon of a child where Jonathan's spirit was now. As night tapped on the windows with fingers of wind that flung handfuls of brittle gray flakes, Tempest realized dimly that the ordeal was, with the waning of the day, winding down. His mother was in bed with something the doctor had given her, his father was in his study with a whiskey, the house and animals were all settled, his brothers and sisters gone to their own rooms, the servants in bed. All save Betts. He stood stolid and patient outside Jonathan's door. Tempest felt an overwhelming desire to be with his brother.

"You are a good man, Betts," he said. "But you must be dead on your feet." He clapped his hand over the thin old shoulder. "Go to your rest, man. I'll stand watch for awhile."

He entered the room as a shadow might enter, with motionless tread. The silence reached out like a hand to take hold of him, but he felt no dread, no terror at being alone with the dead. He moved with ease to stand beside his brother's body where, hours before, he had knelt and cradled the breathing, intelligent form in his arms. *He is no longer here. He is truly among the living.* The words came into his mind, and remained.

He moved a chair close to the bed and sat down. He remained there a long time. Many intimations, many impressions came to his open mind. He was not aware of time nor of any other condition or atmosphere save that which surrounded him and held him in place. *Uphold me that I fall, that I faint not.*

He sat in the silence, at ease and resigned. And aware, above and within all else, that he was not alone. He was neither alone nor unheeded nor uncomforted as he sat through the night, attended by the solemn stillness of death in the room and the great wildness of the storm outside.

Chapter Twenty-Seven

Christmas Day marked an ending for Esther, not a beginning. To her there no longer seemed a threshold of hope. They buried Jonathan on a day when the snow had stopped and a weak sun shone down. Her father spoke words of comfort, words of spiritual power, but they meant little to her.

> *For since by man came death, by man came also the res-urrection of the dead. For as in Adam all die, even so in Christ shall all be made alive. . . . The hope of the righteous shall be gladness. . . . Blessed is the man whose hope is the Lord.*

She watched him, dignified and kindly, but she knew he was bereft, bereft as was she of all that mattered. After the services at the grave, Doctor Sterne and Janet came forward, Dorothea and her new husband, and sweet Evaline, sticking close to Sallie Brigman in case her husband turned up.

This is the first Christmas since I was a child that I have not sat in the little bee cottage eating sweets and listening to Sallie's stories while the fire popped and the kettle stewed.

She knew this was in part due to the time and manner of Jonathan's dying, but that signified only a piece of the whole. And would they be shoveling cold earth, snow, and ice on top of him if the Mormon strangers had not come and begun it all? She felt estranged from them, as well as isolated, their differences looming so much larger than all that had once bound them close.

She saw Sarah and Tempest only from a distance, though Sarah lifted her hand to her, and once, looking up, Esther caught Tempest's eye. She could not recognize the expression she saw there. His features looked drawn, almost fierce, like a pony newly broken, chaffing against the self-discipline that had been imposed upon him instead of having been drawn from within.

Even Tempest had a place now, a place of honor that he would grow into, she felt sure. If her father kept *his* position, would it ever be the same for him in this place again? If his superiors condescended to retain him, they would watch his every move like black vultures circling over-head. *Heaven knows*, she reflected, *this is a small enough parish. He has only stayed here because of Mother, because of her grave in the churchyard, and the memories of her presence everywhere else.*

Why can they not just leave him alone! she agonized. *What harm has he done?* But the harm *was* done, if not by him. She thought, with the vehemence of youth, *They have broken his heart.* Yet, for all her passion, her instincts were not far wrong, and sorrow clung to both father and daughter as they walked away from the open grave, and the flakes of snow, like so many whispering shadows, began again to glide through the sky.

The snow stayed, rendering daily tasks tedious and restricting all activity save what was necessary. For over three weeks storms raged inter-mittently, day and night. January, always a long month, seemed to crawl with the maddening tediousness of a snail. The inhospitable skies and the more inhospitable landscape shortened the radius of comings and goings; yet, in the village itself, the Saints managed to keep in daily touch with one another, and plans went forth for some of their number to have place on the ships that would sail, perhaps in late spring.

Doctor Sterne thought that projection unlikely; no one in their little band possessed enough money for passage as yet. Perhaps the later departures in summer, or even the *following* spring after another year's harvests had been gathered, would be more realistic; though he shied from putting forth such a suggestion that would dampen spirits and even hope. He, himself, would stay as long as he was needed, to help all that he might, though at times a desire for Zion would overwhelm him and make him wonder how he would ever be able to wait.

Dorothea Whitely Bidford had no desire to emigrate to an unknown country, but Lucius did. She was just becoming comfortable with her new home and her new status, and she felt it permissible at least to encourage him to wait in the wings and let some of the others try the business out first.

Zachie Kilburn fluctuated hot and cold. There were times he felt a certainty that he could sell his blacksmith shop for a profit and amass enough to take his family of seven to Zion. But then there were days when he broke a wedge or auger and the chimney in the house started leaking, and he wondered how he would ever make do. Louisa encouraged his doubts, though always in a subtle way. As Zachie's confidence waxed, so waxed her fears. Yet, she must *not* let him know; he would be so ashamed of her. If only he did not have such a passion for this religion, she could hope that it all might settle down or wear off a bit. Yet, knowing her husband as she did, and watching his devotion to matters of the Spirit intensify, she entertained little hope. One day at a time, one day at a time, that was all she dare anticipate as the winter wore on.

With Michael and Hannah Bingham, nothing save the safety of their unborn child was as important as this trip to Zion. Michael worked round the clock it seemed, filling every commission he could get his hands on, and the little stack of money piled up. They were already a part of Zion and of Zion's work in their hearts.

In much the same way, so was Paul Pritchard and his family. To sell his mill, which had been in the family for four generations, would be a sacrifice if he let himself think about it. But he had already made contacts in both of the neighboring villages, knowing some men who were both interested and in possession of means. He hoped to pass on a different legacy to his son and daughter, and to other children who may yet come, and he kept his sights on that goal while he and Paisley made their plans together and trusted the rest to the Lord.

Meg Weatherall had her winter's store of herbs in readiness for most of the common ailments: horehound with honey for sore throats and colds in the chest; lovage to ease rheumatism, stimulate the kidneys, and sweeten the bread; marjoram to aid digestion and expel poisons from the body; sweet cicely as a laxative; pennyroyal, tansy, balm, and rue for tonic, which she sold by the jug. Her skills would find place in the new land; she felt certain of that.

Peter Goodall wanted nothing more than to send his two granddaughters to Zion. He expressed as much to the doctor, who assured him that they could travel with any one of the families, if it came to that. One afternoon, during a thaw, his granddaughters scurried over to Sallie's, their cheeks glowing with the cold, their words tumbling over and across one another, as they discussed this possibility that they might make it to Zion with the rest, after all.

"You could travel with Evie here," Sallie said, once they had quieted down a bit. "She intends to go thither herself."

They eyed her up and down and decided they liked that idea. No one was as gentle and kind as Evaline Sowerby.

"Indeed, she has been doing every bit of work she can get her hands on, just to make a hae'penny or two to add to her hoard." Sallie's eyes sparkled as she spoke, for, in truth, she was proud of the girl and hoped that she would make her way to a new life and a chance at happiness, away from the harsh times she had known. One thing that worthless husband had given her was a knowledge of leather, and Evie had become a very skilled glover in her own right, a skill that would serve her well wherever she went.

"Sam and Meg have as good as adopted that Roger lad," Evaline said softly. "He'll be going with them. We ought to try to make the same boat."

She was teasing them. Both girls colored a little and Mary's dimples showed prettily as she smiled. Sallie, looking on, wondered at the revolutionary newness that was going on here. Mormonism—a new way of life. Zion—a place they were suddenly all longing for, whose existence they had not even dreamed of less than a year before!

So it goes, she mused. *They are busy as my bees will be in the springtime. But right now it is all in their thoughts. So much ground has to be covered between the wishing and the doing!* She knew that well enough. She knew there would be many challenges and many surprises before it all came to pass.

Those weeks were quiet weeks at the vicarage. Esther took to her needlework with a vengeance at those times when her mind was in too great a turmoil to read. She forced all desire away from her thoughts and concentrated on making her father as contented as possible. Because of their enforced closeness, there were occasions when he drew her into his confidences again, but these were guarded and few. Some evenings, when the heaviness became too much for them, Esther would read aloud from the old volumes of poetry, or from Thackeray, Jane Austen, or Dickens, and then their own burdens would be buried beneath those of Oliver Twist, Anne Elliott, and the sisters Elinor and Marianne.

A month had passed since Jonathan's funeral, and Esther had heard nothing from the big house. Just when she was beginning to let go, to accept the inevitable, there came a knock at the door and Pearl's voice in conversation with another whose tones were familiar to her.

Pearl entered. "A gentleman to see you, miss. Squire Feather's son; Tempest, I believe, was the name."

"Sit him in the parlor, tell him I shall be there directly." She wanted to gather her wits a bit before seeing his face and having those scrutinizing eyes play over her features.

When she walked into the room, he rose and came toward her. He appeared thinner, and a gauntness haunted his cheekbones and the depths of his eyes.

"Thank you for receiving me." His voice was like sunlight upon water, like the water itself rippling easily over warm stones. "How have you been faring, Esther? You look pale and house-ridden."

"As indeed I am." She smiled; she could not help it. They both sat down again, at ease. "Sarah and the others, how are they? Your mother?"

"The squire's the worst. Jonathan was the goodness in his life, if there's any sense to that, and now he can't seem to find that side of his nature—call it back from following after his dead son."

Esther shuddered. "I am truly sorry."

Tempest nodded. She had thought his eyes were blue, but in this lack of direct light they appeared a dark gray, as deep and unfathomable as a storm sky.

"Ill luck for Jonathan to die at this time of year when there is so little work to be done. My father cannot lose himself in good, cleansing labor."

"Nor you. 'Tis a pity." Esther sighed.

"Ah, I have nae come to greet and moan," Tempest said suddenly, with some life to his voice.

"Greet?"

"'Tis the Scottish word for grieving and mourning. I did not come for that." He straightened his back and sent her a purposeful look. "I came to set eyes on you, lass." If she colored beneath his blunt words, he took no notice. "I had need of the sight of you, after these long weeks in that house. And—" He hesitated. "I have something for you— something Jonathan wanted you to have."

He drew a package out of his deep coat pocket and began to unfold the wrappings that revealed an octagonal wooden box some four or five inches in diameter and height. She put her hand to her mouth; she had taken note of it in Jonathan's room many times.

"I cannot." She shook her head.

Tempest leaned closer. "There are keepsakes in plenty for his family, Esther. This he wanted for you." He held it forth and she noticed the amber ring on his finger, the ring his brother had worn. He followed her gaze. "Aye, the dead move on, where there is no buying and selling, no eating and drinking, no wearing of jewelry and fine apparel." His voice had dropped low, but the emotion in it was only intensified.

"I cannot," she repeated in a near-whisper.

"*He does not want you to forget him, Esther!* You understand that."

She put a trembling hand to her temple. Tempest had spoken of his brother in the present tense: *He does not—he lives still—he needs you to remember him.* She nodded and held out her hand, her fingers closing over the smooth wood, tracing the faint carvings.

"There is more," Tempest was saying. "Open the lid."

Inside rested a miniature of the original owner set in a small oval frame. Esther touched it with a tentative finger; there were tears in her eyes.

"No need for words, lass."

She looked up with the earnest candor of a child. "Thank you," she said weakly. "I wish I could thank him."

"I miss him like the deuce myself," Tempest growled abruptly. "And I do not suspect it will go away."

"He need not be dead, if certain things had not happened!" Esther spoke the words vehemently, surprising even herself with her ardor.

"That ticklish subject again?"

"I mean it! I feel a great deal of anger and resentment—"

"You rave against conjecture and uncertainty."

"That is not true! Vain people make changes they have no right to, altering, hazarding—even destroying—things of value which can never be brought back again."

"It is your heart that is wounded, Esther. Did the Mormons do that? I recall very clearly your championship of them."

"You know nothing of the matter—you know nothing of anything!" She raised her voice to him, but her lips were trembling.

"You are a rare girl, Esther, a rare girl." He rose to his feet. "May I call upon you again?"

She glared at him.

"It would help me, lass, through the winter."

How could he be denied?

"We shall see you then, from time to time," she murmured, "and perhaps Sarah, too?"

She raged inwardly as she walked to the door with him and bade him good-bye. *Through the winter,* she thought, leaning against the closed door. *That may be all the time I shall have left in this house, in my life here. And who else will be gone? All the fine ones will take their way off to Zion, and the whole village will sag with the terrible loss of them, perhaps even wither and die. And who, my brave handsome boy, will you be squire of then?*

❧

Christian felt himself gripped in the hold of winter, its cold hand on his heart. He had spoken of his situation to no one, save Esther. Doctor Sterne he had been careful to avoid. Oh, Nicholas Sheppard had come, blowing like an affronted whale, wallowing in what he considered vindication. *I told you so!* How frightfully Nicholas clearly wanted to say the very words outright. Instead he made it clear by other, just as painful, ways.

"Kindness never gets you anywhere in matters of religion, my old friend. You ought to know that. Opened the door to them, didn't you? Opened it to betrayal and trouble—on your own head, not theirs."

"Christ said that we ought to do unto others as we would wish to be done to ourselves."

"You know he was not speaking of *these* circumstances! You had the church to protect, and your *living*, man! Think of that."

"'Pray for those who hate you and despitefully use you,'" Christian quoted.

"Have you some of the martyr in you, for heaven's sake? Be realistic now and look well to the mess you are in."

So went the tedious conversation, back and forth, forth and back, Christian taking a bleak compensation in baiting his neighbor, revealing the man's virulent self-interest and hypocrisy.

It all came to naught. Sheppard, certainly, went away feeling the smug elation of superiority that was essential for his well-being, Christian merely that exhaustion laced with hopelessness that had beset him of late. His choices were narrow and self-effacing, every one of them. Yet he would not look beyond. *He would not!* He fought with himself, and the solitary battles were grim and terrible indeed.

Chapter Twenty-Eight

After several false starts, spring came on in earnest. The river ran to her banks, swollen with melting snow from the high fens and hills. A sheath of green blanketed the hedgerows, where the earliest flowers—celandine, with its butter-colored petals; wake-robin; and stitchwort—were standing forth, with primroses still hiding modestly in their shade.

The birds were busy re-creating their world anew, as they did each year. The linnet and robin and all the thrushes were preening their feathers and building their nests. The cruel little boys who went bird-nesting would not touch the robins and wrens, for they were believed to be "God Almighty's friends." Martin and swallow were likewise protected, and the throstle thrushes, though their numbers were many, were considered almost sacred in the village which bore their name.

One could *smell* the sun, for the air was as warm and new as the grasses pushing their tiny green heads through the knots of black soil. All was new, all was washed clean and watchful for the many small miracles each day would bring.

Mud was the common side of spring, the unattractive reality that accompanied the wonder of beauty coming alive, reborn. It choked the

village streets, the lanes were ankle deep in it, and the women took gratefully to wearing wooden pattens that would lift them inches above the
morass.

It was early for the fields to be worked, so there was a general inven-
tory and cleaning of tools, household as well as those used in field and
shop, and a turning out of linen and bedclothes—all that the winter had
rendered unhearty or stale. Some of the houses were being freshly white-
washed without, while the table and floorboards within were scrubbed
to the color of pale straw, and housewives polished their grates and their
candlesticks, wax-encrusted during the long winter months.

The mud did not stop the children from launching into their games,
"London Bridge," "Oranges and Lemons," and "Here Come Three
Tinkers," one of the favorites of all. The smaller children played
"Honeypots, honeypots, all in a row! Who will buy my honeypots, O?"
and "Here Comes an Old Woman from Cumberland."

Half a dozen games would be gone through on any given evening,
but there was not a single one of them in which Daniel Pritchard could
take part. His lame leg prevented him from running and jumping with
the rest, yet the itchiness of spring was upon him as it was upon them.
He might pretend indifference, even cheerfulness, but several times
Paisley had caught him sniffling over his flute as he attempted to divert
himself in his solitary way. Her heart went out to the boy, and it was all
she could do at such times to keep herself from bursting into tears of
compassion for the lad.

"'Tisn't fair," she would mutter to herself, "'tisn't fair or right, and
him such a good and faithful son. What will it be like when he grows up
to be a man and starts to look for a wife? And how in heaven's name will
he support her, if he gets one at all?"

She harbored many fears concerning her son and his future, though
Paul had often said to her, "Leave him to God. I feel to do that, Paisley."

"God has more to do than to look after one lame boy," she would
scold back. "It is up to us to do that."

"He tells us not a sparrow falls without Himself taking notice. Do
you not take that, then, for absolute truth?"

Such words silenced her, but did not truly reconcile her, for in her heart she still thought: *Perhaps He might take notice, surely, and feel sorry, and grieve. Yet is it his purpose to do something about every poor sparrow and every poor child?*

✐

The bees were awake, and Sallie took her orders, more or less, from the bees, who cleaned out the debris of the hives themselves, stocking the central cells with eggs and larvae, others with "bee bread," a mixture of honey and pollen. They would soon be ready to swarm. Sallie, through the years, had grown sufficiently watchful and quiet in her patient way to have sometimes heard "the queen's song," that curious piping sound which emanates from her being and controls the bees of her hive. But the new swarms must be followed, caught, distributed or settled into new homes of their own. It was one of the busiest times of the year for Sallie, and she thrived on the work, thrived on the closeness to her bees, for were they not at the very core of Nature's wisdom, regarded with due reverence from the earliest history of mankind 'til now?

Rose's baby was another miracle that she boasted of that spring—a nose like her mother's; small, dove-sweet eyes; and a fuzzing of pale hair on the crown of her head. She was everyone's baby, the first child born into the church in this part of the kingdom, marking Throstleford as a place to be respected and remembered. They named her Grace, for had not the grace of God brought her to them, the crowning of the many blessings that had come into their lives?

✐

Esther felt the spring, flutters of sweet life within her own being, which she had no strength to deny. She had little to do in the way of work, for the parish employed gardeners to care for the grounds and extra maids to help Pearl with the added weight of cleaning work in the house. All securely organized, and herself with no part in it. She'd *heard* that Andrew had fared well during his stay in London and would be leaving to take a permanent place in his uncle's household before the month was up. She'd *heard* that Rose Dubberly had given birth to her daughter and named her Grace. She'd *heard* that there were six, possibly eight places still available on a ship bound for New Orleans, then Zion, scheduled to sail midsummer. She'd *heard* that Tempest Feather was not only settling in well but instituting measures that were looked upon by the most astute farmers and businessmen in the whole area round as canny and wise.

She *heard*, she *heard*! But it was all happening outside her, it was all happening to other people who had, for all intents and purposes, forgotten that she was alive.

✎

The Stragglers' Inn, though it was perched on the edge of such a small village, was nevertheless situated on one of the main roads between York and Durham, and there were travelers in plenty, all times of year. But the winter had still been winter and custom thin, and Harvey Heaton felt like a caged animal, keen for action of any sort.

He had heard his customers talk with admiration and envy of the price Paul Pritchard was likely to get for his mill. "He'll be takin' a goodly chunk of silver with him to the new world, all right," one man asserted.

"Aye, but we're up to lose the best miller we ever had," his friend complained.

Heaton thought this a good place to start, and he laid his plans carefully. Fire was the safest and the surest means of undetected destruction, he surmised. He drew only Smedley into the plan, along with his own sons. Smedley had grown a wild mustache over the winter, and his shaggy eyebrows stretched atop slanted eyes that were as calculated and wicked as a wild cat's. He would send Smedley in to do the actual job.

Getting hold of enough whale oil might have been a problem, but the timing was right for him to place a large order for the use of the inn over the next several months. He dare not increase it by much; he wanted no suspicion drawn to himself. Cannily, he did the opposite and ordered *less.* After all, spring was here and the nights would be shorter now. No one could try to finger him for any inconsistency; rather it would appear that he was frugal in his use of the stuff.

Then he contacted his friend up London way and gave him a generous commission to purchase more oil for him there. That one, delivered discreetly in the dead of night, would never go on the record books, you could be sure. He was pleased with himself.

Now to the time and circumstances; these must be most carefully seen to. April was nearly over when the opportunity presented itself. Part of the roof on Adam Dubberly's cottage had fallen in. The Mormons were gathering to repair the roof and whitewash the walls and who knew what else while they were at it. But the word was round that there would be a meal and dancing to round off the working, right there at the cottage, in the bare fields that had not been plowed or planted as yet.

Heaton bided his time, though the hours of the day seemed interminable. He told Smedley in careful detail exactly what he must do. Darkness still came down quickly enough; in fact, he noticed a slender wind had blown up toward evening, and he grinned at the thought of what further mischief that wind might do.

The oil was to be sprinkled only in the mill itself, not in Pritchard's living quarters. No, Heaton wanted this to look like an accident. Perhaps the house would catch, too, but if the mill was destroyed, that would be loss enough to the braggart.

Smedley was already set up in a well-equipped wagon in the woods past the mill, waiting for nightfall. Heaton had his own alibi in hand; he would spend the evening with friends at an inn in Appleford, past Bunbury, and safely out of the way.

⟨∞⟩

The day went as planned. The wind did not rise until near evening, so the work had gone easily, and, nearly all of the Saints having gathered, they had accomplished even more than they'd planned. Not only was the roof and the whitewashing completed, but the chimney was cleaned, Michael Bingham had repaired a broken table indoors, and

Zachie Kilburn had mended and strengthened the sled Adam used for hauling things out in the yard.

As the sunlight thinned and the first shadows slanted across the meadows, the men put their tools away and sent Daniel to tell the women they were setting up tables so food could be brought out.

It was then that Daniel realized he had left his flute back at the house. He remembered setting it down on a barrel in the mill in order to help his mother carry things out to the wagon. Now what would he do when the ladies wanted him to play a lively tune or two for them?

He confided his frustration to his father, and Constable Johns, overhearing him, offered cheerily to lend Daniel his horse.

"Don't think I could manage him, sir," the boy replied, coloring slightly.

"Then jump on afore me, and we'll go together," Wilford Johns suggested. "We'll be back in two shakes of a lamb's tail that way."

Daniel was elated. It was a treat to sit astride the constable's tall horse and move with such smoothness and ease. The wind on his cheeks cooled him down. He leaned into it and closed his eyes, glad for this bit of luck.

Smedley was nervous from the start. Alone in the mill, he was aware of an awful silence and the feeling of eyes watching him. *Do the thing quickly,* he muttered to himself, *and be gone.* He doused a stack of grain sacks, and another, then spattered the crude oil aimlessly.

He had matches in his pocket, but Heaton had instructed him to find a lamp about the place and smash it, so that it looked like it might have been a natural accident of some sort that set off the blaze. But deuce if he could find one. He muttered under his breath as he kicked and pulled things about. He ought to have waited until it was a little darker, perhaps, but he was in a fever to get out of there quickly before someone came back, or the storm, which was blackening over the far fells, came on the tail of this wind.

Daniel and the constable felt the wind gather and growl at their backs, as though urging them on. Wilford Johns was spooked by it a bit, though he would never have told the lad that. But Daniel knew. He heard voices of his own in the strong current of air, and they prickled the hairs at the back of his neck.

At last, finding nothing, Smedley drew the matches from his pocket, struck one against a wood beam, and watched the blue flame flare up. Without thinking, he dropped it at the spot closest to his own feet, then did a quick two-step back as a line of fire spit its way across the floor-boards. He lit another and tossed it as far as his arm could manage. The pile of sacking was separated from him by the lengthening flame. It would catch in time, and the whole place go up neatly enough; of that he was sure.

He threw one more, watching a new flare hiss into life, backing his way out for a bit, but still watching in fascination the eerie effects of his handiwork. Then he suddenly turned, head thrust forward, with nothing in mind but to get safely out.

As they pulled into the yard, Constable Johns saw Smedley and grunted under his breath. There was nothing to warn him of trouble save the shadowy man. "Stay here, lad," he cried as he pushed Daniel half-roughly off the horse's back. "Look sharp. I'll be back."

The last words were swallowed by the breath of the wind. Daniel steadied himself and coughed. There was debris in the air, and a taste of moisture. He wet his lips. Constable had said to stay here, but he felt he ought to duck into the mill, quick like, and catch up his flute while he still had light.

He perceived the trouble through every nerve in his body before he was all the way up the stairs. He could smell the fire before he could hear it, and hear it before it lashed out to his sight with tongues of red flame.

He did not think of what to do, but seemed to know instinctively.

He found himself kicking at anything at all that stood in the path of the flames as he made his way over to where his father kept three large barrels of water. He grabbed for the hatchet that hung above them and brought it down with a splintering, cracking sound time and time again until water began to ooze from the opening. He tried to drag it out, but the weight was too much for him, so he struck again and again until the opening was enough for him to thrust in one of the small buckets that also hung there, fill it with trembling hands, tug it out through the opening—the weight of the water dragging against it—and throw it on the nearest flame that he came to, going back to repeat the process over again.

For a few moments he thought of nothing, was aware of nothing. Then, of a sudden, it seemed that the heat struck out at him like the huge, rough tongue of a serpent. He took the bucket he had just filled and poured it over his own head, feeling relief at once. A thought came to him, and he somehow lifted his body up until he was kneeling atop one of the other barrels and, with all of his weight, he shoved the open barrel, once, twice—with feet, then with his shoulder—a third time, until it was rocking—until it was off-balance—a fourth—until it toppled over with a crash on one side, splitting in half a dozen places and pouring its precious liquid toward the rivers of flame.

He jumped down, aware of a sharp pain in his lame leg and another pain in his arm, and made his way to a bin that he knew was filled with dozens of coarse burlap bags. He thought he might smother the flames with them, if he worked quickly enough. He did not even see Constable Johns enter the smoke-dimmed interior. His first awareness came when someone pushed him aside, reached into the deep bin, then shoved an armful of bags at him, the weight making him stagger. But he stumbled forth to do what he had purported. Over and over again he spread a bag over a spurt of flame, stamped it down with his foot, or bent over and beat at a place until the air was all gone and the red flames were blackened out.

He was not aware that the constable had opened the other barrels of water and was dousing much of the flame. Nor did he see the storm gathering dense and murky above them, blotting out the deep blue of the evening sky under which the Saints had hoped to eat, dance, and celebrate. He did remember a throstle, blown by the wind, flying past the black hole of a window. He did remember a face bent above his, all dim and wavery before his hot eyes. Then the whole world snuffed out like a candle.

☙

When next Daniel opened his eyes it was to see his father's face, and the doctor's beside it, their eyes smiling and kind. He remembered well what had happened. "The mill—" He asked the question, but the words did not seem to come out right and his lips hurt in forming them.

"You are safe in your own bed. Lie still," Doctor Sterne answered, to his surprise. "You were burned quite badly, Daniel, but we've bandaged you up bravely and you ought to do well."

He was, in truth, more concerned than he let the boy see, and when Daniel struggled again, trying to speak, Archibald leaned close, realizing in a rush what the distress was. "The mill is saved, lad, by and large, thanks to you and the constable."

"Thanks to Daniel first and foremost," he heard Wilford Johns say.

"And thanks to the storm," his father added. Daniel could see, though dimly, that there were tears in his father's eyes.

Inside his own head he was thinking, *This is all thanks to Heavenly Father, really. He helped from the beginning, and he sent the storm.* But he could not form the words, nor even keep his mind on them; everything before him turned dim and drifty again.

"I would like to give him a blessing," Doctor Sterne told his father when Daniel went unconscious another time. "It will give us an edge I believe we shall need."

Paul Pritchard nodded. "An edge, you say? Is that what we pray for— just a mite beyond what we, ourselves, can do?"

Archibald sensed a terrible shame shudder through him; he felt justly chastised. "Forgive me. I truly want God's help, but feel somewhat uncomfortable yet asking for it in this way."

"I understand." Paul's voice was sober. "'Tis a remarkable thing to realize that we have permission, nay, authority, to act for Deity and to literally call down His blessings in such a way."

They began preparations, but Archibald felt a powerful impression to remove himself from the others and seek the guidance of the Spirit. Walking outside he noticed that already some of the men were hacking away at the charred and broken mill beams, and shoring them up with others that still were sound. The storm had come, everyone agreed, out of nowhere, a cloudburst that found access through the collapsed part of the mill's roofing and helped to put out the flames and prevent them from spreading. Then, nearly as soon as it started, the heavy rain stopped. People pondered the circumstances at length, but they did not do much talking about them.

Archibald found a tall, dripping tree, under whose branches he could attain some protection, and offered up the prayers of his heart. The turmoil of his mind must be settled if he were to hear anything stronger than the beatings of his own heart. As he continued to pray, the weariness that had been upon him lifted; his mind became quiet and clear. He believed he could perceive the love of Heavenly Father for this little gathering of His children, here in this village in the core of England, who had raised their desires and their faith to Him, trusting and eager to do his will.

When he returned to the boy's room, only the lad's mother and father were waiting, but he called Zachie Kilburn in to anoint the lad's head with oil. Daniel opened his eyes. "I thought you were giving me a blessing," he said, and his voice was clear.

"Yes. You've no objections to it, have you, Daniel?"

"I've been waiting so long!" he replied, and there was the brightness of tears in his eyes. "Doctor Sterne," he continued, "while you are asking God to heal my burns, will you ask Him to heal my lame leg?"

The room went still; no one spoke, no one ventured any response, and Archibald Sterne did not look round. He did not need to. He met the eyes of the suffering boy. "Do you believe God can heal your leg, Daniel?"

"I have talked to Him about it. I know He can heal it, Doctor; I know that He will."

Doctor Sterne no longer thought of himself and of what he was doing. He closed his eyes, spoke the sacred words, and opened his mind to God, knowing this, above all, was his role in what was happening: he was honored to be a mouthpiece through which a loving Father intended to speak to His son.

He could never recall any of the words he spoke that day, but Paisley remembered them all. She wrote them down before she went to bed that night, or, rather, in the wee hours of the morning. Many long years after that, when Daniel was a man and his mother had been laid to rest beside her husband, he came across her thin, small book and read the faded words of testimony and gratitude, written in her cramped, careful hand. He copied them out in his own hand, seven times over, for each one of his children to have. But only his wife was in the room with him at the time to see him clasp the fragile pages to his breast and cry into the night like a boy.

But in those first moments as a boy still, when Daniel opened his eyes, he knew; he had felt the change in his body. When he met Archibald Sterne's eyes, he saw that the doctor knew, too. "I wish I could stand up this moment," he said, "but my arms hurt too much."

Tears were running down Doctor Sterne's cheeks. "The last price you will have to pay, lad. The very last time."

And so it was. The next morning the fever had left, the morning following the burns were no longer seeping, two mornings after that Daniel stood on two legs that were straight, two feet that were placed firmly and evenly on the ground. He glanced at his parents, who were watching him intently, then took a first step. There was no pain. There was no twist to the leg bone, no humping and rolling of the hip bone. He took another step, and another, and another—then several, more rapidly. His sister, watching from one corner, and Doctor Sterne from another, ran toward one another and clasped arms in a kind of dance. His father's eyes closed, and Daniel knew he was praying. He was praying himself. Like a song of praise he was praying. *I can feel God's joy,* he thought. *I can feel it as surely as I can my mother's when I look into her eyes.*

Thus was Doctor Sterne looked upon by the citizens of Throstleford as a man of God, well and truly; no one doubted it anymore. Some sent their children to wait beside his buggy when he was out doctoring, just to catch sight of the man. Some expected him to look different, but he didn't, though perhaps, it was decided, more gentle and kind. People stopped muttering about the Mormons, but took a step back, in a sort of awe. *Our own doctor!* The women, and even the men, were coming up with stories about him that they suddenly remembered, each one more glowing and wonderful than the last. *A healer among us . . . I always said Doctor Sterne was a terrible good man . . .*

There *were* some inclined to blow off the whole thing, and there were a few who thought dark, tortured thoughts about what had happened, and about how their own plans fell through. Harvey Heaton would have liked to tell Smedley to clear off; he did not want to set eyes on him for at least a year and a fortnight. But Constable Johns had taken the matter in hand, and Smedley talked enough to assure Heaton that he, too, was in the hot seat and had best mind his manners from here on out. The constable had been required to return to the mill to help put out the fire, but he had seen Smedley's clothes close enough to identify him, and the back of Heaton's wagon as it lumbered out of the trees. Nothing could be proved—nothing needed to be—and when Constable Johns stood facing the angry inn owner, they both knew that.

Heaton knew at heart that it was his own fault. He had been a fool to trust Smedley, and he was paying for that in humiliation, the most bitter sort of humble pie. Over the next weeks he became as testy as a caged beast, and he took out his ire on his sons. Marjorie knew she had nothing to fear from him, as long as she kept out of his way. He needed her services too keenly to do harm to her, or to force her to pack up and leave. But it was his youngest son, Ben, who bore the brunt of his cruelty, and she could scarcely bear that.

"Go away," she told him, every time they were alone together. "You do not belong in this place. You are a good worker, and I daresay you could find a situation with ease."

"The old man would come after me."

"He would not. I suppose he would wash his hands of you, because of his pride."

"'Cause of his pride, he would come after me and kill me."

It always ended like that. And she feared for him, and she could do nothing about it, however she tried.

April, light on her feet—dropping blue bells, anemones, and marigolds from each toe and heel print—tripped across the fens and over the far hills one day. And the villagers, waiting and watching and planning, welcomed in the May.

Chapter Twenty-Nine

❧

*E*sther knew the way May Day would proceed—she had since she was a child. The old women of the village organized every aspect, from the garland and the maypole to the choosing of the May Queen and King. She, herself, had been honored as Queen of the May when she was fifteen. Now there were younger girls to carry on the tradition, and she was glad. She cared most of all for the bare-footed dancing around the beribboned pole, dancing and weaving to the same tunes her ancestors had sung. Being older, she would trail at the back of the procession as the children went forth, then the Queen in a white veil encircled by a daisy crown. All would bear garlands of flowers before them, containing masses of cowslip, for yellow flowers were considered lucky, and cowslips themselves were often made into love potions. The primrose, too, was seen in abundance, for it signified good luck, and the children left blooms of it on the doorsteps to encourage the fairies to bless the houses, along with cowslip balls, given to many of the old people who would faithfully carry them to keep witches away.

When Esther was seventeen, and much enamored of Andrew, she had the good luck to find a primrose with six leaves, and had chanted the encouraging lines to herself: *The primrose, when with six leaves gotten, grace maids, as a true love in their bosom place.* Now Andrew would no longer speak to her when they happened to pass on the street, and in a few weeks he would be truly gone from her life. As Jonathan was; as her mother was.

Bringing in the May always made Esther think of her mother. For the first place the May procession visited was the rectory, and her mother would receive the happy youngsters with glowing cheeks and an armful of blossoms she would scatter among them—for good luck, she said. *For blessing!* Esther could still hear her mother's voice cry out the words, and remember the fragrance of her skin, more sweet and fresh than the flowers themselves.

The children would be gone then, from rectory to the squire's house, then through the village streets, with the wind of May, soft as a fairy's wing, fanning their cheeks: *Come see our new garland, so green and so gay; 'Tis the firstfruits of spring and the glory of May.*

Later there would be bonfires lit, more games for the children, and dancing and food, and the crowning moment of the Queen's day, when a Maid of Honour would snatch the crown from the King's head and another lift off the Queen's veil so that the happy but uncomfortable young man may lean forward to kiss the fair lips of his love. "Again, again!" the young people would chant, and the King must repeat his chaste kiss, over and over again, as long as demands were made.

Oh, to be young and carefree, as it seemed she had been only last year! Esther sighed as her thoughts skipped randomly through the months of the year that had passed their hands over her, sifting her life like so much chaff in the wind, to be blown away, blown and tossed so that she could not grasp it to herself anymore!

Morose thoughts for a May Day, she chided herself. *I will plait my auburn hair round with daisies and wild roses and sprigs from the may tree, or the hawthorn, to bring in the May. I will not pine and grieve for no purpose, and rob myself as only a headstrong and foolish maid can! Mother will watch to see if I am happy, and be glad of it herself, I am sure.* So thinking, she moved lightly and swiftly, and hummed under her breath as she dressed.

❧

If there were separations still, Sallie meant to ignore them on this day. She went early to Lambson's Dairy when the air was awash with birdsong. As she had hoped, gathering there were women of the village whom she now called "sister," others old friends whose associations went back to when she was a child. New life stirring brought all souls together, if given a chance. Thus preparations for the May Day splendors went forward as planned, and it was as easy to work together as it always had been. The men had fastened the maypole with its streamers in place at the village center the day before. That would be their first merriment, as the sun rose over the high fells—all gathered together, with the maids vivid as colorful flowers and the young men like tall, slender reeds. Then the Queen of May would be crowned and the children would head off on their march: *A bunch of may I have brought you, and at your door it stands. It is but a sprout, but it's well put about by the Lord Almighty's hands.* All that was old and all that was new would meet together as one. Sallie recognized the power in that as few people did. She was grateful for one more May Day and one more spring.

Evaline awoke late, so Sallie had left her to straighten the kitchen and get herself ready in leisure after the sun was well up. She enjoyed the quiet and the aloneness; she was never alone anymore. And though Sallie was a lifesaver and the dearest and kindest of women, she did have a tongue that ran on like a bright, chortling brook from earliest morn until night! Nevertheless, Evaline was glad of the many tasks she could do to ease Sallie's rheumatic fingers and back. It pleased her to be needed, to be of real help.

With heedless ease she buttoned the frock round her slender figure, laced up her shoes, then braided her hair, weaving in blossoms of wind flowers and daisies and softly-coloured ribbons Sallie had brought home from Meg Weatherall's shop. "Traded for honey," she had replied when Evaline attempted to thank her. "This and half a dozen other things we are in need of, so don't ye go fretting yourself."

She hummed under her breath. She heard nothing to disturb her, but in the back of Sallie's garden a man was carefully making his way. Edwin Sowerby had happened to see old Sallie leaving that morning and he knew his wife was alone. He had waited months for this opportunity, and eager as a fox he had made his way through the back lanes and paths to the house set like a child's cottage amid trees and gardens—all the better for him. No one would see him and, hopefully, no one would hear him as he taught his wife a lesson. He knew he could put enough fear into her to make her come home, put her back in her place, and give up those highfalutin ideas of going off with the Mormons to God knows where.

He walked as stealthily as he could, for he did not want Evaline to be warned of his coming. If he heard the bees at all, it was only as a gentle background hum in his ears, so that when they came at him he had no warning and no time to take cover. He had no way of knowing that one of the hives was about to swarm, and the bees were irritable and restive. He could not know that the fear and malice he emitted perturbed them, that the odor of him maddened their instinctive senses to fever pitch. As Sallie often said, "Bees *know* if a person is a bully and a liar; the bees know like a shot if a man is mean. And they haven't a bit of mercy in them at such a time. It's the master mind behind them, part of the spirit of the hive."

Too late the reality of this was borne in upon Edwin, as the bees attacked from all sides. He brushed wildly at them, he ran, cursing, away from them, but that did not dislodge them at all. With his arm over his face to protect it, he rolled in the grass, but there were a dozen insects waiting for every one he crushed or destroyed. He was whimpering now, crawling on his knees into the low tangle of bushes, tortured with twistings of sharp spring thorns. He braved their piercings if they could keep the bees off him and, to a degree, this ploy worked. He huddled there, smacking at the bees with foliage and sticks he tore from the hedge, shuddering as the waves of pain broke over him, and his eyes swelled, and he gasped through a burning throat for breath.

❧

Esther, running lightly toward the maypole in the village, did not see her father walk off in the other direction. He had left a note for her with

Pearl, and instructions that it would be late, he was sure, before he came home.

He knew Oliver Morris, the shepherd, would be down in one of the corries, perhaps with others of his kind, digging a circular trench and finding sacred wood for the fire. Very shortly they would begin to weave hoops of rowan or hawthorn for the lambs to pass through. He wanted to be there to help, and yet he walked slowly, tasting the morning as it came to him, harboring time like a well-loved guest within his heart, a guest that would soon desert him. He was glad for the shepherd, he was glad for the morning that could enfold him and defend him against a future that was coming all too fast.

For a good while Marjorie had not really known what was lacking in her life. She seldom had time to think about her own needs, if it came down to that. But spring—spring had the power to disquiet her. Even in the shadows of the inn yard, where the dampness of winter still lingered, she felt the pull.

"How long is it," she asked herself one night a few weeks before May Day, "since I have put on a proper gown and gone into the village? Oh, I've run errands aplenty, with a kerchief tied over my head, and a skirt and shawl that looked like something my grandmother wore!"

In the dim candlelight her combed out hair shone like spun gold, but her face, reddened by work over the hot fire, was not as pale as she'd like. "I could bathe my skin in a preparation of coriander water," she murmured, "trim my nails and wash my hair. I've that frock of flowered muslin that tucks in at my waist and makes me look thin; that would do well enough. And I know as surely as the next lass how to weave flower wreaths." She tapped her brush against the wood of the table on which her bit of a mirror was propped. "Why not? Why not be like the other young girls of my age for once?"

She made her preparations but kept her plans to herself until the last Sabbath before May Day, when Benjamin crept into her kitchen with a bump on his head that was already turning black and blue above an eye that had puffed up to twice its size. She swore under her breath. "Here, jump down, Cobweb," she said, addressing the cat, "while I bathe this and fix up his face a bit."

He drew back at her first touch, and would not meet her eyes.

"'Tis no shame to have a woman take care of you," she reproached, reading his thoughts. "If this were a normal household you'd have a mother to look after your needs, yes, and even fuss over you now and again."

He quieted then, and did not wince beneath her ministrations. And, in those tense moments, the notion came into her head.

"Come with me sunup May Day morning," she suggested. "I'll be getting up early to do my chores and set food enough in the oven that your father will scarcely know I'm gone."

He blinked up at her; he had no idea what she was talking about.

"*May Day!* We'll dance at the pole with the others, and share in all the fine fare—richest food you'll have tasted since Christmas, I promise you. There will be games all day long, and a bonfire when the sun sets."

He was thinking about it; she could see from his eyes.

"And girls, the prettiest girls you can imagine, with white dresses and flowers at their waists and wound into their hair."

She wanted to cry at the expression that came into his eyes then. "Do you believe that I ought?"

"I think that you might. We'll be off so early that it will be hours before anyone can miss us." He was still hesitating. "And you can trot on home after the food, if you think you'd better, and not wait the day out."

So it was agreed, and it seemed she counted those last days by hours, so eager she was. A bit of fun, a bit of fancy—who, even Heaton, could be mean enough to take issue with that?

∞

Sarah spied Esther first, dropped her sister's hand, and hurried up to her. As soon as they had greeted one another, she asked the question that was first in her mind.

"Will you come to the great house with me, Esther? Father says we're to have such a bonfire as you've never set eyes on, and a feast for all. Mother." She twisted a lock of hair round her finger in a nervous gesture. "Well, you know how it is since Jonathan died—"

Esther hesitated. "Have you spoken to your father? Do your parents—"

"Yes, yes, they want you, they will be glad if you will agree to come."

Esther nodded, reluctant still. She had not been back to the squire's since Jonathan was buried. She did not want to walk through that hall—past that door, closed forever over a room that was empty, over a reality that was gone.

Sarah squeezed her hand. "I must go back to the others. But, thank you, Esther, I cannot wait 'til tonight."

Esther watched her skip off, "in fair fettle," as Sallie would say. Feeling guilty and small-minded even as she thought it, she wondered how much Sarah really missed her brother. She had another brother now who had stepped into his place, and she would be going to a finishing school somewhere on the continent come autumn—Jonathan had been only a small, if pleasant, part of her life.

What was he to me? Esther's heart asked, but she did not wish to deal with that question now. More and more people were approaching the maypole, singly or in couples, snatching a streamer that beguiled them and securing a place.

"Over here, lass. I believe I have the two loveliest ribbons, don't you?" Tempest beckoned.

Esther laughed lightly at the insolence in the handsome eyes and face. She took the rose ribbon between her fingers. "Have you ever danced round a maypole before?"

"Here on this common, when I was a lad, at the insistence of my parents."

She smiled. "I can imagine the discomfort of young boys at such times."

"Ah, but I have got over it," he assured her, voice sparkling as much as his eyes. "'Tis the Scots I have to thank again. They take dancing very seriously. Did you know there are war dances the men do to prepare them for battle? You have naught seen any significant cavorting until you have seen the sword dance."

"I am sure of it." She was speaking lightly, but the pounding of the heart within her was anything but light.

She glanced up to see Lucius Bidford approaching with his new wife on his arm. "Dorothea appears ten years younger than she did before she was married," she marveled, not realizing that she had spoken the words out loud.

"Is that so?" Tempest peered at the couple. "A magical elixir, then, marriage? A restorative and a grace."

"Do you make sport of everything?" Esther turned hot eyes on him, and he retreated before them.

"Aye, I believe that *is* what I have come to do. I beg your pardon." His voice was so sincere that she merely blinked back at him, not knowing what she should say. "If truth were known, I believe in marriage as the highest estate men and women can secure in this life. Mind, I had no good example when I was a child."

"Are your parents unhappy, then?" Somehow it seemed all right for her to ask the question; he was being so honest with her.

"Not unhappy—but not *happy*, if that makes sense. Thoroughly unsuited, as most couples are."

"What altered your opinion, then?"

"Watching my aunt and uncle in Scotland, seeing what real love and respect between a man and woman can do for an entire household— how it imbues everything and everyone with kindness and dignity."

"It was like that with my parents. I was only a child, but I felt it. I watched it happening before me."

"And neither of you has ever been the same since she left you."

Tempest spoke with a matter-of-factness so tender that it startled a few wayward tears into her eyes. "*You understand.*" She merely breathed the words, but he heard them, and reached out for her hand.

She let him possess it. His fingers were warm. With a sinewy grace he wound them around hers. They stood thus for a few moments, with no word spoken between them; there was no need to speak.

❧

Daniel Pritchard was up early, for he was to meet with the other children on the green. For the first time in a long time he was among them on equal terms, for the first time their world was open to him. When the other boys ran, for the sheer joy of movement, he ran with them, wondering at the ability of his legs to carry him along. When they skipped round the maypole, he skipped with them, feeling as light as the thistledown that blows up from the hedgerows. He laughed and he sang, and the others laughed with him at the sheer happiness and wonder they saw in his eyes.

Janet Sterne felt like a mere slip of a girl, light on her feet and carefree; it was the effect May Day had on her every time. Archibald thought her the most beautiful of all the women before him, with a stately grace that could not entirely conceal the girlishness in her that he loved. He tried to tell her so, but she blushed and kissed his cheek, laughing his words aside.

So many people here, young and old, he thought, *people I know well and care for. They are caught in the grace of the moment, feeling the strength of centuries of ancestors who went before them, men and women whose voices still echo over this very spot where they, too, were gay.*

Janet was loosing his hand and running to meet Mary and Martha. He watched her go, feasting his eyes and his heart upon the sight of her.

"We did it," Mary cried. "Martha thought we were too old"—she leaned close to Janet's ear—"but I say we are *just* old enough."

"And desperate enough!" Martha laughed in acquiescence.

"'The young maid who the first of May goes to the fields at break of day, and bathes in the dew from the hawthorn tree, will ever after handsome be,'" Janet quoted. "I admit that I did the same many times myself."

"And it worked for you!" Martha smiled.

Janet's cheeks flushed with color again, knowing their admiration of her. "Do not be silly," she said.

"Silly and hopeful," Mary sighed. "Let us hasten to the maypole and find a place—on opposite ends"—she started off at a light run—"beside some handsome lad we have never seen before in our lives."

≈

Marjorie had decided it would be wise to leave a written message for Harvey Heaton, as well as warm food. "I shall come back with you, I believe," she told Benjamin as they trudged along. "Don't want your dad brooding half the day over what I've left undone and thinking how I've slighted him." She smiled at the boy. "You look right splendid with your hair slicked back that way," she said, dodging a harmless blow he sent to cover his discomfiture. "Look! They're already gathering round the maypole! Grab my hand and we'll run."

≈

Oliver had shaded his eyes when he saw Christian approaching, but as soon as he recognized the figure he bent again to his work. It was not until the guest was within a few feet of him that he said, looking up, "Welcome, Pastor. I thought you might be coming out to the high fells one of these days."

Two other shepherds, standing at a short distance, nodded their heads at him. There were hot eggs and oat cakes on a griddle over the fire, and a kettle steaming with tea. "Take your ease, sir." Oliver scrutinized his friend carefully as he bound supple reeds round a circle of hawthorn branches. "Take all the time that you need."

≈

Evaline, humming under her breath still, unlatched Sallie's door, then pulled it shut tight behind her. Ah, but the morning was fair. Sun warm on her head, but the air as cool and fresh as the first morning on earth must have been. *No trouble as yet.* She felt hope, more heady than happiness, surge through her. For just this one day she would push fear away. Surely God, in His mercy, would not let the nightmare return.

Surely God, knowing her heart, would make a small place for her in this Zion of His.

Heel—an—toe, jolly rumble o, we've been up long before the day-o. The patterns were coming together now, like the shifting colors of rainbows above their heads. *To welcome in the summer, to welcome in the May-o, for summer is in-coming in, and winter's gone away-o.*

Esther threw her head back, and found Tempest's eyes upon her, and she dared to look back at him, drawn into the fire of his gaze, warmed by it—lighted by it, as a candle, as a consecrated candle she had carried into the church as a child. All things appeared beautiful to her at that moment—that trembling perfection of time—that she was to carry with her like a warm jewel during the long days ahead.

It was a taggle end of boys who found Edwin. He had crawled out from the bushes after a time and was half-stumbling, half-crawling toward his house in a daze of fever and pain. One had the presence of mind to stay with him while the others raced back to the village green and tugged at the doctor's arm, just as he was placing it round his wife's waist, prepared to give her a kiss.

Of course, he went with them. Of course, like an ill wind, the disturbance ran through the gathered revelers, and Evaline was called, a bit wildly. She came, pale and wide-eyed. Sallie was beside her, and Meg Weatherall right on their heels, both women with the remedies of centuries to apply to his needs.

"You can't take him to my cottage," Sallie lamented, "the bees will not have it."

"Take him home," Evaline said. "I shall look after him there."

"You do not owe him this," Sallie stated roundly. "He was there to do harm to you, Evie, because he knew I was gone."

"I am his wife." Evaline swayed on her feet, and Meg put out a hand to her. "At least for the time being, I must do my duty by him."

So it was arranged, and the women made up herbal preparations of alecost to rub over the bee stings, and borage for both fever and chills, and a poultice from burnet, which was much used in the Slavic countries to cure the wounds of their soldiers. The doctor, after examining Edwin, was worried about fever and possible shock. He had his work cut out for him over the next several hours, and the three women stayed at his side. All thought of spring and the joy and hope it brings was driven from their minds. Evaline, pale as a ghost, stood at times like a statue, at others she fluttered restlessly from one end of the room to the other, such an unhappiness in her eyes that they could scarcely bear to look at her.

The sun had retreated, the thin sky was turning a gravelly gray. Thus evening came on, darkening into night, and not one of them took notice of it at all.

Chapter Thirty

hose left at the green found the merriment they desired more difficult to fan into innocent life again. The children were sent off on their meanderings, oblivious, but the adults found their spirits subdued. Marjorie, however, determined upon one last pleasure, filled her plate from the table of delectable foods—foods she neither had to cook nor to clean up after. Some of the ladies smiled kindly and inquired after her well-being. The squire's handsome son, Tempest, smiled at her. "Marjorie, isn't it?" She nodded and dropped her eyes, feeling color rise to her face. "I am happy to see you here, enjoying yourself for once, eh? Out from under the old scoundrel's thumb."

There were others who had been kind, as well. The potter's son, freckled and sandy-haired and built slight like his father, had his own charm, and he had winked at her and tucked a stray blossom into the strands of her hair.

She noticed Benjamin was in a cluster of young people that included at least three pretty girls. Her heart warmed as she watched him. Given half a chance he'd amount to something fine, something any father could be proud of, she was certain of that. She ate each bite slowly, savoring the taste and the sensation of freedom that was like sauce to the meat.

❧

Esther felt resentment, like an errant flame, flare within her. She tugged her hand out of Tempest's. "It is those Mormons again, stirring trouble, and spoiling what ought to be."

"I would not say that. 'Tis *Sour Sourby*—did you know that is what people call him? He was born to make trouble, Mormons or no Mormons, you see."

"A convenient response, but not entirely true," she steamed. "For, without the Mormons, Evaline would not have left him, and all the rest of this would not have the least chance of happening."

He lifted a thoughtful eyebrow and regarded her. He could deduce some of the other circumstances that were playing havoc with Esther's sensibilities, but he did not like seeing her this way.

"Where is my father?" she demanded suddenly. "I have not seen him all morning. He ought to be here."

Tempest placed his hand on her arm, but she tugged away from him. "I shall just run home quickly and see if anything is the matter."

"May I come with you?" he asked. When she hesitated, he merely started off, with his long strides, and she had to walk hard to keep up. The parsonage looked quiet and cool tucked away as it was behind an expanse of trees, shooting up at their will. Esther sensed her father's absence; she knew before she burst in the door and confronted Pearl that he was not there.

When she read his note her hands began to tremble, and she dropped it as though it had burned her fingers. Tempest took it up in his own. "Why does this distress you—this much?" he asked, and the way he spoke was so tender that she had to blink tears from her eyes and stomp out of the house and away from him. But she heard him following discreetly behind.

After a few moments, he tried again. "Esther, what is it?"

She lifted her hands in a hopeless gesture. "I am unable to explain, and you would be unable to understand. You would have to know the whole history of his life, and the history of his heart."

"But as far as you can tell me—" His persistence, rather than annoying her, somehow engendered an assurance: he would not give up. His concern for her was real, and perhaps would endure anything.

"He has gone to the shepherd for help, a last resort—it is humiliating!"

"You cannot know that."

"I know that before this month is ended he will stand before a spiritual tribunal and be forced to defend himself—*defend his Christlike actions, heaven forbid*—and all on account of *them.*"

Spirited girls Tempest had known in Scotland; they bred them there. But the passion of this gentle woman tore through his heart. *Only pain seems to move her to passion,* he thought, *the pain and suffering of others.* He wanted to draw her into his arms and comfort her, he wanted to fiercely protect her, to make everything right.

"I do not wish to go to your father's house tonight," she was saying. "I wish to sit right here and wait until my father comes home to me." There were tears in her voice.

"You are not doing that. I will not allow it," he heard himself say. "It would ill please your father, and that you know."

She shook her head, and her voice when she spoke was so low that he could scarcely make out the words. "I cannot bear to be around people—I cannot right now."

He made up his mind without even thinking. "I shall be back for you in an hour then. Can you change your clothes into something suitable for riding?"

She lifted her eyes to him, and the trust he read there nearly disarmed him. "I had forgotten—I promised Sarah I would be there."

"I shall take care of that. An hour then?"

She was still gazing at him. His stifled breath burned in his lungs.

"An hour."

He turned on his heel and was gone from her, without looking back. She sat where she was for ten minutes or longer, then rose and walked into the house. She knew just what she would wear. Perhaps he would let her ride swiftly, so that the wind would lift her hair and cool her face and her neck and, after awhile, reach in and deaden the fears in her heart.

⚬

They headed away from the village in the opposite direction, avoiding Windy Strath and the higher moors where the shepherd's camp was. She did not know this land. She rode at his side on a horse the color of honey, and the animal seemed to sense her deep restlessness and respond. Tempest watched her closely, but he let her go faster and faster, until the wind lashed her hair and burned her cheeks and numbed all feeling and thought. A sensation of pure pleasure that nearly drew her out of herself drove her on and on. At length they were prevented from going further by a dense stand of trees with a fence just beyond. She drew her horse up with reluctance, and they both stood panting, and when she looked over at Tempest, there were lights again in her eyes.

"We had best return at an easy canter," he said. "Have some water first." He held out a leather pouch and she grabbed at it eagerly. "I am ravenous," she admitted.

"That will pass," he said, "but I will find you something to eat when we get back."

They rode easily for a while, until Tempest suddenly drew up beside an immense ash tree that stood at the edge of a field all alone. The last of the sun was filtering through its greening branches so that the light appeared almost misty and otherworldly. Esther caught her breath.

"Oak, ash, and thorn," he mused, "the very heart of England. As long as they stand all that is England will prosper and thrive."

"Yes, I know the old legends, too."

"But you take them lightly?"

"No, no, in truth, I do not. I fear rather the other way round." She sighed. She was thinking of her father and what place he would have here in the future, if any.

"We have done with May Day, you and I, in our hearts," he said, "but I must crave the indulgence of a few more moments that I might explain the gift I brought for you." He patted his breast pocket.

She could not pretend disinterest. It gave him pleasure to sense her anticipation. He drew a deep breath.

"Let me guess. You are going to tell me something about Scotland." Her open, girlish laughter caught him offguard.

"I will not allow your mockery to dissuade me," he teased in return. "I fear you will have to indulge me before the present is yours. In all of Scotland, stones, or *stanes,* are often considered sacred, or to have magical qualities. Chiefs are installed standing on a rock or a cairn, oaths are taken upon them, and the Great Stone of Destiny crowned the kings of Scotland for centuries."

"I have heard they can heal," Esther offered, "and protect against the Evil Eye. But are these not ancient legends, indeed?"

"With the power in them as old and as enduring." His eyes were dark, almost colorless. "And I have here—" He reached into his pocket and his long fingers searched there. "I have one of the Covenanter stones of 1639, which tumbled down of their own accord near the Scottish camp at a time when the soldiers sorely needed good fortune to be with them."

He held it up for her to see. It was an oval stone, nearly as large as a hen's egg, perfectly shaped, of a gray color that appeared almost blue, and lined with feathered strains of yellow that the sun's fingers caught and lit, so that they seemed to glow from inside.

"This was carried about in the pocket of one of the soldiers who was twice wounded but survived," Tempest continued, "and lived to bring the stone back to his sweetheart, who became his wife and bore him nine children, only five of which lived."

Esther sighed. "Have you any names?"

"Yes, I am coming to that. One of these children was a daughter, her father's darling, and the stone was given to her by her father on the day that her mother died. Her name was Mairi, and she in turn gave the stone to a daughter who bore her name. This second Mairi swore that the stone protected her and even saved her life upon one occasion, and she gave it, with some reluctance, to her only son when he was going off to battle."

"Thus the stone was returned to its original purpose or setting," Esther mused.

"So it was. And it remained in the hands of sons from then on, passing in time"—he paused—"passing in time into the hands of the Tempest MacGregor for whom I was named."

Esther studied him closely, her curiosity rising. "Did the stone come to your own mother, then, through him?"

"No, it remained in the hands of the sons—her brother, with whom I stayed when I was in Scotland. He gave it to me, said it ought to belong to the namesake of the man who had so highly valued it. *'You are most like him—'* he told me that often—*'and like, I believe, is intrinsically drawn to like.'*"

Esther was becoming confused. "This is very precious to you," she began, "and I thank you for showing it to me."

"Aye, but you know I mean more than that."

"You cannot," she protested.

He was smiling. "You see, I fear I have not told you all. In the beginning the stone was larger, but when it was in Tempest's possession its shape and size were altered. The story goes that at a time when he was being sorely pressed by his enemies, he took it out of his pocket and threw it, striking his foe in the head, but splitting the rock into two separate pieces, both of which he retrieved and had polished and shaped to perfection."

His fingers reached into his pocket again. "The other is much smaller," he said, "and when he found a woman whom he admired above all others, he gave it to her."

Esther was shaking her head. "This is madness. You are mad. I could never accept this! And, what are you trying to say?"

"I am trying to say that, for me, you are that woman."

"You have no right to say that!"

"I have every right." He put a finger under her chin and forced her to face him. "Love is neither courted nor bidden. Love, therefore, has her own rights."

"I will not listen to this!" Esther cried. "I will not permit it!" She dug heels into the horse's sides and attempted to pull away.

Tempest's eyes were smoldering, but he said very gently, "I did not intend to distress you. Perhaps I have spoken too soon." He tugged at the bridle of her horse and drew her closer. "But you are in need of the stone, Esther. You are in need of the love that it brings."

She lowered her head. She would not again look at him.

"There are no obligations on your part," he said. "Only the kindness of acceptance."

She shook her head. "Take me home. Please, I want to go home now, Tempest."

They rode the rest of the way in an awful silence, so heavy and oppressive that Esther trembled beneath it. When they arrived at the parsonage it was already gentled by shadows leaning in from the ancient trees and the even-more ancient stones that marked the narrow, shallow homes of the dead.

Tempest said nothing; indeed, he knew not what to say. He knew he had been unwise, been a fool, too intent on his own desires to see clearly—

"Tempest?"

He lifted his head. His eyes were still shrouded and cloudy. Esther was struggling, and he held his breath, waiting.

"I will not deny that I have tender feelings toward you," she said. "But, you are asking too much—and giving too much."

He drew her hand to his lips and kissed the gloved fingers.

"May I call on you tomorrow?" he said. "May I—*see you*, Esther?"

She nodded, tugged her hand away from his clasp, and slipped into the house, disappearing behind the frail buttress of a door, which may as well have been a barrier of rock and iron with its power to keep him away.

⮾

The flames had sunk to embers that smoldered orange and dull blue. Christian sat in a hollow of shadow with Oliver Morris. The sheep were quiet and the dog lay stretched between them. The scent of the shepherd's pipe curled into Christian's nostrils; that and the sharp smell of the fire mingled with a suggestion of grass and water, so that the minister sighed in temporary content.

Oliver shook out his pipe and bits of fire floated into the air. "I must be on my way," Christian said. "Esther will be worried. I can see her pinched white face now."

"Ah, the merry-making at the squire's will go on for hours yet."

"But I am not certain she is there. If she came back to the parsonage for any reason and saw my note for her—" He let his words trail into the silence where they were at once swallowed up.

"That one is too deep of feeling for her own good," Oliver responded.

"I fear I must agree with you there. But she will live life to the full, and is that not the price providence exacts?"

"Especially, it seems, for women," Oliver mused.

"Which brings me to thank you again," Christian said. He rose, shook the damp grass from his trousers and coat, and bent again to stroke the head of the collie. "Will you think about what I have asked you?"

"Yes—you have made it impossible for me to do otherwise. But, do not hold your breath."

Christian smiled and extended his hand. "Good night, old friend. You have shared with me something more precious than I can express."

❧

Some of the young people had talked Marjorie into making a tragic mistake; a simple, lighthearted decision, really, to go on to Squire's with them and dance for a spell. She hesitated—but when she saw the bright-faced girls tugging at Benjamin's shirtsleeves, teasing him forward, she nodded to him and went on with the happy troupe herself.

Harvey Heaton did not begin stewing until the afternoon waned and his maidservant did not return from the village, and then some of the men in the tavern told him his son—his spineless, soft-eyed youngest son—had gone with that saucy Marjorie and danced on the green, and flirted with the Mormon maidens. He could see it all in his mind.

When he could see that the sun was setting, he knew they would be lighting bonfires at Squire's place, and there would be more dancing and drink, and food—what bits that sluggard had left *him* had long since been consumed. The old bile rose in his throat. How dare she cross him? How dare she drag his son as her escort and make merry right under the nose of those Mormonites?

He fumed, and let indignation seethe in him until it became a flame in his belly and a burning in his chest. How dare Marjorie deal thus with him, after how good he had been to her? How dare she serve him like that? He kicked at the table legs, turned over a chair or two, and kept on drinking the strong whiskey his friends placed before him. When that girl got home, she would get what was coming to her, and then some!

The angry threats may have been all there was to it; Heaton might have slept it all off if Marjorie had stayed late enough, and if Cobweb had not curled himself round the master's feet like a cool gray shadow at just the wrong time—just when a couple of fellows who were in their cups had nettled the landlord and stung him with their attempts at contempt.

He bent down in a sudden swift movement and grabbed the cat by the neck, getting a red slashing of claw across his wrist that made him squeeze all the tighter so that the creature struggled in vain. Then it came to him, out of the murky hazes of his own mind. Still dragging the cat by the neck, he went to the cupboard behind the bar and shuffled through the junk until he pulled out a long length of strong cord.

He barked out a staccato order to one of his mates, who chuckled under his breath at what he saw coming. It took the man three times to manage to coil the rope into a noose and toss it over one of the beams. Then Heaton jumped on a chair and made a noose on the other end, fixed it firmly around the half-strangled neck of the big cat, and set it to swing.

There was a wave of raucous applause and admiration that shivered through the tables of drinking men. The cat's body twisted grotesquely, and one of those who laughed too loudly found his head clouted hard. The lovely gray animal twitched one final time, a tremble running like a breeze through the thick fur, and then it was still.

Heaton stared at it, cursing all women and all worthless sons under his breath.

Janet knew her husband would not return until late, so she forced herself to remain with the others and garner what sweetness she could from the day. She watched the children as they tramped back in happy exhaustion, but she had no heart for the intensified celebrations that would take place at the big house.

"I am going home," she told Dorothea, "to put my feet up."

Dorothea smiled. "An excellent idea, but I doubt I can talk Lucius into it."

Janet watched the two stroll away. This happiness that had come to both of them was a wondrous thing to behold. It made her feel all the more grateful that she was one of the lucky ones. She hurried away, anxious for the quiet and comfort of her own house.

Sarah was disappointed. She kept watching over her shoulder, hoping the two miscreants would return. She was piqued with her brother for cajoling Esther away from her, though she knew in her heart that friendship between girls could never compete with romantic interest. *How much of romance is there?* she wondered. At first she had thought it clever and benign to encourage it, but now she was not so sure. It was not that she got along poorly with her mother and sister; she was happy at home. But she was also restless, and she had wanted some interest of her own making, that belonged to herself alone. Harmless little Esther had provided that interest. But now?

Darkness intruded step by step, so that the fires burned brighter and higher, and Sarah, distracted with half a dozen duties, did not notice the lone horseman lead a riderless mount to the stables, where he unsaddled and tended to the horses himself.

∞

Marjorie knew something was wrong. Shortly after the bonfires were lighted she entreated Ben to come away with her, but he would have none of it.

"I'll get the daylights whipped out of me, as it is. I may as well lap up every last bit of the cream, Marjie." He grinned. "The way Cobweb does."

At last she went on her own, half-running through the darkening ash grove, cutting across fields, boosting herself over fences and finding openings in hedgerows, with this terrible urgency upon her which she could not understand.

As she grew closer to the inn, she felt something shrink inside her, and she opened the side door cautiously, glancing all round before she slipped in and pattered soundlessly down to the kitchen. She breathed a sigh of relief, the first part safely done.

Where would Heaton be now? Drinking upstairs with his cronies and the last die-hard customers, no doubt. Dare she put on her apron and go in as though nothing had happened amiss, and begin to see to her work? She decided yes, it would be the best of her choices.

The common room seemed dirtier than usual, but she had expected that. The smoke smarted her eyes. She put her head down and walked forward, avoiding eye contact but covertly searching for Heaton among the men.

He found her first, coming up from behind and grabbing her by the scruff of her neck. "Slunk back, have ye? Well, you're too late, missy, too late by half." He laughed between his teeth in a way he had that sounded more like a hiss and a threat. She twisted away from him.

"I'll get everything done," she said. "Don't worry. I'll work into the night."

"Generous of you."

"I've never had any time off," Marjorie blurted, "and I left you a note."

"*I* decide such matters, not the likes of you, girl. And do you think I'd let you go off with those Mormons—old Sallie and the doctor and the blacksmith, wretched lot of them—you and *my own son?* What in the name of the devil made you think that?"

His breath was foul with drink. Marjorie took a step back. "I am sorry," she said, her voice lowered. "I shall never do it again."

"Right there! And you're too late with your sniveling." Heaton's teeth parted in an evil grin that sent a chill down her spine. He clamped his hand around her neck again and with the other pushed her forehead back. "Look up there, will you, and see what happens when a chit of a girl tries to cheat Harvey Heaton. Look at what you've done, girl."

Marjorie screamed, and the sound was like shards of glass darting through the room. Some of the men put their hands to their ears, but the rending cry rose and rose until Marjorie crumpled suddenly into a heap on the floor and lay sobbing with her head on her arms.

No one spoke or moved. When at last Heaton took a few stumbling steps toward her, one of his mates muttered, "Leave her alone. Leave her be to cry it out, Heaton, for mercy's sake."

Heaton was glad of the excuse. He reeled away from her, and she lay like a scar on the dark floor, with the body of the dead cat still swinging above her head and a dozen sets of eyes staring at her, not unlike sorry and shamed little boys.

She never remembered getting up from that floor and making her way to her bed. Heaton never did make it up from the table on which his head dropped close to the candle that sputtered and ran rivulets and at last melted into a puddle of wax.

"I loved that cat, I loved that cat!" he kept muttering, swiping now and again at his eyes. "Curses on the girl! I never loved an animal in my whole life the way that I loved that cat."

Chapter Thirty-One

*E*sther awoke early. She had not spoken with her father the previous night. He had wandered in very tired and damp from the night dews, and she had seen him to bed, sensing that he was all talked out and could not tell her what was left in his heart.

She still felt the weight of yesterday's difficulties upon her as she roused herself and made ready for the day. It seemed May and the spring had come in dismally, with nothing to promise save more of the same difficulties. Then she remembered Tempest and a warmth swept through her, though it deepened her sense of confusion. What was he to her? And what could she possibly be to him? "Young squire" now, he should look elsewhere for a wife; he must know that. And, in cruel reality, what had she to offer? Daughter of a parson—daughter of a disgraced parson— who may very soon be kindly escorted out of house and home?

She shook her head as though to dislodge the thoughts from it. When she went downstairs her father was not at the breakfast table.

"Had me bring a tray up to his room," Pearl said darkly. "Doesn't eat enough of late to keep a bird alive, you know."

Esther knew. She played with her own food, her appetite blunted by Pearl's gloomy words. She wondered what had passed between her father and the shepherd up there on the hill. She wondered what plans her father might be considering right now.

≈

May came to be thought of as a long month by many of the villagers before it was through, regardless of spring and her wooing. Evaline was one who had no chance to pay the May any mind.

During the hours she sat beside her husband she worked at her gloves, her dexterous fingers knowing the motions by heart, moving almost of their own accord. She had planned to sell some of these at the county fair in June, and take the rest with her to Zion, where, certainly, she could find work as a seamstress. Doctor Sterne had paid the deposit to secure a berth for her; she knew he held the opinion that she ought to be one of the first ones to go.

Yet she wavered. Edwin would be sick in bed for weeks, the doctor had told her. Perhaps it would soften him, this suffering. Perhaps this meant that she ought to give him another chance.

She spent many of the quiet hours praying while her fingers worked, but it seemed that no answer came through. She would wait—she must wait—there was nothing else she could do.

≈

Marjorie was not thinking clearly. She had awakened before dawn, knowing she must get out of this place, and had packed her things in a sort of daze by the light of one candle. Tears coming and going, like a film over her eyes, blurred her vision and she nearly stumbled going down the steep stairs and out through the kitchen. At that point she sat down hard on the doorstep and started to cry.

It was here Benjamin found her. He squatted on his heels in front of her and took both her hands. "I've cut him down, Marjorie, do you hear me? I'm glad *you* didn't go back in there."

She sniveled, half-choking. "You cut him down?"

"That's right, and I washed and brushed his fur up nicely and laid him out proper-like in a box."

She clutched at the boy. "We have to bury him—but not here!"

"I daresay we can find a more suitable place. What about the edge of the churchyard, just inside the fence?"

Marjorie shook her head. "That's consecrated ground."

"The Lord wouldn't begrudge a foot of it to one of his own creatures—no wise could something that close to the fence be used as a regular grave."

So it was determined. Marjorie rose to her feet. She lifted her satchel.

"What you got there?"

"I'm leaving, Benjamin. Can't face one more day of your father. Not after—"

Benjamin grinned. "I am of the same humor, I've got my things out in the barn."

"But if you leave—"

"I know I said he'd come after me, but I don't think he will. I know a man in Cheapside, comes through here every year, and said if I'm ever in want of adventure I can come to him and he'll give me work." He patted his pocket. "Got his card with the address on it right here. *And* my last month's wages; I'll take no more."

"Will you ride the coach to London?"

"Thought it best to be well and truly gone before he wakes up." The boy's mouth twisted into a woeful expression. "Only thing he'll be mad about is being cheated out of the beating he would have given me."

Marjorie leaned closer and wrapped her arms round the boy. "God bless you, Benjamin. You are too good for the likes of him; you'll make your way just fine."

By unspoken accord, they moved swiftly, Benjamin carrying both his bag and the box that held Cobweb. But when they reached the churchyard the gate was closed, seeming to prohibit admittance. Marjorie leaned against the iron fence and thought, of a sudden, that even if no one noticed them digging, they would see the disturbance, the bare space on the grass the next day when it was done.

She sank down, feeling weary beyond words and wondering vaguely if she could sleep here come night.

"Be on your way," she told Benjamin. "I'll look after the both of us. You've got to go halfway to Bunbury to catch the stage in time."

"I can't leave you here, Marjie." He dropped down to his heels again. Then they both heard a sound, the muffled clopping of a horse's hoofs—a lonely sound in the still of the early-morning shadows.

"What have we here?" It was the doctor's tired voice that questioned them. Benjamin rose to his feet and, with no qualms, unfolded the whole matter to him. The doctor got down from his horse and lifted the tired girl to her feet. "You could come home with me," he suggested, "but it is very near dawn, and I know someone else who will be stirring soon and would not only be happy to have you but happy to provide a fitting resting place for Cobweb." He answered the questions in their faces. "Old Sallie Brigman, the bee woman."

At once Marjorie knew he was right. She hugged Benjamin to her again. "Will you write and let me know how you are doing?"

"Course I will."

"Remember to be kind as well as honest, and keep away from the women who walk those London streets, and—"

"I'll remember all of it, Marjorie!" he cried. "And I'll not forget you!"

He drew away and the doctor pressed a coin into his hand. "I'm sure you'll need a little extra, lad, so do not protest."

The darkness was dense enough still to mask their tears and contorted faces. Marjorie watched Benjamin's slim young back as he walked away until her tears made it impossible to see.

"Ride this last distance, Marjorie," the doctor urged. "I'll lead the horse and carry Cobweb, and we can tie your bag on back here."

The night diffused as the sun pressed against it for admittance, and Marjorie shuddered. But she knew she was riding toward a haven and, if she were lucky, there would be kindness in her life now, and no more fear. She closed her eyes and let the doctor lead the tired horse whither he would.

❧

Harvey Heaton woke at the Stragglers' Inn to a mouth dry as cotton and a head that felt it was split right in two. He missed the girl at once, but he did not miss his son 'til mid-morning when his other boys, daring to approach him, told him what they had found.

"He's no son of mine, do you hear it?" He thrust his chin out defiantly. "You hear me, boys? He'd better never try to come back." He put a hand to his throbbing head. "Never was a proper Heaton, was he?" His sons nodded agreement. "One less mouth to feed—two less." He turned to Spencer. "You and Alan had best go into Bunbury and see if you can hire some wench and get her back here to take care of this place." For the moment, that was enough. His stomach was too sour and his head too muddled to go beyond that.

Marjorie, rousing from a light sleep, found herself the object of much attention, beginning with Mary and Martha, who brought over a loaf of warm bread and a ribbon for her hair that they thought would go well with her eyes. Meg Weatherall came with a pannikin of butter, saying that if Marjorie was worried about wages and living, she could use a bit of help with her herbs once the summer got underway.

Dorothea had the same thought. "Right now Lucius and I have both his place and mine to keep up," she explained. "And there is more to his farm than I expected; I could do with some help."

"There, you see." Sallie smiled when they had left. "The good Lord provides." She spread a thick layer of honey on a slice of Martha's bread. "But, you know, girl, it would please me if ye were to make your home here. Oh, you could hire out of a day and earn not only your keep but money for things that you'll want." Seeing the amazement in Marjorie's eyes, she leaned over and gave her hand a reassuring pat. "I would be glad of your company, *and* of help with the tasks that keep getting harder for me."

Marjorie forced back the tears that kept sliding out at the corners of her eyes. "I don't know what to do with all this kindness," she confessed, "save to promise that I shall not squander it, but work hard to be worthy of so much goodness and trust."

It took most of the day for details to sift down to Esther, who was woefully omitted from the circle of women's communication. And she would have known nothing at all if it had not been for Pearl.

"The Mormons have her then!" she protested hotly. "I should have expected it." Then she thought, *Sallie has someone else to help her now, too, and I know she needs it. Yet, she will certainly have no further want of me.*

Then she realized with a bit of a start, all over again, how much things had changed. More than a year ago *she* was the one who assisted Sallie, and everyone else, with her little basket over her arm, and her good intentions, and her secure place as the vicar's daughter! That awful day came back to her, when she saw the strangers coming up the back way to the doctor's house. What a child she had been then to think good might come of their being here!

Tempest's mother was not pleased that he had gone off riding alone with Esther during the May Day celebration, and he loved his mother well. Indeed, he had learned from her Scottish arm of the family how women ought to be treated by the men who cherished them. He did not wish to hurt her at all, yet he knew what he knew and he was what he was, and he realized more and more every day why he had really come home. He felt Jonathan with him often as he went through his day, and he had taken the last few weeks to pulling his younger brothers in for instruction and lessons on all manner of things. At first they did not take him seriously, but after awhile enthusiasm built in them, and qualities the boys possessed that had never been called upon began to reveal themselves. Tempest was pleased. James had a way with figures, and Nathan a natural touch with animals and a sense for the land. Perhaps together . . .

Every day Tempest found himself loving the old place more. Every day he marveled at what fate had in store for him.

Louisa Kilburn was glad that the berths available on the boat were few. "You are needed here," she told her husband.

"Perhaps for the time being," he conceded. "But in three years or less, the only *here* will be Zion."

"What nonsense! You fancy the whole lot of us will just pick up and leave?"

"That I do. We cannot practice our religion here, Louisa, the way we can there."

"Religion is one thing, husband, but *home* is another! We are Englishmen! Could you really cross the broad ocean and never set eyes upon England again?"

Zachie knew how well-founded her fears were; he sometimes felt them himself. With one burly arm he pulled her over to him. "You are right, love, it will be a terrible hard thing to do."

She pushed her advantage. "Our children would grow up *Americans?* And *their children,* who will have never seen England at all!"

"They will grow up *Saints,*" he said against her hair, kissing the wound coils of it. "And, because of that, things will turn out all right."

Roger was the greatest boon that had ever come into Sam Weatherall's life. Bright he was, and eager to work and go the extra mile, with no thought to himself. Of an evening the man and the boy would sit by the fire and read passages from the Book of Mormon to one another aloud. Meg took pleasure in watching them. Their own children were young yet, and Roger was a good example to them. Time and time again, later when husband and wife were alone together, they marveled at God's kindness to them.

"Not my family as I saw it and wanted it," Sam would say. "For how I would love to draw my brothers in and see them happy. But, since he could not do that, God has given me this youngster to embrace as a younger brother, or son."

Meg agreed. Roger was like one of them in every way, and his devotion to Samuel was a touching thing to behold. *God delights to bless his children.* That's what came into her mind as she watched the two of them by the fire, their faces earnest with enthusiasm, their heads bent over the book.

⌇

It should not have happened, it could not have been meant to happen. Such a small mishap, really, to have cut his hand when a tool slipped. Michael bound it and thought little of it, until it started to swell. At first he paid no heed to Hannah's pleadings, until he woke in the night because the pain was like a fire in his hand shooting up into his arm.

Hannah dressed and walked to the doctor's, praying he would be at home. He was, and came quickly, fearing blood poisoning, and his worst fears were true.

"If we wait any longer," he told the suffering man, "you will lose your whole arm."

"Let it be, then. As well an arm as a hand; as well my life as an arm." There were tears in his eyes as he looked up at the doctor. "I mean to carve for the temple in Zion, the one in the place called Nauvoo. That is what I am living for, Doctor."

"Nonsense. What of your wife and your child—unborn yet? Would you like him to go through life fatherless?"

Michael sunk back, his face ashen against the pillows. "What is the least you can do?"

"This finger that is the worst must go, and a chunk of flesh along here."

"That will pucker and misshape the whole hand."

"Yes, but if we do it right now I can save your thumb and all the bone will remain sound, I believe."

Hannah knelt down by the bedside. She kissed the hot cheek and leaned close enough to whisper. "Michael, let the doctor give you a blessing first, and then we shall trust the rest to the Lord." He raised tortured eyes to her, and she continued. "I know you are meant to use your gifts, the gifts God gave you, in praising Him through the stones of the temple," she continued. "I know it is true."

He moved his head. "What if it is pride, Hannah? What if God wishes to humble me?"

"Pride?" The tears were running down her cheeks now. "There is no chance of that. Perhaps humble you, and cause your faith in Him to grow."

"But, maimed that way, how could I—"

"Hush, Michael, He'll find a way."

"You believe that, truly?"

"Solemnly, Michael, most solemnly."

So Doctor Sterne called in the blacksmith, and together they gave him a blessing, then the larger man held Michael down while the doctor cut away at his hand. He went ashen gray, then fainted altogether, but Hannah stood trembling, watching all the way through. The doctor was worried for the well-being of her and the baby, but she would not be denied.

She knew her husband's suffering was for a purpose, she knew his hand would be healed—enough to do the work God meant for him. She knew it as she knew that she stood there breathing, with the baby alive in her womb and waiting his turn. She understood that Heavenly Father was preparing her Michael that he might find the best within him, which only suffering brings forth, and use *that* to glorify God with his handiwork. She spoke with serenity to her child.

"Father will be well; he will come out of this a better man for it. And, my little one, you and I will help him and love him and encourage him. From our faith, his own will kindle again and burn bright."

Hannah would entertain no doubts; with a woman's love, she was sure. Archibald Sterne, watching her, marveled as he often did at the power of women to touch the Infinite, to understand it, and to bring it, as an offering of humility, to a man's mind and heart.

❧

Edwin opened his eyes; his pain became in places a terrible itching, and he was at once peevish and demanding. Evaline served him in silence, struggling to *feel* the kindness she was exhibiting. Each day seemed to drag longer and longer until one night, as she bent down to lift the tray from his bedside, he grabbed her wrist, and tightened his hold until it became painful.

"You've learned your lesson, I hope. I could take all this suffering of mine out on your hide, you know, and I think I still might."

She wrenched away from him.

"I'll be out of this bed in a few days, and what do you propose to do then?"

The grin that smirked his features sent a pang of revulsion through Evaline. "Nothing has changed, Edwin." She chose her words carefully and spoke with deliberation. "I have secured my plans to take passage to America—"

He threw his head back and laughed. "Little chance of that, with you poor as a church mouse." Then his eyes fell on the small mound of gloves on the table beside him. "I see, my girl, *these* are the livelihood you hope to earn for yourself."

He grabbed at them, sweeping them into his arms at the same time that he leaned up in the bed and tossed them into the fire, many reaching their mark and sizzling into flame.

Evaline groped wildly, rescuing some, tucking her arms around them.

"Get out of my house," Edwin cried. "You heard me—this is *my house*, and I don't want you in here, not now—not ever again."

She moved swiftly, gathering up the remainder of her sewing materials, trying to think of the most essential items she might hope to escape with. He hissed from his bed, "This be *my* house." As he repeated the words something in her shriveled. "Everything in here is mine, do you hear me, Evie?" He reached for her, but she swept past him, turning back upon him with smoldering eyes.

"I am taking my clothing, my books, my mother's miniature. And if you ever try to touch me, Edwin, I'll have the constable here, and he'll be glad to take and throw you into jail, even as you are."

In a matter of minutes she had collected her essentials and stood at the front door. She did not want to turn back. It took all of her effort to make herself do so.

"I forgive you, Edwin," she said. "In the sight of God I forgive you, and wish you well for the rest of your life."

It was over. She half-ran to Sallie's, pounding on the door, falling into her surprised arms, tears and smiles at the same time. "Have you room for me? Will you take me in, even for a few days?"

Sallie glanced over her shoulder. "I believe our Marjie will be willing to share your old bed with you."

Our Marjie! Marjorie, feeling as though warm sunlight had been poured over her shoulders, walked forward and held out her hands.

Chapter Thirty-Two

May was drawing to a restless close. The date was fixed for the bishop to come to Throstleford, review his subordinate, and announce the decision that had been made.

Christian and Esther had talked but little since May Day, but now he drew her aside. "Come out of doors with me," he asked, and led her to a secluded spot close enough to her mother's grave that she could see it through the low-sitting branches of an elm, one of which she used to swing on when she was a child.

Already tears were tightening her throat. "You are not going to make peace with them, are you, Father?" she asked, needing almost frantically to speak the dread words aloud. "You will not plead for forgiveness. You will not be allowed to stay."

He met her gaze, but he could find no words, and she could see the terrible strain on his face. "I must do what is right," he said at last. "My only regret is that I have taken so long."

Then he lifted a hand, as if in protest. "No, that is certainly not my only regret. *You*—I am asking you to do things I scarcely have power to do myself. I have hurt you, confused you and, worst of all, left you *alone*, and I have never done so before that I can recall."

Through glistening eyes she replied, "Well, Father, is that not part of what they call growing up?"

"That's too easy of an out you're trying to provide for me."

She shrugged her shoulders. "No matter. I suppose I shall sort out my own life, in time." She leaned forward. "But *this!* You ask me to leave—this—my mother's grave—everything!" Unconsciously she moved away from him on the bench so that the folds of her dress and the edge of his trousers no longer touched. "Please do not say 'you can take it all with you.' Ah, yes, *in memory.* But that is not really true!" Her voice had risen to a cry now. "And I shall leave far more of myself behind." She rose to her feet, trembling. "So much so, in fact, that I wonder if I shall have enough left . . . to go on with . . ."

He reached for her hand, but she moved yet farther away. Watching her, he knew of a surety that he had made the wrong choice. If he had only drawn her into his confidence—but his own doubts had buffeted and tortured him, and he had known he must not do anything because of Esther, or through Esther. She could so easily influence him, and he had known that he must do what he was doing entirely on his own, so that he would know, and she would know the true root of it for the rest of their lives!

Yet now she was angry, and even bitter, wearing pain itself like a shield against further pain.

"Where will we go, Father?"

She sounded like a little girl again, and he bit hard on his lip to prevent a cry. "There are possibilities."

"Well, I am relieved to hear it." She sighed, just as the wind scuttered under the trees and sighed through the branches above. "We've nothing to worry about then, I suppose." She pulled her shawl more tightly around her shoulders. "It is getting cold, Father. I think I shall go back inside."

"One moment, Esther, my dear. Have you not always trusted me?"

"Yes, Father, I have."

"Can you do so now—neither seeing nor knowing?"

"I can but try."

She gave him a searching look and realized that there was no longer any fear in his face, no weakness nor doubt. Feeling a sudden tenderness, she bent down and kissed his cheek, then walked swiftly away. Whatever he had in mind—and heaven knew what that could be—it would still require her to turn her back on her home—become a wayfarer—and watch strangers possess what was and ought to be hers.

∞

The bishop was to arrive Sunday afternoon. Christian still had the morning worship services to get through.

He arose early and prayed long before preparing himself for the day. His last walk was like a kind of Gethsemane. The morning dew touched every leaf, every blade of grass with a benediction of God's power and purity. His heart ached at the loveliness that surrounded him, and he fancied he heard whispers, voices of many of the dead whom he had known and loved, over whose burials in the silent ground around him he had reverently presided.

Could they see him? Did they know what he was doing? Did any of their hearts turn to him now?

He thought the organ music had never sounded more beautiful, the strains more rich and clear. *"God moves in a mysterious way His wonders to perform; He plants his footsteps in the sea and rides upon the storm . . ."*

The ancient building rose before him, with wild roses of white and yellow tumbling over the roof and sides of the recessed entry, and climbing up the long stretch of stone. Stone that had withstood hundreds of years of rains and suns and harsh winters, stone that had harbored generations of mortals, frail and foolish, cruel and gentle, and taken into its inanimate self the whole range of human passion, human suffering, human love.

Small wonder he felt the weight of it as he entered. *His church, his people.* But not really so. Henry VIII separated England from Rome in 1534, three hundred years ago, and this place of worship belonged to the Church of England in every way. *Oh, Mary,* he whispered, *oh, my dear wife, be with me now.*

The prayers and responses had been given, the psalter read. It was time for the minister to mount the pulpit and speak to his flock.

Each one felt his love as he cast his eyes over them.

"My dear friends," he began, "how do I bid farewell to you, how do I separate myself from you, who are part of my life?"

Esther sat alone in her narrow pew, watching her father, seeing his gaze, heavy with sadness, but clear with intelligence and faith. And it came to her that he did not stand alone, but that her mother was with him, there by his side.

"I feel as though I am failing you by leaving, and yet, I would fail you more truly if—when further light and knowledge have come to me—I should close my mind and heart to it, and then expect to go on."

Silence opened her wings, and every heart in the chapel seemed to hover on the breath of his words.

"I would be a shell of a man only, if I were to do that, my friends, and certainly never a man of God."

He paused. An expression, as of wonder, lifted his mouth and softened it. He brought forth a book from within the folds of his surplice and held it out before him that all might see.

"This is the Book of Mormon. I have had it in my possession for many months now. I have read over its pages from cover to cover, not once, but twice." He searched the room again with his quiet gaze. "I have used some of its truths in my sermons. I have tried to use them also in my life."

These last words were not lost on most of his listeners, who knew well of their pastor's patient goodness, his honesty, his humility, his forgiveness and love.

"I step down from my place among you with some reluctance, but not with regret. I intend to do as the Spirit of the Holy Ghost bids me and be baptized into The Church of Jesus Christ of Latter-day Saints, which has been established by a Prophet of God—that God who uses the simple things of the earth to confound the mighty. I have a testimony of the work God has commenced. I wish to join with this Joseph Smith and his people and contribute my portion and part."

Christian waited. He felt many eyes upon him, not only those who were there in the flesh. He felt his wife's presence; of an assurance he knew she was with him. *I am sorry, Mary,* he said within himself, *that I was unable to understand. But you did, and you have gone before me, and you are leading me now.*

Oliver Morris was in his accustomed place near the back of the chamber. He thought he might rise and initiate a proposal of acceptance and thanks from the congregation. But he heard a rustle to the left of him, up near the front, coming from the squire's pew. He saw Tempest's tall figure arise and stand straight as a young tree. Oliver bent forward, patting his collie's head unconsciously, wondering what to expect.

Tempest had come to Sunday services fairly regularly the last few months, and on every Sabbath since May Day. He had felt impelled to do so, though he was not certain why. Now, he knew. He turned to face the congregation.

"I can attest, as most of you can, to the worthiness of your vicar. I, as young squire of the village, would like you to know that I, too, have been converted to Mormonism."

This time the silence gave way. After a few moments he raised his hand for order and continued. "My brother, Jonathan, you see, was in possession of one of their books. I loathed the mere sight of it, and the mere mention of Mormons, because I felt they were responsible for his death."

Esther tried to listen, but a shock had numbed her system. Was this some horrible travesty? First her father, and now Tempest!

"But his dying request was that I read the Book of Mormon, and so I have. At first merely to keep faith with the dead, to honor my promise, but after a time—" He paused and pushed his hand through the tendrils of unruly hair, dull brass in the sunless interior. "I have told no one, not even my worthy father, of what I have been doing—of the testimony of Mormonism which I have gained."

Esther stood, swaying slightly. All she could think was, *I must get out of here!* She stumbled through the side door. The congregation as a body seemed to sigh and Tempest, wide-eyed, sat down again.

"We shall close with a hymn, brothers and sisters," Christian said, "and then I will offer a parting prayer. I must leave you, but I shall ever be with you in spirit, and you in me, in my prayers and my love for you, which have only increased through the increased love I have learned and experienced in my struggles for truth."

Sing praise to him who reigns above, the Lord of all creation, the source of pow'r, the fount of love, the rock of our salvation. . . .

Esther, standing not far off, could hear the music, and the words ran through her mind: *With healing balm my soul he fills and ev'ry faithless murmur stills. To him all praise and glory. . . .*

She moved farther away, so that she heard only dimly, as a far, distant murmur this appeal to an Almighty who could bring to pass what she had seen happen today.

The bishop had not heard the same appeal, so Christian was able to tell him all aspects and particulars of the situation in his own words.

"We shall be out in three days, Your Grace," he promised. He, Pearl, and Esther would be busy packing and sorting, but he felt they could meet the deadline.

"You should have been *out*, sir, sooner than this. You have brought disgrace on the church, and I shall see to it that your name goes down in dishonor and infamy." The bishop was red in the face, and his hands would not be still.

"I never intended nor desired such. It grieves me to have—"

"Silence, Grey! I believe you have uttered enough words for one day. I do not wish to hear more. I would be obliged, however, if you would turn over your keys to me this moment." He held out one anxious hand, drumming his thick fingers of the other hand against the arm of his chair. "Your verger can see to the care and keeping of the building. I want you nowhere near it, man—do you understand?" He stood on his feet, looming large and dark in his rich robes and in the self-assurance of his countenance. Contempt glazed his eyes, and Christian felt himself shrink from it, as from a blow.

It took a surprisingly short time for a man's entire life to disintegrate before his eyes. By the time Pearl saw the churchman out, Christian was feeling the strain. Suddenly he wanted Esther with him, but he was not certain of her whereabouts. He knew that Oliver was waiting down in the kitchen, as he had asked him to do. Slowly he made his way there.

"Went off on horseback with young squire, not entirely of her own accord," the shepherd informed him.

"Can you wait for her return? I should rather—I should very much like to see this thing all the way through tonight."

"*Wait*, you ask, my old friend? That is my occupation, and I can rest my head anywhere if the night gets too late."

They forced down a tea of bread and butter and, while Pearl fed the cats and did up the dishes, the two men retired to the small, seldom-used parlor where the minister lit a tall lamp. *To guide her back*, he thought, *to guide my girl home one last time.* But he did not speak the words out loud.

∞

"*You did not trust me!* You let me rant and rave against the Mormons, while all the while—"

Tempest pressed his finger against Esther's lips to stop her. "Please! It was nothing like that. Hear me out, for mercy's sake, Esther."

She stood with her hands on her hips, the unsaddled horse grazing close beside them, the afternoon sky thinning out, color draining as through a sieve, as Esther felt the color and substance of her own life draining away.

Tempest paced back and forth beneath the ash tree, his hands in his pocket, his blue eyes bleached of light, like the sky. "I was angry with Jonathan for extracting such a promise from me; I thought it under-handed, even for a dying man. I dared not tell *you* what I was doing; I did not wish to further distress you so soon after he died."

In her heart she grudgingly acknowledged his reasoning, but merely nodded her head for him to go on.

"By the time my interest was drawn, by the time I began to

experience a change of heart, I—I feared it might alienate you—and above almost everything I did not want that."

"When and how did you think you would finally tell me?"

He lowered his head. "I hardly knew. I prayed something would happen, something to—it has not been easy, Esther!" He had glanced up too late and caught the expression in her eyes. "So often did I want to unburden my heart to you, but you were struggling already with so many difficult things—"

"You did not trust me. I already said that." Her voice had gone cold and monotone.

"See it that way, then, if you like."

"You on one hand, my father on the other, neither one trusting me."

"*Fools! Men!* Call us what you will, Esther! But, it was all done for love."

"Mighty words, and I suppose they make *you* feel better." Esther sighed, and covered her eyes with the palm of her hand. "I am weary, Tempest. Will you take me home?"

They rode in silence. As they drew nearer the parsonage, Esther asked, "What shall Squire and your mother do? Will your father disown you?"

"He very well might. It is the hurting him that tears at me, disappointing his prospects, and his faith."

"And yourself, what of your own life from now on?"

"I have my plans."

"*You and my father!*" She slid down from the horse's back and took a few steps away.

"You leave me then, like this?"

"I must face my father, and you face yours," she called over her shoulder. But she did not turn around, and therefore did not see how long he stood his horse watching after her, before he had the strength to ride on.

Christian had gone to Doctor Sterne's house and revealed to him all that had happened, and requested to be baptized.

The doctor had to sit and gather his senses about him. "I had no idea," he confessed. "Why did you tell no one? We might have—"

"You must see why. You, in particular, would have been implicated if you had known. Even Esther can honestly say, if questioned, that she knew nothing at all." There was a peace in Christian's face that Archibald recognized.

"I cannot tell you," the doctor said, as his old friend rose to go, "how much you are wanted, and needed. Yes, needed: your leadership, wisdom, and love."

"I am glad of it," Christian replied, his eyes warm with happiness, a happiness he recognized as something he had not felt within him since before Mary died.

He waited now, impatiently, for the return of his daughter. When she came into the house he coaxed her to sit down quietly before him, and rehearsed the whole thing again: his struggles with his conscience, his sense of loyalty and fears for the future if he were to turn his back on his livelihood, his growing testimony as he pondered and prayed. But, with Esther, there was more to add.

"You wonder why I went to see Oliver," he began.

"He was Mother's friend," she answered.

"Yes, and she had shared some things with him that she had not shared with me. It was these of which I wanted to be sure." He nodded to the shepherd, who had been sitting with them in the stiff, tense room while Christian talked.

"I gave you an idea of such yourself, when you came to me, Esther."

"Yes, I remember it well."

"Your father was aware of your mother's doubts, but only in a vague sense which it was easy—and necessary—for him to ignore. He came in hopes that I knew further of the matter."

"And you did." Esther felt a tingling sensation, like a series of little shocks, along her flesh.

The shepherd leaned forward, his eyes intense and dark. "Your mother told me of a dream she had in which she was walking through a beautiful green meadow toward a building which was bathed all in light, a white building of exceeding beauty. The closer she drew, the greater was her sense of joy, and the light seemed to reach out and enfold her, so that she felt it even inside her own being."

Christian took up the narrative. "She looked round for me, for her husband, and could not find me, but then, at length, she saw me at a distance toiling over a dark, barren rock land. She turned and called to me as loudly as she could, yet I seemed not to hear. She called again and held her arms out to me, but I did not look up, and the light she was seeking seemed to dim and withdraw from her. She stood undecided, tormented, looking with longing both ways, then the light retreated and my figure faded, and she stood on the green plain with her hands to her face, crying as bitterly as a lost child."

Esther was still. She knew the truth of the story, she felt it way down inside. She looked into the eyes of her gentle father, whom she trusted, and into those of the shepherd, which were as full of uprightness and love as the minister's were.

"My mother knew, then," she whispered. "She was given a vision of truth, and she hungered for it the rest of her life."

"She knew there was more, more of truth than that which her husband was teaching," Oliver explained. "She told me so. She felt that was what the dream had to tell her."

"And then she died."

Christian reached out and placed his hand on his daughter's shoulder. "She has the truth now. She tried to guide me, and you—but I have not let her! *But she left the dream with me.* And I discovered it at last, thanks to heaven for that."

"And you and I are to be baptized and evicted, perhaps on the same day. What then, Father?"

"I have made arrangements to rent a farm five miles outside the village. It has a nice cottage on the grounds, and a barn as well. I was good at farming as a young man, and I shall raise a great number of chickens and keep a few goats for milk."

Esther shook her head, as though to dislodge his words from it. "This makes no sense!"

"You can help with the livestock, if you will. Archibald tells me that Michael Bingham met with an accident recently and would be grateful for some help in his little shop, sanding and staining. I could surely do that."

"Bits and pieces of work with which to get by."

"There is no shame, daughter, in that."

She looked at her father. He really believed what he was saying. He seemed to feel no sense of loss or humiliation, of a great fall in status among the villagers who had always looked up to him. What would they think of him now?

"It will not be for long, Esther. I have enough put away to help keep us, and to pay for two ship's fares to"—he hesitated just slightly—"to Zion."

"You should have—" She raised her arms and waved them a bit helplessly.

"I know. It was very wrong of me, but I thought it the best way. Can you forgive me, Esther?"

"I have to think about—*everything!*" She backed away from him. "I want to go to my room."

She escaped just in time, before sobs shook through her body, like the winter storms slash and tear through the trees. There were so many sources of pain that she could not disentangle nor identify them. She could not understand—because she did not *wish* to understand! Like a child waking out of a nightmare, she wanted someone to hold her tight and soothe her, she wanted someone to say, *There, there, it was just a dream. Nothing has happened, nothing is changed, my dear one, and you are safe.*

"It's *your* people, Sophia, caused him to speak that way in chapel, like a barbarian! I never looked to be shamed by a son of mine that way." The squire was growling in his usual manner, but his eyes were deeply unhappy. Tempest's mother was crying softly, with her hands in her lap.

"I have tried to explain it to you." Tempest's face was as open and hopeful as a little boy's, tense with desire for understanding. "I did not *seek* this kind of complication. Believe me, I did not."

"I should have thrown that wretched book on the fire! But I could not seem to find it to lay my hands on."

Tempest thought, *I know why—God preserved it for me.* "Father, I love you," he said, "more than I ever thought was possible when I went away. I feel—" He paused, searching for words that his father would accept from him. "I feel honored to be your son."

"So it sounded this morning before the whole village."

"My words brought no shame to you, Father, except in your own mind."

His mother looked up, her eyes red and swollen. "What do you intend to do now?"

"That is up to Father, up to the two of you, really." He glanced to the end of the table where his two brothers sat, waiting. "I shall continue to work here for you, if you want me, as long as I can." He paused, then continued when no word was said. "James and Nathan there, I've been training them in the ways of a squire, and I believe you would be proud of them both."

"You cannot stay here," Squire spoke up. "That bishop would style me a sympathizer if I let you remain in my house."

"Very well. I *have* put you in an awkward position; I see that. There is a small farm I can let, work with the horses they raise, as well as put in a little farming. Then by fall or next spring—"

"You will return to Scotland? You know your aunt and uncle would welcome you," his mother added, hoping against hope for his well-being.

"Aye, and how I would love to go to them!" Tempest drew a breath and pushed his unruly hair from a forehead creased in furrows of pain.

"*Where* are you thinking to go, then," his father pressed, "if not there?"

"To America, Father."

"The boy has gone out of his mind."

"You have two good sons who will do you honor, Father, when it is time for them to step into your place." There were tears in Tempest's words and his voice was shaking.

His father glanced up at him, not wild-eyed, but with an expression as cold and gray as tempered steel. "You are no longer my son. Gather your things and get out of here. I never want to see you again."

Tempest stood frozen for a moment. His limbs had gone stiff and he thought if he tried to move them, he would fall flat on his face. His father waited, nothing in his expression altering or softening. At last, with a shudder, Tempest took a step, then another, then turned his back on them all, and somehow climbed the stairs to the room which had become very much his own, which held the few little treasures of his brother's now bequeathed to him. He had set them out here and there to keep him company, to remind him of Jonathan and the part he still played in his life.

This was the room where Tempest had first knelt to pray, putting Moroni's words to the test: "*And if ye shall ask with a sincere heart, with real intent, having faith in Christ, he will manifest the truth of it unto you, by the power of the Holy Ghost. And by the power of the Holy Ghost ye may know the truth of all things.*"

He knelt now, dropping to his knees as a child would, full of hunger and seeking and pain. He felt he must be whimpering, and put his hand to his mouth lest a cry should escape. He prayed a long time, his head resting on his arms, the shadows in the cold room lengthening, tracing dull gold patterns across the rug and the stuffed velvet chair and the tartan coverlet that he had thrown over his bed. He prayed, unmindful of the chill in the room and the cramp in his long legs. He prayed as a wounded son, longing for the tenderness and comfort that only a loving Father could give.

Chapter Thirty-Three

er father brought her the Book of Mormon as Esther had requested. It made her think only of the days spent with Jonathan, so that she picked it up, held it close against her, and closed her eyes. She had been praying, but her heart was not entirely in her prayers. Now she sat very still and let memories sift over her spirit the way sunlight filters into a room, more delicate than the breath of a baby or water sifted by wind, yet each miniscule speck carrying the power of the whole sun with it, from whence it came.

She felt her memories came from some pure source that was both within her and somewhere she could not see. She remembered words Jonathan had spoken and expressions that had come over his face.

"There is nothing like this bit, Esther. Listen: 'For he that diligently seeketh shall find; and the mysteries of God shall be unfolded unto them, by the power of the Holy Ghost, as well in these times as in times of old, and as well in times of old as in times to come; wherefore, the course of the Lord is one eternal round.'"

She remembered how long they had talked about that verse, feeling the wisdom of truth entering their thoughts and expressions as it never had in their lives. She thumbed haphazardly through the pages. Here was another verse that spoke to her deeply. "*For behold, I am God; and I am a God of miracles; and I will show unto the world that I am the same yesterday, today, and forever; and I work not among the children of men save it be according to their faith.*"

What faith Jonathan had possessed. *Much like my father's,* Esther thought. He had planned to rise from his sickbed and be baptized, and then go about doing good. "It is simple, my dear girl," he had said. "Love. And try to help and serve others. I wish I had started on such a course long before."

"You have, from all accounts I have heard of you," Esther had maintained.

"But I see so much more now." His eyes would be alight with an emotion for which she had no name. *Anticipation . . . perhaps anticipation . . .*

And now he was gone—up to that world which also contained her mother, that world where both of them knew *of a surety* what they had only guessed at and desired before. Esther wondered if perhaps they would meet one another, and speak of her. It was a girlish daydream, but she liked the thought of it, and it stuck in her mind. Surely, such a thing would not be impossible. They would like one another, and she enjoyed picturing the friendship the two of them might experience, with nothing of the earth and the flesh to get in their way.

But I am here, she realized, with a terrible impact. *And I still must make my way.* The realization overwhelmed her, and a new wave of vulnerability swept through her.

What was this? "*Nevertheless, I did look unto my God, and I did praise him all the day long; and I did not murmur against the Lord because of mine afflictions. . . .*"

Esther drew in her breath. She knew she was being willfully blind, willfully childish, almost willfully weak. *Unworthy.* The word came to her like a stone dropped into the troubled pool of her soul. Her eyes caught another verse, one that her father had underlined. She read the words in a hushed voice out loud: "He that will harden his heart, the same receiveth the lesser portion of the word; and he that will not harden his heart, to him is given the greater portion of the word, until it is given unto him to know the mysteries of God until he know them in full."

She felt her soul expand as eternity touched it, as something eternal within *her* cried out for joy. She closed her eyes and prayed as though God himself stood in the room with her, listening to her, loving her. She remembered suddenly that other spring day when she had seen the two strangers approaching Throstleford from the lonely back road. She remembered the strange sensation that had overtaken her: anticipation, and a delicious warmth she could not explain. She remembered this book, and the feelings she had experienced when first she read its words.

Slowly a sorting began to take place in her mind, so that she could identify and understand the many divergent elements that had worked in her life and her father's, and in Throstleford itself. Clarity came as a calm blessing to her spirit, then she said in her heart, *I do not think I could have done this, in any way, without you, Mother dear. I was not brave enough, nor wise enough.* Her whole being cried out with gratitude that her mother was there still, a part of her life! A part of all that would happen, that was meant to happen—*not to me, nor to Father,* she marveled, *but to us, as a family.*

She rose, anxious to go to her father, anxious to reveal to him what had happened and to feel the last shreds of darkness and confusion fall from her heart.

⧼

Tempest grieved; he could not prevent this fierce longing for home, hearth and kin. *'Tis the Scots in me,* he told himself a bit angrily. And he thought it an odd sort of irony that he, who had prided himself on going his own way, cared deeply for the welfare of his father, cared for his father's good name, and shrank from taking a path in opposition to him. Yet, he knew that he must. What is more, he knew that Jonathan would be with him on this new path, would walk by his side every day.

As to *other things,* he could do nothing but wonder, and desire. He had prayed for Esther, oh, how he had prayed. But he had felt no confirming answer, no comfort, and when Sarah came to him in tears, desolate, he did not know what to do to comfort her, he did not know what to say.

"How can *religion* be important enough to spoil everything else?" she wailed.

"Religion *is* everything else."

"That makes no sense."

"Sarah, a man or woman is the sum total of their beliefs and their desires, and the translation of these into actions as they go through their lives. Religion defines and informs and illuminates—"

She shook her head. "It does not matter if I understand, or if I don't. You will still leave me—both of you."

"You will find happiness, Sarah. I pray that you will."

He felt alienated, as though an invisible shield separated him from the people with whom he moved and talked. It was as though he could not hear them, and they could not hear him. *Lost to each other. Would it remain that way?* With all his heart he hoped not.

He slept restlessly that night, in his own bed, as his mother had insisted. But he had not seen his father since he'd walked out of that room. On the morrow he would be baptized. He and the pastor—and who else? He pondered, he agonized, he prayed. He knew he must walk by faith, not expecting the kind of answers he desired to be always granted him, not even by God.

It happened much as Esther had predicted. They would be baptized in the morning and begin to flit, or move house, in the afternoon. She did not care, she was unable to think of anything right now that was ordinary or mundane. She had done her best to prepare her spirit for what it was about to receive. She had gone into the churchyard shortly after the sun had risen, when dew drooped like drops of pearls from spiderwebs in the corners and from leaf and frond at her feet. She had knelt and prayed at her mother's grave, at her mother's feet. For a few moments she had felt a gentle pressure on the top of her head, as of the impress of a hand resting upon her; she could almost feel of its warmth as much as of its weight. And she *saw* her mother in the power of the Spirit as though she were there.

She had prayed also with her father in his study before, hand in hand together, they'd walked out of the house. Pearl, bless her heart, was in tears. She understood none of this, nor the necessity of it, and she did not wish to serve a new pastor when those she loved were no longer there.

"You could come with us," Christian had offered, doing all he could to draw out her thoughts and imagination toward such an end. But her desires, after all, were of a nature that closed such pathways to her. So he left her instead with his blessing, a blessing that became a living strength to her for the rest of her life.

Tempest rose in solitude and prepared himself quietly for the day. When he walked down the stairs and into the wide front hall, he saw his mother step out of the shadows where she had been waiting for him.

Sophia MacGregor Feather, who had left her home to marry an English squire, possessed that reticent Scottish nature which does not speak nor communicate much, keeping its own counsel in almost all things. Now she stood before this glorious young son, longing to share with him the things in her heart.

Tempest knew, by the very fact of her presence, the strength of those emotions she held in check. He took one look at her face, then gathered her into his arms. "I love you, Mother," he said at length, "I shall always love you, and I shall try all my life to bring honor to you and your name."

"Go with my blessing, Tempest." Her words were little more than a hoarse whisper against the curve of his neck where her cheek rested. With reluctance, she lifted her tear-stained face and moved away.

He wanted to cry out to her! He wanted to be a little boy again, and dissolve the heavy weights of manhood that rested upon his shoulders! He lifted her hand and pressed it to his lips. Their hearts cried out to one another, though there were no words to say.

He walked through the door. He had already removed his things from the house; he would not return here. But he walked with the love of his mother like a light warming the cold loneliness of his soul.

⬡

It was nearly too much to believe. The little cluster of Mormons, the minister's friends, gathered around Doctor Sterne like wide-eyed children to hear the tale.

"Surely, God is good," Peter Goodall murmured.

"Surely, he loves his children," old Sallie agreed.

There was joy and rejoicing, there were prayers of gratitude in every heart gathered there, and a vocal prayer offered for the help and strength of the goodly parson and his daughter, that Heavenly Father would bless and uphold them throughout this challenging time.

"I cannot wait to get my arms around Esther again," Janet confessed.

"Oh, how we shall celebrate!" Evaline cried. "Will you make one of your pies for her, Janet? And Sallie and I shall make honey cakes—"

"And I," Hannah offered, "the currant scones that she loves."

"*I* cannot wait to hear Christian Grey preach again," Paul Pritchard chuckled. "With the truth in his mouth, what a power he'll be."

They made preparations for Monday morning by the river when, with the sacred authority vested in them, the elders of Throstleford would take their beloved brother into the waters of baptism and render him one of their own.

The hedgerows were bursting with blossoms and the bright bees that fed on them: there were woodruff; bluebells; and wild hyacinth, called goosy gander; all entwined with flowering crab apple and blackthorn and a cascade of hawthorn blooms. The blackbirds were searching for worms and the throstles for snails, and the hedge sparrows perched and chattered the fair morning in.

Marjorie walked along with the others; she felt at ease among them. She would like to be baptized herself, but was reluctant to speak yet of her desire. She would finish the book, read the Book of Mormon all the way through; Roger had said he would help. She closed her eyes and lifted her face to let the sun warm her eyelids and hair. Back home at Sallie's, for so she thought of it, a little treasure awaited her, a long gray kitten with fur like silk, one black paw, and a streak of black along the top of his nose.

"One of Cobweb's, to be certain," Dorothea had told her. "Found it among the litter in the barn, and Lucius said I could bring it to you."

Friends. Marjorie had never known people could behave in this manner, could truly care about what happened to their neighbors, could live in peace. Her own parents had spent every thought and effort, every waking moment on figuring out how to get by. Life was a day-to-day matter, with nothing left over at the end of the long, exhausting hours, and nothing to look forward to but more of the same. In this atmosphere Marjorie was discovering her own spirit, that *self* that she had sometimes sensed, often struggled for, but had, in truth, been a stranger to. She secretly rejoiced at what others seemed to take for granted. She wanted to be part of such companionship, she wanted to contribute her portion and, thereby, belong.

Esther saw Tempest before he saw her. He was riding his tall gelding, Phantom, its slate coat so dark that it looked like a gray autumn sky, wet through with rain. His blue eyes were wide with wonder and, was it, anticipation? Oh, but he sat a horse well, his long back straight, yet relaxed, his head as erect, yet somehow at a watchful angle, his hands, with their long fingers, lightly balancing the reins. She wondered what had happened at the squire's house last night and this morning. She wondered how things would fall out or come together once this day's work was complete.

Suddenly Esther's musing was interrupted by a great noise, that of many feet moving and many voices murmuring together. She looked up and gasped. Over the rise it appeared a large body of people was approaching, moving with some purpose and determination. She put her hand to her mouth. Were they coming to make trouble, to throw stones and bash heads? She looked for her father, but he had moved away from her. Suddenly Tempest was there, stretching a hand down to her.

"Climb up behind me, lass, until we see what this swarm is about."

She did as he bade, quite happily, counting from her vantage point ten men and fourteen women, with nearly a dozen children between them. Then she drew in her breath and leaned forward to squeeze Tempest's arm.

"This isn't a rabble," she hissed. "It cannot be. Every one you see is a parishioner of my father's; good, sober people all of them—"

They surrounded Christian now, moving like the tall meadow grasses move when a wind swells through their ranks. Some reached out in order to touch his hand. Others clapped him on the back or the shoulder. They smiled, and their faces were soft and ashine.

"That is right, Parson," she heard, "we've come to baptize ourselves along with you."

"Do you know what you are doing?" Her father's voice held a thrill of incredulity and, Esther thought, hope.

"That we do," he was assured by another. "We have always trusted your word because it was backed by example."

"You see, sir," a woman added, "we all met last night and voted together to cast our lot with you—to find what you have found—"

"We saw that light in your eyes. And the peace of it. We still feel to trust you, Parson."

Christian stood in the midst of them with tears in his eyes. Esther leaned forward, wishing she could go to him. She felt a hand fumble for hers, warm, sinewy fingers wrapped round her fingers lightly, but with a toughened strength. She could feel the pulse of the man's heartbeat in those fingers, his soul, his life. Then she wanted to lean her head against the long lean back and rest there awhile.

But the happy commotion was reaching out to them still, drawing them in. Tempest slid from the saddle, lifted her down, then secured his horse to a tree.

"We shall have to wait our turn, it appears," he said to her. "Who would have imagined this?"

"Not I," she admitted. "There will surely be a different kind of commotion when the bishop hears." Suddenly fearful, she clutched at his sleeve. "Tempest, what if they are so angry that they run us out of the village?"

"My little lass, what a worrier you are! Where is your faith?" He leaned closer, and she could feel the sweetness of his breath on her face. "Look for yourself, the lot of us is more than the lot of *them,* any day."

He made her smile and relax, which was his intention. He wished he could draw her for comfort into his arms. But that day would come; surely, that day would come for him.

The congregation drew round. One of the elders began the proceedings. He had such kind eyes. When they rested on Esther he smiled at her in such a way that she drew encouragement from it and felt he must, surely, know who she was, and what it meant for her to be there today.

"The Spirit of God like a fire is burning. . . ." Daniel began the melody on his flute, and the thin notes floated and then hung suspended on the cool, fragrant air. The people sang with force and conviction, most of them seeming to know the words by heart.

Esther, listening, realized that she could admit to herself how much this song moved her, how her spirit rose in response to it. Always before she had held herself behind a barrier, poised for flight, never opening her soul entirely so that truth and joy could flow in.

" *. . . the Lord is extending the Saints' understanding, restoring their judges and all as at first. The knowledge and power of God are expanding; 'The veil o'er the earth is beginning to burst. . . . We'll sing and we'll shout with the armies of heaven, hosanna, hosanna to God and the Lamb. . . ."*

She realized that Tempest, beside her, was singing along with the rest. He picked up the music easily, and his rich tenor voice sent a thrill through her. Everything in her wanted to "sing and shout" in praise of what she was feeling inside.

As she gazed out, Windy Strath had the blush of May upon it, and Ash Water was high in its banks, swelled with the winter runoff and the early spring rains. But where it widened into a pool the water was calm and low enough to suffice. There were people on the bridge, people dotting the rounded rise of Blind Man's Knoll, and all had peace in their eyes.

Esther lifted her gaze and saw the shepherd with his long staff and his dog walking sedately toward her. She waved a hand to him, and he nodded his head.

"I have come to be with you and your father," Oliver stated simply as he drew closer. "But I see I am not the only one who had that in mind."

When she explained, a slow smile broke over his features. "This would please her—your mother," he said. "I believe she is here with the rest of us, Esther."

"Yes, I think you are right."

Her father came up and, resting one arm across Esther's shoulder, held out his hand to the shepherd, who leaned forward and grasped it with both of his.

"I shall be happily beholden to you for the rest of my days," Christian said.

"To Mary, you mean, as many of us are," was the shepherd's reply.

"Have you come to join us?" Christian asked, but the words were a gentle tease, for he knew what his answer would be.

"I'll wait my time out here, if it be all the same to you," Oliver said. He put his hand over his eyes and scanned the horizon. "I shall lay my bones down in these hills with my sheep," he mused, "and that is how it should be."

He dropped his hand and turned his gaze on the pastor, looking long and searchingly into his eyes. "You shall tend sheep in other hills than these. I can see it, though dimly. Very high and rocky hills that rise in a far-off place. In time you shall lay your bones down among them, and that, too, is how it should be."

"You will watch over *her*, then, when I am gone?" Christian murmured the words softly, and there were tears in his eyes.

"It will be my honor to fulfill such a trust, for your sake," Oliver replied.

And then another voice: "It is time now—"

Someone was calling them forward. Both men stepped aside so that

Esther might pass first to the water's edge. She lifted her gaze and rested it for a moment upon the three men who stood watching her, and realized that each one was dear to her in his own way.

Then there was a hand on her arm, and her feet touched the water, and the chill of the blue pool reached up her legs. *"And now, as ye are desirous to come into the fold of God, and to be called his people, and are willing to bear one another's burdens, that they may be light . . ."*

The water had reached to her waist. It rippled around her in little pools. *"Yea, and are willing to mourn with those that mourn; yea, and comfort those that stand in need of comfort, and to stand as witnesses of God at all times and in all things, and in all places that ye may be in . . ."*

Esther took a few steps forward, drew a deep breath, and steadied her feet on the smooth, uneven rocks beneath her. *"Now I say unto you, if this be the desire of your hearts, what have you against being baptized in the name of the Lord . . . that he may pour out his Spirit more abundantly upon you?"*

She placed her hand in that of the man who was standing beside her, and, as he raised his right arm to the square, she closed her eyes.

Light. Light fragmented, flowing. Rays of gold, strings of silver-white light, penetrating and warm; light purifying her gaze, permeating her whole being with healing and delight. *"Delight thyself also in the Lord . . ."*

She came up out of the water, sputtering a little, pushing the wet strands of hair from her face. The man beside her still held her hand, and guided her uncertain walking against the weight of the pool with his other hand on her arm. She saw before her an expanse of faces smiling, eyes glistening with tears. She felt she was smiling with every pore of her being, she felt the light flowing into her and out of her in waves of gladness. She held out her arms. *"And now when the people had heard these words, they clapped their hands for joy, and exclaimed: This is the desire of our hearts."*

She watched her father take his turn in the water. She met his eyes as he stood afterward and gazed at her—and through her, at things she could not see.

She watched the tall young man with the untamed eyes and the unruly hair go down into the water at last. She was aware of him in a way she had never been before, as though he were familiar to her, not in any way a stranger, but deeply known. She felt his pleasure—and she felt the pleasure of his dead brother, whose shining spirit was still so happily, so gloriously alive.

Chapter Thirty-Four

◦◦◦◦◦◦◦

There were so many people helping to clean and scrub, heft, move, and organize the minister's belongings that in a matter of hours all was in order and ready for father and daughter to move in.

Esther had thought she would despise the little house, feel ill at ease and cramped there, but instead the walls seem to fold comfortingly around her, and the square rooms, much smaller than those at the parsonage, wore a clean, sparse dignity that appealed to her senses: she felt at home from the first moment she walked in and sat down.

Darkness came as a friend to their weariness; the helpful neighbors went to their own homes. There was food in the kitchen: soup which that good soul, Pearl, had sent over, warm bread from Martha's oven, scones and honey cakes, and one of Janet's mouth-watering pies.

Too much, really. They ate sparingly of the bread and soup, and only tasted the sweets. "These will wait until tomorrow," Esther said. Tomorrow she would return to the parsonage and collect the clippings of plants and bushes that she had set out, and she would round up the cats and the kittens. "Will they stay in a new place?" she asked her father.

"The same food, the same voice, the same love to assure them. I hope that they will."

She leaned back in her chair and closed her eyes. The day had been nearly too much for her, and she wished to record every moment in her journal—each impression, each thought. Tempest had left early. "I shall be back in the morning," he'd promised, "with something for you."

He was spending the night further down the road at the farm he had rented. Alone. She did not like to think of him that way and hoped that he, like she, would be too weary to feel much of anything but the craving for sleep.

When she knelt to say her prayers she realized, with a start, that she was a new person, newly born of water and of the Spirit, with a clean whiteness before her, unmarred by any of the shadows and mistakes that had in any way tarnished her young life. She sensed the freedom of it. *I have a new heart within me,* she thought, *and I shall keep it pure. I pray tonight for the very first time as a Latter-day Saint.* Those words still had an awkward feel to her. But she knew that, in time, she would fit herself into them, and they would fit themselves into her.

Tempest kept his word, but he did not come too early. He found her feeding and naming the new chickens that had just been delivered. He cajoled her away to sit beneath a wide, gnarled oak that had so broad a girth and so magnificent a crown that it must have been planted in the days of Doomsday record under William the Conquerer. Throstles darted, alighting on branches above them, filling the air with their song.

"I am off to Scotland," he announced. "A short trip, I regret, but a necessary one."

She looked at him quizzically. "Necessary?"

"Yes, there are things I must do. And once I begin working the farm and the horses, I shan't get away."

"Are you going alone? Is that wise?"

"Actually, Mother is urging Father into allowing one of my brothers to ride with me, to meet the family in Scotland." He appeared a bit anxious. "But, that is not why I am here."

Esther leaned forward, interested, yet trying not to appear too much so.

"Do you remember this?" Tempest drew from his pocket the polished blue-gray stone he had tried to give her before. Beneath the touch of the morning sun the yellow streaks stood out like pathways of gold that dug deep into the interior of the rock, and yet trembled on the surface, seeming to have a life of their own.

Esther held out her hand and Tempest placed the peculiar offering into it.

"A protection, a talisman," he reminded her. "Will you keep it, Esther?"

She knew to refuse him would be cruel. She nodded her head. He cupped her small hand in his and closed her fingers over the smooth stone, then kissed those fingers, and the touch of his lips was warmer than any touch of air or sun she had ever felt.

"You will miss our first Sabbath," she said, realizing this suddenly.

"It cannot be helped. By the time I return you and your father will be settled in." He attempted a smile, but the expression on his face was one of uncertainty. "Then we can turn our attentions to—other things."

"You speak enigmatically, sir." Esther smiled, half-teasing him. Reluctantly, he removed his hand from hers and, not realizing it, Esther sighed.

They walked to the house together, but said little. He mounted his smoky horse.

"Be careful," she cried again and, as he turned away from her, "Hurry back."

Why did I say that? she demanded of herself. *Just like a starry-eyed girl!* Yet, in truth, she had left girlhood behind her, and what she felt now was an emotion of deep and lasting import, and she wondered at it as she watched Tempest ride away.

The week passed quickly. There were new things to be done, it seemed, every day. Only at night, crawling into bed, bone-weary, did Esther realize how happy she was. Part of this came, she knew, from working hand in hand with her father and from leaving the tedious realm of ideas behind. They were one with the sun and the soil, with green things growing, with beast and fowl that were in daily need of their care. Esther could feel a lessening of the tensions that had strung her taut, she felt her whole being relax—her young body, supple and alive, in harmony with her spirit and mind.

The Sabbath came upon them by surprise. Christian shook his head in wonder when he realized it was Saturday night. "How is it that I have spent an entire week and not thought once of my sermon—of what I ought to be reading, considering, and preparing." It disconcerted him a little.

"We have been so pleasantly occupied," Esther explained.

Zachie Kilburn had insisted on sending his horse-drawn cart for them to ride in. "Please, sir, we would all prefer to have you and Miss Esther . . . well-provided for, in this little way."

He acquiesced. The concern they showed touched him so deeply, he was unable to tell Esther what he felt when they passed close by the churchyard and heard the bells reach out to them, rich and deep-throated. He could name every bell, and had himself rung more than one of them in his day. It was the first Sabbath in twenty-five years that he had not stood at his pulpit and greeted the array of faces before him: most weary, some eager, some hard and closed, others too hurt for believing, scarcely daring to hope.

Yet, many of them would be with him this very day, and they would take this journey into the future together. And he would still have the opportunity of holding their hands and encouraging them, as he had always done.

⬯

Tempest had, after all, traveled alone to Scotland. His father would not permit his brother to accompany him, which was a shame. The words the squire had spoken echoed through his mind: *"You are no longer my son. I never want to see you again."* Had his father's hurt cut so deep then that he would never rescind? Tempest shuddered as he rode alone through the lengthening days.

But as he approached Scotland he began to relax into a sort of happiness. He loved it here; he had forgotten how much: wilder country, wilder manner, but gentler hearts. Weakening, he allowed himself to contemplate what it would be like to return here with Esther beside him. They could make a good life, they could—ah, yes! They could do many things—but they could not very easily be Latter-day Saints. Entirely on their own. Yet, Throstleford had started with Doctor Sterne and just a few others . . . he permitted himself to muse on.

With much ceremony, ancient and steeped in the mystical, Christian Grey had entered the ministry. Now he was ordained in a very different way, with hands laid on his head and those simple words spoken over him, which thrilled through him, confirming all that was taking place.

" . . . *By the power of the holy Melchizedek Priesthood which we hold, we lay our hands upon your head and ordain you . . .*"

He felt the difference; so gentle, yet so undeniable. He felt, above all, love. *Charity, the pure love of Christ.* He knew it was that which was being bestowed on him. He knew it was this kind of love that he *desired,* desired to possess in his own heart, desired to give.

Tempest's aunt and uncle, who were at first pleased to see him, became quiet and almost stern when he announced his errand to them. They took the book gingerly from his hands.

"It will nae burn you," he laughed at them. "'Tis precisely how I felt the first time, as well."

He told them of Jonathan's death, of his dying desire. He told them of Esther, and here, at last, he brought forth some smiles.

"We must meet her," they insisted.

"God willing, you shall."

He remained longer than he had intended. He felt more at home and alive here each day. He helped Ewan and the others with any work that needed doing out in the field or the yard. He went on long rides with Margaret and discussed Scottish heroes and Scottish tragedies. But there was a tension, a hesitance toward him at times that he could not deny. Surely these people, who loved him for what he was, would not turn away, would not withdraw their affections from him.

The night before his departure, very late, he answered a knock on his door to find his uncle standing outside. He drew him in, his heart suddenly constricted within him, and all his nerves alive.

"Lad, I have come, as is proper, to speak for the lot of us—" he hesitated.

"Concerning?"

"I think you know what."

"Surely not religion, not Mormonism?"

"And why not, lad? 'Tis a thing of importance in the life of a man."

"Precisely! And I have—"

"Nae, hear me out, Tempest. You see, I've a letter here from your father that arrived yesterday."

"To warn you against me?"

"To tell of his disappointment and displeasure. And, yes, to request our support."

Tempest stood very still. He had heard the words spoken, but he could not believe them; they appeared to him as meaningless sounds. "Surely not you? You have such a fine mind, a courageous vision—" He stumbled forward, speaking his own thoughts aloud.

"Loyalty to family. That comes first with the Scots, Tempest; you ought to know that." The older man drew himself up with a terrible solemnity of purpose. "Squire says you have entirely broken your mother's heart."

Of course, her own brother, standing sternly before him, would object most to that. And, of what use for Tempest to attempt to deny it? Attempt to explain?

"Och, lad, we love you, we shall always love you. But it is my advice that you put away this madness, disentangle yourself from these people—before it is too late."

Tempest stood facing this man he loved, with no words to speak to him. He watched his uncle take out a book from among the folds of his jacket. "I had determined to throw this on the fire," he admitted, "but thought better of destroying property that, no matter how distasteful it may be to me, is not mine."

Tempest reached for it. "I thank you for that, sir. It was my brother's, you know."

"Think it over the night," his uncle said, "and we'll have a word on the matter in the morning, lad, before you start home."

Home. A word in the morning. So that was it. He shut the door and leaned against it. Did his uncle truly believe that this was all it would take to bring him to his senses?

Tempest paced the long room, the room in which he had lived, grown up, blundered from boyhood to young manhood, discovered himself. Suddenly he realized that this gentle, strong-minded family knew how much they meant to him, knew what a vital part each one had played in his life. If their love and entreaty could not touch him—then, aye, they would look upon him as lost, lost indeed.

Home. A word in the morning. And, without the right word in the morning, he would never go home again.

He slept little that night. He had not expected his convictions, his testimony to be tried so early, and so hard. *He who will not leave father and mother and take up his cross and follow me is not worthy of me.* The words went something like that. He lit a candle and sat in the cushioned alcove where he had spent many a long night dreaming and planning at a time when he was yet a lad, and the untried world lay before him— and such a day as this could not have been even imagined.

He opened the Book of Mormon on his lap and began to search through it. He had better be sure of some of the pronouncements of Deity, of the testimonies of the great Nephite prophets. He needed their wisdom, he needed their strength with him as the dark border night, windy and noisy as usual, settled upon him and he was alone.

This was unfair advantage; this was too pitiless to bear. Not only his uncle but the whole lot of them braved the chill of the morning to stand, stomping their feet and rubbing their cold hands together, while he mounted his horse.

His aunt kissed his cheek, but she kept her eyes averted; Margaret found his hand and pressed it. The others stood awkwardly by.

"Have ye a word for us, lad, in parting?"

"If I could but say it as it ought to be said," Tempest cried, "then, indeed, yes, I do."

They looked on him and waited. He thought in his heart: *Love is more painful, more powerful to destroy, than any other emotion.* He uttered a silent prayer.

"I love you. I have never known such love as I have known in this house. I regard you with respect and admiration. I owe much of what I am to you . . . and I shall carry you always, as a very real strength, in my heart."

He drew a deep breath, and it seemed to burn through him. "But that heart belongs to my Lord and Savior, Jesus Christ, who has restored the keys of His gospel in this day, *my* day, and I intend to go where He calls me, and to do whatever He requires of me."

They continued to stare. There were tears in Margaret's eyes. Tempest wished he had the power to draw them, altogether, into the fierce embrace of his arms.

No word. They had not expected to hear such a response from him. He drew up the reigns and turned the gray to face the long slender road ahead. Each step rang loudly on the packed gravel. He and the horse seemed to move in slow motion, drawing out the agony, drawing thin the fine cord that bound them and that must, eventually, snap.

Harvey Heaton had to scramble to maintain his self-respect and superiority, for it had become slim pickings now.

"All things come to those who wait," he told his sons and his mates, down in the musty cellars beneath the inn. "These Mormons are lunatics, they plan to walk clean out of here; sell up, cut their losses." He rubbed his thick, calloused hands together. "And so they shall."

It peeved him to see the blank looks on the faces gazing up at him. "Do I have to spell it out for you?" He clipped Jem Irons on the side of the head, just to wake up the whole lot of them. "We'll buy 'em up cheap, hold out for the lowest price possible—making sure no one else hereabouts dares to outbid us! Farmland, the smithy, the mill—even Weatherall's market—and perhaps a dozen good houses. Unbelievable what some people will do." He chuckled in that dry, scaly way that made the hearer's skin prickle. "Won't be long now, lads, and we'll be sittin' pretty as princes, you can bet your mother's best hat on that."

So Heaton said, so it would be. The others were inwardly relieved that little was expected of them. Being of the cowardly sort, they enjoyed watching suffering more if they did not have to inflict it by facing dangers and discomforts. And that seemed always their lot when Heaton took to ordering them around.

Chapter Thirty-Five

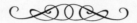

*T*empest did not come. Esther found it difficult to admit, even to herself, how much she missed him, or that she fretted about him when no one could see. She did not have a sense of good things happening to him. Another Sunday went by. A few asked about him and, from the tone in their voices, she could sense a certain distrust of him: *Of course, young squire, difficult for him to make such a change in life, to commit such an outrage against the traditions that everyone expected him to uphold.*

Esther wondered herself. She did not know why he had gone to Scotland; she did not really know what was in his heart or his mind. So she pondered, until one night late in May when spring snarled and turned her back on them, and the hounds of the wind took up baying and spitting rain. Folk herded their beasts indoors, covered their plants with protective sacking, battened down anything that was not attached, and prepared to wait out the storm.

Esther watched the storm with a growing sense of unease. *Was Tempest caught out in it?* she wondered. She could hear the wind raise its voice and howl, she could feel its weight pressed against the walls of the house. She missed the big trees at the parsonage that had set up a windbreak and protected her more than she'd realized. She felt vulnerable here, in these new surroundings, and restless as well.

At supper her father smiled in an absentminded manner, and she realized that his mind was elsewhere. The doctor had asked him to preach a sermon on the following Sunday, and she knew he had much to consider and think about. She was tired, too tired to settle over her books, though she wished that she might. Marjorie had come for several hours the day before to help Esther with laundry and other heavy tasks, and had promised she would come every week. But the daily upkeep of things fell almost entirely upon Esther now, and it was a new and prickly challenge to say the least.

She went up to her room, realizing that she was droopy-eyed tired, yet her weariness fought with her restlessness as she made preparations for bed. She found her place in the scriptures and sat down to read, but the wind poked its cold fingers into her concentration and, after a few verses, she closed the book and got down on her knees.

She shut her eyes and began to pray. Ever since her mother died, prayer had been a comfort to her; she felt at ease talking to God in heaven, for he seemed as real as her mother, once she knew her mother was there.

Tonight, as she began to speak her thoughts and express her desires, the faces of the two brothers rose up before her mind's eye. She saw the beauty and tranquility of the one, and the terrible sorrow of the other. The image made her eyes fly open in astonishment. When she closed them again she found herself praying fervently for Tempest Feather's well-being. Well-being more than protection, and she found that a bit odd.

Before she climbed into bed she took her candle over to the dresser and drew the Scottish stone from its nighttime resting place, cradling it in the palm of her hand. She could almost see him beside her, smell the tangy fresh scent of him, feel his blue, blue eyes on her face. *A protection, a talisman*, he had said. She blew out the candle and got under the covers, the stone still in her hand. Even in the darkness she could trace the pattern of the yellow lines upon its surface. She did so over and over again, then lifted the stone to her lips and pressed them gently against the cool surface. "God, keep him," she said. She slipped the stone beneath her pillow, tucked the coverlet around her, and let sleep cheat the night of its remainder of shadows and fears.

∞

A weight had pressed on Tempest all the way home, every inch of ground that he covered. It was as though once he stated clearly his stand, Satan would give him no peace. He felt weary and drained of energy, angry and discouraged, and it seemed all the tainted emotions reared up in him, contending against one another, and leaving him weak.

When he spied the ash grove down below, he turned Phantom toward it, traveling several yards until he realized, with a painful start, that he could not go down there. He had already ridden past the turnoff to his new home, and he felt everything within him recoiling as he made the necessary adjustments and took his tedious way back. It was Saturday evening and would be too late when he arrived to call upon Esther. Just as well. For he could not, would not, approach her in such a foul mood. The Sabbath tomorrow; a further test of—everything. He pressed on, step by step, breath by breath, allowing himself to think of nothing but the moment when he could slide down from his horse and stumble into a bed.

∞

Untamed nature had withdrawn in the night, and the sun shone as usual over a newly washed and, somehow, tranquil world. The animals, led out into the warmth, blinked their eyes and shook the straw and dust of the barn from their sides. Esther's cats chased each other's tails like so many kittens, and flowers that had withstood the storm's beating stood supple and bright on their slender stems.

Esther prepared for meeting with that sensation of newness still clinging to her, a sensation not altogether comfortable. She wondered if her father was content with his preparations for the sermon he would

give. She could not imagine how he would feel, standing up on the dusty
floor of Paul Pritchard's mill room, with nary a roster in sight. What
would he rest his elbows on? Where spread out his huge, cumbersome
Bible, from which he would read?

But as soon as she entered the big room, something warm seemed
to reach out and engulf her, and the meeting itself held a sense of affec-
tionate intimacy. Her father spoke with splendid insight and power, not
using his Bible at all. Michael Bingham spoke also, thanking his
"brothers and sisters" for their generosity and support, and preached a
strong sermon on faith, drawn from the experiences he had lately been
through.

"My wife tells me," he said, "that for a man to be worthy to work on
the holy temple of the Lord, he must be tried and proved true. And I
have here in my hand a statement made by the Prophet Joseph, following the terrible trials he and his people suffered in Kirtland. May I read it
to you?"

He had a rough time doing so, for tears kept rising in his throat to
choke his speech. But the words he quoted brought tears to many other
eyes, too.

"'It was clearly evident that the Lord gave us power in proportion to the
work to be done, and strength according to the race set before us,' the Prophet
said, 'and grace and help as our needs required.' I testify, brothers and sisters, that it has been so with us. And I thank God for it, for His gracious
kindness to Hannah and me."

They sang another of the songs of Zion to close the meeting, one that
Esther particularly loved. "Now let us rejoice in the day of salvation. No
longer as strangers on earth need we roam. Good tidings are sounding to us
and each nation, and shortly the hour of redemption will come. . . . We'll love
one another and never dissemble but cease to do evil and ever be one. . . ."

A benediction was offered by Charlie Bates, the potter, and the meeting dismissed, but only to have the members turn in eagerness to one
another, talking softly, encouraging, praising.

Esther marveled. Every man—even women—able to speak, able to give, able to learn. *Equality before God*—that is what she thought of. *All men the same in his eyes.*

Then she saw him. He was standing all alone, leaning against one of the posts that held up the tall ceiling. His hands were hidden, clasped behind his back. His eyes were shadowed with pain and an almost boy-ish misery that made Esther want to cry out.

How out of place he must feel here, she thought. *Lonely. Lonely and frightened.* She started to move toward him and something spoke in her heart: *I am the only one who can help him. I know where he comes from, I know who he is. I can understand.*

She approached slowly, and she was aware of his beauty, the physi-cal comeliness of his features and build, the sensitive insights and hungers of his soul, and that intensity of his nature that at times burned him up. When at last he looked about and his searching eyes found her, she felt her whole being smile. She moved more quickly then and, when she drew close to him, she reached out her hand. There was an expres-sion of gratitude in his beautiful eyes as he took it gently into his own, and his touch seemed the most natural thing in the world to Esther.

"I have been watching for you." She sighed. "I have been worried about you."

"I have suffered disappointments," Tempest replied, "and I have endured a lonely and discouraged spirit since then." He was telling her! Why in the world was he opening his heart to her in this way?

"Were you present for much of the meeting?" Esther questioned. "Did you hear the quote of the Prophet Joseph Smith which Michael Bingham read?"

"I did. I heard those amazing words." His eyes had darkened, like the blue of a river darkens as it reaches its depths.

"And they lifted your spirit. I can tell they did—the first bit of light and hope held out to you since you left Scotland," she said.

He nodded.

"They shall be our motto," she breathed, tightening her fingers around his. "You and I."

She drew the stone from her pocket and held it out, tracing the golden paths along its surface with her little finger. "A talisman, a protection," she recalled, "a bond between your spirit and mine."

Tempest smiled, despite himself. "Why have you this power to—" He shook his head in frustration, lacking the words he desired. But she understood.

"Make you more of yourself than you would be if I were not there?" Esther did no more than whisper the words, and her cheeks blushed to have said such a thing out loud.

He pulled her close to him, ever so gently. "I have known for a long time that you were my happiness," he said.

She wanted to cry—she wanted to lift her face heavenward and shout her joy to the sky.

Someone came up to shake his hand. "Welcome, Brother Feather," he said. Then another and another, and the ladies crowding behind them, with offers of aid to help him get settled in, and food for the first while until they found him a girl who could cook.

He shook his head; he became almost shy in their presence. "I cannot afford a cook," he said.

"I shall cook for both you and Father," Esther announced boldly, "and you shall take all of your meals with us. That is—" she glanced round at the kind, happy faces. "That is if Sallie and Marjorie and Mary and Martha will help me a bit."

The laughter followed them as Tempest tugged at the hand he still held and led her out of the room. Here were trees and empty space in abundance. He found a low-spreading birch, dragged her with him until they stood leaning against the broad trunk. Then he kissed her—her lips, her forehead, her hair—at last drawing her cheek against his and resting there.

Christian watched the two from a distance. He knew what it was they felt. He was overwhelmed by the generosity of love God had bestowed upon him and upon this precious daughter he loved.

Stay with us, Mary, he murmured in his soul. *No matter how difficult the journey may seem at times, I shall not forget; I know it is you who brought us here. I know you will be there waiting for us when we come home.*

Author's Note

The information in this novel about throstles and other birds is accurate, as is that about bees. In the vein of "truth is stranger than fiction," the cruelties inflicted upon Evaline Sowerby by her husband were all, in reality, inflicted upon my great-great-grandmother on the Isle of Bute in Scotland, after she joined the Church, and before she came to Utah to join with the Saints. And the name Tempest Feather (spelled Tempist), I found on a stone in the graveyard of Haworth Parish, whose crowded gloom is flanked on one side by the church and on the other by the parsonage where the Brontë sisters lived and wrote, and where two of them died. I found it the most incongruent, intriguing name I have ever encountered, and was determined one day to bring it back to life within the pages of a book.